CHILLING
AND
KILLING

Books by Joan Kahn

Ladies and Gentlemen Said the Ringmaster

To Meet Miss Long

Open House

See Saw

You Can't Catch Me

EDITOR

The Edge of the Chair

Some Things Dark and Dangerous

Some Things Fierce and Fatal

Some Things Strange and Sinister

Some Things Weird and Wicked

Hanging by a Thread

Trial and Terror

Open at Your Own Risk

Chilling and Killing

CHILLING
AND
KILLING

EDITED AND WITH
AN INTRODUCTION BY

Joan Kahn

PREFACE BY

Jacques Barzun

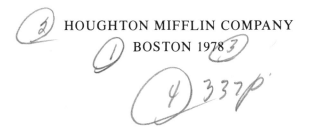

HOUGHTON MIFFLIN COMPANY
BOSTON 1978

Library of Congress Cataloging in Publication Data

Main entry under title:

Chilling and killing.

   1. Detective and mystery stories, English.
2. Detective and mystery stories, American.
3. Crime and criminals. I. Kahn, Joan.
PZ1.C436 1978 [PR1309.D4]   823'.0872   77-20093
ISBN 0-395-26287-9

Printed in the United States of America

V 10 9 8 7 6 5 4 3 2 1

"The Raspberry Patch" by Berton Roueché. Copyright 1968 by Berton Roueché. This story appeared originally in *Evergreen Review*, Vol. 12, No. 58. Reprinted by permission of the author.

"The Man Hunt" by Milton MacKaye. Reprinted from *Dramatic Crimes of 1927* by Milton MacKaye. Copyright 1928 by Milton MacKaye. Reprinted by permission of Doubleday & Company, Inc.

"Another Solution" by Gilbert Highet. Copyright © 1951 by *Harper's Magazine*. All rights reserved. This story appeared originally in *Harper's Magazine*, November 1951. Reprinted by permission of the author.

"Miss Hinch" by Henry Sydnor Harrison. Originally published in *McClure's Magazine*, September 1911, Volume 32. Copyright 1911 by *McClure's Magazine*.

"The Withered Arm" by Thomas Hardy. Originally published in *Blackwood's Magazine*, January 1888.

"The Old Shell Collector" by H. R. F. Keating. Copyright © 1970 by H. R. F. Keating. This story appeared originally in *Ellery Queen's Mystery Magazine*, July 1970. Reprinted by permission of A. D. Peters & Co. Ltd.

"The Man Who Murdered Papa Désiré" by Lassister Wren. Reprinted from *Masterstrokes of Crime Detection* by Lassister Wren. Copyright 1929 by Doubleday & Company, Inc. Reprinted by permission of the publisher.

"A Jury of Her Peers" by Susan Glaspell. Copyright 1946 by Susan Glaspell. Reprinted by permission of Curtis Brown, Ltd.

For
JOYCE HARTMAN
an editor's editor
par excellence

Preface
by Jacques Barzun

WHY PREFACES? The author's own opening remarks have point in that they tell us what the book intends and promises. But the intrusion of an outsider before the show begins has to be justified by some unusual circumstance, for an ordinary good book can and should stand on its own merits. And surely it is a bore to hear what the previewing reader chooses to say about this or that luscious bit: we want to find them for ourselves — and most likely they will be different bits altogether. What an imported prefacer alone can do is to suggest the special place that an uncommon book occupies within its kind and praise the author for his or her originality.

The volume in hand has had four predecessors, but its originality remains, for all four were the work of Joan Kahn, whose unique merit is to have seen that connoisseurs of crime fiction are also readers of true crime and amateurs of ghost stories. Dorothy L. Sayers had joined two of these interests but not all three. There is of course a paradox in this combination of tastes. One would suppose that taking pleasure in the neat artifice of a good crime tale would make one reject the messy incoherence of an actual murder; and the paradox is redoubled when one couples the lust for a solution in detective stories with the forever lingering doubt and wonderment in a truly enjoyable experience with ghosts.

But the fact is there. We who read tales, as well as novels properly so called, want all three types of mystery. The samples of each must of course be of superior quality; they must respect the demands of the worldly intellect and exhibit the virtues of literature. This is where Joan Kahn's talents shine and give her rank as Prime Anthologist. As editor of crime fiction at Harper's she has in effect been compiling over the years a huge "anthology" through the selection of the best works by modern masters of the genre — Nicholas Blake, Michael Gilbert, Andrew Garve, Dick Francis, Nicolas Freeling, John Dickson Carr, E. Richard Johnson, Robert Van Gulik, and a host of others of smaller output but equal worth — as may be ascertained in *A Catalogue of Crime*, another by-product of Miss Kahn's tireless devotion to her craft.

When in 1967 she decided to put together a volume of shorter works which she called *The Edge of the Chair,* she set a new standard for such collections. To begin with, most of the matter was new; it was not to be found in the many dozens of previous anthologies. Second, the bouquet she made of the three aforementioned types was an admirably balanced whole. Next, she provided each bloom with a short statement designed to enhance pleasure in reading and develop in the innocent a critical attitude. And finally, the book was of such a generous size that the variety it afforded proved a revelation to those who think the three genres repetitive, bound down to formula, cut-and-dried.

Joan Kahn has pursued her encyclopedic reading and produced novelty at each fresh gathering of judiciously chosen pieces. No need to anticipate and itemize the contents of this fifth and (I hope) not final harvesting. I shall only say that as a seasoned reader of this literature, I found my zest for reading roused to the utmost when I discovered that of the baker's score of narratives I knew only two.

Contents

Introduction
by Joan Kahn

EVEN THOUGH I'd been an editor of books for many years, when I was first persuaded to become an anthologist, I was uneasy, insecure, dubious. I had read many anthologies, and had admired some of them, but I wasn't at all sure I could produce one myself. Where did one find the material? How did one put an anthology together?

Where one found the material turned out to be mainly in secondhand bookstores. This was doubly rewarding, as I've loved such stores and found them romantic ever since I read *The Haunted Bookshop* by Christopher Morley. Secondhand bookstores: the best of them have a mustiness all their own, they're cramped and crowded, and often one has to go up and down a series of strange staircases into dark underground caverns or climb up to dimly lit attics — and somehow the farther in one burrows and the dirtier one's hands get, the better the results. (I'm not much good at climbing ladders, and I'm fairly short, so the books I've found are mainly five feet and under on the shelves.) I've also discovered that, on the whole, the darker and more battered the book's binding, the more rewarding its contents.

It turned out that there were a lot of grubby, full-of-treasure books around. Somehow I think there may be too many — because I seem to have become an old-book addict (not a rare-book one, just an old-book one) and now my apartment has begun to resemble an old bookstore, and it's getting to be difficult to find a chair that hasn't a pile of books on it (all my bookshelves are full to overflowing) and that old bookstore mustiness may be closing in around my dining room table. (Romantic? Well, perhaps all that atmosphere is better in a store.) However, I found material enough, and several anthologies later I'm *still* finding it.

And it turned out that to put together an anthology one could manage all right if one tried not to use overly familiar material, and to use material that scared or interested the anthologist herself. An anthology can be rewarding, not only because of the treasure hunting and the collecting, but because one is uncovering, from dark and dusty corners, exciting material that has been too long buried and forgotten, and deserves a second or new audience.

My anthologies have been (as much of my book editing has been) in the field of mystery and suspense. Dorothy L. Sayers, whom I admire almost as much for her skills as an anthologist as for her Lord Peter Wimsey novels, said in her introduction to her *Third Omnibus of Crime,* "Here is a book of stories nearly all about dead bodies and wicked people; stories designed to make you feel that it is good to be alive and that, while alive, it is better, on the whole, for you to be good." The stories and the nonfiction pieces in this new collection are about the dead and the wicked, too, some rising up from the past to frighten you, some from the present.

Several of the stories that follow I didn't discover on any old, mysterious shelves; I'm delighted to say they were put into my hands by their authors. And one of the pieces has never appeared in book form before; it's "The Trial of Jane's Aunt," and it was written by a Cleveland lawyer who's a Jane Austen fan and whose book of essays, *Innocence and Arsenic,* I edited recently.

The other stories and articles were gathered together from a marvelous assortment of volumes — such as *The Mammoth Book of Thrillers, Ghosts and Mysteries,* edited by J. M. Parrish and John R. Crossland and published by Odham Press, Ltd., London, 1936, where I found the E. F. Benson story, and *A*

Book of Long Stories, selected and edited by Arthur H. Nethercat, Ph.D., assistant professor of English, Northwestern University, Macmillan, 1927 — which led me to the Thomas Hardy chiller, "The Withered Arm"; and *Nation-Famous New York Murders*, repictured by Alfred Henry Lewis (author of *Faro Nell and Her Friends* and *The Apaches of New York*), published by G. W. Dillingham in 1914, and dedicated "as a mark of friendship by the author to William W. McLaughlin, Chief Inspector of the New York Police, retired."

Chilling and Killing includes, whatever the source of its contents, a variety of pretty scary stuff. Berton Roueché, delightfully friendly company off paper, is terrifying in print in "The Raspberry Patch," and Robie Macauley's "The Invaders" may make you feel very nervous indeed the next time you're sitting on a beach, while Gilbert Highet's "Another Solution" should keep you away from the water for some time to come, and Lassiter Wren's "The Man Who Murdered Papa Désiré" may make you shudder a bit when anyone says Paris.

All in all, the authors you're about to meet, present and past, can handle words with such skill that you should be properly frightened by them — in a most entertaining manner, of course. At least that has been my fervent intent.

FICTION

WHAT WAS IT?

by Fitz-James O'Brien

"I heard the creature beneath me panting in the darkness,
and felt the violent throbbing of a heart."

IT IS, I confess, with considerable diffidence that I approach the
strange narrative which I am about to relate. The events which I
purpose detailing are of so extraordinary a character that I am
quite prepared to meet with an unusual amount of incredulity
and scorn. I accept all such beforehand. I have, I trust, the literary courage to face unbelief. I have, after mature consideration,
resolved to narrate, in as simple and straightforward a manner as
I can compass, some facts that passed under my observation, in
the month of July last, and which, in the annals of the mysteries
of physical science, are wholly unparalleled.

I live at No. — Twenty-sixth Street, in New York. The house
is in some respects a curious one. It has enjoyed for the last two
years the reputation of being haunted. It is a large and stately
residence, surrounded by what was once a garden, but which is
now only a green enclosure used for bleaching clothes. The dry
basin of what has been a fountain, and a few fruit trees ragged
and unpruned, indicate that this spot in past days was a pleasant,
shady retreat, filled with fruits and flowers and the sweet murmur of waters.

The house is very spacious. A hall of noble size leads to a
large spiral staircase winding through its center, while the various apartments are of imposing dimensions. It was built some fifteen or twenty years since by Mr. A——, the well-known New

York merchant, who five years ago threw the commercial world into convulsions by a stupendous bank fraud. Mr. A——, as everyone knows, escaped to Europe, and died not long after, of a broken heart. Almost immediately after the news of his decease reached this country and was verified, the report spread in Twenty-sixth Street that No. — was haunted. Legal measures had dispossessed the widow of its former owner, and it was inhabited merely by a caretaker and his wife, placed there by the house agent into whose hands it had passed for the purposes of renting or sale. These people declared that they weie troubled with unnatural noises. Doors were opened without any visible agency. The remnants of furniture scattered through the various rooms were, during the night, piled one upon the other by unknown hands. Invisible feet passed up and down the stairs in broad daylight, accompanied by the rustle of unseen silk dresses, and the gliding of viewless hands along the massive balusters. The caretaker and his wife declared they would live there no longer. The house agent laughed, dismissed them, and put others in their place. The noises and supernatural manifestations continued. The neighborhood caught up the story, and the house remained untenanted for three years. Several persons negotiated for it; but, somehow, always before the bargain was closed they heard the unpleasant rumors and declined to treat any further.

It was in this state of things that my landlady, who at that time kept a boardinghouse in Bleecker Street, and who wished to move further uptown, conceived the bold idea of renting No. — Twenty-sixth Street. Happening to have in her house rather a plucky and philosophical set of boarders, she laid her scheme before us, stating candidly everything she had heard respecting the ghostly qualities of the establishment to which she wished to remove us. With the exception of two timid persons — a sea-captain and a returned Californian, who immediately gave notice that they would leave — all of Mrs. Moffat's guests declared that they would accompany her in her chivalric incursion into the abode of spirits.

Our removal was effected in the month of May, and we were charmed with our new residence. The portion of Twenty-sixth

Street where our house is situated, between Seventh and Eighth avenues, is one of the pleasantest localities in New York. The gardens back of the houses, running down nearly to the Hudson, form, in the summertime, a perfect avenue of verdure. The air is pure and invigorating, sweeping, as it does, straight across the river from the Weehawken heights, and even the ragged garden which surrounded the house, although displaying on washing days rather too much clothesline, still gave us a piece of greensward to look at and a cool retreat in the summer evenings, where we smoked our cigars in the dusk and watched the fireflies flashing their dark lanterns in the long grass.

Of course we had no sooner established ourselves at No. — than we began to expect ghosts. We absolutely awaited their advent with eagerness. Our dinner conversation was supernatural. One of the boarders, who had purchased Mrs. Crowe's *Night Side of Nature* for his own private delectation, was regarded as a public enemy by the entire household for not having bought twenty copies. The man led a life of supreme wretchedness while he was reading this volume. A system of espionage was established, of which he was the victim. If he incautiously laid the book down for an instant and left the room, it was immediately seized and read aloud in secret places to a select few. I found myself a person of immense importance, it having leaked out that I was tolerably well versed in the history of supernaturalism and had once written a story the foundation of which was a ghost. If a table or a wainscot panel happened to warp when we were assembled in the large drawing room, there was an instant silence, and everyone was prepared for an immediate clanking of chains and a spectral form.

After a month of psychological excitement, it was with the utmost dissatisfaction that we were forced to acknowledge that nothing in the remotest degree approaching the supernatural had manifested itself. Once the black butler asseverated that his candle had been blown out by some invisible agency while he was undressing himself for the night; but as I had more than once discovered this colored gentleman in a condition when one candle must have appeared to him like two, I thought it possible that, by going a step further in his potations, he might have reversed this phenomenon, and seen no candle at all where he ought to have beheld one.

Things were in this state when an accident took place so awful and inexplicable in its character that my reason fairly reels at the bare memory of the occurrence. It was the tenth of July. After dinner was over I repaired, with my friend Dr. Hammond, to the garden to smoke my evening pipe. Independent of certain mental sympathies which existed between the Doctor and myself, we were linked together by a vice. We both smoked opium. We knew each other's secret and respected it. We enjoyed together that wonderful expansion of thought, that marvelous intensifying of the perceptive faculties, that boundless feeling of existence when we seem to have points of contact with the whole universe — in short, that unimaginable spiritual bliss, which I would not surrender for a throne, and which I hope you, reader, will never — never taste.

Those hours of opium happiness which the Doctor and I spent together in secret were regulated with a scientific accuracy. We did not blindly smoke the drug of paradise and leave our dreams to chance. While smoking, we carefully steered our conversation through the brightest and calmest channels of thought. We talked of the East, and endeavored to recall the magical panorama of its glowing scenery. We criticized the most sensuous poets — those who painted life ruddy with health, brimming with passion, happy in the possession of youth and strength and beauty. If we talked of Shakespeare's *Tempest*, we lingered over Ariel and avoided Caliban. Like the Guebers, we turned our faces to the East, and saw only the sunny side of the world.

This skillful coloring of our train of thought produced in our subsequent visions a corresponding tone. The splendors of Arabian fairyland dyed our dreams. We paced the narrow strip of grass with the tread and port of kings. The song of the *Rana arborea*, while he clung to the bark of the ragged plum tree, sounded like the strains of divine musicians. Houses, walls, and streets melted like rain clouds, and vistas of unimaginable glory stretched away before us. It was a rapturous companionship. We enjoyed the vast delight more perfectly because, even in our most ecstatic moments, we were conscious of each other's presence. Our pleasures, while individual, were still twin, vibrating and moving in musical accord.

On the evening in question, the tenth of July, the Doctor and myself drifted into an unusually metaphysical mood. We lit our large meerschaums, filled with fine Turkish tobacco, in the core of which burned a little black nut of opium, that, like the nut in the fairy tale, held within its narrow limits wonders beyond the reach of kings; we paced to and fro, conversing. A strange perversity dominated the currents of our thought. They would *not* flow through the sun-lit channels into which we strove to divert them. For some unaccountable reason, they constantly diverged into dark and lonesome beds, where a continual gloom brooded. It was in vain that, after our old fashion, we flung ourselves on the shores of the East and talked of its gay bazaars, of the splendors of the time of Haroun, of harems and golden palaces. Black afreets continually arose from the depths of our talk, and expanded, like the one the fisherman released from the copper vessel, until they blotted everything bright from our vision. Insensibly, we yielded to the occult force that swayed us, and indulged in gloomy speculation. We had talked some time upon the proneness of the human mind to mysticism, and the almost universal love of the terrible, when Hammond suddenly said to me, "What do you consider to be the greatest element of terror?"

The question puzzled me. That many things were terrible, I knew. Stumbling over a corpse in the dark; beholding, as I once did, a woman floating down a deep and rapid river, with wildly lifted arms and awful, upturned face, uttering, as she drifted, shrieks that rent one's heart while we, spectators, stood frozen at a window which overhung the river at a height of sixty feet, unable to make the slightest effort to save her, but dumbly watching her last supreme agony and her disappearance. A shattered wreck, with no life visible, encountered floating listlessly on the ocean, is a terrible object, for it suggests a huge terror, the proportions of which are veiled. But it now struck me, for the first time, that there must be one great and ruling embodiment of fear — a King of Terrors, to which all others must succumb. What might it be? To what train of circumstances would it owe its existence?

"I confess, Hammond," I replied to my friend, "I never considered the subject before. That there must be one Something more terrible than any other thing, I feel. I cannot attempt, however, even the most vague definition."

"I am somewhat like you, Harry," he answered. "I feel my capacity to experience a terror greater than anything yet conceived by the human mind — something combining in fearful and unnatural amalgamation hitherto supposed incompatible elements. The calling of the voices in Brockden Brown's novel of *Wieland* is awful; so is the picture of the Dweller of the Threshold, in Bulwer's *Zanoni*; but," he added, shaking his head gloomily, "there is something more horrible still than those."

"Look here, Hammond," I replied, "let us drop this kind of talk, for Heaven's sake! We shall suffer for it, depend on it."

"I don't know what's the matter with me tonight," he replied, "but my brain is running upon all sorts of weird and awful thoughts. I feel as if I could write a story like Hoffman, tonight, if I were only master of a literary style."

"Well, if we are going to be Hoffmanesque in our talk, I'm off to bed. Opium and nightmares should never be brought together. How sultry it is! Good night, Hammond."

"Good night, Harry. Pleasant dreams to you."

"To you, gloomy wretch, afreets, ghouls, and enchanters."

We parted, and each sought his respective chamber. I undressed quickly and got into bed, taking with me, according to my usual custom, a book, over which I generally read myself to sleep. I opened the volume as soon as I had laid my head upon the pillow, and instantly flung it to the other side of the room. It was Goudon's *History of Monsters* — a curious French work which I had lately imported from Paris, but which, in the state of mind I had then reached, was anything but an agreeable companion. I resolved to go to sleep at once; so, turning down my gas until nothing but a little blue point of light glimmered on the top of the tube, I composed myself to rest.

The room was in total darkness. The atom of gas that still remained alight did not illuminate a distance of three inches round the burner. I desperately drew my arm across my eyes, as if to shut out even the darkness, and tried to think of nothing. It was in vain. The confounded themes touched on by Hammond in the garden kept obtruding themselves on my brain. I battled against them. I erected ramparts of would-be blankness of intellect to keep them out. They still crowded upon me. While I was lying still as a corpse, hoping that by a perfect physical inaction I should hasten mental repose, an awful incident occurred. A Something dropped, as it seemed, from the ceiling, plumb upon my chest, and the next instant I felt two bony hands encircling my throat, endeavoring to choke me.

I am no coward and am possessed of considerable physical strength. The suddenness of the attack, instead of stunning me, strung every nerve to its highest tension. My body acted from instinct before my brain had time to realize the terrors of my position. In an instant I wound two muscular arms around the creature and squeezed it, with all the strength of despair, against my chest. In a few seconds the bony hands that had fastened on my throat loosened their hold, and I was free to breathe once more. Then commenced a struggle of awful intensity. Immersed in the most profound darkness, totally ignorant of the nature of the Thing by which I was so suddenly attacked, finding my grasp slipping every moment, by reason, it seemed to me, of the entire nakedness of my assailant, bitten with sharp teeth in the shoulder, neck, and chest, having every moment to protect my throat against a pair of sinewy, agile hands, which my utmost efforts could not confine — these were a combination of circumstances to combat which required all the strength, skill, and courage that I possessed.

At last, after a silent, deadly, exhausting struggle, I got my assailant under by a series of incredible efforts of strength. Once pinned, with my knee on what I made out to be its chest, I knew that I was victor. I rested for a moment to breathe. I heard the creature beneath me panting in the darkness, and felt the violent throbbing of a heart. It was apparently as exhausted as I was; that was one comfort. At this moment I remembered that I usually placed under my pillow, before going to bed, a large yellow

silk pocket handkerchief. I felt for it instantly; it was there. In a
few seconds more I had, after a fashion, pinioned the creature's
arms.

I now felt tolerably secure. There was nothing more to be
done but to turn on the gas, and, having first seen what my midnight assailant was like, arouse the household. I will confess to
being actuated by a certain pride in not giving the alarm before; I
wished to make the capture alone and unaided.

Never losing my hold for an instant, I slipped from the bed to
the floor, dragging my captive with me. I had but a few steps to
make to reach the gas burner; these I made with the greatest caution, holding the creature in a grip like a vice. At last I got within
arm's length of the tiny speck of blue light which told me where
the gas burner lay. Quick as lightning I released my grasp with
one hand and let on the full flood of light. Then I turned to look
at my captive.

I cannot even attempt to give any definition of my sensations
the instant after I turned on the gas. I suppose I must have
shrieked with terror, for in less than a minute afterward my room
was crowded with the inmates of the house. I shudder now as I
think of that awful moment. *I saw nothing!* Yes; I had one arm
firmly clasped round a breathing, panting, corporeal shape, my
other hand gripped with all its strength a throat as warm, as apparently fleshy, as my own; and yet, with this living substance in
my grasp, with its body pressed against my own, and all in the
bright glare of a large jet of gas, I absolutely beheld nothing! Not
even an outline — a vapor!

I do not, even at this hour, realize the situation in which I
found myself. I cannot recall the astounding incident thoroughly.
Imagination in vain tries to compass the awful paradox.

It breathed. I felt its warm breath upon my cheek. It struggled
fiercely. It had hands. They clutched me. Its skin was smooth,
like my own. There it lay, pressed close up against me, solid as
stone — and yet utterly invisible!

I wonder that I did not faint or go mad on the instant. Some
wonderful instinct must have sustained me; for, absolutely, in
place of loosening my hold on the terrible Enigma, I seemed to
gain an additional strength in my moment of horror, and tight-

ened my grasp with such wonderful force that I felt the creature shivering with agony.

Just then Hammond entered my room at the head of the household. As soon as he beheld my face — which, I suppose, must have been an awful sight to look at — he hastened forward, crying, "Great heaven, Harry! what has happened?"

"Hammond! Hammond!" I cried. "Come here. Oh, this is awful! I have been attacked in bed by something or other, which I have hold of; but I can't see it — I can't see it!"

Hammond, doubtless struck by the unfeigned horror expressed in my countenance, made one or two steps forward with an anxious yet puzzled expression. A very audible titter burst from the remainder of my visitors. This suppressed laughter made me furious. To laugh at a human being in my position! It was the worst species of cruelty. *Now*, I can understand why the appearance of a man struggling violently, as it would seem, with an airy nothing, and calling for assistance against a vision, should have appeared ludicrous. *Then*, so great was my rage against the mocking crowd that had I the power I would have stricken them dead where they stood.

"Hammond! Hammond!" I cried again, despairingly. "For God's sake come to me. I can hold the — the Thing but a short while longer. It is overpowering me. Help me! Help me!"

"Harry," whispered Hammond, approaching me, "you have been smoking too much opium."

"I swear to you, Hammond, that this is no vision," I answered, in the same low tone. "Don't you see how it shakes my whole frame with its struggles? If you don't believe me, convince yourself. Feel it — touch it."

Hammond advanced and laid his hand in the spot I indicated. A wild cry of horror burst from him. He had felt it!

In a moment he had discovered somewhere in my room a long piece of cord and was the next instant winding it and knotting it about the body of the unseen being that I clasped in my arms.

"Harry," he said, in a hoarse, agitated voice, for, though he preserved his presence of mind, he was deeply moved, "Harry, it's all safe now. You may let go, old fellow, if you're tired. The Thing can't move."

I was utterly exhausted, and I gladly loosed my hold.

Hammond stood holding the ends of the cord, which bound the Invisible, twisted round his hand, while before him, self-supporting as it were, he beheld a rope laced and interlaced and stretching tightly around a vacant space. I never saw a man look so thoroughly stricken with awe. Nevertheless his face expressed all the courage and determination which I knew him to possess. His lips, although white, were set firmly, and one could perceive at a glance that, although stricken with fear, he was not daunted.

The confusion that ensued among the guests of the house who were witnesses of this extraordinary scene between Hammond and myself — who beheld the pantomime of binding this struggling Something — who beheld me almost sinking from physical exhaustion when my task of jailer was over — the confusion and terror that took possession of the bystanders, when they saw all this, was beyond description. The weaker ones fled from the apartment. The few who remained clustered near the door and could not be induced to approach Hammond and his Charge. Still, incredulity broke out through their terror. They had not the courage to satisfy themselves, and yet they doubted. It was in vain that I begged of some of the men to come near and convince themselves by touch of the existence in that room of a living being which was invisible. They were incredulous but did not dare to undeceive themselves. How could a solid, living, breathing body be invisible, they asked. My reply was this. I gave a sign to Hammond, and both of us — conquering our fearful repugnance to touch the invisible creature — lifted it from the ground, manacled as it was, and took it to my bed. Its weight was about that of a boy of fourteen.

"Now, my friends," I said, as Hammond and myself held the creature suspended over the bed, "I can give you self-evident proof that here is a solid, ponderable body, which, nevertheless, you cannot see. Be good enough to watch the surface of the bed attentively."

I was astonished at my own courage in treating this strange event so calmly; but I had recovered from my first terror and felt a sort of scientific pride in the affair, which dominated every other feeling.

The eyes of the bystanders were immediately fixed on my bed. At a given signal Hammond and I let the creature fall. There was a dull sound of a heavy body alighting on a soft mass. The timbers of the bed creaked. A deep impression marked itself distinctly on the pillow and on the bed itself. The crowd who witnessed this gave a low cry and rushed from the room. Hammond and I were left alone with our Mystery.

We remained silent for some time, listening to the low, irregular breathing of the creature on the bed and watching the rustle of the bedclothes as it impotently struggled to free itself from confinement. Then Hammond spoke.

"Harry, this is awful."

"Ay, awful."

"But not unaccountable."

"Not unaccountable! What do you mean? Such a thing has never occurred since the birth of the world. I know not what to think, Hammond. God grant that I am not mad and that this is not an insane fantasy!"

"Let us reason a little, Harry. Here is a solid body which we touch, but which we cannot see. The fact is so unusual that it strikes us with terror. Is there no parallel, though, for such a phenomenon? Take a piece of pure glass. It is tangible and transparent. A certain chemical coarseness is all that prevents its being so entirely transparent as to be totally invisible. It is not *theoretically impossible*, mind you, to make a glass which shall not reflect a single ray of light — a glass so pure and homogeneous in its atoms that the rays from the sun will pass through it as they do through the air, refracted but not reflected. We do not see the air, and yet we feel it."

"That's all very well, Hammond, but these are inanimate substances. Glass does not breathe, air does not breathe. *This* thing has a heart that palpitates — a will that moves it — lungs that play, and inspire and respire."

"You forget the phenomena of which we have so often heard of late," answered the Doctor, gravely. "At the meetings called 'spirit circles,' invisible hands have been thrust into the hands of those persons round the table — warm, fleshly hands that seemed to pulsate with mortal life.''

''What? Do you think, then, that this thing is . . .''

''I don't know what it is,'' was the solemn reply; ''but please the gods I will, with your assistance, thoroughly investigate it.''

We watched together, smoking many pipes, all night long, by the bedside of the unearthly being that tossed and panted until it was apparently wearied out. Then we learned by the low, regular breathing that it slept.

The next morning the house was all astir. The boarders congregated on the landing outside my room, and Hammond and myself were lions. We had to answer a thousand questions as to the state of our extraordinary prisoner, for as yet not one person in the house except ourselves could be induced to set foot in the apartment.

The creature was awake. This was evidenced by the convulsive manner in which the bedclothes were moved in its efforts to escape. There was something truly terrible in beholding, as it were, those secondhand indications of the terrible writhings and agonized struggles for liberty which themselves were invisible.

Hammond and myself had racked our brains during the long night to discover some means by which we might realize the shape and general appearance of the Enigma. As well as we could make out by passing our hands over the creature's form, its outlines and lineaments were human. There was a mouth; a round, smooth head without hair; a nose, which, however, was little elevated above the cheeks; and its hands and feet felt like those of a boy. At first we thought of placing the being on a smooth surface and tracing its outlines with chalk, as shoemakers trace the outline of the foot. This plan was given up as being of no value. Such an outline would give not the slightest idea of its conformation.

A happy thought struck me. We would take a cast of it in plaster of Paris. This would give us the solid figure and satisfy all our wishes. But how to do it? The movements of the creature would disturb the setting of the plastic covering and distort the mold. Another thought. Why not give it chloroform? It had respiratory organs — that was evident by its breathing. Once reduced to a state of insensibility, we could do with it what we would. Doctor X—— was sent for; and after the worthy physician had recovered from the first shock of amazement, he proceeded to administer the chloroform. In three minutes afterward we were enabled to remove the fetters from the creature's body, and a modeler was busily engaged in covering the invisible form with the moist clay. In five minutes more we had a mold, and before evening a rough facsimile of the Mystery. It was shaped like a man — distorted, uncouth, and horrible, but still a man. It was small, not over four feet and some inches in height, and its limbs revealed a muscular development that was unparalleled. Its face surpassed in hideousness anything I had ever seen. Gustav Doré, or Callot, or Tony Johannot never conceived anything so horrible. There is a face in one of the latter's illustrations to *Un Voyage où il vous plaira* which somewhat approaches the countenance of this creature, but does not equal it. It was the physiognomy of what I should fancy a ghoul might be. It looked as if it were capable of feeding on human flesh.

Having satisfied our curiosity and bound everyone in the house to secrecy, it became a question of what was to be done with our Enigma? It was impossible that we should keep such a horror in our house; it was equally impossible that such an awful being should be let loose upon the world. I confess that I would have gladly voted for the creature's destruction. But who would shoulder the responsibility? Who would undertake the execution of this horrible semblance of a human being? Day after day this question was deliberated gravely. The boarders all left the house. Mrs. Moffat was in despair and threatened Hammond and myself with all sorts of legal penalties if we did not remove the Horror. Our answer was, "We will go if you like, but we decline taking this creature with us. Remove it yourself if you please. It appeared in your house. On you the responsibility rests." To this there was, of course, no answer. Mrs. Moffat could not obtain for love or money a person who would even approach the Mystery.

The most singular part of the affair was that we were entirely ignorant of what the creature habitually fed on. Everything in the way of nutriment that we could think of was placed before it but was never touched. It was awful to stand by, day after day, and see the clothes toss, and hear the hard breathing, and know that it was starving.

Ten, twelve days, a fortnight passed, and it still lived. The pulsations of the heart, however, were daily growing fainter, and had now nearly ceased. It was evident that the creature was dying for want of sustenance. While this terrible life struggle was going on, I felt miserable. I could not sleep. Horrible as the creature was, it was pitiful to think of the pangs it was suffering.

At last it died. Hammond and I found it cold and stiff one morning in the bed. The heart had ceased to beat, the lungs to inspire. We hastened to bury it in the garden. It was a strange funeral, the dropping of that viewless corpse into the damp hole. The cast of its form I gave to Doctor X——, who keeps it in his museum in Tenth Street.

As I am on the eve of a long journey from which I may not return, I have drawn up this narrative of an event the most singular that has ever come to my knowledge.

THE RASPBERRY PATCH

by Berton Rouechè

He stood in the stifling storeroom, watching the boy and the girl in the garden.

THE TELEPHONE RANG, and I heard Mrs. Logan answer it at her desk.

"It's for you, Mr. Jeffries," she said.

I finished with my depositor and put the sign under my grille and closed my cash drawer and walked over to the telephone, and it was Mother.

"Yes," I said. "What is it, Mother?"

But I couldn't hear her. All I could hear was a babel of voices and then a lot of laughing.

"For heaven sakes," I said. "You've got the TV on. Turn it down."

The laughter ended with a gulp.

"I don't know what you're talking about," Mother said.

"Well," I said. "What is it?"

"Edward," she said.

"Yes?"

"I meant to tell you at lunch," she said, "but you left in such a rush."

"Tell me what?"

"You don't have to shout at me, Edward."

"All right, Mother," I said, "but Mrs. Logan wants to use her desk. What is it?"

"I'm trying to tell you, Edward," she said. "I want you to stop at the drugstore on your way home and get me some Empirin. I've got one of my headaches. I've had it ever since breakfast."

"Empirin?" I said. "What's the matter with aspirin? You've got aspirin. I put the bottle on your table this morning."

"I can't take aspirin anymore," she said. "It doesn't agree with my bloat medicine. If you ever listened to me, you would know that."

"All right," I said. "OK. But I've got to go now."

"And, Edward," she said.

"Mother," I said, "it's after two. It's almost closing time."

"I want you to be sure and get the large bottle," she said.

"All right," I said, and hung up.

I took a deep breath and held it as long as I could. That's an exercise I learned at a yoga class I went to before Mother had her second stroke. It always seems to help. Then I took a Gelusil tablet and went back to my cage. I could already feel the tension subsiding. Yoga breathing and Gelusil — they really work. I don't know what I'd do without them. But I wasn't very proud of myself. I'd come pretty close to actually losing my temper. I suppose, in a way, it was partly Mother's fault, but that isn't any excuse. That's the way Mother is. She just doesn't understand about business. It was the same when Father was alive. Mother has always been a world unto herself.

Frank Palmer and I left the bank together. It was twenty past four and we were almost the last to leave. I don't know what Frank's trouble was, but mine was my drawer. I thought I'd never get it proved. There wasn't anything really wrong. We came out of the passage and into the heat of the street, and Frank stopped and lit a cigarette.

"Well," I said.

"Wait a minute," Frank said. "I'm meeting Martha for a drink at the Domino. How about joining us?"

"I'd like to," I said, and I meant it. I was flattered. Frank is at least ten years younger than I. And I've always liked Martha Palmer. But then I thought of Mother. "I'd like to, Frank, but I guess I'd better not. I really ought to get home."

"It isn't that late," he said. "Besides, it's Friday."

"All right," I said. It wasn't really late. Mother likes to eat early, but I could still get home in time to have dinner ready by six. "But I've got to stop at the drugstore first and get some medicine for Mother."

"OK," he said. "How *is* your mother, Ed?"

"Oh, she's fine," I said. "She's coming along fine. She still spends most of her time in her chair, but she's beginning to get around pretty well with a cane."

"She sounds like a wonderful woman," he said.

"She is," I said. "She really is."

The Domino was dark and cool, and Martha was already there. She waved to us from a booth across from the bar. She looked pretty and smiling, and it made me feel good to see her.

"Why, Ed," she said, "this is great." She looked at Frank. "And you — I hope you realize how late you are."

"I had nothing to do with it," he said. He slid into the seat beside her.

"A beautiful girl tried to pick me up. I almost didn't get away."

"I don't blame her," Martha said. She leaned over and kissed him on the cheek. "And now order me something long and cold and delicious. I've never been so thirsty."

"One beer," Frank said. "What about you, Ed?"

"A beer sounds fine," I said.

We all had beer. The beer was cold and it tasted good, but after a few swallows, I didn't really enjoy it. I liked sitting here in the cool and the dark with the juke box playing and having a drink at the end of the week with my friends, but I didn't feel right. I had a kind of empty feeling and I couldn't seem to get relaxed. But I made myself finish my beer. I sat back with my glass and listened to Frank laughing about a funny twenty that turned up in the Star Lanes deposit and watched Martha smiling and listening to every word he said and tried to look calm and comfortable. And then I couldn't stand it any longer.

"Well," I said. I put down my glass and tried to smile. "I'm afraid I've got to go."

"Go?" Martha said.

"Why, we only just got here," Frank said.

"I know," I said, "and I wish I could stay. But Mother's alone and . . ."

I walked back to the bank and around to the parking lot in back and got my car and drove home along the river road. The clock in the big Esso station under the bridge said twenty-five past five. The Domino had been a mistake, but I wasn't really late. I touched my pocket to make sure the bottle of Empirin was still there, and turned into our street and down the block to our house. There was a car parked in the driveway of the old Hamilton house next door. It was a red Volkswagen, and I remembered that I had seen it there at noon. And all of the windows in the house were open. The Hamilton house had been vacant for over a year, but it looked as if somebody had finally taken it. I drove on past and up our drive and put the car in the garage, got out and closed the doors and went in the kitchen door. I could hear the TV talking in the living room. I went through the dining room and across the hall.

"I'm home," I said.

Mother was sitting erect with her hands on the arms of her chair.

"Edward," she said. "Where in the world have you been? It's almost six o'clock."

"I've got your Empirin," I said. I got the package out of my pocket and put it with the other things on her table. "That's a hundred tablets. It's the largest size they had."

Mother unwrapped the bottle and looked at the label and put it back on the table. "Well," she said. "Aren't you even going to kiss me?"

I bent down and touched her cheek.

"You've been drinking," she said.

"I had a beer with one of the fellows at the bank," I said. "He asked me to."

"I see," she said. "And I suppose you have to do everything you're asked?"

I didn't say anything. I was looking out the window at the backyard next door. Old Mr. Hamilton had been a gardener, and most of the yard was garden and most of the garden was a raspberry patch. A girl in a jersey and tight blue jeans was standing there in the tangle of canes. She looked very pretty in her tight blue pants against the pale leaves and the bright red berries. And young. She looked even younger than Martha Palmer. She looked about twenty-five. She said something to somebody in the house and laughed. I turned away.

"I'd better go and change," I said. "Do you want me to get you anything first?"

"You could fill my water glass," she said. "I might want to take an Empirin."

"How is your headache?" I said.

"I think it's coming back," she said.

I took the glass out to the kitchen and filled it from the cooler in the refrigerator and brought it back and put it on the table.

"I'm going up now," I said. "OK?"

She nodded. I went up to my room and took off my coat and tie and rolled up my shirtsleeves and went into the bathroom and washed and came back down again. I looked in the living room.

"I'm going to start dinner," I said. "And I thought I'd make some iced tea. I thought that might taste good."

"If that's what you want," she said, "but be sure and make it strong enough."

I went out to the kitchen and got the rest of last night's roast out of the refrigerator and sliced off four or five slices. Then I got out a package of frozen green beans and a package of frozen potatoes. I set the table in the dining room and came back and put the kettle on to boil.

"Edward!"

I went back and across the hall to the living room.

"Yes?"

"There isn't a breath of air in here," Mother said. "It's even worse than it was this afternoon. I think I'll have to have the fan."

"I don't think you should," I said. "You know what Dr. Tillinghast said about drafts."

"I know what he said," she said. "But he didn't intend for me to suffocate. This room is stifling and I want the fan. It's up in the storeroom closet."

"All right," I said.

I went back up the stairs. The storeroom was under the eaves and it was really stifling. I opened the window to let in some air. The girl next door was still in the raspberry patch. Only now she wasn't just standing there. She had a dish or a bowl or something and she was picking raspberries. I stood at the window and watched her. She was younger than Martha Palmer, and prettier, too. I heard a screen door slam. A man in a T-shirt came out of the house and across the yard and down the garden path. That would be her husband, but he wasn't much more than a boy. He was only just a boy. The girl was squatting down between the canes. The boy came up behind her and gave her a pat on her tight blue bottom. She looked up and smiled and pushed a raspberry into his mouth.

I moved away from the window and opened the closet door. It was dark in there and even hotter than the room. I waited a minute until I could see. The closet was full of Father's things — his fishing rods, his waders, his shotgun, his golf clubs in their big leather bag. The fan was on the shelf. I reached it down and my hand touched something else. It was a box of shotgun shells. I shook it. There were shells inside. I put down the fan. My heart was beating hard, and I felt heavy and out of breath. It was all I could do to breathe. I put out my hand and picked up Father's shotgun and broke it open and held it up to the light. It was a double-barreled shotgun, and both barrels looked dark and linty, but a little dirt wouldn't make much difference.

I loaded the gun and backed out of the closet and knelt down at the open window. They were still down there picking raspberries. I sighted on the boy and squeezed the trigger the way Father always said. There was hardly any noise. I hardly heard a thing. But the boy sat down and fell back in the canes. I squeezed the other trigger. The girl stood up and took a step and fell across the boy.

I pulled back the gun and closed the window. I stood there for a moment. Then I took a deep breath and held it as long as I could. Then I stood the gun back in the closet and closed the door and picked up the fan and went out of the room and down the hall.

Mother was standing at the foot of the stairs.

"Edward," she said, and she had the strangest look on her face. She didn't look like Mother. She looked almost frightened. "What was that noise? What happened?"

"I was up in the storeroom," I said. "You said you wanted your fan."

NONFICTION

THE MAN HUNT

by Milton MacKaye

"The three men leaped into the engineer's cabin, yelling,
'Stick 'em up or we'll blow your damned heads off!' "

THIS IS THE STORY of the greatest man hunt in criminal annals, a
more astounding and costly and widespread search than any
ever prosecuted by the cockney bloodhounds of Scotland Yard.

It was not a man hunt in the Uncle Tom tradition, that is, a
scouring of the swamps with shotguns and lynching rope and
melancholy, cadaverous dogs; on the contrary, there was something of a mechanical majesty about it. The punitive agencies of
the United States were brought into play, with all the tremendous resources at government command. Science did its part.
The resultant triumph dusted off and restored to its proper place
that article in the credo of the timid lawbreaker which a Prohibi-
tion statute had tarnished and deposed — namely, that federal
officers always get their man.

On the night of October 11, 1923, a Southern Pacific express
train, pulled by one of the monster locomotives designed for
mountain traffic, was puffing up the long grade in the Klamath
Range of southern Oregon. The tracks were almost in the
shadow of Mount Shasta, and the fireman shivered in the cold
blast as he left his great blaze for a moment to peer from the window of the cab.

The pace of the Limited grew slower. The grade was steep,
and Siskiyou Tunnel, a half-mile bore through the rock of the
mountain, was approaching.

As the headlights of the locomotive picked out the black mouth of the opening, three men muffled in greatcoats might have been seen in the darkness at the edge of the right of way. They raced, panting, alongside the moving cars, their breath smoking in the chilly air and their shoes tearing sharply at the stones. Two scrambled into the blind baggage, but the third, carrying a small satchel and clutching frantically for a step, almost slipped beneath the wheels. A hand caught him and pulled him aboard.

The three men, shadowy there in their hiding place, were just behind the coal tender. Now, as the locomotive whistled hoarsely and plunged into the tunnel, they straightened the grim masks that hid their faces and crawled forward on all fours. The roar of the pistons in the narrow confines of stone drowned the sound of the tumbling coal, and a moment later the three of them leaped into the engineer's cabin, and screamed in one hysterical voice:

"Stick 'em up or we'll blow your —— damned heads off!"

The engineer sat transfixed at the throttle, startled even beyond thought of the great engine of death he drove. The fireman recovered more quickly. He dropped his shovel where he stood and slowly raised his black and sweaty arms.

The shortest of the three visitors crossed quickly to the engineer and ran his hands over him for weapons. He spoke:

"Stop this train."

The engineer was staring as though he had just waked from a nightmare, but he complied, automaton-like. The brakes screamed and ground, and the Southern Pacific express drew to a sobbing halt.

Now the satchel was opened, and the engineer and fireman pushed roughly from the cab. Two guns guarded them while a third bandit a few yards away fumbled beneath a mail car. He was having trouble, and he cursed in a low voice as he tinkered with an unseen mechanism. Suddenly, with relief, he raised himself erect. A fuse was carried down the tracks. Ten seconds later there was a terrific explosion that shook the mountain and made of the tunnel a madhouse of reverberant roars. The mail car had been dynamited.

Back in the sleeping car, the passengers were jerked awake, and alarmed hands pulled back the green curtains. What had happened? A wreck! was the first thought. Men pushed to the exits. The brakeman had already swung himself off and was running forward through the darkness, a fusee signaling over his head.

He had reached the baggage car when a man stepped through the smoke and gas that billowed toward the stone ceiling of the tunnel. The man raised his arm, fired.

The brakeman staggered as though he had stepped in a hole, but he still pushed forward. He raised his hands, trying to ward off some unseen blow.

"Wait a minute, boys," he said — and then fell forward, dead.

The gas was becoming bad, and the three bandits coughed and rubbed their eyes as they tried to uncouple the smoking mail car. The whole end had been torn out of it by the blast. They were working hysterically; passengers would soon be cutting their way through the fumes.

The original plan, it was evident, had been to make the engineer pull the mail car out of the tunnel, where it could be looted. But the mail car was in flames. The engineer, compliant at last, was ordered back in the locomotive. The fireman was pinioned against the wall with a gun at his ribs. The automatic electric bell on the engine clanged unceasingly. Madness bit into the minds of the three baffled outlaws. They had made a botch of their holdup. Without warning, the man who covered the engineer turned full upon him and shot him through the head. The fireman dropped from the bullet of another gun.

Three figures in greatcoats fled down the tracks and out in the clean mountain air. They were sobbing as they ran. All the murderous hate had died out of them when they plunged at last into the woods.

The great Siskiyou Tunnel holdup was over. Three men had been shot down and killed. They were Sidney Bates, the engineer; Marvin Seng, the fireman; and Coyle Johnson, the brakeman. And in the mail car E. E. Daugherty, the mail clerk, stunned by the explosion, had breathed the gases and the hot vapors freed by a broken steam line until he choked to death.

Railroad men and police soon reached the burning train from both directions. When they had extricated the clerk's charred body, they went to work. Here was a crime that was blundering, amateurish, fiendish, appalling — and clueless. It was obvious that it was not the work of experienced train robbers. They would not have used a charge of explosive so strong that it destroyed the currency and registered mail they sought and drove them from the tunnel before they had the chance for loot. Only a novice or novices could have been so stupid.

But that knowledge was of little help in solving the crime. When the news of the tragedy reached the outside world the next day and a great outcry for vengeance had arisen, there was almost nothing to work on. No one had seen the bandits. True, fleeing from the sight of the holocaust they had created, the bandits had left behind them several articles. The magneto with which the dynamite had been fired lay beside the tracks. An automatic pistol had been dropped, and on it were fingerprints. A knapsack, in which overshoes had been carried, and a pair of grimy overalls were found not far away.

The fingerprints, however, would be valuable only in the event they belonged to some criminal who had "done time" and whose thumb marks were in the archives of the police departments of the country. The rest of the stuff was apparently worthless.

Several days passed. Every spot in the near neighborhood of the crime was covered. The bodies of the dead men were shipped to their homes. The debris of the mail car fire was removed by tireless crews of immigrant section hands. The public grew restless. Only the overalls seemed to the detectives to provide them with a lead. The result was that they arrested, as the most likely suspect, a garage worker in one of the towns close by. The investigators had concluded that certain dark smears on the working clothes were motor oil. Also, the batteries in the magneto seemed to have been purchased at the garage where the man was employed, and the overalls fitted him perfectly. To make the case even more plausible, he was an ex-convict — a man with a record.

The garage worker, however, made strenuous denial of participation in the murders, and the alibi he developed seemed to have a certain, unmistakable ring of truth. The detectives were unwilling to admit defeat, but eventually they were forced to conclude they were holding the wrong man.

Now the investigation of the Siskiyou tragedy seemed to have steered up a blind alley. There were no more clues, and the guilty man or men — how could the detectives know how many had been involved? — still were at liberty. The investigators became sullen before the inquiries of newspapermen; they chewed savagely on their stumps of cigars and tore up and tossed into wastebaskets the countless telegraphic appeals for action from railroad executives.

At last they raised their hands, unwillingly admitted defeat, and called for help. Thus, Professor Edward Oscar Heinrich was brought into the case. Professor Heinrich was not one of these fabled scientific detectives of whom we read so much in the popular fiction of the time. He was not a detective at all. Instead, he was a serious, retiring, studious, even pedantic gentleman who was an instructor at the University of California and never ventured from his little laboratory there in Berkeley. Heinrich was a chemist, and he spent all of his days over the test tubes and Bunsen burners and reagents of his profession.

The professor did not come to the Siskiyou Tunnel to look over the scene. He was able to work miracles at a distance. The articles found after the dynamiting were sent to him. He took them into his private laboratory and began study. The first report was that the splotches on the overalls, which the detectives had judged to be grease from motor cars, was not grease at all. The splotches were gum from pine or fir trees. The news was relayed, and the next day the garage worker was freed.

Next Heinrich emerged from his researches with this astounding announcement:

The man who wore these overalls was a left-handed, brown-haired lumberjack, not more than twenty-five years old. He was about five feet eight inches tall, thickset, fastidious in his personal habits, and clean-shaven. He had recently been working in northwestern Oregon or western Washington in the camps where fir trees were being felled. He was one of three men who committed the crime.

It sounded like Sherlock Holmes or Craig Kennedy. The scientist had little more than a pair of dirty overalls to work on. How could he have spelled out such a fund of information without recourse to a crystal ball or a Baker Street hypodermic? The detectives were at first both astonished and incredulous. They were soon convinced.

The size and cut of the overalls had determined the size and probable build of the owner. Under the left-hand flap were deposits of pitch, showing the man had taken off his clothes with his left hand, for the flap on the right side was clean. The determination of the color of the bandit's hair was easy. From one of the buttons, the professor took one or two hairs that caught there when the owner pulled the suspenders over his head to dress or undress.

From the right-hand pocket of the overalls Heinrich extracted tiny slivers and chips of the wood and needles of the Douglas fir. They grow only in northwestern Oregon or western Washington, and that revealed where the bandit had recently been employed. There was also in the same pocket some extremely fine fingernail filings and parings. What did that prove? It established the point of fastidiouness, for no hardened and slovenly lumberjack takes such care of his hands.

All of these substances were studied under microscopes and thus identified. The hair was magnified and compared with standard tables showing the condition of human hair during the various ages of man. Thus it was possible, in what may seem almost a miraculous way, to tell that the man in question was under the age of twenty-five.

The wear on one side of his overalls strengthened the evidence of the pitch that he was left-handed, for it showed that he stood with his right side nearest the trees when he was swinging his heavy woodsman's ax.

But how did Professor Heinrich determine that there were three bandits involved in that attack on the Southern Pacific train? The usefulness of the overalls was exhausted; it took further investigation to substantiate his hypothesis. The knapsack found at the scene had been used to carry creosote-soaked overshoes which were to baffle bloodhounds, if any were used.

The chemist, after painstaking scrutiny, found in the knapsack three or four grains of rock salt.

At this point Heinrich temporarily abandoned absolute science for a venture in the field of speculation. He made the prediction that a cattleman's cabin would be found in the vicinity of Siskiyou Tunnel (cattlemen used rock salt for their stock), and that evidence would be found there that the bandit or bandits had used the cabin as a hideaway.

The detectives in the field made a hurried survey of the surrounding country and they found, surely enough, a lonely house squatting in a little hollow not five miles away. Within, there was more evidence. A towel hung on the nail, and there were a few odd parts of the magneto rusting on a pantry shelf.

The towel, placed under the microscope, revealed whisker cuttings and shaving debris from three faces. The difference in the shade and quality of hair and skin particles established the fact that three men had made their temporary home there, and other evidence proved that they had remained about a week — long enough for the frantic pursuit of the train vandals to die away, and long enough to make their leisurely flight practicable.

When the chemist's report was all in, it furnished concrete evidence of what the scientific man may accomplish with a minimum of materials. It had silenced once and for all the sneers of professional policemen at the impracticabilities of the sedentary expert. With a few odds and ends, Professor Heinrich had provided a better description of at least one of the criminals than could have an untrained and casual eyewitness, if there had been one on the spot.

Even so, the man hunt had not advanced greatly. The keystone of the structure had been laid, but only the tireless work of less imaginative men could carry it further. There were (to quote Mr. Edward H. Smith, writing in the *New York Times*) "hundreds of lumber camps, thousands of lumberjacks, hundreds of thousands of men of the age and size noted. And there was a world to hide in."

At just about this time Charles Riddiford, the postal inspector at Spokane, Washington, boarded a train for the national capital. Riddiford controlled the postal district which includes Oregon,

Washington, Idaho, Montana, and Alaska. He was speeding eastward for the purpose of appealing to the Postmaster General to allow him unlimited funds and the utmost cooperation in his search for the men who had attempted robbery in the Klamath Mountains and who had allowed a clerk in the mail car there to strangle to death.

After he entered the long gray stone building on Pennsylvania Avenue that houses the Post Office Department, and was ushered into the presence of his superior, he drew from his brief case a photograph. It was a picture of three of the men murdered in the tunnel, a picture snapped as they lay there dead beside the tracks. A moment later he heard Postmaster General New speak.

"The scoundrels who murdered these men must be caught," said Mr. New. "You've got to get them."

Riddiford went back to Spokane with full authority to look to the ends of the earth for his quarry.

Armed with the information that Professor Heinrich had furnished, postal inspectors now went up and down the lengths of the West, seeking out principally the lumber camps. They succeeded in hiring themselves out as lumberjacks, teamsters, cooks, paymasters, barbers, clerks in timber-town general stores. Always they sought three men who had disappeared in October of 1923. They never disclosed their real purpose in the questionings — ostensibly they were hunting old friends, or distant relatives, or men who owed them money. There were many false clues and futile raising of hopes. For months the search was fruitless. The problem was that of the old proverb, but, this time, there were three needles in a haystack to be found.

Finally two men, posing as workers, came into Eugene, Oregon. They haunted the club rooms and speakeasies of the little lumber town, the places where the radicals and malcontents of the camps congregated. There they first crossed the trail of three brothers who bore the name d'Autremont. The d'Autremonts had been incendiary young fellows while in Eugene, they heard; fellows who were bitter against constituted authority and egotistical of their own prowess. Yes, they had disappeared without notice in the fall of 1923, but only disappeared as had a hundred other transient laborers, leaving no trace behind.

The two inspectors visited the little cottage in town where the three young men had resided. That night the telegraph wires carried messages in code to Tacoma and Spokane and San Francisco. The next day there were other detectives in Eugene. Bits of evidence were gathered from the deserted dwelling — hairs, nail filings, pieces of cloth, and, most important of all, fingerprints. They were sent in haste to Professor Heinrich at Berkeley.

A week later the walls of every post office in the United States, from Bangor, Maine, to San Jose, carried this notice:

Wanted: $15,000 reward; Hugh d'Autremont, 19; Roy d'Autremont, 23; Ray d'Autremont, 23. Charged with the murder of four men in the Siskiyou Tunnel holdup.

And who were the three d'Autremonts, the young brothers who were hunted? They were sons of a barber who, until early in 1923, had lived in Artesia, New Mexico, and done Artesia's shaving and trimming. Roy and Ray had been wanderers from their earliest years. Hugh was different. He was the bright boy of the three, and his parents had intended to send him to college to make him the gentleman of the family, the professional man.

That spring, Hugh graduated from high school as one of the leaders of his class. He was self-assertive and confident, popular among both his boy and girl classmates, a boxer and foot-racer and debater. His teachers believed Hugh would "make his mark" if he only curbed his imagination a little and worked hard. He was clever enough, but he was argumentative and dissatisfied. If that dissatisfaction could be turned into the proper channels it would furnish him with driving power. But there was one thing his teachers and his parents did not note. Contained in Hugh was a tremendous admiration for Robin Hood and that more modern outlaw, Jesse James. Hugh loved their boldness and their defiance. He read all the dime novels which dealt with the exploits of Jesse James, and he took the role of Jesse always when the lads of the neighborhood played at bandit. Later, the childish admiration remained so strong in him that he used the name himself, or changed it slightly, for caution's sake, to E. E. James.

Hugh was not destined for college. After he graduated from

school that spring, the wanderlust bit him; he could not wait for excitement. His two older brothers were already in Oregon, and they invited him to come on. And so Hugh bade good-bye to New Mexico for good and all. At Eugene, he joined Roy and Ray. He was right in the heart of the big-tree country.

Lumbering was not too hard for the youngster. He was sturdy and well built. After a few lessons he could handle his ax as well as the next man.

With his brothers now, Hugh found new followers, and rash ones, for his leadership. Ray, five years his elder, furnished the yeast of their unrest, but the imagination of Hugh directed the channels in which it should flow. Ray was a hard, bitter young man. He had spent a year in the Washington State Reformatory at Monroe during the war for criminal syndicalism. Ray in reality, however, was not a radical at all. Probably he couldn't have quoted a single paragraph from Karl Marx before his arrest, and certainly he could not have explained satisfactorily the difference between syndicalism, Christian socialism, and philosophical anarchism. His revolt was entirely an emotional thing. He was merely against the established order, a lusty underdog. But a year's confinement gave him time to brood, and when he came out, youthful enthusiasm had turned into a snarling hatred for all that the law represented. A man should get ahead no matter whom he tramped down, that was his dogma, and soon he had imbued his twin with the same savage unrest, the same unreasonable rebellion.

It was Hugh who turned this philosophy into action. He began talking of retaliation and hazard. His talents as a high school debater were called into action in the club rooms and meeting places of the lumberjacks in Eugene. He spouted and spouted in public and was laughed down for his pains. Then one day he made a concrete suggestion. The d'Autremont boys, like the James boys, would prove their mettle by banditry, he told his receptive brothers; they would rob a bank along the Pacific Highway. It was easy, and they were too smart to be caught.

Dubiously at first, then with enthusiasm, Roy and Ray agreed. The bank robbery, however, never took place. Before they could carry out the project, Hugh had come forward with a suggestion infinitely more glamorous. They would hold up a train.

The next day the three boys disappeared from Eugene, and they were never seen there again.

So much for the history of the d'Autremonts. With the posting of the federal placards the hunt for them was on in earnest. The government had pictures, clipped from old Artesia high school annuals, and full descriptions of each. They had Ray's fingerprints. Everything considered, it seemed highly probable the robber hunt would be a short-lived and successful one. The three youths had no money to aid them in escape; they had fled empty-handed from the burning mail car. They had no moneyed friends and no previous experience in eluding the police.

Six months passed, and still they were free. All lumber camps had been watched and the haunts of the I.W.W. raided repeatedly in search of them. A year passed. Still the pursuit was vain. The unheard-of was happening. Three young novices at crime were defeating all the vigilance of the law. Half a million policemen, federal officers, sheriffs, and rural constables, scattered through every state and county in the union, were on the watch, hungry for the huge reward that had been offered. The net covered the nation from Maine to California. Every mail brought wispy and conflicting clues to the Post Office Department, clues that were religiously checked in the hope that the law of averages would produce one that was authentic.

There were arrests, of course — many of them. A hundred civic-minded individuals every day looked askance at their train mates or road companions and decided that they resembled the d'Autremonts. Sometimes their testimony convinced the police, always eager to take someone into custody when it is a matter of discretion. In Canada "Hugh d'Autremont" was seized and newspapers carried headlines heralding his capture until the admission of error was made. In Montana "Roy d'Autremont" was arrested and held. He was found to be just a cowboy full of bad liquor. In Michigan "Ray d'Autremont" was found reading a Communist newspaper and was thrown into a dirty cell, until it had been established that he was only an agitator come out of Chicago to wake the iron miners to a realization of their wage slavery.

One day a New York state trooper interfered in a brawl in Bay Shore, Long Island, and put handcuffs on one surly young man who defied his authority. Later the face of the boy haunted him, and he went back to the jail at Islip. Midway in their interview the thought dawned on the trooper that this prisoner resembled the fugitive Hugh. Within thirty minutes there was a postal inspector at Islip. The prisoner did look much like the bandit, he talked like him, he had apparently been in the West and he said he was a roving sideshow and carnival worker. But a day's inquiry revealed him only as a runaway and talented liar from Boston.

One of the most complete fiascos occurred in a small town in Maine. The postal inspector at Boston was informed over long-distance telephone that Roy and Ray d'Autremont were there. The informant was a private detective, and it was plain from his speech that he was already planning ways to spend the reward. The Boston inspector did not put too much faith in the "tip-off," but the more he considered it, the more earmarks of truth the story had. The Maine village was a lumber town, and the d'Autremonts were lumberjacks; the two men were twins and looked much alike; their age was approximately correct. Several federal operatives were hustled north.

At the station late at night they were met by the triumphant detective. The big-time fellows had nothing on him! One at a time the inspectors drifted casually uptown and surrounded a little lunchroom. The local officer and one agent entered the café and engaged the proprietor in conversation. Yes, he had two such men working for him. They were queer and silent and they were twins. Just at midnight the twins entered the restaurant. The waiting officers pounced before the men could draw guns — and found they had seized two innocent Polish cooks.

There were five hundred false arrests in all, and once the father of the fugitive boys identified a body found in the Columbia River as that of one of his sons. But the Post Office was not convinced, and when eighteen months had passed, the officials went into solemn conference to discuss new ways and means of prosecuting the search.

It was clearly apparent by this time that the government had no easy chase on its hands, but, instead, the most difficult man hunt in criminal history. The d'Autremont boys had got away to a good start, and they had mixed themselves up in no more escapades. The murder of four men had satisfied their blood lust; a fruitless robbery had cured their desire to emulate the James brothers. Shortly before, the nationwide pursuit of Gerald Chapman and Dutch Anderson, famous New York bandits, had been successful after two years of effort. But Anderson and Chapman were professional criminals who looked like criminals and were certain to drift to the underworld of any city in which they made hiding place. Eventual capture, for them, had been certain from the start. The Siskiyou Tunnel bandits had no acquaintance with the underworld, and they did not frequent the haunts of the habitually unrighteous.

The gray-haired men in the Washington swivel chairs studied the matter deeply at their solemn conference. They had determined to catch the d'Autremonts, and catch them they would if it cost a million dollars. The result, then, of that conference was the formulating of a new and tremendous program. The government would try the methods of modern advertising; it would circularize the whole world with posters of the fugitive bandits. It would make their name a household word, and their photographed faces as familiar as those of motion picture stars or baseball players or ex-Presidents.

Two million posters were printed and sent to points as distant as Central Asia and the Transvaal. Dentists everywhere received private communications from the government which asked them to look for the three men and furnished a technical description of all their dental work. Opticians and optometrists in all countries were given the eyeglass prescriptions of Ray and Roy. Public libraries were asked to be on the watch for men of their description who would ask for books on socialism and volumes of verse — and who showed a marked liking for the he-man jingles of Robert W. Service. Any pity the nation might have felt for Hugh d'Autremont was thus dammed by the information that he had a weakness for reciting "The Spell of the Yukon."

This new crusade cost over $500,000 and yet three years

passed without a hint of the fugitives' whereabouts. The three young men, not so young now, had long since parted company, but they must have felt, with reason, that the danger of apprehension was past. Still the federal officers kept doggedly on. Riddiford would not give up, and he was supported fully by his superiors.

What eventually happened might seem, at first glance, to have been blind luck. But the most careful and painstaking hunt in history had made possible that luck. A discharged soldier strolled into a San Francisco post office one morning to send a money order. While he waited to be served he cast his eyes idly over a poster there that said "Wanted: $15,000 reward; Hugh d'Autremont." He started, and then he looked at the poster again and scrutinized closely one of the photographs. He whistled softly and strolled up to the postal window.

"Say," he drawled to the clerk, "I served with that guy there in the Philippines."

Six weeks later on a steaming hot day in Manila, a sergeant of infantry halted drill and read off the name of a private in ranks.

"James C. Price," he called.

James C. Price stepped forward. He was stripped of his arms and sent to the guardhouse at the point of eight bayonets. Hugh d'Autremont was under arrest.

After a first and futile bluff, the handsome young soldier readily admitted his identity and was taken back to the United States for trial. Three years and four months had elapsed since the Siskiyou holdup, and the hunt had followed him 9000 miles from the scene and halfway around the world from Chicago, where he had enlisted.

The government redoubled its efforts to locate Roy and Ray. The crafty Hugh maintained that he had no knowledge of their whereabouts, and pressure failed to make him say more. The radio was pressed into service, and descriptions of the men were sent into almost every home in the country by the channels of the ether. Seventy-five thousand additional circulars were printed.

One day the Department of Justice received a note from

Steubenville, Ohio. Someone there believed he had seen the d'Autremont twins. The officials sighed wearily and sent men to investigate. The clue sounded false, but it was worth inquiry.

The operatives found that living in a rooming house in the foreign section were, indeed, twin brothers who were known as Elmer and Clarence Goodwill. One was married and had a small child almost a year old. They were employed by a Wheeling Steel Corporation mill. Both previously had worked in a Detroit automobile factory and they had come to Steubenville from Hanging Rock, Ohio. There they lived in a community of "moonshiners," where there were no inquiries into the next fellow's business. The hair of one of the men, however, did not tally with printed descriptions of the bandits. It was very light, as though it had been bleached with peroxide.

Hugh d'Autremont was to go to trial in Medford, Oregon, on June 9. On June 8, Roy d'Autremont was arrested in Steubenville as he came from work in the mill. The police and federal agents then went in a motor car to the house where he lived.

A detective knocked on the door. Ray answered it.

"Your brother has been injured at the mill and wants you," he was told.

A look of horror crossed Ray's face. Hunted, always in fear of capture, his own identity sacrificed, Roy was the only person in the world he could trust as a friend. If Roy died . . .

He thrust on his hat and walked hurriedly to the motor car, where four men waited. There he found four guns covering him, and he submitted quietly to arrest. Ray's wife was called. She carried her young child in her arms as she stepped dazedly to the street.

"Well, good-bye, Hazel," Ray said.

"Good-bye," she echoed, and she stood there, desolate, as the car moved away.

When Ray arrived at police headquarters, he found Roy waiting for him.

"If you had come in my house I would have killed you and then shot myself," Ray told one of the federal agents. "My life is worth nothing to me now, for I know what I am up against."

It had been almost four years since three boys in greatcoats climbed aboard a train in the shadow of Mount Shasta, but the d'Autremonts at last were under arrest. The greatest man hunt in history had been successful.

The three were found guilty of first-degree murder and were sentenced to life imprisonment. Just before they went to the state prison at Salem, Oregon, all made full confessions of their guilt. And here is what Hugh, still the boy rhetorician, said:

"The hand of the potter wavered and poured into the mold of the d'Autremonts too much guts."

ANOTHER SOLUTION

by Gilbert Highet

"This night was a terrible adventure; but he would live to
tell about it."

JUST BEFORE the boat capsized, Victor noticed that the sun was
beginning to touch the water. He had never seen a sunset from
the level of the sea: now he turned to watch the glow sucked
down into that motionless green; but one of the girls, at the bow,
screamed. Her long appalling cry echoed back instantly from the
cliffs.

Within the same moment, there was a shock. Everyone in the
boat seemed to be struck by an enormous fist. The boom whipped round and smashed Pedro in the face. Concha, sitting on the
bulwark, was hurled backward into the water; her head must
have struck something, for Victor did not see her again. Pepa
was always afraid of the sea — she could swim only a little, and
she had been sitting in the hold with her knees below the deck-
planking to make herself feel safe. As it turned over, the boat
took her with it into the depths.

The last thin sector of the sun was exactly on Victor's eye
level as he kicked his way to the surface. There was nothing else
on the whole face of the sea, except Concha's handkerchief. He
dived several times as well as he could. He was not a good
swimmer, and all he could do was to duck his head under the
surface, trying to kick his way down through the vague luminous
water, in the hope of finding one of his friends, struggling or unconscious. Once he got down about fifteen feet and saw dim

shapes near him. Concha and Pedro? He could touch nothing when he swam across under water, and afterward he thought it was only reflected light slanting down from the surface. There was nothing else within his reach.

Then he swam round and round in great circles, sometimes cutting across and turning back on his course, in case a body floated up to the surface. Nothing. He swam farther out to sea, dived again and again, until he felt sick. Nothing, nothing. His friends, Pedro, Pepa, Concha, were all drowned. He was suddenly alone.

His mind was clear. His friends were dead. He had to save himself. He had to save himself — that was the problem. He had often heard of threatened men thinking clearly and swiftly: it was true that they could. Think.

He was alone, without a boat, in the Mediterranean, at nightfall, below the enormous cliffs of Majorca. He had eaten a good meal an hour before and was not tired. After the boat capsized, he had kicked off his clothes easily enough. It was summer, so the water would not be unbearably cold at any time during the night. The weather was calm: cloudless sky, no moon, but the first stars were appearing. It would be quite dark in fifteen minutes. Already the cliffs seemed to exude a brown vapor, and above them the sky of night was luminous.

The first way of escape was to bring help by shouting. Difficult. As far as he knew, this coast was made of solid lava blocks cast up and shorn off in one abrupt and forbidding front. When the water was bright and still, the cliffs could be seen continuing down, far beneath it, to horrible depths. The island was only an incident in the Mediterranean; it rested on the sea floor, and under its cliffs were miles of water, the waves of the deep. There were no coastwise villages, no houses nearer than the Archduke's deserted villas high on the hill. Over the water, a shout will carry for miles; but Victor knew it would be useless to shout until much later, when a boat might be out for nightfishing. He must try other solutions. Meanwhile, he was slowly treading water and beginning to feel a little tired.

Second, then. Was it possible to swim to the cliffs and climb them? He looked up. Gulfs of dark space opened before him — a smooth wall with one long slow crack extending diagonally upward, out of sight. Leaving Concha's handkerchief still floating, he swam toward the lower end of the fissure. Every stroke took him into a deeper angle of midnight. The water was a quiet purple darkness all round him. He reached the black rock, and gripped. But he might as well have tried to climb an iceberg. For yards above his head the protuberances were all rounded off by years of waves. His hands slipped off every grip he took. The cliff was impossible. Dark and deathly, it towered above him, forcing him down.

Involuntarily, he struck out into the open sea, away from the black echoing mass of stone. He could see the floating handkerchief as a tiny interruption in that smooth water in which his own movements made only large ripples. It was so small and lonely that he was glad when he reached it. Now, a third way of escape —

The last light was being sucked out of the air. Victor stopped treading water and began to jump. Standing upright in the water, he drew up his legs and jerked them sharply downward. At the same time, he thrust his hands into the face of the sea, palms under. This relieved his muscles, and raised him above the surface with every leap. He looked southward, in the direction of Otonozar, where his friends lived — had lived. Nothing there; not a light, not even a movement in the surface glimmer of the sea. Ten miles lay between him and home. Paddling slowly on his back, he considered the third escape. Could he swim back to Otonozar? Could he swim all night? Could he even float until he was rescued?

As the night breeze blew in from the sea, he knew that he could do neither. He was not a good swimmer, like poor Pedro. Once, with Pedro and two other Majorcans, he had swum out a mile to meet their motorboat at La Foradada; but he was exhausted and sick after it, and had had to come home in the boat. Now the distances lengthened out in the darkness before him. Ten miles. Twenty thousand strokes. To count them, and hear yourself panting, and count, and kick and plunge in the darkness, for hours, for hours, still to struggle on, through the water always colder and stranger, and at last to be engulfed in an unknown place, forever lost, not even beside his friends. No.

It was quite dark. Eleven. The quiet stars shone to one another without a thrill of movement. Silent night. The sea lay in leaden stillness, broken only by the recurrent thrust of Victor's strokes. They were slower now.

He turned over and swam ahead. He must think of some way to keep alive, not to die after a few hours of ignominious and futile survival. Four solutions: all useless. Could he swim along the coast to find a landing place?

No, not even that. The cliffs were never less than five hundred feet high, and always beaten smooth by the stormy waves. There was no place where they could be climbed. He remembered that his friends had never been able to go swimming except at the village: there was no way down, no way up the cliffs. They were broken sharp off by the volcano, and smoothed by the busy sea which now waited so quietly. The fifth solution was hopeless. Only one remained.

Victor felt something brush his head, and knew it for Concha's handkerchief, floating just below the surface. This was where to die. He grasped the little rag; he said a prayer for the souls of his friends and one for himself; he let himself sink. He would wait until he had sunk some distance before breathing the water into his lungs. Drowning was, they said, a blend of sickness and sleep.

Slowly, on his back, he sank. Above him the dark-shining surface would become smooth again; when it was beyond reach, he would breathe. First, the sickness; then, the sleep.

It seemed he was hardly under water before his back felt a pain. There was something firm and sharp beneath him. It was a rock.

Victor sprang into movement — his lungs were still full of air. In his struggles, he ground his shoulder on the rock with a welcome pang, and his first gasp after he reached the surface was choked by his splashing. He swallowed a great deal of water, which made him shiver and cough with nausea. But he was happy, breathing in great gulps of air. Escape was found; a solution was found. It was only one tall thin wedge of rock rising from the sea floor, or from some deep-sunken buttress of the cliff. It there had been a wide shelf, he would have touched it long before as he swam about; but it was easy enough to miss this — he felt it now with his feet — this blade six inches wide. After swimming over and over this place, he had thought of it only as a chasm of deep sea, with his friends buried far below. The boat was sunk and he had never thought of the rock which had sunk it.

As he cautiously put his weight on his feet, he felt ill with relief and hope and horror to think that he might have drowned two fathoms away from his safety. Here was the seventh, the unexpected solution. Now he had a firm foothold, his head and shoulders were out of the water, and there were no waves, so he could stand still and rest. The tide would not rise more than an inch. He could stand all night on this rock and bear the chill — never so dreadful. And in the morning there would be fishermen; in the morning at the earliest light of dawn. Night was not long. For a moment the whole scene was friendly, and the stars were companions. He felt the solid grateful rock with his feet; bent his strained muscles. This night was a terrible adventure; but he would live to tell about it.

A piece of seaweed touched his foot, and he pushed it away. It drifted back, and he kicked it off. When it returned and glided along his knee, he lowered one arm to catch it. Perhaps it was not seaweed; perhaps it was poor Concha's handkerchief.

As he felt about in the water, something gripped his knee. Instantly, the same grip was on his hand. He could not move. He glared down into the dark water, where beside his own body he saw nothing. But it was not necessary to see the gray shape with the long arms, the great octopus which clung to the rock and now grasped both his wrists and threw another tentacle round his waist and drew him down. He had not thought of that.

FICTION

MISS HINCH

by Henry Sydnor Harrison

Wherein the world's greatest woman detective hunts the
world's cleverest woman murderer.

IN GOING FROM a given point on 126th Street to a subway station
at 125th, it is not usual to begin by circling the block to 127th
Street, especially in sleet, darkness, and deadly cold. When two
people pursue such a course at the same time, moving unobtrusively on opposite sides of the street, in the nature of things the
coincidence is likely to attract the attention of one or the other of
them.

In the bright light of the entrance to the tube they came almost
face to face, and the clergyman took a good look at her. Certainly she was a decent-looking old body, if any woman was:
white-haired, wrinkled, spectacled, and stooped. A poor but
thoroughly respectable domestic servant of the better class she
looked, in her black hat, neat veil, and nondescript gray cloak;
and her brief glance at the reverend gentleman was precisely
what it should have been from her to him — deference itself.
Nevertheless, he, going more slowly down the drafty steps, continued to study her from behind with a singular intentness.

An express was just thundering in, which the clergyman,
handicapped as he was by his clubfoot and stout cane, was
barely in time to catch. He entered the same car with the woman
and took a seat directly across from her. It must have been then
well past midnight, and the wildness of the weather was dis-

couraging to travel. The car was almost deserted. Even here under the earth the bitter breath of the night blew and bit, and the old woman shivered under her cloak. At last, her teeth chattering, she got up in an apologetic sort of way and moved toward the rear of the car, feeling the empty seats as she went, in a palpable search for hot pipes. The clergyman's eyes followed her; he watched her sink down, presently, into a seat on his own side of the car. A young couple sat between them now; he could no longer see the woman, beyond glimpses of her black knees and her faded bonnet, fastened on with a long steel hatpin.

Nothing could have seemed more natural or more trivial than this change of seats on the part of a thin-blooded and half-frozen passenger. But it happened to be a time of mutual doubts and general suspiciousness, when men looked askance into every strange face, and the smallest incidents might take on an hysterical importance. Through days of intense searching for a fugitive outlaw of extraordinary gifts, the nerves of the city had been visibly strained. All jumped now when anybody cried "Boo!" and the hue and cry went up falsely twenty times a day.

The clergyman pondered; mechanically, he turned up his coat collar and fell to stamping his feet. He was an Episcopal clergyman, by his garb — rather short, very full-bodied, not to say fat, bearded, and somewhat puffy-faced, with heavy cheeks cut by deep creases. Well lined against the cold though he was, however, he, too, began to show signs of suffering, and presently rose and moved in his turn, seeking out a new place where the chilled heating apparatus might give a better account of itself. He found a seat just beyond the old serving woman, limped into it, and relapsed into his own thoughts.

The young couple, half a dozen seats away, appeared thoroughly absorbed in each other's society. The fifth traveler, a withered old gentleman sitting across and down the aisle, napped fitfully upon his cane. The woman in the shapeless cloak sat in a sad kind of silence; and the train hurled itself roaringly through the tube. After a time, she glanced through her spectacles at the meditating clergyman, and her look fell swiftly from his face to the "ten o'clock extra" in his hand. She removed her gaze and let it travel casually about the car; but before long it returned again, as if magnetized, to the newspaper. Then, with some obvious hesitation, she bent forward and said, above the noises of the train:

"Excuse me, Father, but would you please let me look at your paper a minute, sir?"

The clergyman came out of his revèrie instantly, and looked at her with a quick smile.

"Certainly. Keep it, if you like: I am quite through with it. But," he said, in a pleasant deep voice, "I am an Episcopal minister, not a priest."

"Oh, sir — I beg your pardon! I thought . . ."

He dismissed the apology with a nod and a good-natured hand.

The woman opened the paper with decent cotton-gloved fingers. The garish headlines told all the story: EARTH OPENED AND SWALLOWED MISS HINCH, SAYS INSPECTOR — POLICE CONFESS "PRACTICALLY NO CLUE" — EVEN JESSIE DARK — so the bold capitals ran on — SEEMS "STUMPED." Below the spread was a luridly written but flimsy narrative, "By Jessie Dark," which at once confirmed the odd implications of the caption. "Jessie Dark," it appeared, was one of those most extraordinary of the products of yellow journalism, a woman "crime expert," now in action. More than this, she was a "crime expert" to be taken seriously, it seemed — no mere office-desk sleuth, but an actual performer with, unexpectedly enough, a somewhat formidable list of notches on her gun. So much, at least, was to be gathered from her paper's boxed display of "Jessie Dark's Triumphs":

March 2, 1901. Caught Julia Victorian, alias Gregory, the brains of the "Healy Ring" kidnapers.
October 7–29, 1903. Found Mrs. Trotwood and secured the letter that convicted her of the murder of her lover, Ellis E. Swan.
December 17, 1903. Ran down Charles Bartsch in a Newark laundry and trapped a confession from him.
July 4, 1904. Caught Hélène Gray, "Blackmail Queen," and recovered the Stratford jewels.

And so on — nine "triumphs" in all; and nearly every one of them, as the least observant reader could hardly fail to notice, involved the capture of a woman.

Nevertheless, it could not be pretended that the "snappy" paragraphs in this evening's extra seemed to foreshadow a new or tenth triumph for Jessie Dark at an early date; and the old serving woman in the car presently laid down the sheet with a look of marked depression.

The clergyman glanced at her again. Her expression was so speaking that it seemed almost an invitation; moreover, public interest in the curious case had created a freemasonry which made conversation between total strangers the rule wherever two or three were gathered.

"You were reading about this strange mystery, I suppose?"

The woman, with a sharp intake of breath, answered: "Yes, sir. Oh, sir, it seems as if I couldn't think of anything else."

"Ah?" he said, calmly. "It certainly appears to be a remarkable affair."

Remarkable indeed the affair seemed. In a tiny little room within ten steps of Broadway, at half past nine o'clock on a fine evening, Miss Hinch had killed John Catherwood with the light sword she used in her famous representation of the Father of his Country. Catherwood, it was known, had come to tell her of his approaching marriage; and ten thousand amateur detectives, stimulated by the unprecedented "rewards," had required no further motive of a creature already notorious for fierce jealousy. So far the tragedy was commonplace enough, and even vulgar. What had redeemed it to romance from this point on was the extraordinary faculty of the woman, which had made her celebrated while she was still in her teens. Violent, unmoral, criminal she might be, but she happened also to be the most astonishing impersonator of her time. Her brilliant act consisted of a series of character changes, many of them done "in full view of the audience" with the assistance only of a small table of properties half concealed under a net. Some of these transformations were so amazing as to be beyond belief, even after one had sat and watched them. Not the woman's appearance only, but voice, speech, manner, carriage, all shifted incredibly to fit the new part; so that she appeared to have no permanent form or fashion of her own, but to be only so much plastic human material out of which her cunning could mold at will man, woman, or child, great lady of the Louisan court, or Tammany chieftain with the modernest of East Side modernisms upon his lips.

With this strange gift, hitherto used only to enthrall large audiences and wring extortionate contracts from managers, the woman known as Miss Hinch — she appeared to be without a first name — was now fighting for her life somewhere against the police of the world. Without artifice, she was a tall, thin-chested young woman with strongly marked features and considerable beauty of a bold sort. What she would look like at the present moment nobody could venture a guess. Having stabbed John Catherwood in her dressingroom at the Colisseum, she had donned hat and coat, dropped two wigs and her make-up kit into a handbag, and walked out into Broadway. Within ten minutes the dead body of Catherwood was found and the chase begun. At the stage door, as she passed out, Miss Hinch had met an acquaintance, a young comedian named Dargis, and exchanged a word of greeting with him. That had been ten days ago. After Dargis, no one had seen her. The earth, indeed, seemed to have opened and swallowed her. Yet her natural features were almost as well known as a President's, and the newspapers of a continent were daily reprinting them in a hundred variations.

"A very remarkable case," repeated the clergyman, rather absently; and his neighbor, the old woman, agreed mournfully that it was. Then, as the train slowed and quieted for the stop at 86th Street, she spoke again, with sudden bitterness:

"Oh, they'll never catch her, sir — never! She's too smart for 'em all, Miss Hinch is."

Attracted by her tone, the stout divine inquired if she was particularly interested in the case.

"Yes, sir — I got reason to be. Jack Catherwood's mother and me was at school together, and great friends all our life long. Oh, sir," she went on, as if in answer to his look of faint surprise, "Jack was a fine gentleman, with manners and looks and all beyond his people. But he never grew away from his old mother — no, sir, never! And I don't believe ever a Sunday passed that he didn't go up and set the afternoon away with her, talking and laughing just like he was a little boy again. Maybe he done things he hadn't ought, as high-spirited lads will, but oh, sir, he was a good boy in his heart — a good boy. And it does seem too hard for him to die like that — and that hussy free to go her way, ruinin' and killin' —''

"My good woman," said the clergyman presently, after glancing about, "compose yourself. No matter how diabolical this woman's skill is, her sin will assuredly find her out."

The woman dutifully lowered her handkerchief and tried to compose herself, as bidden.

"But oh, she's that clever — diabolical, just as ye say, sir. Through poor Jack we of course heard much gossip about her, and they do say that her best tricks was not done on the stage at all. They say, sir, that, sittin' around a table with her friends, she could begin and twist her face so strange and terrible that they would beg her to stop, and jump up and run from the table — frightened out of their lives, sir, grown-up people, by the terrible faces she could make. And let her only step behind her screen for a minute — for she kept her secrets well, Miss Hinch did — and she'd come walking out to you, and you could go right up to her in the full light and take her hand, and still you couldn't make yourself believe that it was her."

"Yes," said the clergyman, "I have heard that she is remarkably clever — though, as a stranger in this part of the world, I, of course, never saw her. I must say, it is all very interesting and strange."

The express had started again with a jolt, and the rumbling and roaring all but drowned out his voice. He turned his head and stared through the window at the dark flying walls. At the same moment the woman turned her head and stared full at him. When he turned back, her gaze had gone off toward the door.

The clergyman picked up the paper thoughtfully and read for a while. But when, just outside of Grand Central Station, the train came to a nameless halt, he at once resumed the conversation.

"I'm a visitor in the city, from Denver, Colorado," he explained in an easy way, "and knew little or nothing about the case until an evening or two ago, when I attended a meeting of

gentlemen here. The Men's Club at St. Matthias' Church —
perhaps you know the place? Upon my word, they talked of
nothing else. I confess they got me quite interested in their gossip. So tonight I bought this paper to see what this extraordinary
woman detective it employs had to say about it. We don't have
such things in the West, you know. But I must say I was disappointed, after all the talk about her."

"Yes, sir, indeed, and no wonder, for she's told Mrs. Catherwood herself that's she's never made such a failure as this, so
far. It seemed like she could always catch women, up to this. It
seemed like she knew in her own mind just what a woman would
do, where she'd try to hide, and all, and so she could find them
time and time when the men detectives didn't know where to
look. But oh, sir, she's never had to hunt for such a woman as
Miss Hinch before!"

"No? I suppose not," said the clergyman. "Her theorizing
here certainly seems very sketchy."

"*Theorizing*, sir! Bless my soul!" suddenly exploded the old
gentleman across the aisle, to the surprise of both. "You don't
suppose the clever little woman is going to show her hand in those
newspaper stories, with Miss Hinch in the city and reading every
line of them! In the city, sir — such is my positive conviction!"

He had roused from his nap, it seemed, just in time to over-
hear the episcopate criticism. Now he answered the looks of the
old woman and the clergyman with an elderly cackle.

"Excuse my intrusion, I'm sure! But I can't sit silent and hear
anybody run down Jessie Dark — Miss Matthewson in private
life, as perhaps you don't know. No, sir! Why, there's a man at
my boarding place — remarkable fellow named Hardy, Tom
Hardy — who's known her for *years*! As to those *theorizings*,
sir, I can assure you she puts in there *exactly the opposite of
what she really thinks*!"

"You don't tell me!" said the clergyman.

"Yes, sir! Oh, she plays the game! She has her private ideas,
her clues, her schemes. The woman doesn't live who is clever
enough to hoodwink Jessie Dark. I look for developments any
day, sir!"

A new voice joined in. The pair down the car, their attention caught by the old man's pervasive tones, had been frankly listening: and it was illustrative of the public mind at the moment that, as they now rose for the station, the young fellow felt perfectly free to offer his contribution.

"Dramatic situation, isn't it, when you stop to think? Those two clever women pitted against each other in a life-and-death struggle — fighting it out in the underground somewhere — keen professional pride on one side and the fear of the electric chair on the other . . ."

"Oh, yes! Oh, yes!" exclaimed the old gentleman, rather testily. "But, my dear sir, it's not professional pride that makes Jessie Dark so resolute to win. It's *sex jealousy* — if you follow me — no offense, madam! Yes, sir! Women never have the slightest respect for each other's abilities — not the slightest. No mercy for each other, either! I tell you, Jessie Dark'd be ashamed to be beaten by another woman. Read her stories between the lines, sir — invincible determination — no mercy! You catch my point?"

"It sounds reasonable," answered the Colorado clergyman, with his quick smile. "Women, we are told . . ."

"Oh, I'm for Jessie Dark, all right!" the young fellow broke in — "especially since the police have practically laid down. But . . ."

"Why, she's told my friend Hardy," the old gentleman rode him down, "that she'll find Hinch if it takes her lifetime! Knows a thing or two about actresses, she says. Says the world isn't big enough for the creature to hide from her. Well! What do you think of that?"

"Tell what we were just talking about, George," prompted the young wife, with an admiring gaze.

"But oh, sir," began the old woman timidly, "Jack Catherwood's been dead ten days now, and . . ."

"Woman got on my car at nine o'clock tonight," suddenly shouted the guard, who, having flung open the doors, was listening to the symposium eagerly — "wore a brown veil and goggles. I'd 'a' bet every dollar I had . . ."

"Ten days, madam! And what is that, pray?" barked the old

gentleman, rising abruptly but triumphantly. "A lifetime, if necessary! — never fear! Mrs. Victorian was considered pretty clever, eh? Wasn't she? Remember what Jessie Dark did for her? Nan Parmalee, too — though the police did their best to steal her credit. She'll do just as much for Miss Hinch — you may take it from me!"

"But how's she going to make the capture, gentlemen?" cried the young fellow, getting his chance at last. "That's the point my wife and I've been discussing. Suppose she succeeds in spotting this woman-devil, what'll she do? Now . . ."

"Do, sir! Yell for the police! I say . . ."

"And have Miss Hinch kill her — and then herself, too? Wouldn't she have to . . ."

"Grand Central!" cried the guard for the second time; and the young fellow broke off reluctantly as his bride towed him strongly toward the door.

"Hope she nabs her soon," he called back to the clergyman over his shoulder. "Getting on my nerves! One of these kindergarten reward-chasers followed my wife five blocks, just because she's got a pointed chin. Don't know what might have happened if I hadn't come along and . . ."

Doors rolled shut behind him, and the train flung itself on its way. Within the car, a silence ensued. The clergyman stared at the floor, and the old woman fell back upon the borrowed "extra." She appeared to be rereading the observations of Jessie Dark with considerable care. Presently she lowered the paper and began a quiet search for something under the folds of her cloak; and at length, her hands emerging empty, she broke the silence, in a lifted voice:

"Oh, sir — have you a pencil you could lend me, please? I'd like to mark something in the piece to send to Mrs. Catherwood. It's what she says here about their hide-outs, as she terms them."

The obliging divine felt in his pockets, and, after a good deal of hunting, produced a pencil — a white one, with thick blue lead. She thanked him gratefully.

"How is Mrs. Catherwood bearing all this strain and anx-

iety?'' he asked suddenly, in the loud, empty car. ''Have you
seen her today?''

''Oh, yes, sir. I've been spending the evening with her since
nine o'clock, and am just back from there now. Oh, she's dreadful broke up, sir.''

She glanced at him with an uncertain air. He stared straight in
front of him, saying nothing, though conceivably he had learned,
in common with the rest of the world, that Jack Catherwood's
mother lived, not on 126th Street, but on West 8th Street. Possibly his silence had been an error of judgment? Perhaps that mis-
statement of hers had not been a slip, but something cleverer?

Eagerly the woman went on: ''Oh, sir, I only hope and pray
those gentlemen may be right, but it does look to Mrs. Catherwood, and me, too, that if Jessie Dark was going to catch her at
all, she'd have done it before now. Look at those big, bold, blue
eyes she had, sir, with lashes an inch long, they say, and that
terrible long chin of hers. They do say she can change the color
of her eyes, not forever, of course, but put a few of her drops
into them and make them look entirely different for a time. But
that chin, ye'd say . . .''

She broke off; for the clergyman, without preliminaries of any
sort, had picked up his heavy stick and suddenly risen.

''Why! Here we are at Fourteenth Street!'' he said, quite astonished. ''I must change here — well, well! You go farther,
perhaps? Good night! Success to Jessie Dark, I say.''

He was watching the woman's sad, faded face, and he saw
break into it a look of quick surprise which, it may be, was just
what he had expected.

''Fourteenth Street, sir! I'd no notion at all — for I've paid no
notice of the stops. It's where I change too, sir, the express not
stopping at my station.''

''Ah?'' said the clergyman, smiling a little.

He led the way, limping and leaning on his stick. They
emerged upon the chill and cheerless platform, not exactly together, yet still with some reference to their acquaintanceship on
the car. But the clergyman, after stumping along a few steps, all
at once realized that he was walking alone, and turned. The
woman had halted. Over the intervening space their eyes met.

"Come," said the man gently. "Come, let us walk about a little to keep warm."

"Oh, sir — it's too kind of you," said the woman, slowly coming forward.

From other cars two or three chilled travelers had got off to make the change; one or two more came straggling in from the street; but, scattered over the bleak narrow expanse, they detracted little from the isolation that seemed to surround the woman and the clergyman. Step for step, the odd pair made their way to the extreme northern end of the platform.

"By the way," said the clergyman, halting abruptly, "may I see that paper again for a moment?"

"Oh, yes, sir — of course," said the woman, producing it from under her cloak. "I thought you had finished with it, and I . . ."

He said that he wanted only to glance at it for a moment; but he fell to looking through it page by page, with rather a searching scrutiny. The woman glanced at him several times. At last she said hesitatingly:

"I thought, sir, I'd ask the ticket-chopper could he say how long before the next train. I'm very late as it is, sir, and I still must stop to get something to eat before I go to bed."

"An excellent idea," said the clergyman, putting the newspaper in his pocket. Side by side, they retraced their steps down the platform, questioned the chopper with scant results, and then, as by tacit consent, started slowly back again. However, before they had gone very far, the woman all at once stopped short and, with a drawn face, leaned against a pillar.

"Oh, sir, I'm afraid I'll just have to stop and get a bite somewhere before I go on. You'll think me foolish, sir, but I missed my supper entirely tonight, and there is quite a faint feeling coming over me."

The clergyman eyed her with apparent concern. He said: "Do you know, your mentioning something to eat a moment ago reminded me that I myself am all but famishing." He glanced at his watch, appearing to deliberate. "Yes — it will not take long. Come, we will find some modest eating place together."

"Oh, sir," she stammered, "but — you wouldn't want to eat with a poor old woman like me, sir."

"Why not? Are we not all equal in the sight of God?"

They ascended the stairs together, like any prosperous parson and his poor parishioner, and coming out into 14th Street, started west. On the first block they came to a little restaurant, a brilliantly lighted, tiled, and polished place of the quick-lunch sort, well filled with late patrons. But the woman timidly preferred not to stop here, saying that the glare of such places was very bad for her old eyes. The divine accepted the objection, without comment. A block farther on they found on a corner a quieter resort, an old-fashioned establishment which boasted a Ladies' Entrance down the side street.

They entered and sat down at a table, facing each other. The woman read the menu through, and finally, after some embarrassed uncertainty, ordered poached eggs on toast. The clergyman ordered the same. The simple meal was soon served. Just as they were finishing it, the woman said apologetically:

"If you'll excuse me, sir — could I see the bill of fare a minute? I think I'd best take a little pot of tea to warm me up, if they do not charge too high."

"I haven't the bill of fare," said the clergyman.

They looked diligently for the cardboard strip, but it was nowhere to be seen. The waiter drew near.

"Yes, sir. I left it right there when I took the order."

"I'm sure I can't imagine what's become of it," repeated the clergyman.

He looked rather hard at the woman and found that she was looking hard at him. Both pairs of eyes turned instantly.

The waiter brought another bill of fare; the woman ordered tea; the waiter came back with it. The clergyman paid for both orders with a bill that looked hard-earned.

The tea was very hot; it could not be drunk down at a gulp. The clergyman, watching the woman sidewise as she sipped, seemed to grow more and more restless. His agile fingers drummed the tablecloth; he could hardly sit still. All at once he said: "What is that calling in the street? It sounds like newsboys."

The woman put her old head on one side and listened. "Yes, sir. There seems to be an 'extra' out."

"Upon my word," he said, after a pause. "I believe I'll go get one. Good gracious! Crime is a very interesting thing, to be sure!"

He rose slowly, took down his shovel hat from the rack near him, and, grasping his heavy stick, limped to the door. Leaving it open behind him, much to the annoyance of the proprietor in the cashier's cage, he stood a moment, looking up and down the street. Then he took a few slow steps eastward, beckoning with his hand as he went, and so passed out of sight of the woman at the table.

The eating place was on the corner, and, outside, the clergyman paused for half a breath. North, east, south, and west he looked, and nowhere he found what his flying glance sought. He turned the corner into the cross street and began to walk, at first slowly, continually looking about him. Presently his pace quickened, quickened so that he no longer even stayed to use his stout cane. In another moment he was all but running, his clubfoot pounding the sidewalk heavily as he went. A newsboy thrust a paper under his nose, and he did not see it.

Far down the street, nearly two blocks away, a tall figure in a blue coat stood and stamped in the freezing sleet, and the divine was speeding straight toward him. But he did not get very near. For, as he passed the side entrance at the extreme rear of the restaurant, a departing guest dashed out so recklessly as to run full into him, stopping him dead.

Without looking at her, he knew who it was. In fact, he did not look at her at all, but turned his head hurriedly up and down, sweeping the dark street with a swift eye. But the old woman, having drawn back with a sharp exclamation as they collided, rushed breathlessly into apologies:

"Oh, sir — excuse me! A newsboy popped his head into the side door just after you went out, and I ran to him to get you the paper. But he got away too quick for me, sir. I . . ."

"Exactly," said the clergyman in his quiet, deep voice. "That must have been the very boy I myself was after."

On the other side, two men had just turned into the street, well muffled against the night, talking cheerfully as they trudged along. Now the clergyman looked full at the woman, and she saw that there was a smile on his face.

"Well! As he seems to have eluded us both, suppose we now return to the subway?"

"Yes, sir; it's full time I . . ."

"The sidewalk is so slippery," he went on gently. "Perhaps you had better take my arm."

Behind the pair in the dingy restaurant, the waiter came forward to shut the door, and lingered to discuss with the proprietor the sudden departure of his two patrons. After listening to some unfavorable comments on the ways of the clergy, the waiter returned to his table to set it in order.

On the floor in the carpeted aisle between tables lay a white piece of cardboard, which his familiar eye recognized as a torn scrap of one of his own bills of fare, face downward. He stooped and picked it up. On the back of it was some scribbling, made with a blue lead pencil.

The handwriting was very loose and irregular, as if the writer had had his eyes elsewhere while he wrote, and it was with some difficulty that the waiter deciphered this message:

Miss Hinch 14th St. subway Get police quick

The waiter carried this curious document to the proprietor, who read it over a number of times. He was a dull man, and had a dull man's suspiciousness of a practical joke. However, after a good deal of irresolute discussion, he put on his overcoat and went out for a policeman. He turned west, and halfway up the block spied an elderly bluecoat standing in a vestibule. The policeman looked at the scribbling, and dismissed it profanely as a wag's foolishness of the sort that was bothering the life out of him a dozen times a day. He walked along with the proprietor, and as they drew near to the latter's establishment, both became aware of footsteps thudding nearer up the cross street from the south. As they looked, two young policemen, accompanied by a man in a uniform like a street-car conductor's, raced around the corner and dashed into the restaurant.

The first policeman and the proprietor ran in after them and found them staring about rather vacantly. One of the arms of the law demanded if any suspicious characters had been seen about the place, and the dull proprietor said no. The officers, looking rather flat, explained their errand. It seemed that a few moments before, the third man, who was a ticket-chopper at the subway station, had found a mysterious message lying on the floor by his box. Whence it had come, how long it had lain there, he had not the slightest idea. However, there it was. The policeman exhibited a crumpled strip, torn from a newspaper, on which was scrawled in blue pencil:

Miss Hinch Miller's Restaurant police quick

The first policeman, who was both the oldest and the fattest of the three, produced the message on the bill of fare, so utterly at odds with this. The dull proprietor, now bethinking himself, mentioned the clergyman and the old woman who had taken poached eggs and tea together, called for a second bill of fare, and departed so unexpectedly by different doors. The ticket-chopper gasped out that he had seen the same pair at his station. They had come up, he said, and questioned him about trains. The three policemen were momentarily puzzled by this testimony. However, it was soon plain to them that if either the woman or the clergyman really had any information about Miss Hinch — a highly improbable supposition in itself — they would never have stopped with peppering the neighborhood with silly, contradictory messages.

"They're a pair of old fools tryin' to have sport with the police, and if I catch 'em, I'll run 'em in for it," growled the fattest of the officers, and this was the general verdict.

The conference broke up. The dull proprietor returned to his cage, the waiter to his table; the chopper, crestfallen, departed on the run for his chopping box; the three policemen passed out into the bitter night. They walked together, grumbling, and their feet, perhaps by some subconscious impulse, turned eastward toward the subway. And in the middle of the next block a man came running up to them.

"Mister! Look what I picked off'n the sidewalk!"

He held up a white slab which proved to be half of a bill of fare from Miller's Restaurant. On the back of it the three peering officers saw, almost illegibly scrawled in blue pencil:

Police! Miss Hinch 14th subw

The hand trailed off on the *w* as though the writer had been suddenly interrupted. The fat policeman blasphemed and threatened arrests. But the second policeman, who was young and wiry, raised his head from the bill of fare and said suddenly: "Tim, I believe there's something in this."

"There'd ought to be thirty days on the Island in it for thim," growled Tim.

"Suppose, now," said the other policeman, staring intently at him, "the old woman was Miss Hinch herself, f'r instance, and the parson was shadowing her while pretendin' he never suspicioned her, and Miss Hinch not darin' to cut and run for it till she was sure she had a clean getaway. Well now, lissen, what better could he do . . ."

"That's right!" exclaimed the third policeman. "'Specially when ye think that Hinch carries a gun, an'll use it, too! Why not have a look in at the subway station, anyway, the three of us?"

The proposal carried the day. The three officers started for the subway, the citizen following. They walked at a good pace and without more talk; and both their speed and their silence had a subtle psychological reaction. As the minds of the men turned inward upon the odd behavior of the pair in Miller's Restaurant, the conviction that, after all, something important might be afoot grew and strengthened within each one of them. Unconsciously their pace quickened. It was the young, wiry policeman who first broke into an open run, but the two others had been for twenty paces on the verge of it.

However, these consultations and vacillations had taken time. The stout clergyman and the poor old woman had five minutes' start on the officers of the law, and that, as it fell out, was all that the occasion required. On the street, as they made their way arm in arm to the station, they were seen, and remembered, by several belated pedestrians. It was observed by more than one that the woman lagged as if she were tired, while the clubfooted cleric, supporting her on his arm, steadily kept her up to his own brisk gait.

So walking, the pair descended the subway steps, came out upon the bleak platform again, and presently stood once more at the extreme uptown end of it, just where they had waited three quarters of an hour before. Nearby, a porter had at some time overturned a bucket of water, and a splotch of thin ice ran out and over the edge of the concrete. Two young men, taking turns up and down, distinctly heard the clergyman warn the woman to look out for this ice. Far away to the north was to be heard the faint roar of an approaching train.

The woman stood nearest the track, and the clergyman stood in front of her. In the vague light their looks met, and each must have been struck by the pallor of the other's face. In addition, the woman was breathing hard, and her hands and feet betrayed some nervousness. It was, of course, difficult now to ignore the fact that for an hour they had been clinging rather desperately to each other, at all costs; but the clergyman made a creditable effort to do so. He talked without ceasing, in a voice sounding only a little unnatural, for the most part of the deplorable weather, with a good deal about a train to Jersey, which he had not previously mentioned. And all the time both of them kept turning their heads toward the station entrances, as if expecting some arrival.

As he talked, the clergyman kept his hands quietly busy. From the bottom edge of his black sack-coat he drew a pin and stuck it deep into the ball of his middle finger. He took out his handkerchief to dust the hard sleet from his hat; and under his overcoat he pressed the handkerchief against his bleeding finger. While making these small arrangements, he held the woman's eyes with his own, talking on; and, still holding them, he suddenly broke off his random talks and peered at her cheek with concern.

"My good woman, you've scratched your cheek somehow! Why, bless me, it's bleeding quite badly."

"Never mind — never mind," said the woman, hurriedly, and swept her eyes toward the steps.

"But, good gracious . . . Just allow me — Ah!"

Too quick for her, he leaned forward and, through the thin veil, brushed her cheek hard with the handkerchief; removing it, he held it up so that she might see the blood for herself. But she did not glance at the handkerchief, and neither did he. His gaze was riveted upon her cheek, which looked so smooth and clear where he had smudged the clever wrinkles away.

Down the steps and upon the platform pounded the feet of the three hurrying policemen. But it was evident now that the on-coming train would thunder in just ahead of them. The clergy-man, standing close in front of the woman, took a firmer grip on his heavy stick and a look of stern triumph came into his face.

"You're not so terribly clever, after all!"

The woman had sprung back from him with an irrepressible exclamation; and in that instant she was aware of the police.

However, her foot slipped on the treacherous ice — or it may have tripped on the stout cane, when the clergyman suddenly shifted its position. In the next breath the train roared past.

By a curious chance, the body of the woman was not mangled or mutilated at all. There was a deep blue bruise on the left tem-ple, but apparently that was all; even the old black hat remained on her head, skewered fast by the long pin. It was the clergyman who first made out the body, huddled at the side of the dark track where the train had flung it — he who covered the still face and superintended the removal to the platform. Two eyewitnesses pointed out the ice on which the unfortunate woman had slipped, and described their horror as they saw her companion spring forward just too late to save her.

Not wishing to bring on a delirium of excitement among the clustered bystanders, the oldest policeman drew the clergyman aside and showed him the three mysterious messages. Much af-fected by the shocking end of his sleuthery as he was, he readily admitted having written them. He briefly recounted how the woman's strange movements on 126th Street had arrested his at-tention, and how, watching her closely on the car, while en-couraging every opportunity for conversation, he had finally detected that she wore a wig. Unfortunately, however, her suspicions had been aroused by his interest in her, and thereafter a long battle of wits had ensued between them — he trying to summon the police without her knowledge, she dogging him close to prevent that, and at the same time watching her chance to give him the slip. He rehearsed how, in the restaurant, when he had invented an excuse to leave her for a minute, she had made a bolt and narrowly missed getting away; and finally how, having brought her back to the subway, and seeing the police at last near, he had decided to risk exposing her make-up, with this unexpectedly shocking result.

"And now," he concluded in a shaken voice, "I am naturally most anxious to know whether I am right — or have made some terrible mistake. Will you look at her, officer, and tell me if it is indeed — she?"

But the old policeman shook his head over the well-known ability of Miss Hinch to look like everybody else in the world but herself.

"It'll take God Almighty to tell us that, sir — saving your presence. I'll leave it f'r headquarters," he continued, as if that were the same thing. "But, if it is her, she's gone to her reward!"

"God pity her!" said the clergyman.

"Amen! Give me your name, sir. They'll likely want you in the morning."

The clergyman gave it: Rev. Theodore Shaler, of Denver; city address, a street and number near Washington Square. Having thus discharged his duty in the affair, he started sadly to go away; but, passing by the silent figure stretched on a bench under the ticket-seller's overcoat, he bared his head and stopped for one last look at it.

The parson's gentleness and efficiency had already won favorable comments from the bystanders, and of the first quality he now gave a final proof. The dead woman's little handbag, which somebody had recovered from the track and laid at her side, had slipped to the floor; and the clergyman, observing it, stooped silently to restore it. This last small service chanced to bring his head close to the drooped head of the dead woman;

and, as he straightened up, her projecting hatpin struck his cheek and ripped a straight line down it. This in itself would have been a trifle, since scratches soon heal. But it happened that the point of the hatpin caught under the lining of the clergyman's perfect beard and stripped it clean from him; so that, as he rose, with a suddenly shrilled cry, he turned upon the astonished onlookers the bare, smooth chin of a woman, curiously long and pointed.

There were not many such chins in the world, and the urchins in the street would have recognized this one. Amid a sudden uproar which ill became the presence of the dead, the police closed in on Miss Hinch and handcuffed her with violence, fearing suicide, if not some new witchery; and at the station house an unemotional matron divested her of the last and best of all her many disguises.

This much the police did. But it was everywhere understood that it was Jessie Dark who had really made the capture, and all the papers next morning printed pictures of the unconquerable little woman, and of the hatpin with which she had reached back from another world to bring her greatest adversary to justice.

THE WITHERED ARM

by Thomas Hardy

Gertrude's nightly prayer was "O Lord, hang some guilty
or innocent person soon!"

I

A Lorn Milkmaid

It was an eighty-cow dairy, and the troop of milkers, regular
and supernumerary, were all at work; for, though the time of
year was as yet but early April, the feed lay entirely in water
meadows, and the cows were "in full pail." The hour was about
six in the evening, and three fourths of the large, red, rectangular
animals having been finished off, there was opportunity for a little conversation.

"He do bring home his bride tomorrow, I hear. They've come
as far as Anglebury today."

The voice seemed to proceed from the belly of the cow called
Cherry, but the speaker was a milking woman, whose face was
buried in the flank of that motionless beast.

"Hav' anybody seen her?" said another.

There was a negative response from the first. "Though they
say she's a rosy-cheeked, tisty-tosty little body enough," she
added; and as the milkmaid spoke she turned her face so that she
could glance past her cow's tail to the other side of the barton,
where a thin, fading woman of thirty milked somewhat apart
from the rest.

"Years younger than he, they say," continued the second,

with also a glance of reflectiveness in the same direction.

"How old do you call him, then?"

".Thirty or so."

"More like forty," broke in an old milkman near, in a long white pinafore or "wropper," and with the brim of his hat tied down, so that he looked like a woman. " 'A was born before our Great Weir was builded, and I hadn't man's wages when I laved water there."

The discussion waxed so warm that the purr of the milk streams became jerky, till a voice from another cow's belly cried with authority, "Now then, what the Turk do it matter to us about Farmer Lodge's age, or Farmer Lodge's new mis'ess? I shall have to pay him nine pound a year for the rent of every one of these milchers, whatever his age or hers. Get on with your work, or 'twill be dark afore we have done. The evening is pinking in a'ready." This speaker was the dairyman himself, by whom the milkmaids and men were employed.

Nothing more was said publicly about Farmer Lodge's wedding, but the first woman murmured under her cow to her next neighbor, " 'Tis hard for *she*," signifying the thin worn milkmaid aforesaid.

"Oh no," said the second. "He ha'n't spoke to Rhoda Brook for years."

When the milking was done they washed their pails and hung them on a many-forked stand made of the peeled limb of an oak tree, set upright in the earth and resembling a colossal antlered horn. The majority then dispersed in various directions homeward. The thin woman who had not spoken was joined by a boy of twelve or thereabout, and the twain went away up the field also.

Their course lay apart from that of the others, to a lonely spot high above the water meads and not far from the border of Egdon Heath, whose dark countenance was visible in the distance as they drew nigh to their home.

"They've just been saying down in barton that your father brings his young wife home from Anglebury tomorrow," the woman observed. "I shall want to send you for a few things to market, and you'll be pretty sure to meet 'em."

"Yes, Mother," said the boy. "Is Father married then?"

"Yes . . . You can give her a look and tell me what's she's like, if you do see her."

"Yes, Mother."

"If she's dark or fair, and if she's tall — as tall as I. And if she seems like a woman who has ever worked for a living, or one that has been always well off and has never done anything, and shows marks of the lady on her, as I expect she do."

"Yes."

They crept up the hill in the twilight and entered the cottage. It was built of mud walls, the surface of which had been washed by many rains into channels and depressions that left none of the original flat face visible; while here and there in the thatch above a rafter showed like a bone protruding through the skin.

She was kneeling down in the chimney corner, before two pieces of turf laid together with the heather inward, blowing at the red-hot ashes with her breath till the turves flamed. The radiance lit her pale cheek and made her dark eyes, that had once been handsome, seem handsome anew. "Yes," she resumed, "see if she is dark or fair, and if you can, notice if her hands be white; if not, see if they look as though she had ever done housework, or are milker's hands like mine."

The boy again promised, inattentively this time, his mother not observing that he was cutting a notch with his pocket knife in the beech-backed chair.

II

The Young Wife

The road from Anglebury to Holmstoke is in general level; but there is one place where a sharp ascent breaks its monotony. Farmers homeward-bound from the former market town, who trot all the rest of the way, walk their horses up this short incline.

The next evening, while the sun was yet bright, a handsome new gig, with a lemon-colored body and red wheels, was spinning westward along the level highway at the heels of a powerful mare. The driver was a yeoman in the prime of life, cleanly shaven like an actor, his face being toned to that bluish-vermilion hue which so often graces a thriving farmer's features when returning home after successful dealings in the town. Beside him sat a woman, many years his junior — almost, indeed, a girl. Her face too was fresh in color, but it was of a totally different quality — soft and evanescent, like the light under a heap of rose petals.

Few people traveled this way, for it was not a main road; and the long white riband of gravel that stretched before them was empty, save of one small scarce-moving speck, which presently resolved itself into the figure of a boy, who was creeping on at a snail's pace and continually looking behind him — the heavy bundle he carried being some excuse for, if not the reason of, his dilatoriness. When the bouncing gig party slowed at the bottom of the incline above mentioned, the pedestrian was only a few yards in front. Supporting the large bundle by putting one hand on his hip, he turned and looked straight at the farmer's wife as though he would read her through and through, pacing along abreast of the horse.

The low sun was full in her face, rendering every feature, shade, and contour distinct, from the curve of her little nostril to the color of her eyes. The farmer, though he seemed annoyed at the boy's persistent presence, did not order him to get out of the way; and thus the lad preceded them, his hard gaze never leaving her, till they reached the top of the ascent, when the farmer trotted on with relief in his lineaments — having taken no outward notice of the boy whatever.

"How that poor lad stared at me!" said the young wife.

"Yes, dear; I saw that he did."

"He is one of the village, I suppose?"

"One of the neighborhood. I think he lives with his mother a mile or two off."

"He knows who we are, no doubt?"

"Oh yes. You must expect to be stared at just at first, my pretty Gertrude."

"I do — though I think the poor boy may have looked at us in the hope we might relieve him of his heavy load, rather than from curiosity."

"Oh no," said her husband offhandedly. "These country lads

will carry a hundredweight once they get it on their backs; besides his pack had more size than weight in it. Now, then, another mile and I shall be able to show you our house in the distance — if it is not too dark before we get there." The wheels spun round, and particles flew from their periphery as before, till a white house of ample dimensions revealed itself, with farm buildings and ricks at the back.

Meanwhile the boy had quickened his pace, and turning up a by-lane some mile and a half short of the white farmstead, ascended toward the leaner pastures, and so on to the cottage of his mother.

She had reached home after her day's milking at the outlying dairy, and was washing cabbage at the doorway in the declining light. "Hold up the net a moment," she said, without preface, as the boy came up.

He flung down his bundle, held the edge of the cabbage net, and as she filled its meshes with the dripping leaves she went on, "Well, did you see her?"

"Yes; quite plain."

"Is she ladylike?"

"Yes; and more. A lady complete."

"Is she young?"

"Well, she's growed up, and her ways be quite a woman's."

"Of course. What color is her hair and face?"

"Her hair is lightish, and her face as comely as a live doll's."

"Her eyes, then, are not dark like mine?"

"No — of a bluish turn, and her mouth is very nice and red; and when she smiles, her teeth show white."

"Is she tall?" said the woman sharply.

"I couldn't see. She was sitting down."

"Then do you go to Holmstoke church tomorrow morning; she's sure to be there. Go early and notice her walking in, and come home and tell me if she's taller than I."

"Very well, Mother. But why don't you go and see for yourself?"

"*I* go to see her! I wouldn't look up at her if she were to pass my window this instant. She was with Mr. Lodge, of course. What did he say or do?"

"Just the same as usual."

"Took no notice of you?"

"None."

Next day the mother put a clean shirt on the boy and started him off for Holmstoke church. He reached the ancient little pile when the door was just being opened, and he was the first to enter. Taking his seat by the font, he watched all the parishioners file in. The well-to-do Farmer Lodge came nearly last; and his young wife, who accompanied him, walked up the aisle with the shyness natural to a modest woman who had appeared thus for the first time. As all other eyes were fixed upon her, the youth's stare was not noticed now.

When he reached home his mother said "Well?" before he had entered the room.

"She is not tall. She is rather short," he replied.

"Ah!" said his mother, with satisfaction.

"But she's very pretty — very. In fact, she's lovely." The youthful freshness of the yeoman's wife had evidently made an impression even on the somewhat hard nature of the boy.

"That's all I want to hear," said his mother quickly. "Now, spread the tablecloth. The hare you caught is very tender; but mind that nobody catches you . . . You've never told me what sort of hands she had."

"I have never seen 'em. She never took off her gloves."

"What did she wear this morning?"

"A white bonnet and a silver-colored gownd. It whewed and whistled so loud when it rubbed against the pews that the lady colored up more than ever for very shame at the noise, and pulled it in to keep it from touching; but when she pushed into her seat, it whewed more than ever. Mr. Lodge, he seemed pleased, and his waistcoat stuck out, and his great golden seals hung like a lord's; but she seemed to wish her noisy gownd anywhere but on her."

"Not she! However, that will do now."

These descriptions of the newly married couple were continued from time to time by the boy at his mother's request, after any chance encounter he had had with them. But Rhoda Brook, though she might easily have seen young Mrs. Lodge for herself by walking a couple of miles, would never attempt an excursion toward the quarter where the farmhouse lay. Neither did she, at the daily milking in the dairyman's yard on Lodge's outlying second farm, ever speak on the subject of the recent marriage. The dairyman, who rented the cows. of Lodge and knew perfectly the tall milkmaid's history, with manly kindliness always kept the gossip in the cow-barton from annoying Rhoda. But the atmosphere thereabout was full of the subject during the first days of Mrs. Lodge's arrival; and from her boy's description and the casual words of the other milkers, Rhoda Brook could raise a mental image of the unconscious Mrs. Lodge that was realistic as a photograph.

III

A Vision

One night, two or three weeks after the bridal return, when the boy was gone to bed, Rhoda sat a long time over the turf ashes that she had raked out in front of her to extinguish them. She contemplated so intently the new wife, as presented to her in her mind's eye over the embers, that she forgot the lapse of time. At last, wearied with her day's work, she too retired.

But the figure which had occupied her so much during this and the previous days was not to be banished at night. For the first time Gertrude Lodge visited the supplanted woman in her dreams. Rhoda Brook dreamed — since her assertion that she really saw, before falling asleep, was not to be believed — that the young wife, in the pale silk dress and white bonnet, but with features shockingly distorted, and wrinkled as by age, was sitting upon her chest as she lay. The pressure of Mrs. Lodge's person grew heavier; the blue eyes peered cruelly into her face; and then the figure thrust forward its left hand mockingly, so as to make the wedding ring it wore glitter in Rhoda's eyes. Maddened mentally, and nearly suffocated by pressure, the sleeper struggled; the incubus, still regarding her, withdrew to the foot of the bed, only, however, to come forward by degrees, resume her seat, and flash her left hand as before.

Gasping for breath, Rhoda, in a last desperate effort, swung out her right hand, seized the confronting specter by its obtrusive left arm, and whirled it backward to the floor, starting up herself as she did so with a low cry.

"Oh, merciful heaven!" she cried, sitting on the edge of the bed in a cold sweat; "that was not a dream — she was here!"

She could feel her antagonist's arm within her grasp even now — the very flesh and bone of it, as it seemed. She looked on the floor whither she had whirled the specter, but there was nothing to be seen.

Rhoda Brook slept no more that night, and when she went milking at the next dawn they noticed how pale and haggard she looked. The milk that she drew quivered into the pail; her hand had not calmed even yet, and still retained the feel of the arm. She came home to breakfast as wearily as if it had been suppertime.

"What was that noise in your chimmer, Mother, last night?" said her son. "You fell off the bed, surely?"

"Did you hear anything fall? At what time?"

"Just when the clock struck two."

She could not explain, and when the meal was done went silently about her household work, the boy assisting her, for he hated going afield on the farms, and she indulged his reluctance. Between eleven and twelve the garden gate clicked, and she lifted her eyes to the window. At the bottom of the garden, within the gate, stood the woman of her vision. Rhoda seemed transfixed.

"Ah, she said she would come!" exclaimed the boy, also observing her.

"Said so — when? How does she know us?"

"I have seen and spoken to her. I talked to her yesterday."

"I told you," said the mother, flushing indignantly, "never to speak to anybody in that house, or go near the place."

"I did not speak to her till she spoke to me. And I did not go near the place. I met her in the road."

"What did you tell her?"

"Nothing. She said, 'Are you the poor boy who had to bring the heavy load from market?' And she looked at my boots, and said they would not keep my feet dry if it came on wet, because they were so cracked. I told her I lived with my mother, and we had enough to do to keep ourselves, and that's how it was; and she said then, 'I'll come and bring you some better boots, and see your mother.' She gives away things to other folks in the meads besides us."

Mrs. Lodge was by this time close to the door — not in her silk, as Rhoda had seen her in the bedchamber, but in a morning hat, and gown of common light material, which became her better than silk. On her arm she carried a basket.

The impression remaining from the night's experience was still strong. Brook had almost expected to see the wrinkles, the scorn, and the cruelty on her visitor's face. She would have escaped an interview, had escape been possible. There was, however, no back door to the cottage, and in an instant the boy had lifted the latch to Mrs. Lodge's gentle knock.

"I see I have come to the right house," said she, glancing at the lad, and smiling. "But I was not sure till you opened the door."

The figure and action were those of the phantom; but her voice was so indescribably sweet, her glance so winning, her smile so tender, so unlike that of Rhoda's midnight visitant, that the latter could hardly believe the evidence of her senses. She was truly glad that she had not hidden away in sheer aversion, as she had been inclined to do. In her basket Mrs. Lodge brought the pair of boots that she had promised to the boy, and other useful articles.

At these proofs of a kindly feeling toward her and hers, Rhoda's heart reproached her bitterly. This innocent young thing should have her blessing and not her curse. When she left them a light seemed gone from the dwelling. Two days later she came again to know if the boots fitted; and less than a fortnight after that paid Rhoda another call. On this occasion the boy was absent.

"I walk a good deal," said Mrs. Lodge, "and your house is the nearest outside our own parish. I hope you are well. You don't look quite well."

Rhoda said she was well enough; and, indeed, though the paler of the two, there was more of the strength that endures, in her well-defined features and large frame, than in the soft-cheeked young woman before her. The conversation became quite confidential as regarded their powers and weaknesses; and when Mrs. Lodge was leaving, Rhoda said, "I hope you will find this air agree with you, ma'am, and not suffer from the damp of the water meads.''

The younger one replied that there was not much doubt of it, her general health being usually good. ''Though, now you remind me,'' she added, ''I have one little ailment which puzzles me. It is nothing serious, but I cannot make it out.''

She uncovered her left hand and arm; and their outline confronted Rhoda's gaze as the exact original of the limb she had beheld and seized in her dream. Upon the pink round surface of the arm were faint marks of an unhealthy color, as if produced by a rough grasp. Rhoda's eyes became riveted on the discolorations; she fancied that she discerned in them the shape of her own four fingers.

''How did it happen?'' she said mechanically.

''I cannot tell,'' replied Mrs. Lodge, shaking her head. ''One night when I was sound asleep, dreaming I was away in some strange place, a pain suddenly shot into my arm there, and was so keen as to awaken me. I must have struck it in the daytime, I suppose, though I don't remember doing so.'' She added, laughing, ''I tell my dear husband that it looks just as if he had flown into a rage and struck me there. Oh, I daresay it will soon disappear.''

''Ha, ha! Yes . . . On what night did it come?''

Mrs. Lodge considered, and said it would be a fortnight ago on the morrow. ''When I awoke I could not remember where I was,'' she added, ''till the clock striking two reminded me.''

She had named the night and the hour of Rhoda's spectral encounter, and Brook felt like a guilty thing. The artless disclosure startled her; she did not reason on the freaks of coincidence; and all the scenery of that ghastly night returned with double vividness to her mind.

''Oh, can it be,'' she said to herself, when her visitor had departed, ''that I exercise a malignant power over people against my own will?'' She knew that she had been slyly called a witch since her fall; but never having understood why that particular stigma had been attached to her, it had passed disregarded. Could this be the explanation, and had such things as this ever happened before?

IV

A Suggestion

The summer drew on, and Rhoda Brook almost dreaded to meet Mrs. Lodge again, notwithstanding that her feeling for the young wife amounted well-nigh to affection. Something in her own individuality seemed to convict Rhoda of crime. Yet a fatality sometimes would direct the steps of the latter to the outskirts of Holmstoke whenever she left her house for any other purpose than her daily work; and hence it happened that their next encounter was out of doors. Rhoda could not avoid the subject which had so mystified her, and after the first few words she stammered, "I hope your — arm is well again, ma'am?" She had perceived with consternation that Gertrude Lodge carried her left arm stiffly.

"No; it is not quite well. Indeed it is no better at all; it is rather worse. It pains me dreadfully sometimes."

"Perhaps you had better go to a doctor, ma'am."

She replied that she had already seen a doctor. Her husband had insisted upon her going to one. But the surgeon had not seemed to understand the afflicted limb at all; he had told her to bathe it in hot water, and she had bathed it, but the treatment had done no good.

"Will you let me see it?" said the milkwoman.

Mrs. Lodge pushed up her sleeve and disclosed the place, which was a few inches above the wrist. As soon as Rhoda Brook saw it, she could hardly preserve her composure. There was nothing of the nature of a wound, but the arm at that point had a shriveled look, and the outline of the four fingers appeared more distinct than at the former time. Moreover, she fancied that they were imprinted in precisely the relative position of her clutch upon the arm in the trance; the first finger toward Gertrude's wrist, and the fourth toward her elbow.

What the impress resembled seemed to have struck Gertrude herself since their last meeting. "It looks almost like finger marks," she said, adding with a faint laugh, "my husband says it is as if some witch, or the devil himself, had taken hold of me there and blasted the flesh."

Rhoda shivered. "That's fancy," she said hurriedly. "I wouldn't mind it, if I were you."

"I shouldn't so much mind it," said the younger, with hesitation, "if — if I hadn't a notion that it makes my husband — dislike me — no, love me less. Men think so much of personal appearance."

"Some do — he for one."

"Yes; and he was very proud of mine, at first."

"Keep your arm covered from his sight."

"Ah — he knows the disfigurement is there!" She tried to hide the tears that filled her eyes.

"Well, ma'am, I earnestly hope it will go away soon."

And so the milkwoman's mind was chained anew to the subject by a horrid sort of spell as she returned home. The sense of having been guilty of an act of malignity increased, affect as she might to ridicule her superstition. In her secret heart Rhoda did not altogether object to a slight diminution of her successor's beauty, by whatever means it had come about; but she did not wish to inflict upon her physical pain. For though this pretty young woman had rendered impossible any reparation which Lodge might have made Rhoda for his past conduct, everything like resentment at the unconscious usurpation had quite passed away from the elder's mind.

If the sweet and kindly Gertrude Lodge only knew of the scene in the bedchamber, what would she think? Not to inform her of it seemed treachery in the presence of her friendliness; but tell she could not of her own accord — neither could she devise a remedy.

She mused upon the matter the greater part of the night; and the next day, after the morning milking, set out to obtain another glimpse of Gertrude Lodge if she could, being held to her by a gruesome fascination. By watching the house from a distance the milkmaid was presently able to discern the farmer's wife in a ride she was taking alone — probably to join her husband in some distant field. Mrs. Lodge perceived her, and cantered in her direction.

"Good morning, Rhoda!" Gertrude said, when she had come up. "I was going to call."

Rhoda noticed that Mrs. Lodge held the reins with some difficulty.

"I hope — the bad arm," said Rhoda.

"They tell me there is possibly one way by which I might be able to find out the cause, and so perhaps the cure, of it," replied the other anxiously. "It is by going to some clever man over in Egdon Heath. They did not know if he was still alive — and I cannot remember his name at this moment; but they said that you knew more of his movements than anybody else hereabout, and could tell me if he were still to be consulted. Dear me — what was his name? But you know."

"Not Conjuror Trendle?" said her thin companion, turning pale.

"Trendle — yes. Is he alive?"

"I believe so," said Rhoda, with reluctance.

"Why do you call him conjuror?"

"Well — they say — they used to say he was a — he had powers other folks have not."

"Oh, how could my people be so superstitious as to recommend a man of that sort! I thought they meant some medical man. I shall think no more of him."

Rhoda looked relieved, and Mrs. Lodge rode on. The milkwoman had inwardly seen, from the moment she heard of her having been mentioned as a reference for this man, that there must exist a sarcastic feeling among the workfolk that a sorceress would know the whereabouts of the exorcist. They suspected her, then. A short time ago this would have given no concern to a woman of her common sense. But she had a haunting reason to be superstitious now; and she had been seized with sudden dread that this Conjuror Trendle might name her as the malignant influence which was blasting the fair person of Gertrude, and so lead her friend to hate her forever, and to treat her as some fiend in human shape.

But all was not over. Two days after, a shadow intruded into the window pattern thrown on Rhoda Brook's floor by the afternoon sun. The woman opened the door at once, almost breathlessly.

"Are you alone?" said Gertrude. She seemed to be no less harassed and anxious than Brook herself.

"Yes," said Rhoda.

"The place on my arm seems worse, and troubles me!" the young farmer's wife went on. "It is so mysterious! I do hope it will not be an incurable wound. I have again been thinking of what they said about Conjuror Trendle. I don't really believe in such men, but I should not mind just visiting him, from curiosity — though on no account must my husband know. Is it far to where he lives?"

"Yes — five miles," said Rhoda backwardly. "In the heart of Egdon."

"Well, I should have to walk. Could not you go with me to show me the way, say tomorrow afternoon?"

"Oh, not I — that is," the milkwoman murmured, with a start of dismay. Again the dread seized her that something to do with her fierce act in the dream might be revealed, and her character in the eyes of the most useful friend she had ever had be ruined irretrievably.

Mrs. Lodge urged, and Rhoda finally assented, though with much misgiving. Sad as the journey would be to her, she could not conscientiously stand in the way of a possible remedy for her patron's strange affliction. It was agreed that, to escape suspicion of their mystic intent, they should meet at the edge of the heath at the corner of a plantation which was visible from the spot where they now stood.

V

Conjuror Trendle

By the next afternoon Rhoda would have done anything to escape this inquiry. But she had promised to go. Moreover, there was a horrid fascination at times in becoming instrumental in throwing such possible light on her own character as would reveal her to be something greater in the occult world than she had ever herself suspected.

She started just before the time of day mentioned between

them, and half an hour's brisk walking brought her to the south-eastern extension of the Egdon tract of country, where the fir plantation was. A slight figure, cloaked and veiled, was already there. Rhoda recognized, almost with a shudder, that Mrs. Lodge bore her left arm in a sling.

They hardly spoke to each other, and immediately set out on their climb into the interior of this solemn country, which stood high above the rich alluvial soil they had left half an hour before. It was a long walk; thick clouds made the atmosphere dark, though it was as yet only early afternoon; and the wind howled dismally over the hills of the heath — not improbably the same heath which had witnessed the agony of the Wessex King Ina, presented to after-ages as Lear. Gertrude Lodge talked most, Rhoda replying with monosyllabic preoccupation. She had a strange dislike to walking on the side of her companion where hung the afflicted arm, moving round to the other when inadvertently near it. Much heather had been brushed by their feet when they descended upon a cart track, beside which stood the house of the man they sought.

He did not profess his remedial practices openly, or care anything about their continuance, his direct interests being those of a dealer in furze, turf, "sharp sand," and other local products. Indeed, he affected not to believe largely in his own powers, and when warts that had been shown him for cure miraculously disappeared — which it must be owned they infallibly did — he would say lightly, "Oh, I only drink a glass of grog upon 'em — perhaps it's all chance," and immediately turn the subject.

He was at home when they arrived, having in fact seen them descending into his valley. He was a gray-bearded man with a reddish face, and he looked singularly at Rhoda the first moment he beheld her. Mrs. Lodge told him her errand; and then with words of self-disparagement he examined her arm.

"Medicine can't cure it," he said promptly. " 'Tis the work of an enemy."

Rhoda shrank into herself, and drew back.

"An enemy? What enemy?" asked Mrs. Lodge.

He shook his head. "That's best known to yourself," he said. "If you like, I can show the person to you, though I shall not

myself know who it is. I can do no more; and don't wish to do
that.''

She pressed him; on which he told Rhoda to wait outside
where she stood, and took Mrs. Lodge into the room. It opened
immediately from the door; and, as the latter remained ajar,
Rhoda Brook could see the proceedings without taking part in
them. He brought a tumbler from the dresser, nearly filled it with
water, and, fetching an egg, prepared it in some private way;
after which he broke it on the edge of the glass, so that the white
went in and the yolk remained. As it was getting gloomy, he took
the glass and its contents to the window and told Gertrude to
watch them closely. They leaned over the table together, and the
milkwoman could see the opaline hue of the egg fluid changing
form as it sank in the water, but she was not near enough to
define the shape that it assumed.

"Do you catch the likeness of any face or figure as you look?"
demanded the conjuror of the young woman.

She murmured a reply, in tones so low as to be inaudible to
Rhoda, and continued to gaze intently into the glass. Rhoda
turned, and walked a few steps away.

When Mrs. Lodge came out, and her face was met by the light,
it appeared exceedingly pale — as pale as Rhoda's — against the
sad dun shades of the upland's garniture. Trendle shut the door
behind her, and they at once started homeward together. But
Rhoda perceived that her companion had quite changed.

"Did he charge much?" she asked tentatively.

"Oh no — nothing. He would not take a farthing," said Gertrude.

"And what did you see," inquired Rhoda.

"Nothing I — care to speak of." The constraint in her manner
was remarkable; her face was so rigid as to wear an oldened aspect, faintly suggestive of the face in Rhoda's bedchamber.

"Was it you who first proposed coming here?" Mrs. Lodge
suddenly inquired, after a long pause. "How very odd, if you
did!"

"No. But I am not sorry we have come, all things considered," she replied. For the first time a sense of triumph possessed her, and she did not altogether deplore that the young

thing at her side should learn that their lives had been antagonized by other influences than their own.

The subject was no more alluded to during the long and dreary walk home. But in some way or other a story was whispered about the many-dairied lowland that winter that Mrs. Lodge's gradual loss of the use of her left arm was owing to her being "overlooked" by Rhoda Brook. The latter kept her own counsel about the incubus, but her face grew sadder and thinner; and in the spring she and her boy disappeared from the neighborhood of Holmstoke.

VI

A Second Attempt

Half a dozen years passed away, and Mr. and Mrs. Lodge's married experience sank into prosiness, and worse. The farmer was usually gloomy and silent; the woman whom he had wooed for her grace and beauty was contorted and disfigured in the left limb; moreover, she had brought him no child, which rendered it likely that he would be the last of a family who had occupied that valley for some two hundred years. He thought of Rhoda Brook and her son; and feared this might be a judgment from heaven upon him.

The once blithe-hearted and enlightened Gertrude was changing into an irritable, superstitious woman, whose whole time was given to experimenting upon her ailment with every quack remedy she came across. She was honestly attached to her husband, and was ever secretly hoping against hope to win back his heart again by regaining some at least of her personal beauty. Hence it arose that her closet was lined with bottles, packets, and ointment pots of every description — nay, bunches of mystic herbs, charms, and books of necromancy, which in her schoolgirl time she would have ridiculed as folly.

"Damned if you won't poison yourself with these apothecary messes and witch mixtures some time or other," said her husband, when his eye chanced to fall upon the multitudinous array.

She did not reply, but turned her sad, soft glance upon him in such heart-swollen reproach that he looked sorry for his words, and added, "I only meant it for your good, you know, Gertrude."

"I'll clear out the whole lot and destroy them," said she huskily, "and try such remedies no more!"

"You want somebody to cheer you," he observed. "I once thought of adopting a boy; but he is too old now. And he is gone away I don't know where."

She guessed to whom he alluded; for Rhoda Brook's story had in the course of years become known to her, though not a word had ever passed between her husband and herself on the subject. Neither had she ever spoken to him of her visit to Conjuror Trendle and of what was revealed to her, or she thought was revealed to her, by that solitary heathman.

She was now five-and-twenty; but she seemed older. "Six years of marriage, and only a few months of love," she sometimes whispered to herself. And then she thought of the apparent cause, and said, with a tragic glance at her withering limb, "If I could only again be as I was when he first saw me!"

She obediently destroyed her nostrums and charms; but there remained a hankering wish to try something else — some other sort of cure altogether. She had never revisited Trendle since she had been conducted to the house of the solitary by Rhoda against her will; but it now suddenly occurred to Gertrude that she would, in a last desperate effort at deliverance from this seeming curse, again seek out the man, if he yet lived. He was entitled to a certain credence, for the indistinct form he had raised in the glass had undoubtedly resembled the only woman in the world who — as she now knew, though not then — could have a reason for bearing her ill will. The visit should be paid.

This time she went alone, though she nearly got lost on the heath and roamed a considerable distance out of her way. Trendle's house was reached at last, however; he was not indoors, and instead of waiting at the cottage, she went to where his bent figure was pointed out to her at work a long way off. Trendle remembered her, and laying down the handful of furze roots which he was gathering and throwing into a heap, he offered to accompany her in her homeward direction, as the distance was considerable and the days were short. So they walked together, his head bowed nearly to the earth, and his form of a color with it.

"You can send away warts and other excrescences, I know," she said; "why can't you send away this?" And the arm was uncovered.

"You think too much of my powers!" said Trendle; "and I am old and weak now, too. No, no; it is too much for me to attempt in my own person. What have ye tried?"

She named to him some of the hundred medicaments and counterspells which she had adopted from time to time. He shook his head.

"Some were good enough," he said approvingly; "but not many of them for such as this. This is of the nature of a blight, not of the nature of a wound; and if you ever do throw it off, it will be all at once."

"If I only could!"

"There is only one chance of doing it known to me. It has never failed in kindred afflictions — that I can declare. But it is hard to carry out, and especially for a woman."

"Tell me!" said she.

"You must touch with the limb the neck of a man who's been hanged."

She started a little at the image he had raised.

"Before he's cold — just after he's cut down," continued the conjuror impassively.

"How can that do good?"

"It will turn the blood and change the constitution. But, as I say, to do it is hard. You must get into jail and wait for him when he's brought off the gallows. Lots have done it, though perhaps not such pretty women as you. I used to send dozens for skin complaints. But that was in former times. The last I sent was in 'thirteen — near twenty years ago."

He had no more to tell her; and, when he had put her into a straight track homeward, turned and left her, refusing all money as at first.

VII

A Ride

The communication sank deep into Gertrude's mind. Her nature was rather a timid one; and probably of all remedies that the white wizard could have suggested there was not one which would have filled her with so much aversion as this, not to speak of the immense obstacles in the way of its adoption.

Casterbridge, the county town, was a dozen or fifteen miles off; and though in those days, when men were executed for horse-stealing, arson, and burglary, an assize seldom passed without a hanging, it was not likely that she could get access to the body of the criminal unaided. And the fear of her husband's anger made her reluctant to breathe a word of Trendle's suggestion to him or to anybody about him.

She did nothing for months, and patiently bore her disfigurement as before. But her woman's nature, craving for renewed love, through the medium of renewed beauty (she was but twenty-five), was ever stimulating her to try what, at any rate, could hardly do her any harm. "What came by a spell will go by a spell surely," she would say. Whenever her imagination pictured the act she shrank in terror from the possibility of it. Then the words of the conjuror, "It will turn your blood," were seen to be capable of a scientific no less than a ghastly interpretation; the mastering desire returned, and urged her on again.

There was at this time but one county paper, and that her husband only occasionally borrowed. But old-fashioned days had old-fashioned means, and news was extensively conveyed by word of mouth from market to market, or from fair to fair, so that, whenever such an event as an execution was about to take place, few within a radius of twenty miles were ignorant of the coming sight; and, so far as Holmstoke was concerned, some enthusiasts had been known to walk all the way to Casterbridge and back in one day, solely to witness the spectacle. The next assizes were in March; and when Gertrude Lodge heard that they had been held, she inquired stealthily at the inn as to the result, as soon as she could find opportunity.

She was, however, too late. The time at which the sentences

were to be carried out had arrived, and to make the journey and obtain admission at such short notice required at least her husband's assistance. She dared not tell him, for she had found by delicate experiment that these smoldering village beliefs made him furious if mentioned, partly because he half entertained them himself. It was therefore necessary to wait for another opportunity.

Her determination received a fillip from learning that two epileptic children had attended from this very village of Holmstoke many years before with beneficial results, though the experiment had been strongly condemned by the neighboring clergy. April, May, June, passed; and it is no overstatement to say that by the end of the last-named month Gertrude well-nigh longed for the death of a fellow creature. Instead of her formal prayers each night, her unconscious prayer was, "O Lord, hang some guilty or innocent person soon!"

This time she made earlier inquiries, and was altogether more systematic in her proceedings. Moreover, the season was summer, between the haymaking and the harvest, and in the leisure thus afforded him her husband had been holiday-taking away from home.

The assizes were in July, and she went to the inn as before. There was to be one execution — only one — for arson.

Her greatest problem was not how to get to Casterbridge, but what means she should adopt for obtaining admission to the jail. Though access for such purposes had formerly never been denied, the custom had fallen into desuetude; and in contemplating her possible difficulties, she was again almost driven to fall back upon her husband. But, on sounding him about the assizes, he was so uncommunicative, so more than usually cold, that she did not proceed, and decided that whatever she did she would do alone.

Fortune, obdurate hitherto, showed her unexpected favor. On the Thursday before the Saturday fixed for the execution, Lodge remarked to her that he was going away from home for another day or two on business at a fair, and that he was sorry he could not take her with him.

She exhibited on this occasion so much readiness to stay at

home that he looked at her in surprise. Time had been when she would have shown deep disappointment at the loss of such a jaunt. However, he lapsed into his usual taciturnity, and on the day named left Holmstoke.

It was now her turn. She at first had thought of driving, but on reflection held that driving would not do, since it would necessitate her keeping to the turnpike road, and so increase by tenfold the risk of her ghastly errand being found out. She decided to ride and avoid the beaten track, notwithstanding that in her husband's stables there was no animal just at present which by any stretch of imagination could be considered a lady's mount, in spite of his promise before marriage to always keep a mare for her. He had, however, many cart horses, fine ones of their kind; and among the rest was a serviceable creature, an equine Amazon, with a back as broad as a sofa, on which Gertrude had occasionally taken an airing when unwell. This horse she chose.

On Friday afternoon one of the men brought it round. She was dressed, and before going down looked at her shriveled arm. "Ah!" she said to it, "if it had not been for you this terrible ordeal would have been saved me!"

When strapping up the bundle in which she carried a few articles of clothing, she took occasion to say to the servant, "I take these in case I should not get back tonight from the person I am going to visit. Don't be alarmed if I am not in by ten, and close up the house as usual. I shall be at home tomorrow for certain." She meant then to privately tell her husband; the deed accomplished was not like the deed projected. He would almost certainly forgive her.

And then the pretty palpitating Gertrude Lodge went from her husband's homestead; but though her goal was Casterbridge she did not take the direct route thither through Stickleford. Her cunning course at first was in precisely the opposite direction. As soon as she was out of sight, however, she turned to the left, by a road which led into Egdon, and on entering the heath wheeled round, and set out in the true course, due westerly. A more private way down the county could not be imagined; and as to direction, she had merely to keep her horse's head to a point a little to the right of the sun. She knew that she would light upon a furze-cutter or cottager of some sort from time to time, from whom she might correct her bearing.

Though the date was comparatively recent, Egdon was much less fragmentary in character than now. The attempts — successful and otherwise — at cultivation on the lower slopes, which intrude and break up the original heath into small detached heaths, had not been carried far. Enclosure Acts had not taken effect, and the banks and fences which now exclude the cattle of those villagers who formerly enjoyed rights of commonage thereon, and the carts of those who had turbary privileges, which kept them in firing all the year round, were not erected. Gertrude, therefore, rode along with no other obstacles than the prickly furze bushes, the mats of heather, the white watercourses, and the natural steeps and declivities of the ground.

Her horse was sure, if heavy-footed and slow, and though a draft animal, was easy-paced; had it been otherwise, she was not a woman who could have ventured to ride over such a bit of country with a half-dead arm. It was therefore nearly eight o'clock when she drew rein to breathe the mare on the last outlying high point of heathland toward Casterbridge, previous to leaving Egdon for the cultivated valleys.

She halted before a pool called Rushy Pond, flanked by the ends of two hedges; a railing ran through the center of the pond, dividing it in half. Over the railing she saw the low green country; over the green trees the roofs of the town; over the roofs a white flat façade, denoting the entrance to the county jail. On the roof of this front specks were moving about; they seemed to be workmen erecting something. Her flesh crept. She descended slowly, and was soon amid cornfields and pastures. In another half hour, when it was almost dusk, Gertrude reached the White Hart, the first inn of the town on that side.

Little surprise was excited by her arrival; farmers' wives rode on horseback then more than they do now. Though, for that matter, Mrs. Lodge was not imagined to be a wife at all; the innkeeper supposed her some harum-scarum young woman who had come to attend ''hang-fair'' next day. Neither her husband nor herself ever dealt in Casterbridge market, so that she was unknown. While dismounting she beheld a crowd of boys stand-

ing at the door of a harness-maker's shop just above the inn,
looking inside it with deep interest.

"What is going on there?" she asked of the ostler.

"Making the rope for tomorrow."

She throbbed responsively, and contracted her arm.

"'Tis sold by the inch afterward," the man continued. "I
could get you a bit, miss, for nothing, if you'd like?"

She hastily repudiated any such wish, all the more from a
curious creeping feeling that the condemned wretch's destiny
was becoming interwoven with her own; and having engaged a
room for the night, sat down to think.

Up to this time she had formed but the vaguest notions about
her means of obtaining access to the prison. The words of the
cunning man returned to her mind. He had implied that she
should use her beauty, impaired though it was, as a passkey. In
her inexperience she knew little about jail functionaries; she had
heard of a high sheriff and an under sheriff, but dimly only. She
knew, however, that there must be a hangman, and to the
hangman she determined to apply.

VIII

A Waterside Hermit

At this date, and for several years after, there was a hangman
to almost every jail. Gertrude found, on inquiry, that the Casterbridge official dwelled in a lonely cottage by a deep slow river
flowing under the cliff on which the prison buildings were situate
— the stream being the self-same one, though she did not know
it, which watered the Stickleford and Holmstoke meads lower
down in its course.

Having changed her dress, and before she had eaten or drunk
— for she could not take her ease till she had ascertained some
particulars — Gertrude pursued her way by a path along the
waterside to the cottage indicated. Passing thus the outskirts of
the jail, she discerned on the level roof over the gateway three
rectangular lines against the sky, where the specks had been
moving in her distant view; she recognized what the erection
was, and passed quickly on. Another hundred yards brought her

to the executioner's house, which a boy pointed out. It stood close to the same stream, and was hard by a weir, the waters of which emitted a steady roar.

While she stood hesitating, the door opened, and an old man came forth shading a candle with one hand. Locking the door on the outside, he turned to a flight of wooden steps fixed against the end of the cottage, and began to ascend them, this being evidently the staircase to his bedroom. Gertrude hastened forward, but by the time she reached the foot of the ladder he was at the top. She called to him loudly enough to be heard above the roar of the weir; he looked down and said, "What d'ye want here?"

"To speak to you a minute."

The candlelight, such as it was, fell upon her imploring, pale, upturned face, and Davies (as the hangman was called) backed down the ladder. "I was just going to bed," he said; "'Early to bed and early to rise,' but I don't mind stopping a minute for such a one as you. Come into house." He reopened the door and preceded her to the room within.

The implements of his daily work, which was that of a jobbing gardener, stood in a corner, and seeing probably that she looked rural, he said, "If you want me to undertake country work I can't come, for I never leave Casterbridge for gentle nor simple — not I. My real calling is officer of justice," he added formally.

"Yes, yes! That's it. Tomorrow!"

"Ah! I thought so. Well, what's the matter about that? 'Tis no use to come here about the knot — folks do come continually, but I tell 'em one knot is as merciful as another if ye keep it under the ear. Is the unfortunate man a relation; or, I should say, perhaps" (looking at her dress) "a person who's been in your employ?"

"No. What time is the execution?"

"The same as usual — twelve o'clock, or as soon after as the London mail coach gets in. We always wait for that, in case of a reprieve."

"Oh — a reprieve — I hope not!" she said involuntarily.

"Well — hee, hee! — as a matter of business, so do I! But still, if ever a young fellow deserved to be let off, this one does; only just turned eighteen, and only present by chance when the rick was fired. Howsomever, there's not much risk of it, as they are obliged to make an example of him, there having been so much destruction of property that way lately."

"I mean," she explained, "that I want to touch him for a charm, a cure of an affliction, by the advice of a man who has proved the virtue of the remedy."

"Oh yes, miss! Now I understand. I've had such people come in past years. But it didn't strike me that you looked of a sort to require blood-turning. What's the complaint? The wrong kind for this, I'll be bound."

"My arm." She reluctantly showed the withered skin.

"Ah! —'tis all a-scram!" said the hangman, examining it.

"Yes," said she.

"Well," he continued, with interest, "that *is* the class o' subject, I'm bound to admit! I like the look of the place; it is truly as suitable for the cure as any I ever saw. 'Twas a knowing man that sent 'ee, whoever he was."

"You can contrive for me all that's necessary?" she said breathlessly.

"You should really have gone to the governor of the jail, and your doctor with 'ee, and given your name and address — that's how it used to be done, if I recollect. Still, perhaps, I can manage it for a trifling fee."

"Oh, thank you! I would rather do it this way, as I should like it kept private."

"Lover not to know, eh?"

"No — husband."

"Aha! Very well. I'll get 'ee a touch of the corpse."

"Where is it now?" she said, shuddering.

"It? — *he*, you mean; he's living yet. Just inside that little small winder up there in the glum." He signified the jail on the cliff above.

She thought of her husband and her friends. "Yes, of course," she said; "and how am I to proceed?"

He took her to the door. "Now, do you be waiting at the little wicket in the wall, that you'll find up there in the lane, not later than one o'clock. I will open it from the inside, as I shan't come home to dinner till he's cut down. Good night. Be punctual; and if you don't want anybody to know 'ee, wear a veil. Ah — once I had such a daughter as you!"

She went away, and climbed the path above, to assure herself that she would be able to find the wicket next day. Its outline was soon visible to her — a narrow opening in the outer wall of the prison precincts. The steep was so great that, having reached the wicket, she stopped a moment to breathe; and, looking back upon the waterside cot, saw the hangman again ascending his outdoor staircase. He entered the loft or chamber to which it led, and in a few minutes extinguished his light.

The town clock struck ten, and she returned to the White Hart as she had come.

IX

A Rencounter

It was one o'clock on Saturday. Gertrude Lodge, having been admitted to the jail as above described, was sitting in a waiting room within the second gate, which stood under a classic archway of ashlar, then comparatively modern, and bearing the inscription, COVNTY JAIL: 1793. This was the façade she had seen from the heath the day before. Near at hand was a passage to the roof on which the gallows stood.

The town was thronged and the market suspended; but Gertrude had seen scarcely a soul. Having kept her room till the hour of the appointment, she had proceeded to the spot by a way which avoided the open space below the cliff where the spectators had gathered; but she could, even now, hear the multitudinous babble of their voices, out of which rose at intervals the hoarse croak of a single voice uttering the words, "Last dying speech and confession!" There had been no reprieve, and the execution was over; but the crowd still waited to see the body taken down.

Soon the persistent girl heard a trampling overhead, then a hand beckoned to her, and, following directions, she went out and crossed the inner paved court beyond the gatehouse, her knees trembling so that she could scarcely walk. One of her arms was out of its sleeve, and only covered by her shawl.

On the spot at which she had now arrived were two trestles, and before she could think of their purpose she heard heavy feet descending stairs somewhere at her back. Turn her head she would not, or could not, and, rigid in this position, she was conscious of a rough coffin passing her shoulder, borne by four men. It was open, and in it lay the body of a young man, wearing the smock-frock of a rustic, and fustian breeches. The corpse had been thrown into the coffin so hastily that the skirt of the smock-frock was hanging over. The burden was temporarily deposited on the trestles.

By this time the young woman's state was such that a gray mist seemed to float before her eyes, on account of which, and the veil she wore, she could scarcely discern anything; it was as though she had nearly died, but was held up by a sort of galvanism.

"Now!" said a voice close at hand, and she was just conscious that the word had been addressed to her.

By a last strenuous effort she advanced, at the same time hearing persons approaching behind her. She bared her poor cursed arm; and Davies, uncovering the face of the corpse, took Gertrude's hand, and held it so that her arm lay across the dead man's neck, upon a line the color of an unripe blackberry, which surrounded it.

Gertrude shrieked: "the turn o' the blood," predicted by the conjuror, had taken place. But at that moment a second shriek rent the air of the enclosure; it was not Gertrude's, and its effect upon her was to make her start round.

Immediately behind her stood Rhoda Brook, her face drawn and her eyes red with weeping. Behind Rhoda stood Gertrude's own husband; his countenance lined, his eyes dim, but without a tear.

"D——n you! what are you doing here?" he said hoarsely.

"Hussy — to come between us and our child now!" cried Rhoda. "This is the meaning of what Satan showed me in the vision! You are like her at last!" And clutching the bare arm of the younger woman, she pulled her unresistingly back against the wall. Immediately Brook had loosened her hold the fragile young Gertrude slid down against the feet of her husband. When he lifted her up she was unconscious.

The mere sight of the twain had been enough to suggest to her that the dead young man was Rhoda's son. At that time the relatives of an executed convict had the privilege of claiming the body for burial, if they chose to do so; and it was for this purpose that Lodge was awaiting the inquest with Rhoda. He had been summoned by her as soon as the young man was taken in the crime, and at different times since; and he had attended in court during the trial. This was the "holiday" he had been indulging in of late. The two wretched parents had wished to avoid exposure; and hence had come themselves for the body, a wagon and sheet for its conveyance and covering being in waiting outside.

Gertrude's case was so serious that it was deemed advisable to call to her the surgeon who was at hand. She was taken out of the jail into the town; but she never reached home alive. Her delicate vitality, sapped perhaps by the paralyzed arm, collapsed under the double shock that followed the severe strain, physical and mental, to which she had subjected herself during the previous twenty-four hours. Her blood had been "turned" indeed — too far. Her death took place in the town three days after.

Her husband was never seen in Casterbridge again; once only in the old marketplace at Anglebury, which he had so much frequented, and very seldom in public anywhere. Burdened at first with moodiness and remorse, he eventually changed for the better, and appeared as a chastened and thoughtful man. Soon after attending the funeral of his poor young wife he took steps toward giving up the farms in Holmstoke and the adjoining parish, and, having sold every head of his stock, he went away to Port-Bredy, at the other end of the county, living there in solitary lodgings till his death two years later of a painless decline. It was then found that he had bequeathed the whole of his not inconsiderable property to a reformatory for boys, subject to the payment of a small annuity to Rhoda Brook, if she could be found to claim it.

For some time she could not be found; but eventually she reappeared in her old parish — absolutely refusing, however, to have anything to do with the provision made for her. Her monotonous milking at the dairy was resumed, and followed for many long years, till her form became bent and her once abundant dark hair white and worn away at the forehead — perhaps by long pressure against the cows. Here, sometimes, those who knew her experiences would stand and observe her, and wonder what somber thoughts were beating inside that impassive, wrinkled brow, to the rhythm of the alternating milk streams.

THE OLD SHELL COLLECTOR

by H. R. F. Keating

They really shouldn't have annoyed Mr. Peduncle
so much.

THEY MADE their presence felt down there on the beach from the
moment they arrived. Not that it was a scene of intense solitude
and quiet beforehand. There were children running up and down
the dark wet sand, shouting and calling. More than one mother
was trying to make some toddler return to the family encamp-
ment without herself getting up off the beach towel spread over
the pebbles which the now receding tide had not reached; and all
this required a good deal of increasingly irritated yelling. There
was also a game of cricket being played, a tense affair in which a
boy of seven or eight was standing worriedly in front of a set of
bright yellow plastic stumps while his thick-waisted father strove
at the bowling end to revive younger days; and this naturally resulted in more and more sharply uttered words floating up into
the August air. So it was not really a tranquil scene.

But there were areas of comparative quiet. There was, for instance, a row of deck chairs drawn up just underneath the rust-
stained concrete wall of the promenade, where it was thought
the sharp breeze would not strike with quite as much force as
elsewhere; and here a number of elderly citizens grimly sat, the
men wrestling with wind-teased newspapers, their spouses
mostly knitting away for dear life, one or two determined souls
actually succeeding in dozing in the illusory warmth of the sun.

It was one of these half-sleeping gentlemen, the oldest probably of the whole deck-chair row, who received the brunt of the
arrival.

With a wild outburst of whooping they came tearing along the
half-deserted front, sending the staid gulls wheeling and crying;
and, for some reason or other, when they got to the exact point
underneath which the old gentleman was letting the late hours of
his life glide harmlessly away, the girl who happened to be in
front of the racing, jostling mob elected to jump down onto the
beach. She gave a piercing shriek, echoing out even above the
noise the rest of them were making, and took off with long slim
legs held together aiming for some point on the stony beach below.

And the tips of her outstretched toes just brushed against the
flat white cap that protected the old man's head from the sun.
They sent the incongruously jaunty piece of headgear spinning
and rolling over the pebbles and put the old boy into a state of
alarm which the sight of the rest of the crowd jumping one by
one onto the beach on either side of him did nothing to dispel.

The girl who had landed first took a look at the flinching oc-
togenarian and turned quickly away. Evidently she was not the
type to brazen out any such accident that occurred in her rackety
progress about her world. But others of the party — there were
no more than eight of them in fact, though to the quiet folk on the
beach it must have seemed as if scores of the vandals had descended — were more hardfaced. Another of the girls, a pert-
figured redhead in a saucily diminutive green bikini, turned to
the boy beside her and commented on the incident in a voice
which rang round the whole beach.

"They shouldn't let 'em out that old," she shouted cheerfully.
"It's enough to make you sick just seeing them."

And then with a renewed full-throated whoop she set off leap-
ing over the pebbles toward the somewhat more inviting area of
the dark water-gleaming sand.

Once down on the sand the newcomers proceeded brazenly to
take over the whole area. They ran races from end to end of the
level stretch, and woe betide anyone foolish enough to remain in
their way. They indulged in short games sessions with an enor-

mous brightly colored rubber ball they had brought with them, bouncing it once right onto the carefully laid-out sandwich boxes and thermos bottles of a family eating an early lunch. And all the while they kept up a running commentary on their own activities, delivered at the tops of their voices and interspersed with braying inconsequential laughter.

So bit by bit the whole of the sand was given over to them, mothers sharply calling their children back onto the pebbles, middle-aged fathers darting furious glances at the mob but equally withdrawing to places that were safer, if a good deal more uncomfortable.

Only one determined parent, father of two small boys and a girl, resolutely refused to budge. He was engaged on serious business. From the moment the sea had retreated beyond the pebbles he had been busy constructing an immensely elaborate sand castle. With the aid of their little pails, his children had been dragooned into amassing a sufficient quantity of sand while he himself, equipped, not with any plastic seaside spade, but with a proper no-nonsense garden tool, had toiled manfully to dig out a foot-deep trench all round the area of his proposed edifice. Once or twice as the crowd of newcomers had run whooping and shrieking past he had looked up briefly and a quick frown of annoyance had shown itself on his dedicatedly intense face above the sober pair of spectacles which rested as firmly on the bridge of his nose here on the beach as they did at his office desk.

And as was almost inevitable, before long these two parties staking claim to the sand, each determined in a different way, came into conflict.

It was the girl who had first jumped down onto the beach who was responsible. Jacky, they called her, yelling insults at her in their friendly and thoroughly uninhibited way. She must have been about seventeen by the look of her, certainly no more. And it was in the course of one of their brief but violent games with the big rubber ball — a heavy object some two feet in diameter — that the incident occurred.

Jacky was standing just above the newly built sand castle, which its architect was busy giving a final shaping to, not without sharply reproving advice to his underlings, and the ball had come bouncing along toward her. She made a dash for it, swerved when it bounced askew, and went sprawling frankly spread-eagled right over the delicate structure. In an instant it was reduced from fantasy to flattened nothingness.

She heaved herself up on her elbows and looked across at her companions.

"Oh, God," she shouted, "I've got sand all down inside my bikini!"

And since this time she could hardly pretend she had not been responsible for the damage, she entirely ignored it. She pushed herself to her knees, digging two deep pits in the soft sand by way of final insult added to injury, then staggered upright and ran down toward the sea, pulling the bikini top away from her body and shimmying wildly to get rid of the sand.

"You've spoiled our castle," exclaimed its builder, looking at her retreating back. "You've made a complete mess of it!"

None of the group paid the least attention to him. Jacky was for the time being the focus of their interest. The four boys rushed up and eagerly surrounded her, beginning vigorous and by no means disinterested efforts to help her get rid of more sand.

This activity, as might have been expected, drew a great deal of covert interest from the holiday-makers on the pebbly area. They had all been pretending to ignore the usurpers, but nonetheless they had kept a constant eye on their activities; and by now they had some idea of their different personalities and which name to attach to each of them. And they watched with relished disapproval while Mike, the blatantly handsome and self-assured one, Bob the blond muscle boy, the serious-looking Herbert, who had already raised more than one chorus of strident booing by perpetrating frightful puns, and the smallest of the bunch, little bespectacled Dickie, all set upon the shrieking Jacky and pulled and tugged at her bikini and patted and brushed her body, pretending, with enough shouting to encourage a football team, that she was still thickly sand-covered.

But this was hardly to the liking of the other girls, especially — it looked to the greedy censorious eyes watching from the pebbles — of the pert redhead (was her name Jo?) who had been noted as showing a particular interest in the handsome Mike.

And so — with a great deal of "Hey, leave the silly twit alone" and "What do you want to go and knock over the poor old man's sand castle for?" — they succeeded at last in diverting the boys' attention from little Jacky into a sprint across the sand ("First to touch the breakwater" and "Last there's a sissy"), in which as usual the muscular, and proud of it, Bob was first home.

When they had all arrived at the breakwater and had begun a new outburst of shouting, arguing, and minor horseplay, the first heavy drops of rain began to fall from a suddenly clouded-over sky. The noisy group took no notice, except that the girl in the white swimsuit with the deep, deep tan complained in a loud voice that she would not be able "to get even five minutes of sunbathing." But the rest of the beach, of course, promptly retreated in face of this unpleasant manifestation of unfair Nature. Towels were hastily folded and draped over husbandly arms, sandwiches were stuffed, sand-speckled as they were, back into their plastic boxes, children were summoned, spades and pails were frantically gathered, and small procession after small procession made its way back to the cheerless prospect of boardinghouse bedrooms.

When the invaders noticed this sensible mass retreat it seemed only to heighten their spirits and they set off on a monster leap-frog chase all the way across to the other side of the beach, still ignoring the progressively heavier raindrops. Then the boys began a game of stone-throwing, aiming first at one object until it had been hit and then moving on to something else, a discarded beach shoe, a seaweed-draped spur of rock, a soggy ice-cream carton.

The girls made bets on their prowess.

"Hit it, hit it, Mike," screeched Jacky. "I'll give you such a kiss if you do."

"You'll keep your thieving little hands off him," Jo, the pert redhead, yelled almost as loudly.

"I'll bet Bob gets it, I bet he does," shoued Christine, who was blond and wore her hair piled high on her head.

"Bob," the punster Herbert boomed out, "I bet a bob he can't."

"Darling Bob, hit it for God's sake, this rain's getting cold," the white-swimsuited, well-tanned Liz begged, her voice not much less strident than the others'.

And at that moment the rain abruptly came down in sheets.

The group looked wildly round for shelter. And there, not fifty yards away, was the old Shell Museum.

The words were painted out on a long sun-bleached board running all the way across the front of the single-storied barnlike building just at the edge of the beach. A broad flight of sea-smoothed wooden steps led up to its veranda and the open double-doors beyond.

The group set off like a stampede of horses toward it, the girls screaming as the cold rain struck them, the boys shouting in sheer animal spirits.

And that was when they met old Mr. Peduncle.

He was sitting just inside the doors at a small oilcloth-covered table on which were scattered dozens of little shells, sitting where he had been all morning in his old brown-varnished wheelchair with the mottled brown Leatherette seat and back. He was a big man, filling the chair like a great mound of wheat in his old shabby check suit, and he had a large head, deep pink in hue and mound-shaped, descending from a round skull covered with sparse white hairs to two big cheeks. He sat almost immobile, only his hands moving restlessly but with method among the shells on the table, sorting and shifting, and his eyes, bright and beady behind a tiny pair of gold-rimmed pince-nez in the middle of that big expressionless face, darting quickly here and there.

"Hey," demanded Mike, the handsome one, as they all crowded up into the shelter of the veranda, "is this place open? Can we come in like?"

Mr. Peduncle looked up at the white-painted board beside the open doors, its black letters fretted by the sea winds.

"Admission threepence," he said in a voice that was quiet but plainly audible. "Children, one penny."

"That'll be a penny for this one then," said the boy with the glasses, Dickie, pushing Jacky sharply forward.

Mr. Peduncle took no notice. He slipped open the drawer in the table in front of him and brought out two rolls of cardboard tickets, one pink, one blue, a tall black leather-bound book and a small bottle of India ink with a steel-nibbed pen.

"There is also a two-and-sixpenny season ticket," he said. "Or life membership at three guineas."

He turned back the cover of the big black book. Its paper, once white, had faded to a uniform shade of buff, but the ink of the entries on the first page stood out still bold and black. There were only seven names. The first of them had next to it the date: August 12, 1910.

Liz, the suntanned one in the white swimsuit, spoke sharply from outside on the veranda.

"For God's sake," she said, "pay him, somebody, will you? I'm freezing."

But she was to wait before she got into the comparative warmth of the sea-battered building. Her remark produced, as all remarks made in that company tended to, a whole minor outbreak of noisy verbal warfare.

The redhead, Jo, was first in with a crack.

"Freezing?" she called out cheerfully. "Some people are never happy unless they're lying there baking in the sun."

"Yes," little Jacky came yelling in. "And with half a dozen boys dangling round too."

And then the blond muscular Bob came roaring to Liz's rescue.

"And who's never happy unless she's lying there doing something else? Eh, Jo girl, eh?"

"Nothing wrong with a bit of that," Jo shouted back, perfectly unabashed.

"All right, all right," Bob yelled. "I'm queuing up, old Jo."

"When you like, boy, when you like."

"Hey, Mike, you hear that?" little Dickie called out, though the handsome Mike, or anybody, would have had to be deaf not to have heard.

However, Mike took no notice of the crack, smiling noncommittally and busying himself with fishing in an inner pocket of his bathing trunks and producing a handful of half-crowns. He sprawled them thunderingly onto Mr. Peduncle's table, displacing two or three of the neatly ranged little shells.

"Make it season tickets for one and all," he said. "You never know, this old place might come in useful."

Without a word Mr. Peduncle brought out from his drawer eight green cards and handed one to each of them as they stepped past his table and into the dark of the museum itself.

"I'll switch on the electric light for you," he said when they were all in. "If it's overcast outside it's difficult to see the specimens properly."

"There's nothing wrong with a bit of dark," said the blond Christine, seizing the muscular Bob's arm with one hand and the handsome Mike's with the other.

But Mr. Peduncle was not to be put off. With surprising speed and dexterity he maneuvered his wheelchair round, shot down the alleyway between the two rows of glass-topped showcases that ran the length of the big room, and came to rest beside a small door marked PRIVATE. There he reached up to a pair of switches and clicked one of them on.

It was not a particularly strong light that hung on a chain from one of the wooden beams across the ceiling but it did serve to show the accumulated specimens moderately well. There were hundreds of them. All the walls right up to the high windows were lined with them, hung in thin wire frames and each carefully labeled with its Latin name, its common name, and its place of origin. There were the pink and yellow and brown-spotted tapering cylinders of the volutes; the prickly murexes in an infinity of rock-colored shades; the miters, fit headgear for miniature bishops, darkly red in the interior or vividly orange-splotched; the augers, wickedly pointed and delicately spotted, the many cones with their extraordinary variety of pattern; the wide-spreading scallops, the rapas, the chanks, and the turrids.

And in the two long rows of glass cases were the prize specimens, big and small — the chambered nautilus, the golden cowries, little Aristotle's lanterns, a big startlingly pink queen conch, the lace-edged strombus, the wrinkled scorpion, the striped helmet, with its alternate lines of white and golden-yellow, and the delicately cross-hatched dunker's triton.

Mr. Peduncle swished his old chair back to the table by the entrance from which he could look out over the rain-beaten beach and returned to his minute examination of the pile of shells he had been working on, apparently ignoring his visitors. The group wandered aimlessly round, with the solemn-faced Herbert the only one to pay much attention to the exhibits and then only to read out an occasional label with the object of perpetrating one of his terrible puns, a diversion which did little to raise the spirits of the others who seemed suddenly to have run out of steam.

But it was not long until the provocative redhead, Jo, always somewhat of a pioneer, hit on something a little more to the taste of her friends. She reached up and pretended to put her ear to a wide-mouthed conch hanging on the wall and then exclaimed in a loud voice, "What are the wild waves saying?"

She pretended to listen more intently.

"Oh," she shouted, "there's a little murmur in here says someone in this room's going to get married before they're much older."

She glanced significantly over at the handsome and moneyed Mike.

"Mind you," she bawled, "you never can tell with a boy."

Roars of laughter. And all the girls now must reach up and listen to shells of their own. Impudent Dickie joined them.

"Listen to this, listen to this," he shouted above the general hubbub. "I've news here from the wild waves that an engagement broken by mutual consent may be renewed before long."

Christine, the girl with the piled-up blond hair, stepped backward from the shell she had her ear to.

"Cut it out, Dickie," she said, cold anger showing in her eyes and the taut line of her neck.

But Dickie was not one to learn.

"In spite of many and varied adventures," he intoned, "a certain person is confidently expected to return before long to her first and true love."

And now Mike intervened. He came rapidly up behind little Dickie and seized his arms in a swift lock.

"Whatever there was between Chris and me," he said, "is over and I'll thank you not to make any cracks."

He stood holding the helpless Dickie, and began slowly and painfully twisting Dickie's arms behind his back. There was a smile on his handsome mouth.

"Hey, let go," Dickie exclaimed, the pain putting an undertow of anxiety into his voice.

"When you've been taught your lesson," Mike replied.

Little Dickie gave a sudden sharp gasp.

"Let him go, you great big bully," young Jacky jumped in, loud as ever.

"When I'm ready to," Mike replied.

Dickie let out a long whimper. The others stood round, watching. It was an unpleasant moment. Then an unexpected voice broke in.

"Perhaps I can tell you something of the history of the museum?"

It was Mr. Peduncle, swiftly and silently beside them in his dark wheelchair.

"I've been here thirty years, you know," he said in those quiet but carrying tones of his. "I've not actually left the place in all that time. It wouldn't be possible. They'd have to bring along a crane for my chair."

Curly-haired, straight-nosed, cleft-chinned Mike let little Dickie go. They stood looking at Mr. Peduncle, uneasily suspicious.

"Yes," he said, "I just have a red flag I can hoist as a signal if anything should happen to go wrong, but otherwise I'm quite on my own here. Yet, do you know, I'm perfectly content. I have my work, you see."

"Work?" said the pert Jo.

She glanced round at the yellowy varnished wooden walls with their rows and rows of shells, at the heavy old-fashioned display cases, at the table by the entrance doors with its scattering of black mussel shells and the little tiny white whorls of other British mollusks.

"Oh, yes," said Mr. Peduncle, "this is my work. The study and comparison of shells. I pay the children on the beach a penny a bucket for them, and in summer it takes me all my time to go through what they bring in. And every now and again in a moment of discovery I hit on some difference in one particular shell that is significant, something that adds a drop to the ocean of knowledge. That makes it all worthwhile."

It was at this point that Jacky began to laugh. She put back her seventeen-year-old head and laughed and laughed.

"Shells," she gurgled out. "Spending a lifetime going over and over a lot of moldy old shells."

"You think it humorous," said the old man, unruffled. "Well, let me tell you that systematic study in any field of knowledge is always worthwhile. The making of observations, the carrying out of comparisons. They pay in the end. Sometimes in quite unexpected ways."

A ray of pale sunlight came suddenly in through the high windows above his head, effacing the pale glare of the light.

"Hey, the rain's stopped," shouted Bob, the muscle boy.

He gave the pertly provocative Jo a friendly slap.

"Race you to the sea, Jo girl," he yelled.

And in less than ten seconds the whole group was out.

While the sun shone they continued to sport on the beach and the more timid holiday-makers, creeping out again with the better weather, once more were forced to give up most of the flat area of the sand to their activities. They ran races, jumping over any obstacle and careless of whom they bumped into. They played with the big rubber ball. They grabbed a child's plastic pail and started throwing water over each other, as well as over a good many onlookers.

Only the already deep-brown Liz dropped out after a while to take advantage of the shining sun and lie full length on the sand, improving an unimprovable tan. For a little she succeeded in securing the muscular Bob as an attendant, but before long red-headed Jo, never content for anyone to be doing nothing if she could help it, came up and started whispering into Bob's ear, and he leaped to his feet and began discussing some sort of handicap race from one sea-worn breakwater all the way across to the other.

They ran it too. Bob gave Jo a short start and she won by a yard. And this, of course, in its turn started a series of other races between girls and boys, Jacky against Bob, squealing all over the beach when he outdistanced her, Jo with the same handicap against first Herbert, who dead-heated with her, and then Mike, whom she failed to beat and ended up tussling with, to the great disgust of a group of old biddies up in deck-chair row.

And eventually even Liz, deprived of any sort of male attention, got to her feet and issued a challenge to Jo. She nearly beat her too, for all the sultry laziness of her appearance; but at the last moment up by the edge of the pebbles Liz's breath gave out and she collapsed moodily onto the scuffed sand.

And shortly after this, as suddenly as they had come, the whole group disappeared. They made for the promenade, still talking at the tops of their voices, laughing and shrieking. And then came the roar of the engine of young Mike's sports car and they were gone.

"Good riddance," came the mutters from the staid row of deck chairs, also beginning to break up as the sun dipped toward the distant sea horizon.

But they came back again late in the evening. The noise of the car was heard coming to a squealing halt somewhere at the far end of the promenade, and some of them came down to the beach again in the soft light of the very last of the long day.

Old Mr. Peduncle was taking the air on his veranda. When Jo and Bob glanced back at the wooden structure of the Shell Museum, after they had climbed over the long weed-decked breakwater and dropped down into the darkness on the far side, a tiny glitter of light struck off from the little pair of pince-nez that Mr. Peduncle wore perched on his broad pink-colored nose. It sent a brief flash out into the oncoming night . . .

The group did not visit the museum at all the next day. Mr. Peduncle saw them, of course. Anyone keeping even half an eye on the beach could not have failed to see them. They made, if possible, even more of a nuisance of themselves than they had the day before. From morning till dusk it was nothing but shouting, "Hey, Mike." "Hey, Dickie." "Watch it, Herbert." "Go on, Jo."

Mr. Peduncle noted the facts, as he noted all the facts that came his way. He saw how friendly the redheaded Jo and the handsome, moneyed Mike seemed to be. He saw Dickie going to immense pains, while the serious castle-building father was away at lunchtime, to undermine the new and even more elaborate structure he had built that day, so that when the poor man came back ready to add a few last refinements, the whole thing collapsed as soon as he knelt in front of it.

He noted that the blond Christine had succeeded in playing off Herbert against Dickie most of the morning, to her visible satisfaction. He saw that in the afternoon Liz, who had actually managed to sun-bathe all morning and was doing the same thing again now, had persuaded both Herbert and Bob to sit beside her.

He saw all this and he sorted through some two hundred shells that the penny-a-bucket children had brought him.

And on the next day, when naturally enough it did rain, the group burst into the museum once more. None of them had kept the green season ticket but Mr. Peduncle did not mind.

"I remember you," he said.

Again there was no one else in the big beam-crossed room, and again the group made a fair nuisance of themselves, here as elsewhere.

They had not been inside long and the rain was still beating down on the black-tarred roof in a steady thrumming when the redheaded Jo announced that she must have a drink.

"Bob," she proclaimed, "you're the fastest on your feet; sprint along to the stand and get us all something to drink. I'm parched."

"Yes, Joanna," Bob said, with unexpected acquiescence, considering how hard the rain was coming down.

He squared his shoulders at the entrance doors and in a moment was off, pounding over the pebbles below at a tremendous rate.

He must have kept it up all the way to the ice-cream stand and all the way back with his big paws wrapped round eight cartons of orange drink. But when he handed them over — "Here you are, Joanna" — he got little thanks.

She took one long suck through her pair of plastic straws and jerked her head up in disgust.

"Nuts," she said. "It's not cold; it's hot. Who the hell wants a drink of tepid orange?"

She flung her carton down in a corner.

"Tepid, is it?" shouted Herbert, the pun-maker. "When the chap at the stand poured it out he didn't look which *tep he'd* used."

The others were prepared to accord him the customary noisy groan, but Jo thought differently.

"Did you think your drink was cold then?" she snapped at him.

He blinked. "Well," he said, "I did think it was coolish, as a matter of fact."

"Then you're as big a fool as you look."

And then little Dickie caught the rough edge of her tongue. The rain had slackened, and he was the first to notice it.

"Hey, Jo," he called. "Sun's coming out. How about I race you to the sea? Same prize as Bob got the first day?"

Jo looked at him. "No, thank you," she said bluntly.

They left then, as noisily as they had come. And Mr. Peduncle took his chair across to his private quarters at the back, fetched a walking stick, and used it upside down to jockey Jo's drink carton laboriously across the floor, out onto the veranda, and down onto the pebbles of the beach.

Then he went back to sorting shells . . .

The next day was brilliantly sunny; for once really hot. And Jo died.

They had been playing the burying-in-the-sand game. Each of them in turn had volunteered or been noisily cajoled into lying in the soft dry sand just beside one of the high breakwaters and been covered all over by the others, with eventually only two plastic straws from an orange-drink carton left to breathe through. A sort of competition had evolved out of the game: it was a matter of completing the burial and then leaving the victim deserted for as long as possible.

It had begun as a practical joke and developed into a cruel-edged test of endurance. The rules seemed to be that each one of the party went off in a different direction, and the one whose nerve broke first and who came back to release the victim from the heavy covering of sand was the next to be buried.

More or less everybody on the beach was aware of the rules. The loud shouts in which they had been arrived at insured this.

Jo, bright red hair encased in a bathing cap that matched the vivid green of her minimal bikini, was the last of them to submit to the burying process, and, so it appeared later, she had been covered up a little more deeply than any of the others, so that it had really been impossible for her to have kicked her way to freedom.

However, she had her two straws to breathe through and they were well clear of the sand over her. So she had been in no real danger. Until somehow a pail of sand had been tipped over the place where the straws pointed up to the serenely blue sky. The police surgeon gave it as his opinion that death would have come very quickly.

Of course when the tragedy was discovered — little Dickie had been the one whose nerve had broken this time and who had come back to find the brazenly noisy Jo no longer alive — there was a tremendous fuss. The local constable had been summoned by Bob, who had run in his bathing trunks all the way through the little town looking for him, and in his turn the constable had sent for his superior officers from farther along the coast. Then the various auxiliaries had been brought in — the police surgeon, the ambulance men, the shirt-sleeved detectives with measuring tapes and elaborately operated cameras.

And the local C.I.D. chief, glaringly incongruous on the beach in his heavy dark brown suit, frequently removing his battered soft hat to wipe a sweaty forehead, had questioned at length each of the individuals of the group. And, for all that the town constable prowled stolidly in a sort of invisible circle round the spot where the interrogations took place, the main outlines of the matter percolated quickly enough to the remaining holiday-makers on the beach, all studiously pretending not to notice the activity going on near the breakwater.

It seemed that each member of the group had wandered far from the place they had buried Jo in an attempt to hold out longest from rescuing her, and that none of them had seen any of the others after a couple of minutes from their simultaneous departure. Nor had any of them kept much of an eye on the time. They were all totally vague about everything. None seemed to have been back before any of the others, though they were all converging on the spot again when little Dickie had made his discovery. None certainly had been near enough, so they said, to have seen whether anybody else had chanced to go near Jo's recumbent body.

Much the same result came out of the slow inquiries which half a dozen detectives, sand trickling into their solid shoes, made among the other holiday-makers. Nobody had taken much notice when the noisy little group had moved away. They had got on thankfully with their own affairs, reading the newspapers, knitting, cricket-playing, sand-castle–building.

So at the end of an investigation that had taken almost the rest of the day, the C.I.D. chief's final word to the remaining seven had been taken everywhere as the official verdict. "Of course," he had said, "there'll have to be an inquest, though I don't see that it'll really get us much forrader." And he had added a request that the group not leave the district until after the inquest had been held.

The next day, which was also brilliantly sunny, the reduced group made a much muted appearance, contenting themselves with sitting along the top of the wall overlooking the beach, and wearing reasonable clothes in spite of the heat.

But the day after, when massively building-up clouds threatened thunder and it seemed hotter than ever, their attitude was not so decorous. They continued to sit on the sea wall just above the black-tarred roof of the Shell Museum, but they were by no means as quiet as they had been the day before. They were, in fact, decidedly quarrelsome, and not at all careful to keep their voices down.

Little waves of shock ran all the way along the row of deck chairs at the foot of the wall, back and forth with each new outbreak from above.

Then the storm came. There was one eerie flash of purplish lightning, which seemed to illuminate and transform the whole beach, and almost simultaneously a single peal of thunder cracked out from directly overhead. And then the rain began, pelting down with tropical violence.

The group got inside the museum in seconds.

Mr. Peduncle was seated as always in his battered old wheel-chair at the table by the entrance doors, his huge body still and mound-shaped, his hands moving over the shells spread out in front of him, his little bright blue eyes sharp behind the tiny gold-rimmed pince-nez that seemed almost lost on his large face. He watched the seven of them push their way past into the dim interior of the shell-surrounded room and offered no comment.

The talk now was all of "getting out of this bloody place" and "to hell with telling that idiot inspector." They spoke to each other in sharp, biting phrases, which echoed and clashed noisily in shadowy confines of the museum.

Bob, with his body almost bursting the blue T-shirt and white cotton trousers he wore, came and stood for a moment at the open doors, looking impatiently at the thundering rain. He seemed half-determined to repeat his dash through the downpour of three days earlier.

"Damn it," he said to no one in particular, "Jo was a nice kid but she's dead and there's nothing we can do for her."

The declaration appeared to strike Mr. Peduncle with particular force. His fingers abruptly stopped moving over the shells on his table as Bob pronounced the dead girl's name. He looked up at Bob intently.

"You will tell me it's not my business," the old shell collector said, "but you ought to wait a little longer."

Christine, the blonde with the high-piled hair, swung round.

"No," she said loudly, "it isn't any of your business. And when we're ready to go, we'll go."

Mike glared out at the rain.

"Just as soon as this stops," he promised, "I'm off. The car's just at the end of the prom, and you won't see me for dust."

Curiously, Mr. Peduncle did not at that moment repeat his advice. Instead he opened the drawer at his table and felt about inside it. Apparently he could not find what he wanted, because after half a minute he brought out the tall black book, opened it with a little sigh which might have been audible to some of them had they not gone back to their noisy bickering, and tore out a sheet from the back. He then uncapped his bottle of India ink and with the steel-nibbed pen wrote a few words on the torn-out page, folded it over, wrote again, and finally tucked the whole into a pocket of his old check suit.

Little Dickie was now looking out at the rain.

"I think it's not so bad now," he announced. "Let's go."

The statuesque Liz glanced through the open doors.

"Go out in this?" she said. "You have to be crazy."

And certainly the rain was still beating down with considerable force.

"Well, I'm not staying cooped up here more than another few minutes," Dickie, once so cheerful, announced with distinct viciousness.

Mr. Peduncle abruptly swung his chair along the sand-scattered floor of the museum and stopped it by the door at the back marked PRIVATE. Here there was a lanyard running up through a little hole in the roof. Mr. Peduncle untwisted the thin rope and pulled it energetically.

Herbert, the serious, saw him.

"What the hell are you doing?" he demanded.

Mr. Peduncle looked at him through his tiny glasses.

"I was pulling up my red signal flag," he replied tranquilly. "There's something I want."

He wheeled his chair back to the entrance doors but stopped now in front of his table instead of behind it so that he almost completely blocked the exit.

"There is something I ought to tell you," he announced. "I know which one of you killed Jo."

They all turned to face him. He sat there in the doorway, the hands which had moved rapidly over the shells on the table, sorting and sifting, lying quite still now on the arms of the chair. For a long moment they looked steadily at him, and then as though on a given signal their glances flickered from one to the other, as if a wordless conspiracy was beginning to form.

"I mentioned the other day," Mr. Peduncle remarked steadily, "that I have a mind accustomed by long training to observe first and then to classify. You were disparaging about that process. Yet observation and comparison have led me to my answer."

The self-assured Mike gave a little twist of a smile.

"The armchair detective, eh?" he said, "Well, name your name."

"Certainly," said Mr. Peduncle.

At the placid conviction in his voice the unity of the group inside the dim museum visibly shivered. The glances that were exchanged now were no longer conspiratorial but probing.

"I have had a good deal of opportunity of observing you all since you came to the beach," Mr. Peduncle said. "Both here in the museum and outside as you played at your various games. So when I learned how Jo died, I asked myself if one of you might be responsible. Certainly no one else was going to murder her. It is hardly likely that the gentleman whose sand castle you destroyed would go to such lengths for revenge. No, I had only to look among the seven of you."

Again a flicker of uneasiness passed round the group. Only Mike resisted it.

"You said you could name a name," he challenged.

"So I can," replied Mr. Peduncle. "You see, when I asked myself who among you had reason to hate that girl enough to kill her but was concealing that hatred — and one of you was — the answer came to me soon enough. As I sifted over the facts about you I hit on one quite evident thing standing out as decidedly out of the ordinary."

"Here, let's just go," Herbert broke in, looking not quite as sedately serious as usual.

"No," said Mike, "I want to hear the man."

"No, don't go," Mr. Peduncle said firmly. "Not until I've told you about the races you ran. And the one that had an unexpected winner."

His big head moved suddenly and the twinkling little eyeglasses were focused sharply on the muscle boy, Bob.

"Yes," said Mr. Peduncle, "you, Bob, are the fastest runner of the lot — even the girl Jo said so. Yet when you ran against her she won."

It was little Dickie who broke in here, staring insolently down at Mr. Peduncle.

"You big goop," he said. "That was a handicap race."

"Oh, yes, I know Jo had a head start," Mr. Peduncle replied unperturbed. "But she had exactly the same start over Mike a few minutes later, and Mike beat her easily."

He let the silence fall over them. His eyes were fixed on Bob.

Bob took a step forward.

And at that moment there came the sound of rapidly running feet mounting the steps outside. Everybody wheeled.

A curious headless figure in bright red mackintosh shot up onto the veranda. Once under the shelter it flipped back the plastic raincoat it had been wearing over its head to reveal itself as a boy of about ten.

"Hello, Mr. Peduncle," he said. "I saw your flag up, and Mum said I'd better run over and see if you were in trouble."

"Oh, no," Mr. Peduncle answered. "No trouble. Just a note I wanted delivered."

And he pulled the little folded slip of paper out of his pocket, leaned forward, and thrust it into the boy's hand. The boy took a look at what had been written on the outside. His eyes widened.

"Right ho," he said, and instantly vanished from the veranda.

Mr. Peduncle turned back to Bob.

"I think," he said, "you were just going to tell me that you lost that race on purpose. It was a bet between you and Jo, wasn't it? Rather a secret kind of bet, of course. But one which brought you your reward later that night. Isn't that so?"

Bob tilted up his smooth face. "Yes, it did, if you want to know," he said.

"Yes," said Mr. Peduncle. "I simply used that instance as an illustration of the sort of unusual thing I was looking for, and of the danger of not taking all the associated facts into consideration. I might just as well have chosen to consider the race that Liz ran."

He gave a flick to the wheel at his side and the old brown chair swung round so that he was directly facing the dark-tanned sun-worshiping Liz.

"If the evident thing about Bob was that he could run faster than any of you," he said, " the evident thing about Liz is that she does not like running at all, and whenever the sun shines she simply lies there enjoying it. But then on one occasion she challenged Jo to a race."

They were all looking at Liz now, even Mike, and with a degree of accusation in all their looks. Here was one of them who had been a bit of an "odd girl out."

"Yes," Mr. Peduncle went on, "and one could easily imagine a motive for Liz. Jo had taken the boys away from her. I mean simply that she had just taken Bob, who was sitting by her, off to play beach games. But I am sure Jo could have taken the other boys away in the long term too."

Mr. Peduncle's gaze moved quietly over the shells in their wire holders on the wall all round.

"You see," he went on, "there was another example of the small variation that seems to mean a great deal. But, of course, you have to look at all the facts. Some variations are significant; others are just accidental. And plainly this instance of Liz getting to her feet and running a race was just accidental. She had been deprived of her temporary escort, she hoped she could gain a victory over Jo, she failed. Not exactly a reason for murder."

"Hey," said little Dickie to the rest of them, "you know what the old fool's going to do? He's going to cook up some sort of story about each one of us, and none of them's going to mean any more than any of the others. Look, the rain's definitely got less now. Let's get out of here."

There was a chorus of agreement. The group began coming toward Mr. Peduncle.

He made no attempt to move.

"I see," he said, "that I must admit I have been keeping you under false pretenses."

"Then you don't know who it was," Christine said sharply.

"Oh, yes, I know. But I was, I confess, a trifle unsure how the rest of you would take what I had to tell you. Suppose, I said to myself, they feel their loyalty to their dead companion is greater than any loyalty to society. They might combine to attack me and help the guilty one escape."

It was Mike who laughed. "You know, we might," he said.

"That is why I tried to detain you with suppositions," Mr. Peduncle explained gravely.

"So we'll be off then," Herbert said, recovering his assurance.

"You'll go and six of you will never know who killed her?" Mr. Peduncle asked with a flash of his beady blue eyes behind the gold-rimmed pince-nez.

Their steps slowed. They came to a halt.

"Oh, all right, tell us," Mike said.

Mr. Peduncle looked out of the open doors of the museum. It was still raining, though not as torrentially as before. And the wet and dreary beach appeared totally deserted.

"Well," he said, "I told you that I was on the lookout for slight but significant variations in behavior. And something that was said shortly after you came in here just now gave it to me. 'Jo was a nice kid but she's dead.' Those were the words. And at once they put me in mind of something. Something curious."

They were paying him an almost awed attention now.

"You all," he continued, "used to call her Jo. All except one of you. And he only started to call her Joanna after the first evening you were here."

The gaze behind the tiny pince-nez traveled slowly round.

"Didn't you, Bob?" said Mr. Peduncle. "And didn't you switch back to calling her Jo after she was dead?"

Bob did not reply.

"Now why does a young man suddenly take to calling a girl by her formal name?" Mr. Peduncle resumed. "Is this a significant variation? Well, coupled with the bet that Bob won, the bet that entitled him to that evening walk to a secluded spot behind the breakwater, undoubtedly it was significant. What was the somewhat coarse expression that Jo herself used? Yes: you never can tell with a boy. No, Bob, you didn't come up to expectations, did you? And Jo, when she was disappointed in her little treats, whether it was a boy or a carton of orangeade, could be unpleasantly spiteful, bitterly wounding, couldn't she?"

Suddenly Bob moved. He took one long bound across the width of the room and from the shell-covered wall he snatched one particular shell. Mr. Peduncle knew what it was at once. It was his prize specimen of *Terebra maculata,* commonly known as the marlin spike, a sharp-pointed auger almost nine inches long, tough as steel, and no mean weapon.

"All right," Bob shouted. "You know a hell of a lot, don't you? Well, if you're silenced I'll take a risk with my friends."

And he launched himself with bunched athlete's muscles at the chair-bound Mr. Peduncle.

Chair-bound, but wheelchaired. Mr. Peduncle's big hands flicked hard at the wheels beside him. His chair shot forward at a sharp angle. Bob tried to turn to catch him, skidded on the sand-dusted floor, and crashed heavily to his side.

Before he even had time to get up, the local constable was thumping up the stairs of the veranda, in answer to Mr. Peduncle's summons.

THE MAN WHO MURDERED PAPA DÉSIRÉ

by Lassiter Wren

"At first Voirbo could not be brought to tell what he had done with the victim's head."

PARIS was again in the throes of a murder mystery, and a grim one. During the Christmas and New Year's celebrations merry-makers were repeatedly shocked at police reports of finding bits of human remains — some floating in the Seine, some wrapped in packages and disposed of in various parts of the city. None of the gruesome discoveries bore any clue to the identity of the victim, and the head had not been found. A proprietor of a river-side laundry related that on the nineteenth of December he had seen a man throwing into the river handfuls of scraps of meat. Questioned, the man had said boldly: "I am a keen fisherman. Tomorrow is a holiday and I am baiting the river for a big day's sport!"

The laundry man could say only that the eager fisherman was short and wore a long coat and a tall hat. Paris shivered and wondered.

When Lampon, proprietor of a small restaurant in the Rue Princesse, then drew from his well a package containing a human leg, he ran with his tale of horror to police officer Ringué, a friend of his. Whereupon Ringué wished he had detained a man whom he remembered meeting late at night on December 22 near the Rue Princesse. He had indeed stopped and questioned him, for the man was carrying a large parcel in one hand and a hamper in the other, and there had recently been robberies in the neighborhood. The answer had been straightforward: "I have just arrived by train from Nantes, and, being unable to find a cab at the station at this hour, I am obliged to carry home my luggage myself. The packages contain several fine hams. You may see here on the parcels the label of the railroad company."

Verifying the presence of the railway label, Ringué had accepted the explanation and allowed the wayfarer to continue on his way. He had said he lived in the Rue Princesse. Of course the stranger might have been telling the truth — but Ringué now recalled that the man had been short, wearing a long coat and a tall hat.

Ringué ran in great haste to the police commissioner of the quarter with the news of the discovery in Lampon's well. The young commissioner, M. Gustave Macé, went at once to the Rue Princesse and made a thorough examination of the package and the well. Lampon had pulled the package up with a large iron hook, with the result that it had been considerably damaged. It yielded no clues, but M. Macé was more fortunate in his investigation of the well; it gave up another package which contained a leg, without doubt the mate of the first discovered.

The wrappings of this second package were extremely interesting to M. Macé. An inner wrapper made of part of a trouser leg of iron gray cloth was covered by a piece of glazed black calico, a yard square, simply knotted at each end and the middle sewn up with black thread. The limb was covered by a long cotton stocking, drab in color. Hanging to the lower part of the stocking was a fragment of a short sock which had been stitched over it. On this sock M. Macé was elated to find his first clue to the victim's identity — the initial B, stitched in red cotton with a small cross on either side, thus: +B+

A very slender clue, but a clue. The long stocking seemed the only possible indication of the sex of the victim. Perhaps influenced by this stocking, the examining doctors pronounced the legs those of a woman, and added that the dismemberment had been neatly but unprofessionally accomplished, with the aid of a butcher knife. The well was emptied, but nothing else was found.

While Parisians wondered who the unfortunate victim could be, M. Macé threw himself into his difficult task with all the ardor and amazing skill and patience which were soon to bring him worldwide fame as a detective. Acting on the doctor's decision that the legs were those of a woman, he painstakingly investigated every case of women reported missing for the previous six months — *eighty-four in number*. From these choosing fourteen as most likely, he finally reduced them to three. And then all three were proved to be alive and well.

But just as M. Macé came to this discouraging blank wall, Dr. Tardieu, the great French physician, examined the remains and pronounced an unhesitating verdict that a grave error had been made by the original medical examiners. It was a man's body, he said. The opinion of the great doctor, accepted as final in all cases of this kind, was corroborated by the aged chief attendant at the morgue, who also insisted that the police were off on the wrong trail. Dr. Tardieu said:

> These remains are those of a man advanced in years. My colleagues who stated otherwise were in error, why I cannot say. The feet are larger than those of a woman. The dismemberment has been done skillfully by a cleaver or chopper. The cuts were made soon after death. There has been a considerable effusion of blood. I observe also that there is a clearly marked scar on one leg, only recently healed. But without the head it will not be easy to establish the identity, and the murderer appears to have taken good care to conceal that most important piece of evidence.

The clues to the identity of the murdered were thus few enough, and those to the murderer even less, but M. Macé, in his examination of the black calico package taken from Lampon's well, had come to certain conclusions regarding the man who had made it. He knew that black glazed calico of that particular kind was used extensively by tailors, and the knotted ends and black cotton stitching, in his opinion, pointed in the same direction. Inquiry at the house in the Rue Princesse developed that no tailors lived there. Moreover, all the occupants were known as reputable persons.

However, the old woman who acted as concierge said that it was easy for anyone to get in at any time, provided he knew of the existence of a push button in the wall, which worked a spring latch and opened the door. With this information, M. Macé inclined to the opinion that the murderer was not a resident of the house but someone who had formerly lived or visited there, who knew of the push button and thus obtained access to the well. Certainly it would not seem likely that a resident would poison his own well in such a manner, or risk the discovery being made so near to him.

M. Macé led the garrulous old concierge on to talk of lodgers, past and present. Finally he was rewarded by hearing of a Mademoiselle Dard, who had formerly lived in the house and had worked as a seamstress. He asked eagerly if the concierge knew where the young woman had gone and learned that she no longer worked as seamstress for the tailors, but had gone on the variety stage and was singing at café concerts.

"For what tailors did she work?" asked M. Macé.

"Oh! For half a dozen people. They used to bring the things to her. One man in particular came often, and I had fine work, with him spilling the water on my stairs!"

"Water? What water?" asked M. Macé blandly.

"The water he carried up from the well for her."

This fitted in so nicely with M. Macé's theory that he hastened to find out more about Mlle. Dard and her tailor. A chemist on the opposite side of the street recalled that the tailor's Christian name was Pierre, but he did not know his last name. He said that "Pierre" often brought white waistcoats to be made by Mlle. Dard, and believed he lived in the Rue Mazarin.

Mlle. Dard was hunted up and brought to M. Macé for questioning. She was a pretty, bright-looking little thing, with a turned-up nose and merry eyes. She spoke in a straightforward manner and answered questions intelligently, giving the names of a half-dozen employers for whom she had worked as tailoress.

"And which one was it who carried up water for you from the well?" asked M. Macé.

"That was Monsieur Voirbo."

"Where does he live?"

"He used to live in the Rue Mazarin; then he got married and moved — I don't know where."

"What did you know of him? Was he well off? How did he live?"

"He never worked much, yet always seemed to have money, played cards, drank, frequented cafés. I believe he was mixed up in politics somehow, for he spoke at public meetings."

"Had he any relations or friends?"

"Regarding the first I cannot say. I know he had one particular friend, an ordinary-looking little old man. They often came to the Café Beulgant together. Voirbo called him by his Christian name — *Désiré*, or Papa Désiré, I think he used to call him."

"When did you see this Papa Désiré last? Was it with Voirbo or without him?"

"A couple of months ago, at the café, with Voirbo. At that time Papa Désiré's aunt was with them. She is a bandage-maker, I believe, and lives in the Rue de Nesles. She goes by the name of — yes — Madame Bodasse."

Madame Bodasse, fetched by a special messenger, proved to be a respectable old woman who was quite willing to talk. Yes, Désiré was her nephew — Désiré Bodasse — and lived in the Rue Dauphine. He had been a tapestry worker and had saved money, and now lived on his means, but he was eccentric and a miser. She had not seen him for a month.

Asked if she was not anxious about him, she replied:

"Oh, no. He has often disappeared for weeks. Sometimes he shuts himself up in his place for days and days. Once he was a patient in a hospital for six weeks under a false name and address. That was to avoid paying for his keep."

"Is he married?"

"Yes, but he does not live with his wife. They quarreled years ago, and she went back to her people in the country."

"Were you and Désiré good friends?"

"Oh, yes, perfectly. He took me out to cafés and concerts sometimes. Sunday, the thirteenth of December, was the last time — Désiré and I and Pierre Voirbo, his friend. He took me home afterward and I have not seen him since."

"This Voirbo — describe him, please."

Her reply bought to M. Macé hope that he was on the right trail: "He was short," she said, "and generally wore a long overcoat and a tall hat."

M. Macé at once took Mme. Bodasse to the morgue, where the long stocking, with the sock attached, and the fragments of iron gray trousers were placed before her. She immediately and unhesitatingly identified them as belonging to her nephew Désiré Bodasse. She testified that she herself had marked the socks with the red B between two crosses, and because Désiré liked to wear long stockings to keep him warm but found it hard to get any with large enough feet, she had stitched a sock to each stocking top. Mme. Bodasse also remembered that her nephew had fallen on the jagged edge of a broken bottle and cut his leg severely. This would account for the scar on the leg, mentioned by Dr. Tardieu.

M. Macé was now certain of the identity of the victim, and almost as certain that he knew who had committed the murder. But a visit to Number 50 Rue Dauphin, where Bodasse had his apartment, proved disappointing. After pounding on the door of the apartment and getting no reply (which, of course, was what he expected), M. Macé went downstairs to question the concierge. To his amazement, both the concierge and his wife said that Bodasse was in his apartment. Only the night before, they said, they had noticed a light and a shadow crossing the window. The old man, they said, often locked himself in his room for weeks at a time, and at such times would not even open the door to receive mail. If a letter came, it was poked under his door. Besides, the concierge's wife believed that she had seen him in the street that very morning — he had stopped to speak to someone at the entrance of the Passage du Commerce, she said.

M. Macé was sorely puzzled, and, to make matters worse, Mme. Bodasse now wavered in her belief that the stocking and trouser leg in the morgue belonged to her nephew. For, she said, if there had been lights in Désiré's room and if someone had seen him in the street, she believed she must have been mistaken in her identification. In view of her lack of certainty, M. Macé did not feel justified in forcing entry to the apartment, so he left a letter to be slipped under the door.

In the meantime the commissioner visited the old address of Voirbo, the tailor, in the Rue Mazarin. This Voirbo seemed very unpopular with his old neighbors, though they said they believed he had given up his habits of dissipation now that he was married to a wife with a good dowry. The newlyweds lived in the Rue Lamartine. Voirbo's old servant was interviewed. She had been employed by him to clean his apartment. She knew all about him. Moreover, she was acquainted with Papa Désiré Bodasse. She testified that the two were inseparable friends, and she wondered at the fact that Bodasse had not been present at Voirbo's wedding. Indeed, the tailor himself had appeared hurt at this neglect, she said, and had remarked that "it was a fine time for the old fool to decide to go off on a long journey." He had wished Papa Désiré to be his principal witness at the wedding, he had told her. But, continued the servant, for all that they were such good friends, there were sometimes differences between them, growing out of the extreme stinginess of Bodasse. He had firmly refused to lend Voirbo 10,000 francs toward his marriage, though the latter had begged him to do so.

M. Macé smiled grimly to himself and hastened to the concierge of Papa Désiré's apartment house. Here he learned that the letter which he had poked under the door of the recluse's room was undisturbed. He decided to enter.

The place was in perfect order, but a layer of dust was on the furniture. The bed was made and had not been slept in. In one corner stood Papa Désiré's favorite walking stick. A large silver watch and chain hung from a nail on the wall, and the only hat which the recluse was known to possess (a tall "stovepipe") stood in its place. No one had ever seen him without these "inseparables."

On the mantelpiece stood two cardboard boxes of a kind in which eight candles are customarily sold. One box was empty; the other contained a single candle. Two tall copper candlesticks each contained a candle end, almost consumed, and there were layers of wax below, as though many candles had been burned, one after the other, without removing the wax remaining from each. Below the mantel, in front of the fireplace, were seventeen lucifer matches; fifteen were partially burned and two had missed fire. It was plain that fifteen candles had been burned, for here was a burned match for each candle missing from the two boxes. The candle left in the box would burn for about three hours, and the concierge said that he had noticed the light from eight to eleven o'clock in the evening. Moreover, he had noticed it just about fifteen times in the previous six weeks.

The clock in one corner was ticking regularly. It was a cuckoo clock in a wooden case, but the cuckoo and alarm had been removed. Artful touches, these — someone was impersonating Désiré Bodasse. Did someone think it necessary to assure the neighbors of his presence in his apartment? M. Macé asked himself.

Now, Papa Désiré had confided to Mme. Bodasse, his aunt, the location of his strongbox, hidden in a secret compartment of an old bureau. He had instructed her: "If anything happens to me you will find all my papers and valuables in there. I keep them in an old green pocketbook." But this secret drawer was empty. Bodasse was well-to-do and, like many Frenchmen of the period, he preferred to keep his fortune under his own roof rather than entrust it to a bank.

M. Macé hunted everywhere for some clue to the former contents of the strongbox. At last, inside the case of the large silver watch, he came upon a slip of paper bearing a list of numbers of Italian securities. These securities were "payable to bearer."

M. Macé was now almost certain that Voirbo, the tailor, was the man who had murdered Papa Désiré and that he was cleverly attempting to stave off any investigation into the disappearance of the old man, or examination of his apartment. But more definite proofs were needed. To obtain these, M. Macé planned to hide several of his men in the apartment with instructions to arrest anyone who entered. Through a clerical error they were not told, however, that Voirbo was the man wanted, which lack of information on their part led to an unexpected complication in the plans for capture. For it developed that Voirbo was a minor spy of the secret political police, so the policemen accepted his presence with perfect trust and even told him of the plans to catch the murderer! Well posted, therefore, Voirbo was wary and desperate and had to be handled with extreme care.

While the underlings were engaged unconsciously in ruining M. Macé's plans, the commissioner himself had been industriously gathering further damning evidence. Mme. Bodasse had last seen her nephew on December thirteenth; in fact, she had written on that date, in a letter to a friend: "Désiré has just left me." He had told her he was on the way to see his optician. The optician was found. He testified that Bodasse had visited his shop on the thirteenth, accompanied by a younger man. This younger man had also been with him at his customary restaurant, according to other testimony given, and had accompanied him to the Peacock Baths, too.

An especially suspicious piece of information was volunteered by Voirbo's old servant. Arriving to clean his apartment on the morning of December seventeenth, she had found Voirbo already up and dressed and his room thoroughly cleaned and set to rights. He had even washed up the tiled floor, she said, for in places the tiles were still wet. She had been greatly astonished, for she knew the tailor as a lazy fellow who never troubled to clean his own room. He explained that an old lady had come with a pair of trousers for him to mend and, while there, had dropped a large bottle of kerosene which she was carrying. The smell, he said, had been so disagreeable that he could not stand it and had gone to spend the night with Papa Désiré, returning early in the morning to clean up the floor.

Still more damning, if possible, was another fact that the indefatigable M. Macé dug up. About to move from his old address in the Rue Mazarin, Voirbo had paid his rent from a 500-franc share of Italian stock, which the landlord had cashed for him at a moneychanger's at the corner. At the shop of the moneychanger the counterfoil of the share was produced. The number corresponded with one of the numbers on the list found in the watchcase of Papa Désiré.

All this valuable evidence, however, failed to console M. Macé for the failure of his men. To clinch the case, another plan must be put into execution. He determined to work with Voirbo himself, for according to French methods it is permissible for the police to cross-examine a suspect and to lay cunning traps for him in the hope that he will inadvertently supply the evidence desired against himself. Therefore, Voirbo was politely summoned to pay a visit to the commissioner's office.

He arrived — a short, very stout young man of thirty, with a large nose, brown eyes, black hair and mustachios, small ears, and large strong hands with thick fingers. It was M. Macé's first sight of the villain who had caused him such grueling work. The man's bearing was calm; his answers were prompt, precise, and unhesitating.

The tailor boldly claimed great anxiety over the fate of his old friend Papa Désiré. He explained that he was himself a member of the secret political police, and said he had gone to his own chief to offer his services in fathoming the mystery. He had the effrontery to add that he had thought of consulting with M. Macé but had understood that the case was soon to be taken out of his hands on account of his youth and inexperience! In the grand manner, he offered his assistance. And M. Macé, with magnificent acting, became duly impressed and accepted the proffer.

So, hunter and hunted, police commissioner and the suspected murderer, "worked together," meeting frequently. But Voirbo was too cunning to give himself away. He was always on his guard, always resourceful, and almost too "helpful." His help consisted of a bold and clever attempt to throw suspicion on another man — a butcher named Rifer, who had been a crony of Papa Désiré. Rifer was a gambler and drunkard, a frequenter of low cafés and dives. Voirbo introduced M. Macé to such a haunt, pointed out Rifer, and intimated that "he could tell a good deal if he would."

Rifer and two companions were checked up by Macé and were found to have been often in the company of Papa Désiré. They were questioned but they answered everything and displayed no anxiety whatever. All but Rifer were found to have been in prison at the time of the disappearance of Papa Désiré. Nevertheless, all were watched.

In the meantime Voirbo had taken Rifer in hand and was doing his best to see that the unfortunate man drank himself to death in short order. Soon he was in the throes of delirium tremens and in a fit of madness began smashing his furniture with an ax and throwing the pieces out the window. Passing policemen arrested him and took him to the station. He was then sent to an asylum, and died the same night.

The news of his death came to Voirbo, and in his eagerness to see how matters now lay, the tailor rushed to the office of the commissioner. M. Macé sat at his desk. As Voirbo poured forth on the "manifest guilt of the deceased Rifer," the commissioner, under pretense of writing an urgent letter, scribbled instructions to his secretary for the surrounding of the murderer.

As Voirbo discoursed, all exits were quietly closed and locked. An office messenger entered the room, made up the fire, and withdrew, unobtrusively carrying with him the heavy fire irons. The secretary entered with a letter to be signed and placed himself in readiness to guard the window. Two policemen outside awaited the signal from M. Macé. And Voirbo talked on, his views artfully encouraged by the commissioner at the desk.

Was it not clear, said the tailor, that others besides Rifer shared the guilt for the murder? See! He had an address he wished to give M. Macé — but in extracting the address from his pocketbook, Voirbo dropped a card. With great politeness M. Macé immediately picked it up and returned it to him, noting as he did so that it bore the name of a steamship company with offices in Paris. The arrest had been decided upon none too soon.

The stage was now set. M. Macé struck a gong. Voirbo was surrounded. He shuddered slightly and surrendered, for his captors were four to one. When searched, his pocketbook yielded a receipt for a steamship passage. He had booked under a false name and on a false passport. He was to have started that afternoon for Le Havre.

Before the *juge d'instruction* Voirbo was defiant. He refused to answer any questions. He refused indignantly to be photographed, declaring that he would make such faces it would be impossible to photograph him. The commissioner ordered that he be guarded well, and departed to find certain missing links in the case.

Arriving at the address where M. and Mme. Voirbo had lived since their marriage, he interviewed the tailor's wife. She was the orphaned daughter of a wealthy tailor and had brought

Voirbo as her dowry the considerable sum of 15,000 francs in French securities.

She contrasted strangely with her plump, sly husband — she was pale, delicate, and pious. At the time she met Voirbo she had been about to enter a convent and take the veil. She had been completely deceived by the man, and M. Macé pitied her. He disliked to cause her suffering, but she had to know the truth. Obtaining permission from the unfortunate wife, he forced the lock of the strongbox where the French securities (payable to bearer) which she had brought Voirbo were kept. The box was empty. Mme. Voirbo said the box had also contained Italian securities worth 10,000 francs, which had been her husband's contribution to the marriage.

No securities had been found in Voirbo's possession when he was searched at police headquarters, so M. Macé immediately made a careful search of the premises. The securities could not be found, but some interesting objects came to light. The implements in Voirbo's workshop included several deadly weapons — two pairs of huge shears, recently sharpened; heavy flatirons; a terrible mallet of metal (such as those formerly used by housebreakers), and a large butcher's cleaver. There was an old iron spoon, which had apparently been used for melting lead; and M. Macé gathered up a hank of cord. It was similar to that which had tied up the bundles found in Lampon's well. Several railway labels were also found, such as those on the parcels carried by the man who had been questioned by policeman Ringué on the night of December 22. The last bits of the case were fitting together.

M. Macé proceeded to Voirbo's cellar. It contained nothing but two casks of wine. However, in flashing his light over them, the commissioner saw that the bung in one of them stood out above the head of the cask. He removed the bung and discovered a black string, which was attached to it. The string hung down inside the cask. M. Macé drew it up and there came a small tin cylinder, with its top soldered down. Inside this tin, when it had been broken open, were the Italian securities listed in the memorandum found inside the watch of Papa Désiré. Only one was missing — the one which Voirbo had exchanged to pay his rent before he left the Rue Mazarin.

There was still one point on which M. Macé wanted stronger evidence for his case, the actual dismembering of the victim by Voirbo. There must be nothing lacking in this case.

He took the tailor, under heavy guard, to the house which he had formerly occupied in the Rue Mazarin, where the crime must have been committed. His old apartment was now occupied by a young man and his wife, and the arrangement of the furniture in the room was different from that in Voirbo's time. The concierge explained what the former arrangement had been. Under the window the workbench had stood, to the left of the sewing machine; there was a fireplace, opposite which had stood a chest of drawers; the bed had been in an alcove formed by two clothes cupboards. There were, besides, a stove and chairs; and in the center of the room had been a large round table. When M. Macé had all these details well in mind he commanded Voirbo to be brought in.

The commissioner had reasoned that the murderer must have laid the body of his victim on the table in the middle of the room, for, from the quantity and arrangement of the furniture at the time, it was the only place in the room where the difficult task of dismembering could have been done conveniently. And from the first the acute Macé had noticed something peculiar about the room. The tiled floor sloped downward from the window toward the bed in the alcove. And there especially the young commissioner showed his detective genius.

Picking up a jug of water which stood on the table, he mused aloud:

"I notice a slope in the floor. Now, if a body had been cut up on a table here in the center of the room, the effusion of blood would have been great, and the fluid must have followed this slope. Any other fluid thrown down here must follow the same direction. I will empty this jug on the floor and see what happens!"

At these words, terror leaped into the face of Voirbo, the accused. He grew gray with fright, clenched his hands, and followed with staring eyes the tilted jug in the hands of M. Macé. The water gushed to the floor and flowed straight to the bed, collecting beneath it in two large pools.

The areas covered by these pools then were carefully sponged dry, and a mason was summoned to take up the tiles. Beneath was found a quantity of dark stuff which resembled dried blood. Later the tiles and mortar removed were analyzed by chemists. The dark substance was indisputably human blood.

This was too much even for the cold-blooded Voirbo. When he saw how, in spite of all his caution in washing up the floor, the blood of Papa Désiré had nevertheless appeared to condemn him, he confessed fully to the crime.

The following details are taken from his confession:

Having begged Papa Désiré repeatedly to lend him 10,000 francs to help him toward his marriage with the dowered orphan, and having been firmly refused by the old man, Voirbo decided to kill and rob him. He invited the victim to his apartment in the Rue Mazarin. As his guest stood beside the table, suspecting nothing, the tailor came from behind, struck him on the head with a heavy flatiron, and finished the deed with a knife. He then dismembered the body and with a great caution, by slow degrees, proceeded with the dangerous task of its disposition.

At first Voirbo could not be brought to tell what he had done with the victim's head. Finally he confessed that he had melted lead, weighted the head with it, and then sunk it to the bottom of the Seine. In melting the lead he had used the iron spoon found in his room. He believed, he said, that if he could dispose of the head so that no one would ever find it, it would be impossible for the body to be identified.

On his way to prison Voirbo made a desperate, and very nearly successful, attempt to escape.

Later he stood awaiting his turn to be inscribed on the prison register. Under his arm he was carrying a long loaf of bread, when suddenly he tore the loaf open, extracted a razor, and cut his own throat. So died Pierre Voirbo, one of the most cold-blooded murderers in the annals of crime. How he had obtained the suicide weapon has never become known.

The brilliant young M. Macé subsequently became Chief of Police of Paris and solved many another baffling crime, but never one quite so slender of clue, and so grim in its detail, as that of the man who murdered Papa Désiré.

A JURY OF HER PEERS

by Susan Glaspell

"Somebody slipped a rope round his neck and strangled
him, and you didn't wake up?"
"I didn't wake up. I sleep sound," she said.

WHEN MARTHA HALE opened the storm door and got a cut of the
north wind, she ran back for her big woolen scarf. As she hurriedly wound that round her head her eye made a scandalized
sweep of her kitchen. It was no ordinary thing that called her
away — it was probably farther from ordinary than anything that
had ever happened in Dickson County. But what her eye took in
was that her kitchen was in no shape for leaving: her bread all
ready for mixing, half the flour sifted and half unsifted.

She hated to see things half-done; but she had been at that
when the team from town stopped to get Mr. Hale, and then the
sheriff came running in to say his wife wished Mrs. Hale would
come too — adding, with a grin, that he guessed she was getting
scary and wanted another woman along. So she had dropped everything right where it was.

"Martha!" now came her husband's impatient voice. "Don't
keep folks waiting out here in the cold."

She again opened the storm door, and this time joined the
three men and the one woman waiting for her in the big two-
seated buggy.

After she had the robes tucked around her she took another
look at the woman who sat beside her on the back seat. She had

met Mrs. Peters the year before at the county fair, and the thing she remembered about her was that she didn't seem like a sheriff's wife. She was small and thin and didn't have a strong voice. Mrs. Gorman, the sheriff's wife before Gorman went out and Peters came in, had a voice that somehow seemed to be backing up the law with every word. But if Mrs. Peters didn't look like a sheriff's wife, Peters made it up in looking like a sheriff. He was to a dot the kind of man who could get himself elected sheriff — a heavy man with a big voice, who was particularly genial with the law-abiding, as if to make it plain that he knew the difference between criminals and noncriminals. And right there it came into Mrs. Hale's mind, with a stab, that this man who was so pleasant and lively with all of them was going to the Wrights' now as a sheriff.

"The country's not very pleasant this time of year," Mrs. Peters at last ventured, as if she felt they ought to be talking as well as the men.

Mrs. Hale scarcely finished her reply, for they had gone up a little hill and could see the Wright place now, and seeing it did not make her feel like talking. It looked very lonesome this cold March morning. It had always been a lonesome-looking place. It was down in a hollow, and the poplar trees around it were lonesome-looking trees. The men were looking at it and talking about what had happened. The county attorney was bending to one side of the buggy, and kept looking steadily at the place as they drew up to it.

"I'm glad you came with me," Mrs. Peters said nervously, as the two women were about to follow the men in through the kitchen door.

Even after she had her foot on the doorstep, her hand on the knob, Martha Hale had a moment of feeling she could not cross that threshold. And the reason it seemed she couldn't cross it now was simply because she hadn't crossed it before. Time and time again it had been in her mind, "I ought to go over and see Minnie Foster" — she still thought of her as Minnie Foster, though for twenty years she had been Mrs. Wright. And then there was always something to do and Minnie Foster would go from her mind. But *now* she could come.

The men went over to the stove. The women stood close together by the door. Young Henderson, the county attorney, turned around and said:

"Come up to the fire, ladies."

Mrs. Peters took a step forward, then stopped. "I'm not — cold," she said.

The men talked for a minute about what a good thing it was the sheriff had sent his deputy out that morning to make a fire for them, and then Sheriff Peters stepped back from the stove, unbuttoned his outer coat, and leaned his hands on the kitchen table in a way that seemed to mark the beginning of official business. "Now, Mr. Hale," he said in a sort of semiofficial voice, "before we move things about, you tell Mr. Henderson just what it was you saw when you came here yesterday morning."

The county attorney was looking around the kitchen.

"By the way," he said, "has anything been moved?" He turned to the sheriff. "Are things just as you left them yesterday?"

Peters looked from cupboard to sink; from that to a small worn rocker a little to one side of the kitchen table.

"It's just the same."

"Somebody should have been left here yesterday," said the county attorney.

"Oh — yesterday," returned the sheriff, with a little gesture as of yesterday having been more than he could bear to think of. "When I had to send Frank to Morris Center for that man who went crazy — let me tell you, I had my hands full *yesterday*. I knew you could get back from Omaha by today, George, and as long as I went over everything here myself . . ."

"Well, Mr. Hale," said the county attorney, in a way of letting what was past and gone go, "tell just what happened when you came here yesterday morning."

Mrs. Hale, still leaning against the door, had that sinking feeling of the mother whose child is about to speak a piece. Lewis often wandered along and got things mixed up in a story. She hoped he would tell this straight and plain, and not say unnecessary things that would just make things harder for Minnie Foster. He didn't begin at once, and she noticed that he looked queer —

as if standing in that kitchen and having to tell what he had seen there yesterday morning made him almost sick.

"Harry and I had started to town with a load of potatoes," Mrs. Hale's husband began.

Harry was Mrs. Hale's oldest boy. He wasn't with them now, for the very good reason that those potatoes never got to town yesterday and he was taking them this morning, so he hadn't been home when the sheriff stopped to say he wanted Mr. Hale to come over to the Wright place and tell the county attorney his story there, where he could point it all out.

"We came along this road," Hale was going on, with a motion of his hand to the road over which they had just come, "and as we got in sight of the house I says to Harry, 'I'm goin' to see if I can't get John Wright to take a telephone.' You see," he explained to Henderson, "unless I can get somebody to go in with me they won't come out this branch road except for a price *I* can't pay. I'd spoke to Wright about it once before; but he put me off, saying folks talked too much anyway, and all he asked was peace and quiet — guess you know about how much he talked himself. But I thought maybe if I went to the house and talked about it before his wife, and said all the womenfolks liked the telephones, and that in this lonesome stretch of road it would be a good thing — well, I said to Harry that that was what I was going to say — though I said at the same time that I didn't know as what his wife wanted made much difference to John . . ."

Now, there he was! — saying things he didn't need to say. Mrs. Hale tried to catch her husband's eye, but fortunately the county attorney interrupted with:

"Let's talk about that a little later, Mr. Hale. I do want to talk about that, but I'm anxious now to get along to just exactly what happened when you got here."

When he began this time, it was very deliberately and carefully:

"I didn't see or hear anything. I knocked at the door. And still it was all quiet inside. I knew they must be up — it was past eight o'clock. So I knocked again, louder, and I thought I heard somebody say, 'Come in.' I wasn't sure — I'm not sure yet. But I opened the door — this door,'' jerking a hand toward the door by which the two women stood, "and there, in that rocker" — pointing to it — "sat Mrs. Wright."

Everyone in the kitchen looked at the rocker. It came into Mrs. Hale's mind that that rocker didn't look in the least like Minnie Foster — the Minnie Foster of twenty years before. It was a dingy red, with wooden rungs up the back, and the middle rung was gone, and the chair sagged to one side.

"How did she — look?" the county attorney was inquiring.

"Well," said Hale, "she looked — queer."

"How do you mean — queer?"

As he asked it he took out a notebook and pencil. Mrs. Hale did not like the sight of that pencil. She kept her eye fixed on her husband, as if to keep him from saying unnecessary things that would go into that notebook and make trouble.

Hale did speak guardedly, as if the pencil had affected him too.

"Well, as if she didn't know what she was going to do next. And kind of — done up."

"How did she seem to feel about your coming?"

"Why, I don't think she minded — one way or other. She didn't pay much attention. I said, 'Ho' do, Mrs. Wright? It's cold, ain't it?' And she said, 'Is it?' — and went on pleatin' at her apron.

"Well, I was surprised. She didn't ask me to come up to the stove, or to sit down, but just set there, not even lookin' at me. And so I said: 'I want to see John.' And then she laughed. I guess you would call it a laugh.

"I thought of Harry and the team outside, so I said, a little sharp, 'Can I see John?' 'No,' says she — kind of dull-like. 'Ain't he home?' says I. Then she looked at me. 'Yes,' says she, 'he's home.' 'Then why can't I see him?' I asked her, out of patience with her now. ''Cause he's dead,' says she, just as quiet and dull — and fell to pleatin' her apron. 'Dead?' says I, like you do when you can't take in what you've heard.

"She just nodded her head, not getting a bit excited, but rockin' back and forth.

"Why — where is he?' says I, not knowing *what* to say.

"She just pointed upstairs — like this" — pointing to the room above.

"I got up, with the idea of going up there myself. By this time I — didn't know what to do. I walked from there to here; then I says: 'Why, what did he die of?'

" 'He died of a rope round his neck,' says she; and just went on pleatin' at her apron."

Hale stopped speaking and stood staring at the rocker, as if he were still seeing the woman who had sat there the morning before. Nobody spoke; it was as if everyone were seeing the woman who had sat there the morning before.

"And what did you do then?" the county attorney at last broke the silence.

"I went out and called Harry. I thought I might — need help. I got Harry in, and we went upstairs." His voice fell almost to a whisper. "There he was — lying over the . . ."

"I think I'd rather have you go into that upstairs," the attorney interrupted, "where you can point it all out. Just go on now with the rest of the story."

"Well, my first thought was to get that rope off. It looked . . ."

He stopped, his face twitching.

"But Harry, he went up to him, and he said, 'No, he's dead all right, and we'd better not touch anything.' So we went downstairs. She was still sitting that same way. 'Has anybody been notified?' I asked. 'No,' said she, unconcerned.

" 'Who did this, Mrs. Wright?' said Harry. He said it business-like, and she stopped pleating' at her apron. 'I don't know,' she says. 'You don't *know*?' says Harry. 'Weren't you sleeping' in the bed with him?' 'Yes,' says she, 'but I was on the inside.' 'Somebody slipped a rope round his neck and strangled him, and you didn't wake up?' says Harry. 'I didn't wake up,' she said after him.

"We may have looked as if we didn't see how that could be, for after a minute she said, 'I sleep sound.'

"Harry was going to ask her more questions, but I said maybe that weren't our business; maybe we ought to let her tell her story first to the coroner or the sheriff. So Harry went fast as he could over to High Road — the Rivers' place, where there's a telephone.''

"And what did she do when she knew you had gone for the coroner?'' The attorney got his pencil in his hand all ready for writing.

"She moved from that chair to this one over here'' — Hale pointed to a small chair in the corner — "and just sat there with her hands held together and looking down. I got a feeling that I ought to make some conversation, so I said I had come in to see if John wanted to put in a telephone; and at that she started to laugh, and then she stopped and looked at me — scared.''

At sound of a moving pencil the man who was telling the story looked up.

"I dunno — maybe it wasn't scared,'' he hastened; "I wouldn't like to say it was. Soon Harry got back, and then Dr. Lloyd came, and you, Mr. Peters, and so I guess that's all I know that you don't.''

He said that last with relief, and moved a little, as if relaxing. Everyone moved a little. The county attorney walked toward the stair door.

"I guess we'll go upstairs first — then out to the barn and around.''

He paused and looked around the kitchen.

"You're convinced there was nothing important here?'' he asked the sheriff. "Nothing that would — point to any motive?''

The sheriff too looked all around, as if to reconvince himself.

"Nothing here but kitchen things,'' he said, with a little laugh for the insignificance of kitchen things.

The county attorney was looking at the cupboard — a peculiar, ungainly structure, half closet and half cupboard, the upper part of it being built in the wall, and the lower part just the old-fashioned kitchen cupboard. As if its queerness attracted him, he got a chair and opened the upper part and looked in. After a moment he drew his hand away sticky.

"Here's a nice mess,'' he said resentfully.

The two women had drawn nearer, and now the sheriff's wife spoke.

"Oh — her fruit," she said, looking to Mrs. Hale for sympathetic understanding. She turned back to the county attorney and explained: "She worried about that when it turned so cold last night. She said the fire would go out and her jars burst."

Mrs. Peters' husband broke into a laugh.

"Well, can you beat the women! Held for murder, and worrying about her preserves!"

The young attorney set his lips.

"I guess before we're through she may have something more serious than preserves to worry about. "

"Oh, well," said Mrs. Hale's husband, with good-natured superiority, "women are used to worrying over trifles."

The two women moved a little closer together. Neither of them spoke. The county attorney seemed suddenly to remember his manners — and think of his future.

"And yet," said he, with the gallantry of a young politician, "for all their worries, what would we do without the ladies?"

The women did not speak; did not unbend. He went to the sink and began washing his hands. He turned to wipe them on the roller towel — whirled it for a cleaner place.

"Dirty towels! Not much of a housekeeper, would you say, ladies?"

He kicked his foot against some dirty pans under the sink.

"There's a great deal of work to be done on a farm," said Mrs. Hale stiffly.

"To be sure. And yet" — with a little bow to her — "I know there are some Dickson County farmhouses that do not have such roller towels."

"Those towels get dirty awful quick. Men's hands aren't always as clean as they might be."

"Ah, loyal to your sex, I see," he laughed. He stopped and gave her a keen look. "But you and Mrs. Wright were neighbors. I suppose you were friends, too."

Martha Hale shook her head.

"I've seen little enough of her of late years. I've not been in this house — it's more than a year."

"And why was that? You didn't like her?"

"I liked her well enough," she replied with spirit. "Farmers'

wives have their hands full, Mr. Henderson. And then . . ." She
looked around the kitchen.

"Yes?" he encouraged.

"It never seemed a very cheerful place," said she, more to
herself than to him.

"No," he agreed; "I don't think anyone would call it cheerful.
I shouldn't say she had the homemaking instinct."

"Well, I don't know as Wright had, either," she muttered.

"You mean they didn't get on very well?" he was quick to
ask.

"No; I don't mean anything," she answered, with decision.
As she turned a little away from him, she added: "But I don't
think a place would be any the cheerfuller for John Wright's
bein' in it."

"I'd like to talk to you about that a little later, Mrs. Hale," he
said. "I'm anxious to get the lay of things upstairs now."

He moved toward the stair door, followed by the two men.

"I suppose anything Mrs. Peters does'll be all right?" the
sheriff inquired. "She was to take in some clothes for her, you
know — and a few little things. We left in such a hurry yesterday."

The county attorney looked at the two women whom they
were leaving alone there among the kitchen things.

"Yes — Mrs. Peters," he said, his glance resting on the
woman who was not Mrs. Peters, the big farmer woman who
stood behind the sheriff's wife. "Of course Mrs. Peters is one of
us," he said, in a manner of entrusting responsibility. "And keep
your eye out, Mrs. Peters, for anything that might be of use. No
telling; you women might come upon a clue to the motive — and
that's the thing we need."

Mr. Hale rubbed his face after the fashion of a showman getting ready for a pleasantry.

"But would the women know a clue if they did come upon it?"
he said; and having delivered himself of this, he followed the
others through the stair door.

The women stood motionless and silent, listening to the
footsteps, first upon the stairs, then in the room above.

Then, as if releasing herself from something strange, Mrs.

Hale began to arrange the dirty pans under the sink, which the county attorney's disdainful push of the foot had deranged.

"I'd hate to have men comin' into my kitchen," she said testily — "snoopin' round and criticizin'."

"Of course it's no more than their duty," said the sheriff's wife, in her manner of timid acquiescence.

"Duty's all right," replied Mrs. Hale bluffly; "but I guess that deputy sheriff that come out to make the fire might have got a little of this on." She gave the roller towel a pull. "Wish I'd thought of that sooner! Seems mean to talk about her for not having things slicked up, when she had to come away in such a hurry."

She looked around the kitchen. Certainly it was not "slicked up." Her eye was held by a bucket of sugar on a low shelf. The cover was off the wooden bucket, and beside it was a paper bag — half-full.

Mrs. Hale moved toward it.

"She was putting this in there," she said to herself — slowly.

She thought of the flour in her kitchen at home — half sifted. She had been interrupted, and had left things half done. What had interrupted Minnie Foster? Why had that work been left half done? She made a move as if to finish it — unfinished things always bothered her — and then she glanced around and saw that Mrs. Peters was watching her —and she didn't want Mrs. Peters to get that feeling she had got of work begun and then — for some reason — not finished.

"It's a shame about her fruit," she said, and walked toward the cupboard that the county attorney had opened, and got on the chair, murmuring: "I wonder if it's all gone."

It was a sorry enough looking sight, but "Here's one that's all right," she said at last. She held it toward the light. "This is cherries, too." She looked again. "I declare I believe that's the only one."

With a sigh, she got down from the chair, went to the sink, and wiped off the bottle.

"She'll feel awful bad, after all her hard work in the hot weather. I remember the afternoon I put up my cherries last summer."

She set the bottle on the table, and, with another sigh, started to sit down in the rocker. But she did not sit down. Something kept her from sitting down in that chair. She straightened — stepped back, and, half turned away, stood looking at it, seeing the woman who had sat there "pleatin' at her apron."

The thin voice of the sheriff's wife broke in upon her: "I must be getting those things from the front room closet." She opened the door into the other room, started in, stepped back. "You coming with me, Mrs. Hale?" she asked nervously. "You — you could help me get them."

They were soon back — the stark coldness of that shut-up room was not a thing to linger in.

"My!" said Mrs. Peters, dropping the things on the table and hurrying to the stove.

Mrs. Hale stood examining the clothes the woman who was being detained in town had said she wanted.

"Wright was close!" she exclaimed, holding up a shabby black skirt that bore the marks of much making over. "I think maybe that's why she kept so much to herself. I s'pose she felt she couldn't do her part; and then, you don't enjoy things when you feel shabby. She used to wear pretty clothes and be lively — when she was Minnie Foster, one of the town girls, singing in the choir. But that — oh, that was twenty years ago."

With a carefulness in which there was something tender, she folded the shabby clothes and piled them at one corner of the table. She looked up at Mrs. Peters, and there was something in the other woman's look that irritated her.

"She don't care," she said to herself. "Much difference it makes to her whether Minnie Foster had pretty clothes when she was a girl."

Then she looked again, and she wasn't so sure; in fact, she hadn't at any time been perfectly sure about Mrs. Peters. She had that shrinking manner, and yet her eyes looked as if they could see a long way into things.

"This all you was to take in?" asked Mrs. Hale.

"No," said the sheriff's wife; "she said she wanted an apron. Funny thing to want," she ventured in her nervous little way, "for there's not much to get you dirty in jail, goodness knows.

But I suppose just to make her feel more natural. If you're used to wearing an apron — She said they were in the bottom drawer of this cupboard. Yes — here they are. And then her little shawl that always hung on the stair door.''

She took the small gray shawl from behind the door leading upstairs.

Suddenly Mrs. Hale took a quick step toward the other woman.

''Mrs. Peters!''

''Yes, Mrs. Hale?''

''Do you think she — did it?''

A frightened look blurred the other thing in Mrs. Peters' eyes.

''Oh, I don't know,'' she said, in a voice that seemed to shrink away from the subject.

''Well, I don't think she did,'' affirmed Mrs. Hale stoutly. ''Asking for an apron and her little shawl. Worryin' about her fruit.''

''Mr. Peters says . . .'' Footsteps were heard in the room above; she stopped, looked up, then went on in a lowered voice: ''Mr. Peters says — it looks bad for her. Mr. Henderson is awful sarcastic in a speech, and he's going to make fun of her saying she didn't — wake up.''

For a moment Mrs. Hale had no answer. Then, ''Well, I guess John Wright didn't wake up — when they was slippin' that rope under his neck,'' she muttered.

''No, it's *strange*,'' breathed Mrs. Peters. ''They think it was such a — funny way to kill a man.''

''That's just what Mr. Hale said,'' said Mrs. Hale, in a resolutely natural voice. ''There was a gun in the house. He says that's what he can't understand.''

''Mr. Henderson said, coming out, that what was needed for the case was a motive. Something to show anger — or sudden feeling.''

''Well, I don't see any signs of anger around here,'' said Mrs. Hale. ''I don't . . .''

She stopped. It was as if her mind tripped on something. Her eye was caught by a dish towel in the middle of the kitchen table. Slowly she moved toward the table. One half of it was wiped

clean, the other half messy. Her eyes made a slow, almost unwilling turn to the bucket of sugar and the half-empty bag beside
it. Things begun — and not finished.

After a moment she stepped back, and said, in that manner of
releasing herself: "Wonder how they're finding things upstairs? I
hope she had it a little more red up there. You know" — she
paused, and feeling gathered — "it seems kind of *sneaking*: locking her up in town and coming out here to get her own house to
turn against her!"

"But, Mrs. Hale," said the sheriff's wife, "the law is the
law."

"I s'pose 'tis," answered Mrs. Hale shortly.

She turned to the stove, worked with it a minute, and when
she straightened up she said aggressively:

"The law is the law — and a bad stove is a bad stove. How'd
you like to cook on this?" — pointing with the poker to the broken lining. She opened the oven door and started to express her
opinion of the oven; but she was swept into her own thoughts,
thinking of what it would mean, year after year, to have that
stove to wrestle with. The thought of Minnie Foster trying to
bake in that oven — and the thought of her never going over to
see Minnie Foster . . ."

She was startled by hearing Mrs. Peters say:

"A person gets discouraged — and loses heart."

The sheriff's wife had looked from the stove to the pail of
water which had been carried in from outside. The two women
stood there, silent, above them the footsteps of the men who
were looking for evidence against the woman who had worked in
that kitchen. That look of seeing into things, of seeing through a
thing to something else, was in the eyes of the sheriff's wife now.
When Mrs. Hale next spoke to her, it was gently:

"Better loosen up your things, Mrs. Peters. We'll not feel
them when we go out."

Mrs. Peters went to the back of the room to hang up the fur
tippet she was wearing. A moment later she exclaimed, "Why,
she was piecing a quilt," and held up a large sewing basket piled
high with quilt pieces.

Mrs. Hale spread some of the blocks out on the table.

"It's log-cabin pattern," she said, putting several of them together. "Pretty, isn't it?"

They were so engaged with the quilt that they did not hear the footsteps on the stairs. Just as the stair door opened Mrs. Hale was saying:

"Do you suppose she was going to quilt it or just knot it?"

The sheriff threw up his hands.

"They wonder whether she was going to quilt it or just knot it!" he cried.

There was a laugh for the ways of women, a warming of hands over the stove, and then the county attorney said briskly:

"Well, let's go right out to the barn and get that cleared up."

"I don't see as there's anything so strange," Mrs. Hale said resentfully, after the outside door had closed on the three men — "our taking up our time with little things while we're waiting for them to get the evidence. I don't see as it's anything to laugh about."

"Of course they've got awful important things on their minds," said the sheriff's wife apologetically.

They returned to an inspection of the block for the quilt. Mrs. Hale was looking at the fine, even sewing, and was preoccupied with thoughts of the woman who had done that sewing, when she heard the sheriff's wife say, in a queer tone:

"Why, look at this one."

She turned to take the block held out to her.

"The sewing," said Mrs. Peters, in a troubled way. "All the rest of them have been so nice and even — but — this one. Why, it looks as if she didn't know what she was about!"

Their eyes met — something flashed to life, passed between them; then, as if with an effort, they seemed to pull away from each other. A moment Mrs. Hale sat there, her hands folded over that sewing which was so unlike all the rest of the sewing. Then she had pulled a knot and drawn the threads.

"Oh, what are you doing, Mrs. Hale?" asked the sheriff's wife.

"Just pulling out a stitch or two that's not sewed very good," said Mrs. Hale mildly.

"I don't think we ought to touch things," Mrs. Peters said, a little helplessly.

"I'll just finish up this end," answered Mrs. Hale, still in that mild, matter-of-fact fashion.

She threaded a needle and started to replace bad sewing with good. For a little while she sewed in silence. Then, in that thin, timid voice, she heard:

"Mrs. Hale!"

"Yes, Mrs. Peters?"

"What do you suppose she was so — nervous about?"

"Oh, *I* don't know," said Mrs. Hale, as if dismissing a thing not important enough to spend much time on. "I don't know as she was — nervous. I sew awful queer sometimes when I'm just tired."

She cut a thread, and out of the corner of her eye looked up at Mrs. Peters. The small, lean face of the sheriff's wife seemed to have tightened up. Her eyes had that look of peering into something. But next moment she moved, and said in her indecisive way:

"Well, I must get those clothes wrapped. They may be through sooner than we think. I wonder where I could find a piece of paper — and string."

"In that cupboard, maybe," suggested Mrs. Hale, after a glance around.

One piece of the crazy sewing remained unripped. Mrs. Peters' back turned, Martha Hale now scrutinized that piece, compared it with the dainty, accurate sewing of the other blocks. The difference was startling. Holding this block made her feel queer, as if the distracted thoughts of the woman who had perhaps turned to it to try to quiet herself were communicating themselves to her.

Mrs. Peters' voice roused her.

"Here's a birdcage," she said. "Did she have a bird, Mrs. Hale?"

"Why, I don't know whether she did or not." She turned to look at the cage Mrs. Peters was holding up. "I've not been here in so long." She sighed. "There was a man last year selling canaries cheap — but I don't know as she took one. Maybe she did. She used to sing real pretty herself."

"Seems kind of funny to think of a bird here." She half laughed — an attempt to put up a barrier. "But she must have had one — or why would she have a cage? I wonder what happened to it."

"I suppose maybe the cat got it," suggested Mrs. Hale, resuming her sewing.

"No; she didn't have a cat. She's got that feeling some people have about cats — being afraid of them. When they brought her to our house yesterday, my cat got in the room, and she was real upset and asked me to take it out."

"My sister Bessie was like that." Mrs. Hale laughed.

The sheriff's wife did not reply. The silence made Mrs. Hale turn around. Mrs. Peters was examining the birdcage.

"Look at this door," she said slowly. "It's broke. One hinge has been pulled apart."

Mrs. Hale came nearer.

"Looks as if someone must have been — rough with it."

Again their eyes met — startled, questioning, apprehensive. For a moment neither spoke nor stirred. Then Mrs. Hale, turning away, said brusquely:

"If they're going to find any evidence, I wish they'd be about it. I don't like this place."

"But I'm awful glad you came with me, Mrs. Hale." Mrs. Peters put the birdcage on the table and sat down. "It would be lonesome for me — sitting here alone."

"Yes, it would, wouldn't it?" agreed Mrs. Hale, a certain very determined naturalness in her voice. She had picked up the sewing, but now it dropped in her lap, and she murmured in a different voice: "But I tell you what I *do* wish, Mrs. Peters. I wish I had come over sometimes when she was here. I wish — I had."

"But of course you were awful busy, Mrs. Hale. Your house — and your children."

"I could've come," retorted Mrs. Hale shortly. "I stayed away because it weren't cheerful — and that's why I ought to have come. I" — she looked around — "I've never liked this place. Maybe because it's down in a hollow and you don't see the road. I don't know what it is, but it's a lonesome

place, and always was. I wish I had come over to see Minnie
Foster sometimes. I can see now —'' She did not put it into
words.

"Well, you mustn't reproach yourself," counseled Mrs. Peters. "Somehow, we just don't see how it is with other folks till
— something comes up."

"Not having children makes less work," mused Mrs. Hale,
after a silence, "but it makes a quiet house — and Wright out to
work all day — and no company when he did come in. Did you
know John Wright, Mrs. Peters?"

"Not to know him. I've seen him in town. They say he was a
good man."

"Yes — good," conceded John Wright's neighbor grimly.
"He didn't drink, and kept his word as well as most, I guess, and
paid his debts. But he was a hard man, Mrs. Peters. Just to pass
the time of day with him —" She stopped, shivered a little.
"Like a raw wind that gets to the bone." Her eye fell upon the
cage on the table before her, and she added, almost bitterly: "I
should think she would've wanted a bird!"

Suddenly she leaned forward, looking intently at the cage.
"But what do you s'pose went wrong with it?"

"I don't know," returned Mrs. Peters; "unless it got sick and
died."

But after she said it she reached over and swung the broken
door. Both women watched it as if somehow held by it.

"You didn't know — her?" Mrs. Hale asked, a gentler note in
her voice.

"Not till they brought her yesterday," said the sheriff's wife.

"She — come to think of it, she was kind of like a bird herself.
Real sweet and pretty, but kind of timid and — fluttery. How —
she — did — change."

That held her for a long time. Finally, as if struck with a happy
thought and relieved to get back to everyday things, she
exclaimed:

"Tell you what, Mrs. Peters, why don't you take the quilt in
with you? It might take up her mind."

"Why, I think that's a real nice idea, Mrs. Hale," agreed the
sheriff's wife, as if she too were glad to come into the atmos-

phere of a simple kindness. "There couldn't possibly be any objection to that, could there? Now, just what will I take? I wonder if her patches are in here — and her things."

They turned to the sewing basket.

"Here's some red," said Mrs. Hale, bringing out a roll of cloth. Underneath that was a box. "Here, maybe her scissors are in here — and her things." She held it up. "What a pretty box! I'll warrant that was something she had a long time ago — when she was a girl."

She held it in her hand a moment; then, with a little sigh, opened it.

Instantly her hand went to her nose.

"Why . . . !"

Mrs. Peters drew nearer — then turned away.

"There's something wrapped up in this piece of silk," faltered Mrs. Hale.

Her hand not steady, Mrs. Hale raised the piece of silk. "Oh, Mrs. Peters!" she cried, "it's . . ."

Mrs. Peters bent closer.

"It's the bird," she whispered.

"But, Mrs. Peters!" cried Mrs. Hale. "*Look* at it! Its *neck* — look at its neck! It's all — other side *to.*"

The sheriff's wife again bent closer.

"Somebody wrung its neck," said she, in a voice that was slow and deep.

And then again the eyes of the two women met — this time clung together in a look of dawning comprehension, of growing horror. Mrs. Peters looked from the dead bird to the broken door of the cage. Again their eyes met. And just then there was a sound at the outside door.

Mrs. Hale slipped the box under the quilt pieces in the basket and sank into the chair before it. Mrs. Peters stood holding to the table. The county attorney and the sheriff came in.

"Well, ladies," said the county attorney, as one turning from serious things to little pleasantries, "have you decided whether she was going to quilt it or knot it?"

"We think," began the sheriff's wife in a flurried voice, "that she was going to — knot it."

He was too preoccupied to notice the change that came in her voice on that last.

"Well, that's very interesting, I'm sure, " he said tolerantly. He caught sight of the cage. "Has the bird flown?"

"We think the cat got it," said Mrs. Hale in a voice curiously even.

He was walking up and down, as if thinking something out.

"Is there a cat?" he asked absently.

Mrs. Hale shot a look up at the sheriff's wife.

"Well, not *now*," said Mrs. Peters. "They're superstitious, you know; they leave."

The county attorney did not heed her. "No sign at all of anyone having come in from the outside, " he said to Peters, in the manner of continuing an interrupted conversation. "Their own rope. Now let's go upstairs again and go over it, piece by piece. It would have to have been someone who knew just the . . ."

The stair door closed behind them and their voices were lost.

The two women sat motionless, not looking at each other, but as if peering into something and at the same time holding back. When they spoke now it was as if they were afraid of what they were saying, but as if they could not help saying it.

"She liked the bird," said Martha Hale, low and slowly. "She was going to bury it in that pretty box."

"When I was a girl," said Mrs. Peters, under her breath, "my kitten — there was a boy took a hatchet, and before my eyes — before I could get there —" She covered her face an instant. "If they hadn't held me back I would have" — she caught herself, looked upstairs where footsteps were heard, and finished weakly — "hurt him."

Then they sat without speaking or moving.

"I wonder how it would seem," Mrs. Hale at last began, as if feeling her way over strange ground — "never to have had any children around." Her eyes made a slow sweep of the kitchen, as if seeing what that kitchen had meant through all the years. "No, Wright wouldn't like the bird," she said after that — "a thing that sang. She used to sing. He killed that too." Her voice tightened.

Mrs. Peters moved easily.

"Of course we don't know who killed the bird."

"I knew John Wright," was Mrs. Hale's answer.

"It was an awful thing was done in this house that night, Mrs. Hale," said the sheriff's wife. "Killing a man while he slept — slipping a thing round his neck that choked the life out of him."

Mrs. Hale's hand went out to the birdcage.

"His neck, Choked the life out of him."

"We don't *know* who killed him," whispered Mrs. Peters wildly. "We don't *know*."

Mrs. Hale had not moved. "If there had been years and years of — nothing, then a bird to sing to you, it would be awful — still — after the bird was still."

It was as if something within her, not herself, had spoken, and it found in Mrs. Peters something she did not know as herself.

"I know what stillness is," she said, in a queer, monotonous voice. "When we homesteaded in Dakota, and my first baby died — after he was two years old — and me with no other then . . ."

Mrs. Hale stirred.

"How soon do you suppose they'll be through looking for the evidence?"

"I know what stillness is," repeated Mrs. Peters, in just that same way. Then she too pulled back. "The law has got to punish crime, Mrs. Hale," she said in her tight little way.

"I wish you'd seen Minnie Foster," was the answer, "when she wore a white dress with blue ribbons, and stood up there in the choir and sang."

The picture of that girl, the fact that she had lived neighbor to that girl for twenty years, and had let her die for lack of life, was suddenly more than she could bear.

"Oh, I *wish* I'd come over here once in a while!" she cried. "That was a crime! That was a crime! Who's going to punish that?"

"We mustn't take on," said Mrs. Peters, with a frightened look toward the stairs.

"I might 'a' *known* she needed help! I tell you, it's *queer,* Mrs. Peters. We live close together, and we live far apart. We all go through the same things — it's all just a different kind of the same thing! If it weren't — why do you and I *understand*? Why do we *know* — what we know this minute?"

She dashed her hand across her eyes. Then, seeing the jar of fruit on the table, she reached for it and choked out:

"If I was you I wouldn't *tell* her her fruit was gone! Tell her it *ain't*. Tell her it's all right — all of it. Here — take this in to prove it to her! She — she may never know whether it was broke or not."

Mrs. Peters reached out for the bottle of fruit as if she were glad to take it — as if touching a familiar thing, having something to do, could keep her from something else. She got up, looked about for something to wrap the fruit in, took a petticoat from the pile of clothes she had brought from the front room, and nervously started winding that round the bottle.

"My!" she began, in a high, false voice, "it's a good thing the men couldn't hear us! Getting all stirred up over a little thing like a — dead canary." She hurried over that. "As if that could have anything to do with — with — My, wouldn't they *laugh*?"

Footsteps were heard on the stairs.

"Maybe they would," muttered Mrs. Hale — "maybe they wouldn't."

"No, Peters," said the county attorney incisively; "it's all perfectly clear, except the reason for doing it. But you know juries when it comes to women. If there was some definite thing — something to show. Something to make a story about. A thing that would connect up with this clumsy way of doing it."

In a covert way Mrs. Hale looked at Mrs. Peters. Mrs. Peters was looking at her. Quickly they looked away from each other. The outer door opened and Mr. Hale came in.

"I've got the team round now," he said. "Pretty cold out there."

"I'm going to stay here awhile by myself," the county attorney suddenly announced. "You can send Frank out for me, can't you?" he asked the sheriff. "I want to go over everything. I'm not satisfied we can't do better."

Again, for one brief moment, the two women's eyes found one another.

The sheriff came up to the table.

"Did you want to see what Mrs. Peters was going to take in?"

The county attorney picked up the apron. He laughed. "Oh, I guess they're not very dangerous things the ladies have picked out."

Mrs. Hale's hand was on the sewing basket in which the box was concealed. She felt that she ought to take her hand off the basket. She did not seem able to. He picked up one of the quilt blocks which she had piled on to cover the box. Her eyes felt like fire. She had a feeling that if he took up the basket she would snatch it from him.

But he did not take it up. With another little laugh, he turned away.

"No; Mrs. Peters doesn't need supervising. For that matter, a sheriff's wife is married to the law. Ever think of it that way, Mrs. Peters?"

Mrs. Peters was standing beside the table. Mrs. Hale shot a look up at her; but she could not see her face. Mrs. Peters had turned away. When she spoke, her voice was muffled.

"Not — just that way," she said.

"Married to the law!" chuckled Mrs. Peters' husband. He moved toward the door into the front room and said to the county attorney:

"I just want you to come in here a minute, George. We ought to take a look at these windows."

"Oh — windows," said the county attorney scoffingly.

"We'll be right out, Mr. Hale," said the sheriff to the farmer.

Hale went to look after the horses. The sheriff followed the county attorney into the other room. Again — for one final moment — the two women were alone in that kitchen.

Martha Hale sprang up, her hands tight together, looking at that other woman, with whom it rested. At first she could not see her eyes, for the sheriff's wife had not turned back since she turned away at that suggestion of being married to the law. But now Mrs. Hale made her turn back. Her eyes made her turn back. Slowly, unwillingly, Mrs. Peters turned her head until her eyes met the eyes of the other woman. There was a moment when they held each other in a steady, burning look in which there was no evasion nor flinching.

Then Martha Hale's eyes pointed the way to the basket in which was hidden the thing that would make certain the conviction of the other woman — that woman who was not there and yet who had been there with them all through that hour.

For a moment Mrs. Peters did not move. And then she did it. With a rush forward, she threw back the quilt pieces, got the box, tried to put it in her handbag. It was too big. Desperately she opened it, started to take the bird out. But there she broke — she could not touch the bird. She stood there helpless, foolish.

There was the sound of a knob turning in the inner door. Martha Hale snatched the box from the sheriff's wife, and got it in the pocket of her big coat just as the sheriff and the county attorney came back.

"Well, Henry," said the county attorney facetiously, "at least we found out that she was not going to quilt it. She was going to — what is it you call it, ladies?"

Mrs. Hale's hand was against the pocket of her coat.

"We call it — knot it, Mr. Henderson."

MISS BRACEGIRDLE DOES HER DUTY

by Stacy Aumonier

"To be found in a strange man's bedroom in the night is bad enough, but to be found in a dead man's bedroom was even worse."

"THIS IS the room, madame."

"Ah, thank you — thank you."

"Does it appear satisfactory to madame?"

"Oh, yes. Thank you — quite."

"Does madame require anything further?"

"Er — if not too late, may I have a hot bath?"

"*Parfaitement, madame*. The ·bathroom is at the end of the passage on the left. I will go and prepare it for madame."

"There is one thing more. I have had a very long journey. I am very tired. Will you please see that I am not disturbed in the morning until I ring?"

"Certainly, madame. "

Millicent Bracegirdle was speaking the truth — she *was* tired. But then, in the sleepy cathedral town of Easingstoke, from which she came, it was customary for everyone to speak the truth. It was customary, moreover, for everyone to lead simple, self-denying lives — to give up their time to good works and elevating thoughts. One had only to glance at little Miss Bracegirdle to see that in her were epitomized all the virtues and ideals of Easingstoke. Indeed, it was the pursuit of duty which had brought her to the Hôtel de l'Ouest at Bordeaux on this summer's night. She had traveled from Easingstoke to London, then without a break to Dover, crossed that horrid stretch of sea to Calais, entrained for Paris, where of necessity she had to spend four hours — a terrifying experience — and then had come on to Bordeaux, arriving at midnight. The reason of this journey being that someone had to come to Bordeaux to meet her young sister-in-law, who was arriving the next day from South America. The sister-in-law was married to a missionary in Paraguay, but the climate not agreeing with her, she was returning to England. Her dear brother, the dean, would have come himself, but the claims on his time were so extensive, the parishioners would miss him so — it was clearly Millicent's duty to go.

She had never been out of England before, and she had a horror of travel and an ingrained distrust of foreigners. She spoke a little French, sufficient for the purpose of travel and for obtaining any modest necessities, but not sufficient for carrying on any kind of conversation. She did not deplore this latter fact, for she was of opinion that French people were not the kind of people that one would naturally want to have conversation with; broadly speaking, they were not quite "nice," in spite of their ingratiating manners.

She unpacked her valise, placed her things about the room, and tried to thrust back the little stabs of homesickness as she visualized her darling room at the deanery. How strange and hard and unfriendly seemed these foreign hotel bedrooms! No chintz and lavender and photographs of all the dear family, the dean, the nephews and nieces, the interior of the cathedral during harvest festival; no samplers and needlework or colored reproductions of the paintings by Marcus Stone. Oh, dear, how foolish she was! What *did* she expect?

She disrobed and donned a dressing gown; then, armed with a sponge bag and towel, she crept timidly down the passage to the bathroom, after closing her bedroom door and turning out the light. The gay bathroom cheered her. She wallowed luxuriously in the hot water, regarding her slim legs with quiet satisfaction.

And for the first time since leaving home there came to her a pleasant moment, a sense of enjoyment in her adventure. After all, it *was* rather an adventure, and her life had been peculiarly devoid of it. What queer lives some people must live, traveling about, having experiences! How old was she? Not really old — not by any means. Forty-two? Forty-three? She had shut herself up so. She hardly ever regarded the potentialities of age. As the world went, she was a well-preserved woman for her age. A life of self-abnegation, simple living, healthy walking, and fresh air had kept her younger than these hurrying, pampered city people.

Love? Yes, once when she was a young girl — he was a schoolmaster, a most estimable, kind gentleman. They were never engaged — not actually, but it was a kind of understood thing. For three years it went on, this pleasant understanding and friendship. He was so gentle, so distinguished and considerate. She would have been happy to have continued in this strain forever. But there was something lacking — Stephen had curious restless lapses. From the physical aspect of marriage she shrank — yes, even with Stephen, who was gentleness and kindness itself. And then, one day — one day he went away, vanished, and never returned. They told her he had married one of the country girls, a girl who used to work in Mrs. Forbes's dairy — not a very nice girl, she feared; one of those fast, pretty, foolish women. Heigho! Well, she had lived that down, destructive as the blow appeared at the time. One lives everything down in time. There is always work, living for others, faith, duty. At the same time she could sympathize with people who found satisfaction in unusual experiences. There would be lots to tell the dear dean when she wrote to him on the morrow: nearly losing her spectacles on the restaurant car; the amusing remarks of an American child on the train to Paris; the curious food everywhere, nothing simple and plain; the two English ladies at the hotel in Paris who told her about the death of their uncle — the poor man being taken ill on Friday and dying on Sunday afternoon, just before teatime; the kindness of the hotel proprietor, who had sat up for her; the prettiness of the chambermaid. Oh, yes, everyone was really very kind. The French people, after all, were very nice.

She had seen nothing — nothing but what was quite nice and decorous. There would be lots to tell the dean tomorrow.

Her body glowed with the friction of the towel. She again donned her night attire and her thick woolen dressing gown. She tidied up the bathroom carefully in exactly the same way she was accustomed to do at home; then once more gripped her sponge bag and towel, and, turning out the light, she crept down the passage to her room. Entering the room, she switched on the light and shut the door quickly. Then one of those ridiculous things happened, just the kind of thing you would expect to happen in a foreign hotel. The handle of the door came off in her hand. She ejaculated a quiet "Bother!" and sought to replace it with one hand, the other being occupied with the towel and sponge bag. In doing this she behaved foolishly, for, thrusting the knob carelessly against the steel pin without properly securing it, she only succeeded in pushing the pin farther into the door, and the knob was not adjusted. She uttered another little "Bother!" and put her sponge bag and towel down on the floor. She then tried to recover the pin with her left hand, but it had gone in too far.

"How very foolish!" she thought. "I shall have to ring for the chambermaid — and perhaps the poor girl has gone to bed."

She turned and faced the room, and suddenly the awful horror was upon her.

There was a man asleep in her bed!

The sight of that swarthy face on the pillow, with its black tousled hair and heavy mustache, produced in her the most terrible moment of her life. Her heart nearly stopped. For some seconds she could neither think nor scream, and her first thought was:

"I mustn't scream!"

She stood there like one paralyzed, staring at the man's head and the great curved hunch of his body under the clothes. When she began to think she thought very quickly and all her thoughts worked together. The first vivid realization was that it wasn't the man's fault; it was *her* fault. *She was in the wrong room.* It was the man's room. The rooms were identical, but there were all his things about, his clothes thrown carelessly over chairs, his collar and tie on the wardrobe, his great heavy boots and the strange yellow trunk. She must get out — somehow, anyhow. She clutched once more at the door, feverishly driving her fingernails into the hole where the elusive pin had vanished. She tried to force her fingers in the crack and open the door that way, but it was of no avail. She was to all intents and purposes locked in — locked in a bedroom in a strange hotel, alone with a man — a foreigner — a *Frenchman*!

She must think — she must think! She switched off the light. If the light was off he might not wake up. It might give her time to think how to act. It was surprising that he had not awakened. If he *did* wake up, what would he do? How could she explain herself? He wouldn't believe her. No one would believe her. In an English hotel it would be difficult enough, but here, where she wasn't known, where they were all foreigners and consequently antagonistic — merciful heavens!

She *must* get out. Should she wake the man? No, she couldn't do that. He might murder her. He might — oh, it was too awful to contemplate! Should she scream? Ring for the chambermaid? But no; it would be the same thing. People would come rushing. They would find her there in the strange man's bedroom after midnight — she, Millicent Bracegirdle, sister of the dean of Easingstoke! Easingstoke! Visions of Easingstoke flashed through her alarmed mind. Visions of the news arriving, women whispering around tea tables: "Have you heard, my dear? Really, no one would have imagined! Her poor brother! He will, of course, have to resign, you know, my dear. Have a little more cream, my love."

Would they put her in prison? She might be in the room for the purpose of stealing or she might be in the room for the purpose of breaking every one of the Ten Commandments. There was no explaining it away. She was a ruined woman, suddenly and irretrievably, unless she could open the door. The chimney? Should she climb up the chimney? But where would that lead to? And then she thought of the man pulling her down by the legs when she was already smothered in soot. Any moment he might wake up. She thought she heard the chambermaid going along the passage. If she had wanted to scream, she ought to have screamed before. The maid would know she had left the bathroom some minutes ago. Was she going to her room?

An abrupt and desperate plan formed in her mind. It was already getting on for one o'clock. The man was probably a quite harmless commercial traveler or businessman. He would probably get up about seven or eight o'clock, dress quickly, and go out. She would hide under his bed until he went. Only a matter of a few hours. Men don't look under their beds, although she made a religious practice of doing so herself. When he went he would be sure to open the door all right. The handle would be lying on the floor as though it had dropped off in the night. He would probably ring for the chambermaid or open it with a penknife. Men are so clever at those things. When he had gone she would creep out and steal back to her room, and then there would be no necessity to give any explanation to anyone. But heavens! What an experience! Once under the white frill of that bed, she would be safe until the morning. In daylight nothing seemed so terrifying. With feline precaution she went down on her hands and knees and crept toward the bed. What a lucky thing there was that broad white frill! She lifted it at the foot of the bed and crept under. There was just sufficient depth to take her slim body. The floor was fortunately carpeted all over, but it seemed very close and dusty. Suppose she coughed or sneezed! Anything might happen. Of course, it would be much more difficult to explain her presence under the bed than to explain her presence just inside the door. She held her breath in suspense. No sound came from above, but under the frill it was difficult to hear anything. It was almost more nerve-racking than hearing everything — listening for signs and portents. This temporary escape, in any case, would give her time to regard the predicament detachedly. Up to the present she had not been able to focus on the full significance of her action. She had, in truth, lost her head. She had been like a wild animal, consumed with the sole idea of escape — a mouse or a cat would do this kind of thing — take cover and lie low. If only it hadn't all happened *abroad*!

She tried to frame sentences of explanation in French, but French escaped her. And then they talked so rapidly, these people. They didn't listen. The situation was intolerable. Would she be able to endure a night of it? At present she was not altogether uncomfortable, only stuffy and — very, very frightened. But she had to face six or seven or eight hours of it, and perhaps even then discovery in the end! The minutes flashed by as she turned the matter over and over in her head. There was no solution. She began to wish she had screamed or awakened the man. She saw now that that would have been the wisest and most politic thing to do; but she had allowed ten minutes or a quarter of an hour to elapse from the moment when the chambermaid would know that she had left the bathroom. They would want an explanation of what she had been doing in the man's bedroom all that time. Why hadn't she screamed before?

She lifted the frill an inch or two and listened. She thought she heard the man breathing, but she couldn't be sure. In any case, it gave her more air. She became a little bolder, and thrust her face partly through the frill so that she could breathe freely. She tried to steady her nerves by concentrating on the fact that — well, there it was. She had done it. She must make the best of it. Perhaps it would be all right, after all.

"Of course, I shan't sleep," she kept on thinking. "I shan't be able to. In any case, it will be safer not to sleep. I must be on the watch."

She set her teeth and waited grimly. Now that she had made up her mind to see the thing through in this manner she felt a little calmer. She almost smiled as she reflected that there would certainly be something to tell the dear dean when she wrote to him tomorrow. How would he take it? Of course he would believe it — he had never doubted a single word that she had uttered in her life — but the story would sound so preposterous. In Easingstoke it would be almost impossible to imagine such an experience. She, Millicent Bracegirdle, spending a night under a strange man's bed in a foreign hotel! What would those women think? Fanny Shields and that garrulous old Mrs. Rusbridger? Perhaps — yes, perhaps it would be advisable to tell the dear dean to let the story go no farther. One could hardly expect Mrs. Rusbridger to not make implications — exaggerate. Oh, dear! What were they all doing now? They would all be asleep, everyone in Easingstoke. Her dear brother always retired at ten-fifteen. He would be sleeping calmly and placidly, the sleep of the just — breathing the clear sweet air of Sussex — not this

— oh, it *was* stuffy! She felt a great desire to cough. She mustn't do that.

Yes, at nine-thirty all the servants were summoned to the library. There was a short service — never more than fifteen minutes; her brother didn't believe in a great deal of ritual — then at ten o'clock cocoa for everyone. At ten-fifteen bed for everyone. The dear, sweet bedroom, with the narrow white bed, by the side of which she had knelt every night so long as she could remember — even in her dear mother's day — and said her prayers.

Prayers! Yes, that was a curious thing. This was the first night in her life experience when she had not said her prayers on retiring. The situation was certainly very peculiar — exceptional, one might call it. God would understand and forgive such a lapse. And yet, after all, why — what was to prevent her saying her prayers? Of course, she couldn't kneel in the proper devotional attitude; that would be a physical impossibility; nevertheless, perhaps her prayers might be just as efficacious — if they came from the heart.

So little Miss Bracegirdle curved her body and placed her hands in a devout attitude in front of her face and quite inaudibly murmured her prayers under the strange man's bed.

At the end she added, fervently:

"Please God protect me from the dangers and perils of this night."

Then she lay silent and inert, strangely soothed by the effort of praying.

It began to get very uncomfortable, stuffy, but at the same time drafty, and the floor was getting harder every minute. She changed her position stealthily and controlled her desire to cough. Her heart was beating rapidly. Over and over again recurred the vivid impression of every little incident and argument that had occurred to her from the moment she left the bathroom. This must, of course, be the room next to her own. So confusing, with perhaps twenty bedrooms all exactly alike on one side of a passage — how was one to remember whether one's number was one hundred and fifteen or one hundred and sixteen? Her mind began to wander idly off into her schooldays. She was always very bad at figures. She disliked Euclid and all those subjects about angles and equations — so unimportant, not leading anywhere. History she liked, and botany, and reading about strange foreign lands, although she had always been too timid to visit them. And the lives of great people, *most* fascinating — Oliver Cromwell, Lord Beaconsfield, Lincoln, Grace Darling — *there* was a heroine for you — General Booth, a great, good man, even if a little vulgar. She remembered dear old Miss Trimmings talking about him one afternoon at the vicar of St. Bride's garden party. She was *so* amusing. She . . . *Good heavens!*

Almost unwittingly, Millicent Bracegirdle had emitted a violent sneeze!

It was finished! For the second time that night she was conscious of her heart nearly stopping. For the second time that night she was so paralyzed with fear that her mentality went to pieces. Now she would hear the man get out of bed. He would walk across to the door, switch on the light, and then lift up the frill. She could almost see that fierce mustachioed face glaring at her and growling something in French. Then he would thrust out an arm and drag her out. And then? O God in Heaven! What then?

"I shall scream before he does it. Perhaps I had better scream now. If he drags me out he will clap his hand over my mouth. Perhaps chloroform . . ."

But somehow she could not scream. She was too frightened even for that. She lifted the frill and listened. Was he moving stealthily across the carpet? She thought — no, she couldn't be sure. Anything might be happening. He might strike her from above — with one of those heavy boots, perhaps. Nothing seemed to be happening, but the suspense was intolerable. She realized now that she hadn't the power to endure a night of it. Anything would be better than this — disgrace, imprisonment, even death. She would crawl out, wake the man, and try to explain as best she could.

She would switch on the light, cough, and say, "Monsieur!"

Then he would start up and stare at her.

Then she would say — what should she say?

"*Pardon, monsieur, mais je* —" What on earth was the French for "I have made a mistake"?

"*J' ai tort. C' est la chambre* — " er — incorrect. "*Voulez-vous* —" er . . .?

What was the French for "doorknob," "let me go"?

It didn't matter. She would turn on the light, cough, and trust to luck. If he got out of bed and came toward her, she would scream the hotel down.

The resolution formed, she crawled deliberately out at the foot of the bed. She scrambled hastily toward the door — a perilous journey. In a few seconds the room was flooded with light. She turned toward the bed, coughed, and cried out boldly:

"Monsieur!"

Then for the third time that night little Miss Bracegirdle's heart all but stopped. In this case the climax of the horror took longer to develop, but when it was reached it clouded the other two experiences into insignificance.

The man on the bed was dead!

She had never beheld death before, but one does not mistake death.

She stared at him, bewildered, and repeated almost in a whisper, "Monsieur! Monsieur!"

Then she tiptoed toward the bed. The hair and mustache looked extraordinarily black in that gray, waxlike setting. The mouth was slightly open, and the face, which in life might have been vicious and sensual, looked incredibly peaceful and far away. It was as though she were regarding the features of a man across some vast passage of time, a being who had always been completely remote from mundane preoccupations.

When the full truth came home to her, little Miss Bracegirdle buried her face in her hands and murmured:

"Poor fellow — poor fellow!"

For the moment her own position seemed an affair of small consequence. She was in the presence of something greater and more all-pervading. Almost instinctively she knelt by the bed and prayed.

For a few moments she seemed to be possessed by an extraordinary calmness and detachment. The burden of her hotel predicament was a gossamer trouble — a silly, trivial, almost comic episode, something that could be explained away.

But this man — he had lived his life, whatever it was like, and now he was in the presence of his Maker. What kind of man had he been?

Her meditations were broken by an abrupt sound. It was that of a pair of heavy boots being thrown down by the door outside. She started, thinking at first it was someone knocking or trying to get in. She heard the ''boots,'' however, stumping away down the corridor, and the realization stabbed her with the truth of her own position. She mustn't stop there. The necessity to get out was even more urgent.

To be found in a strange man's bedroom in the night is bad enough, but to be found in a dead man's bedroom was even worse. They would accuse her of murder, perhaps. Yes, that would be it — how could she possibly explain to these foreigners? Good God! They would hang her. No, guillotine her — that's what they do in France. They would chop her head off with a great steel knife. Merciful heavens! She envisaged herself standing blindfolded, by a priest and an executioner in a red cap, like that man in the Dickens story. What was his name? — Sydney Carton, that was it. And before he went on the scaffold he said, ''It is a far, far better thing that I do than I have ever done —''

But no, she couldn't say that. It would be a far, far worse thing that she did. What about the dear dean; her sister-in-law arriving alone from Paraguay tomorrow; all her dear people and friends in Easingstoke; her darling Tony, the large gray tabby cat? It was her duty not to have her head chopped off if it could possibly be avoided. She could do no good in the room. She could not recall the dead to life. Her only mission was to escape. Any minute people might arrive. The chambermaid, the boots, the manager, the gendarmes. Visions of gendarmes arriving armed with swords and notebooks vitalized her almost exhausted energies. She was a desperate woman. Fortunately now she had not to worry about the light. She sprang once more at the door and tried to force it open with her fingers. The result hurt her and gave her pause. If she was to escape she must *think*, and think intensely. She musn't do anything rash and silly; she must just think and plan calmly.

She examined the lock carefully. There was no keyhole, but there was a slipbolt, so that the hotel guest could lock the door on the inside but it couldn't be locked on the outside. Oh, why didn't this poor dear dead man lock his door last night? Then this trouble could not have happened. She could see the end of the steel pin. It was about half an inch down the hole. If anyone was passing they must surely notice the handle sticking out too far the other side! She drew a hairpin out of her hair and tried to coax the pin back, but she only succeeded in pushing it a little farther in. She felt the color leaving her face, and a strange feeling of faintness came over her.

She was fighting for her life; she musn't give way. She darted round the room like an animal in a trap, her mind alert for the slightest crevice of escape. The window had no balcony, and there was a drop of five stories to the street below. Dawn was breaking. Soon the activities of the hotel and the city would begin. The thing must be accomplished before then.

She went back once more and stared hard at the lock. She stared at the dead man's property, his razors and brushes and writing materials. He appeared to have a lot of writing materials, pens and pencils and rubber and sealing wax. Sealing wax!

Necessity is truly the mother of invention. It is in any case quite certain that Millicent Bracegirdle, who had never invented a thing in her life, would never have evolved the ingenious little device she did, had she not believed that her position was utterly desperate. For in the end this is what she did. She got together a box of matches, a candle, a bar of sealing wax, and a hairpin. She made a little pool of hot sealing wax, into which she dipped the end of the hairpin. Collecting a small blob on the end of it, she thrust it into the hole and let it adhere to the end of the steel pin. At the seventh attempt she got the thing to move.

It took her just an hour and ten minutes to get that steel pin back into the room, and when at length it came far enough through for her to grip it with her fingernails, she burst into tears through the sheer physical tenseness of the strain. Very, very carefully she pulled it through, and, holding it firmly with her left hand, she fixed the knob with her right, then slowly turned it.

The door opened!

The temptation to dash out into the corridor and scream with relief was almost irresistible, but she forebore . She listened. She peeped out. No one was about. With beating heart she went out, closing the door inaudibly; she crept like a little mouse to the room next door, stole in, and flung herself on the bed. Immediately she did so, it flashed through her mind that *she had left her sponge bag and towel in the dead man's room!*

In looking back upon her experience she always considered that that second expedition was the worst of all. She might have let the sponge bag and towel remain there, only that the towel — she never used hotel towels — had neatly inscribed in the corner "M. B."

With furtive caution she managed to retrace her steps. She re-entered the dead man's room, reclaimed her property, and returned to her own. When the mission was accomplished she was indeed well-nigh spent. She lay on her bed and groaned feebly. At last she fell into a fevered sleep.

It was eleven o'clock when she awoke, and no one had been to disturb her. The sun was shining, and the experiences of the night appeared a dubious nightmare. Surely she had dreamed it all?

With dread still burning in her heart, she rang the bell. After a short interval of time the chambermaid appeared. The girl's eyes were bright with some uncontrollable excitement. No, she had not been dreaming. This girl had heard something.

"Will you bring me some tea, please?"

"Certainly, madame."

The maid drew back the curtains and fussed about the room. She was under a pledge of secrecy, but she could contain herself no longer. Suddenly she approached the bed and whispered, excitedly:

"Oh, madame, I am promised not to tell — but a terrible thing has happened! A man, a dead man, has been found in room one hundred and seventeen — a guest! Please not to say I tell you. But they have all been here — the gendarmes, the doctors, the inspectors. Oh, it is terrible — terrible!"

The little lady in the bed said nothing. There was indeed nothing to say. But Marie-Louise Lancret was too full of emotional excitement to spare her.

"But the terrible thing is . . . Do you know who he was, madame? They say it is Boldhu, the man wanted for the murder of Jeanne Carreton in the barn at Vincennes. They say he strangled her and then cut her up in pieces and hid her in two barrels, which he threw into the river. Oh, but he was a bad man, madame, a terrible bad man — and he died in the room next door. Suicide, they think; or was it an attack of the heart? Remorse; some shock, perhaps. Did you say a *café complet*, madame?"

"No, thank you, my dear — just a cup of tea — strong tea."

"*Parfaitement, madame.*"

The girl retired, and a little later a waiter entered the room with a tray of tea. She could never get over her surprise at this. It seemed so — well — indecorous for a man, although only a waiter, to enter a lady's bedroom. There was, no doubt, a great deal in what the dear dean said. They were certainly very peculiar, these French people — they had most peculiar notions. It was not the way they behaved at Easingstoke. She got farther under the sheets, but the waiter appeared quite indifferent to the situation. He put the tray down and retired.

When he had gone, she sat up and sipped her tea, which gradually warmed her. She was glad the sun was shining. She would have to get up soon. They said that her sister-in-law's boat was due to berth at one o'clock. That would give her time to dress comfortably, write to her brother, and then go down to the docks.

Poor man! So he had been a murderer, a man who cut up the bodies of his victims — and she had spent the night in this bedroom! They were certainly a most — how could she describe it? — people. Nevertheless she felt a little glad that at the end she had been there to kneel and pray by his bedside. Probably nobody else had ever done that. It was very difficult to judge people. Something at some time might have gone wrong. He might not have murdered the woman after all. People were often wrongly convicted. She herself. If the police had found her in that room at three o'clock that morning . . . It is that which takes place in the heart which counts. One learns and learns. Had she not learned that one can pray just as effectively lying under a bed as kneeling beside it? Poor man!

She washed and dressed herself and walked calmly down to the writing room. There was no evidence of excitement among the other hotel guests. Probably none of them knew about the tragedy except herself. She went to a writing table and, after profound meditation, wrote as follows:

> My Dear Brother, I arrived late last night, after a very pleasant journey. Everyone was very kind and attentive. The manager was sitting up for me. I nearly lost my spectacles in the restaurant car, but a kind old gentleman found them and returned them to me. There was a most amusing American child on the train. I will tell you about her on my return. The people are very pleasant, but the food is peculiar, nothing plain and wholesome. I am going down to meet Annie at one o'clock. How have you been keeping, my dear? I hope you have not had any further return of the bronchial attacks. Please tell Lizzie that I remembered in the train on the way here that that large stone jar of marmalade that Mrs. Hunt made is behind those empty tins on the top shelf of the cupboard next to the coachhouse. I wonder whether Mrs. Buller was able to come to evensong after all? This is a nice hotel, but I think Annie and I will stay at the Grand tonight, as the bedrooms here are rather noisy. Well, my dear, nothing more till I return. Do take care of yourself.
>
> Your loving sister,
>
> MILLICENT

Yes, she couldn't tell Peter about it, either in the letter or when she went back to him. It was her duty not to tell him. It would only distress him; she felt convinced of it. In this curious foreign atmosphere the thing appeared possible, but in Easingstoke the mere recounting of the fantastic situation would be positively indelicate. There was no escaping that broad general fact — she had spent a night in a strange man's bedroom. Whether he was a gentleman or a criminal, even whether he was

dead or alive, did not seem to mitigate the jar upon her sen-
sibilities, or, rather, it would not mitigate the jar upon the peculiarly sensitive relationship between her brother and herself. To
say that she had been to the bathroom, the knob of the door
handle came off in her hand, she was too frightened to awaken
the sleeper or scream, she got under the bed — well, it was all
perfectly true. Peter would believe her, but — one simply could
not conceive of such a situation in the Easingstoke deanery. It
would create a curious little barrier between them, as though she
had been dipped in some mysterious solution which alienated
her. It was her duty not to tell.

She put on her hat and went out to post the letter. She dis-
trusted a hotel letter box. One never knew who handled these
letters. It was not a proper official way of treating them. She
walked to the head post office in Bordeaux.

The sun was shining. It was very pleasant walking about
amongst these queer, excitable people, so foreign and different-
looking — and the cafés already crowded with chattering men
and women; and the flower stalls and the strange odor of — what
was it? salt? brine? charcoal? A military band was playing in the
square — very gay and moving. It was all life and movement and
bustle — thrilling, rather.

"I spent a night in a strange man's bedroom."

Little Miss Bracegirdle hunched her shoulders, hummed to
herself, and walked faster. She reached the post office and found
the large metal plate with the slot for letters and *R.F.* stamped
above it. Something official at last! Her face was a little flushed
— was it the warmth of the day, or the contact of movement and
life? — as she put her letter into the slot. After posting it, she put
her hand into the slot and flicked it round to see that there were
no foreign contraptions to impede its safe delivery. No, the letter
had dropped safely in. She sighed contentedly and walked off in
the direction of the docks, to meet her sister-in-law from
Paraguay.

A RECORD OF ESCAPE

by Alfred Morain

In which the Préfet de Police, Paris, circa 1907, reports on a
murderer's escape from a prison in Cayenne.

AMONG THE MANY CURIOUS and often unique souvenirs which I
have accumulated during the course of my career, I might almost
give pride of place to the actual record, set down by a French
convict, of his escape from the penal settlement at Cayenne.

The writer was a man convicted of willful murder in the early
years of the present century. He stoutly maintained his innocence, as did his counsel. After his successful escape, his lawyer
gave me the manuscript of the autobiographical story of his bid
for freedom. For obvious reasons the name of the escaped prisoner cannot be given to the public, but his narrative seems to me
to bear every mark of authenticity, and while there is no means
of obtaining any corroboration, it is at any rate certain that he
was a prisoner and that he *did* escape!

The pages of the story dealing with the author's own life, his
alleged crime, and the prison conditions on Cayenne were unfortunately lost before the manuscript came into my hands. I can,
therefore, impart to the reader of this book only the bare account
of the actual escape. This account begins abruptly enough, and
is of course at first a little obscure without the immediately pre-
ceding pages, but I prefer to give it in its actual fragmentary state
rather than attempt to build it up from my own imagination, fal-
sifying fact by the admixture of fiction.

The writer found a good friend in prison with whom he threw

in his lot. It is with mention of this friend, Petit Jean, that the
fragmentary record starts.

During his journeys into the interior of the colony, my friend
Petit Jean had got in touch with an Indian and had partly paid for
the canoe by carrying the small planks of wood [shingles] which
serve as roofing for houses. The Indian sold us the canoe for 150
francs and the transportation of the shingles. This latter my
friend had contrived in secret and without the knowledge of the
authorities.

We had to find among the convicts we knew men who were
courageous and who had a little money. This was pretty difficult,
for many would be fugitives have been betrayed by men who
pretended to be ready to join in their attempts to escape.

It was a great problem. Serving a life sentence, I had to be particularly cautious, for if I had been caught trying to escape I
should have been condemned to two to five years of solitary
confinement. If alive at the end of this time I should have been
sent to one of the Iles du Salut, from which escape is impossible.

Three months before the time I write of, a law still existed
which condemned all convicts undergoing a life sentence to two
to five years of the double chain if caught attempting to escape.
This punishment consisted in wearing a heavy chain attached to
the belt which hung down the length of the leg and finished in a
ring attached to the ankle. It made running impossible, and the
convict who wore it for a year or two became lame. The convicts
complained of this punishment, and solitary confinement was
substituted. This was much more terrible, for at least 75 per cent
of the men undergoing it died of scurvy.

After much hesitation, my pal Petit Jean, formerly a lobster
fisher in Corsica, and I resolved to take with us a man of about
forty, a native of the Drôme. He had been condemned to fifteen
years for having tortured many well-to-do people of that department by burning their feet to make them tell where their money
was hidden. We imagined that to do a thing like that he must
have had some pluck, but we were mistaken. We also chose a
young man of our own age. Each of these two had a little money,
and we took with us a third man who had already escaped once

and had been caught in France and sent back to Cayenne. He had no money but we counted on his experience.

As my pal Petit Jean had found a man willing to sell him a canoe, all we had to do was to make our final preparations. We bought satchels made of sackcloth, painted with oil to make them waterproof, and also some of the linen shirts that the administration provides for the convicts. These were to make a sail. We got a convict blacksmith to make us four large iron bolts and a strong bar, which we needed for fixing a rudder on our canoe.

Thread, needles, medicines — chiefly quinine . . .

When everything was ready the three satchels were entrusted to convicts employed at brick-making, who could smuggle them out of the camp for us and hide them in the bush, the place being agreed on in advance. This was easy for the brick-makers. They went to work in the morning and did not get back till late, so there was nothing strange about their carrying satchels, supposedly full of the provisions they would need.

It was a walk of three quarters of an hour to the brick kiln, the way being along the main road, which had been driven through the bush. Our meeting place was fixed in the bush, opposite the slaughterhouse, which was midway between the prison and this brick kiln.

Tuesday, May 14, 1907, was fixed for our departure.

That morning I asked permission of my chief to go to a Chinese grocer in the village who bought two loaves of bread from me every day. Permission was given me and, at the Chinaman's, I met the man from the Drôme. We both set out to the meeting place, where we were to join our three comrades. We had gone about a quarter of the way when we saw one of the military inspectors in the distance. He was coming toward us. The road was built on an embankment. We climbed down into the ditch on the right-hand side; the tide was high and we found ourselves in water to a depth of eighteen inches. We made a detour of at least a hundred yards . . . It is absolutely impossible to keep a straight course in the bush. Sometimes it is completely impassable and to be able to make one's way one must use a felling knife — a sort of saber with a very broad blade, also called a cutlass.

As we had nothing of the sort, we had to pick our way across the roots and branches. To make a guiding mark for myself I would climb a tree from time to time, and when I had discovered the roof of the slaughterhouse I would get down and off we would go again in the water and mud. I did this perhaps twenty times. We lost a good deal of time, but we did not dare to take to the road again.

After about four hours' walk, we arrived at the meeting place. Here the others had been waiting for at least three hours. They thought we had been captured, and that would have put an end to the whole plan, as they had not enough money on them to undertake the journey without us.

Owing to this delay, we arrived too late at the rendezvous fixed with the brick-makers, who were to give us our satchels. Our provisions were in one of them — bread toasted in order to preserve it the better, tins of corned beef, preserved milk, etc. We realized that we should have to go thirty-six hours without eating. If we had had a cutlass we could have cut down a certain tree which contains a soft pith, which even when cooked is indigestible enough, but we would have been prepared to eat it raw. We decided to hide ourselves in the bush and to pass the night on the branch of a tree.

The next day we set out on a road of firm earth about a yard wide. After walking about a hundred yards down this road we should have arrived at the path which we were to take. This path was cleared through the bush. It was about a yard wide, but, being very near the river — the Maroni — it was more than three feet under water when the tide was high. To make walking possible, two pieces of wood had been planted every five yards. On the cross-shaped wood, tree trunks about as thick as telegraph poles were resting, and one walked on these, supporting oneself with a long stick. One needed to be a bit of an acrobat, for the tree trunks swung to and fro. The telegraph wires run along the side of this path and it is inspected every day by a convict telegraphist. The job is only given to those who have received short sentence and are nearly at the end of their term.

We were a hundred yards from this path when we suddenly

caught sight of one of the military inspectors whom we all knew as a famous manhunter. During his off-time he devoted himself to hunting fugitives so as to gain the rewards and also to get promotion. It was said of him that he shot before giving the customary three challenges. If the convict was killed, he always said that the three challenges had not been heeded, or that the man had resisted arrest. He must have had the deaths of many men on his conscience — twenty, fifty, I don't know how many. As soon as he saw us he put his rifle to his shoulder, and we heard two shots. Luckily, none of us was hit.

If this meeting had taken place on the path and we had had to jump into the water and then wade through mud before we could reach the bush I should not have been alive to write this today.

We had all five resolved to die sooner than be captured. Of the five, three were sincere.

We got into the bush. Luckily it was not too thick for us at that point. We ran as hard as we could. I remember I fell; I got up and again I fell. And so on the whole way.

Trees in the country have roots that stick out of the ground. How long did we run like this? I don't remember. But at last we were completely exhausted. We were breathless. We panted like hot and exhausted dogs; our legs and hands were covered with wounds.

I do not know whether the manhunter pursued us into the bush, as I never looked behind me as I ran. I do not think he did, for he was some distance off and before he reached the place where we were when we first saw him, we were probably lost to sight. But this is simple supposition.

When we had recovered our breath we went on walking. We were lost in the bush but we were going in the right direction. My friend Petit Jean knew the times of the tides and, by the current of a stream that we passed, he was able to tell us that if we followed it upward we should arrive at the path. Night came. We found a dry place and decided to stay there in the company of the mosquitoes. We were soaked and very muddy and the nights in Guiana are rather cool.

At dawn the next day we started off again and, after much

wandering backward and forward, we arrived at last at the path
— the only road which would bring us to the man who had promised to sell us the canoe.

As we were walking along, searching for a place to spend the
day in hiding, a convict appeared. He had been hiding in the
bush for two months with a comrade wounded in the leg. The
latter had been shot by the inspector we had encountered the day
before. The man we met had managed to escape, helping his
wounded comrade. The other two of the party had been killed —
at any rate they had fallen and had not been able to get up. These
two remained in the bush, living on fruit and on animals which
they trapped. They hoped to be able to join another escaping
party, though they were both without money.

He conducted us to his *carbet*, a hut constructed with the
branches of trees, roofed with big leaves — mangrove leaves, I
think. The wounded man's leg was quite black and the wound
was suppurating.

After we had talked it over, we promised to take them with us,
but, as we had not much money to buy food, we told them that
we would drop them in British Guiana, so that the sick man
could be taken to hospital.

As we had to wait until ten o'clock before we could go to the
brick-makers' rendezvous, the sick man's friend proposed to go
to the village, which was about an hour's walk away, to buy a
little bread and some salt fish. I gave him three francs, and he
went off. It was a big risk to go to the village in broad daylight
but he was full of enthusiasm, for with the three francs he could
also buy quinine and boric acid for his friend.

The behavior of this man was sublime. He had never left his
friend and he risked capture when he went to the village in broad
daylight. More especially, considering he had our promise to
take him with us in our canoe. His filthy clothes and his two-
months beard would have given him away to the first manhunter,
civil or military, whom he met. But he went off all the same.

He had been gone for about an hour when he returned, out of
breath. He had seen in the distance a military inspector accompanied by two liberated convincts, who were hunting for us.

As soon as he saw them, he turned back and ran as hard as his legs could carry him to warn us.

We left the sick man in the hut. It was quite impossible to take him with us, as he was suffering too much pain. A stretcher would have been necessary, and with a stretcher we could not have moved in the bush. He knew it himself, and told us, "Leave me, leave me, save yourselves."

We ran, as we had done the day before. And, as we ran, we reminded each other that we must keep together. After zigzagging many times so that our tracks should be lost, we decided to climb a tree and to wait there for some hours. We took great care not to break any of the branches.

We heard voices and then the noise of a motorboat on the river. Probably there were dogs in the boat. Dogs cannot walk on the track, and the men who were hunting us had certainly joined the men in the motorboat at the point where the creek cuts across the path.

When we realized that there were dogs among the party, we knew that we could not stay in the tree. We should certainly have been caught. There was a big swamp about fifty yards away, and we decided to get into the water in order to put the dogs off the scent. It was the only thing to do. There was no wind. We sank in up to our necks. It was just about noon.

It was growing dark when the noise of the motorboat, which had stopped, began again. We had barely time to get to dry land before darkness fell. In that country it is quite dark in a quarter of an hour, and walking when there is no moon is not to be thought of.

The swamp was big, and, as we did not know where we were and were utterly tired out, the only thing to do was to remain on the spot. It was a feast for the mosquitoes. Ah, those mosquitoes!

We lay back to back. Like that, we sometimes had a few minutes' sleep. Then the mosquitoes would wake us up again. However, we were all happy. We were certain that the motorboat had gone off, because we had heard the noise of its engine dying away in the distance.

At daybreak we started off again, and after a time we found the place where the hut had been. It was destroyed, the wounded man had been taken, and we found the traces of dogs.

Our new companion went to visit his traps. He found a lizard (an iguana), and, as our matches were wet, we ate it raw.

That evening, we went to get our satchels. The one containing the provisions had disappeared — stolen, they told us. We did not ask for explanations; we continued on our way. We had cutlasses and, by using them, we could eat cabbage palms, which I have already mentioned. Provisions did not matter so long as we had the tools necessary for our escape.

We were near a village. Our new companion would have been obliged to fetch provisions had we asked him, afraid that if he had refused we should have declined to take him with us. But we asked nothing of him; we were in too dangerous a locality. There was no time to lose; we had to get away — far, far . . .

We arrived at the creek which we had to cross. It was about two hundred yards wide. In that country there is a species of floating wood called *canne à feu*. To support the six of us, we had to make a raft with a draft of nine feet. In spite of that, it sank twenty centimeters under water, for the wood is heavy. We clung to it and swam with our legs to push it along. The two satchels, containing two blankets and the shirts to make a sail, were soaked. But we had put our matches inside a well-corked bottle.

Arrived on the other bank, we had to tramp along the path. We took it by turns to carry a satchel. We did not want to waste time in letting the things dry. I was weak from hunger. I stumbled often — and there satchel and I were, in the mud. My comrades too fell again and again. We were in a hurry to get to the Indian who had sold us the canoe, for we knew we should be able to buy some food from him. This journey lasted four days. We met some convict telegraphists on the way, and they sold us some pieces of bread.

In all, we crossed five creeks, and on the bank of one we came upon a camp of Arabs, freed convicts, who were making charcoal. We understood by their gestures that they were arguing whether or no they should arrest us and claim the reward. There were seven or eight of them, but they were not armed, whilst we had between us three cutlasses, which we had in our hands, ready to cut the *cannes à feu*, in order to make a raft to cross the creek.

We went forward to meet them, all six of us, without giving them time to arm themselves, and we told them that, if they tried to arrest us, we would defend our liberty dearly.

They understood, and their attitude changed at once. If we had not frightened them, they would have got their guns and arrested us.

Whilst three of us busied ourselves cutting *cannes à feu*, others looked for creepers to tie the canes up. But, fearing that the Arabs had changed their minds, we constructed the raft so badly that it was nearly wrecked. Two amongst us could not swim, and the raft was breaking down on one side. Those of the party who could swim would have saved themselves but, if our satchels were lost, it was good-bye to liberty. For my part, I would not have let myself be taken.

It seems these creeks that we crossed, propelling the rafts with our legs, are full of crocodiles. I never saw any, but it seems that there are a great number.

When we had arrived at the Indian's hut, we handed him our whole fortune, excepting about a dozen francs, and he went to the village to fetch the canoe and provisions.

He came back next day with an old worm-eaten canoe about thirty feet long by five feet wide — a canoe which doubtless had been stolen and which seemed to have been submerged, who knows for how long? To judge by its size it was a cargo canoe. The quantity of provisions represented about a quarter of the money which had been given to him.

We had been robbed once more, but that did not astonish us. But because he had behaved like this we lost all confidence in him, and, instead of making our canoe more seaworthy, we resolved to set out just as we were, fearing that he would denounce us to his compatriots. We proposed to land in Dutch Guiana by paddling there. We were in very bad condition to cross the Maroni River. We had a wooden cask, which had held cement and which served as a water keg. When we made a landing on one occasion this keg was upset; the waves being high and the keg not being fastened securely in the canoe, the water was spilled, excepting a few liters, which served us to cook the rice we had with us. It went sour afterward, but we ate it all the same.

It was a very old canoe, much too big and worm-eaten. It was extremely dangerous to embark on it at all, for it was full of holes. To stop them up we stuffed rags from our shirts into them. But there was nothing else to be done. We had to embark. If we had gone into the interior we should have been lost and should have had little chance of finding a village, while as to walking along the bank of the river, there are hundreds of kilometers to get through which are uninhabited. We started off then but, at the first village we sighted, the man we had taken with us for his experience, and because he knew how to steer, declared that he would not go on with the voyage in such a rotten canoe. He landed, and so did the man we had found in the bush. Some people are afraid of water. I learned afterward from other escaped prisoners that fifteen days later they were back in jail.

To strengthen the stern of the canoe, we had the idea of spreading a layer of mud twenty centimeters thick over it. We allowed the mud to dry, and it held throughout the whole voyage. If we had not had this idea, on the first day of bad weather one of the planks of the steering gear would certainly have given way, the water would have rushed in, and that would have been the end. Three days afterward our provisions were finished and it was necessary to revictual.

From a distance we saw on the banks a big red-brick building which we took for a barracks. We landed some hundreds of yards away and my friend Petit Jean went to reconnoiter. He soon came back and told us that the building was in British Guiana and that it was a lepers' hospital.

We steered the canoe into a small creek. When they saw us, the lepers came to visit us. The man from the Drôme, who had worked as a shepherd in the United States and spoke a little English, was our interpreter. He asked the sick men, mostly Negroes and Indians, if they would have the goodness to give us some provisions so that we might continue on our way.

In no time we had a bag of bread, some bits of meat and

cheese, and several green bananas, not good eaten raw but good when cooked.

After thanking them a thousand times we put off at once. But the man from the Drôme warned us that it was dangerous to eat the food. Contact with the lepers had infected it. What did that matter? It seems that leprosy takes seven years to declare itself.

A discussion followed, and the man from the Drôme decided to land, as there was a village not far off. He was right, perhaps, for some of our benefactors were in a sad state.

The perpetual sun had exhausted us. I had lost my hat at sea and I covered my head with a piece of the stuff of my shirt. It was ten days since our voyage had begun, and we had eaten food enough perhaps for three days. Three of us were left and only about a quarter of the voyage was accomplished. We had been told: "When you see mountains on the seacoast, you will have reached Venezuela. To guide you during the night, you must take the two last stars of the Great Bear as your steering point. The head of the canoe must point between the two stars."

This man's departure embarrassed us very much, for the canoe was shipping a great deal of water. We had to bale without stopping, and we arranged that one of us should steer, one bale, and the third sleep.

Our drinking water was brackish. We had taken it from a creek, the same place where we stopped to make our canoe seaworthy. We three talked over matters, and, when we had patched up the leaks in the layer of mud, we decided to take to the open sea as far as the coast of Venezuela.

We put off from the coast, but the tide was too far out. We were stranded in the mud. We had chosen, without knowing it, a very dangerous spot. The beach was nearly level for a considerable distance, so that when the tide rose it was followed by huge waves, regular breakers, like the *mascarets* I have seen in the Dordogne. When we saw them, we flung ourselves out on the mud to get our poor old canoe facing the breakers. If they had caught her sideways, she would have been rolled over, and as she was not very strong, she would have been smashed to bits.

The land was about a kilometer away, and we were too weak to swim so far. At that moment the canoe meant life to us, not only liberty. The breakers reached us. Petit Jean held the canoe by the stern, in order to keep her bow on to the breakers. The other man and I were at either side. She floated. We got in and began to paddle. In these latitudes, the wind comes always from the open sea and never from the land.

The canoe was heavy. It was large and the coating of mud covered the stern, while in addition we had put in big tree branches at the bottom to make weight and also so that we might sleep without getting wet.

Owing to our weakness and our rotten paddles, we had not gone far before the ebb came, and again we were stranded in the mud. In the hope of finding depth, we all got out and pushed the canoe, which glided some inches. But the effort sent us into a quicksand, up to the chest. We had to make a new effort, holding on to the sides of the canoe, to pull ourselves out.

We repeated this maneuver over and over again. The sun grilled us, and the canoe made hardly any progress. This went on for three days. We had no water to wash ourselves with. We were covered with mud and, although we were very careful with them, our provisions were decreasing. We had only nine bananas left when we reached the sea. We divided them — three each.

When we tried to cook our bananas we discovered that we still had matches left but that it was impossible to light them. The stuff on which they are struck was completely worn out. But after all, eating the bananas raw came to much the same in the end; they were perhaps a little more bitter than potatoes.

We ate a banana a day and were three days without food, as we took six days to reach the Trinity Islands, which we had tried — without success — to sail past in the open sea so as not to enter the mouth of the Orinoco, where quantities of escaped convicts are lost among the uninhabited islands. The day before we made the islands a flying fish of about a half a pound in weight fell into the canoe. It was devoured — that is the word — raw.

From the sea we saw palm trees, and thought we would provision ourselves with coconuts. We landed; there were no houses. We tried to climb the trees but failed.

People arrived, and we made them understand that we were

hungry, very hungry. About twenty people came to stare at us and asked in English: "You come from Cayenne?" What were we to say? We dared not answer yes, and shook our heads. We knew that we must make off at once, for if the police surprised us it would mean our return to jail.

We showed the people about ten francs and tried to make them understand that we wished to buy provisions if there was a grocery in the neighborhood. Petit Jean talked, now in French, now in Corsican, now in Italian, which he spoke very well in a Marseilles patois. We had no idea if they understood us, but we heard and understood the word "policeman." We did not wait to hear any more. The canoe was pushed into the water. A black man tried to catch hold of it, but Petit Jean seized a cutlass and the Negro let go. We hoisted our sail. There was a fair wind; the open sea was ours. When we looked back we saw two policemen in uniform making signs to us to return. The called to us in English: "Come back, come back!"

We had only just escaped jail and solitary confinement.

Happily, a small boy had given us a coconut. It was cut into equal shares and the slices divided into three.

There was wind. Out at sea there was too much. We had to take down half the sail. The sea was very rough, and we kept on shipping water. This rough sea lasted four hours, but the canoe was going so fast that we began to see the Venezuelan mountains in the distance.

Then the wind dropped and the sea became as smooth as oil. This was about twenty-four hours after we left the Trinity Islands.

The canoe was at a standstill, but we believed that liberty was in sight.

About eight o'clock that night the wind sprang up again. An hour afterward a storm was on us — thunder, lightning, and rain. The night was pitch black, without a star. The wind whistled against our mast and was so strong that it gave the canoe a big list. Two of us baled out the water that came in, while Petit Jean steered, and all three of us tried to counterbalance the list. Then a big wave lifted the canoe, and by the light of a flash of lightning we saw the sea a black gulf. Not one of us said a word. All at once we heard a loud noise of waves breaking against rocks. If our course had been on an even keel, we should have tried to tack and make for the open sea, but it was impossible. The noise of the waves became louder and louder. Petit Jean, who was still at the tiller, said to me: "Eugène, as soon as we are on the rocks you must jump into the sea and try all you can to prevent the canoe from breaking up."

The other man was to lower the sail. He could not swim so well as I. Petit Jean himself was to unship the rudder so that it should not be broken, and then he was going to jump into the water to help me with the canoe.

We knew that it was absolutely necessary to preserve our canoe. We might land in a country uninhabited for hundreds of miles, or in a desert or in virgin forest.

But it was a hopeless scheme. I heard the noise the waves made against the rocks and I understood that this time, except for a miracle, we were lost. The lightning showed us the mountains of foam that the waves made. It was all over. Waiting for death, I began to pray. I said the Lord's Prayer and a Hail Mary. I was convinced that I was about to die, and I found it quite natural. I had no regrets. I thought of nothing. I waited.

A grinding noise under the canoe. The sea — or at least a huge wave — washed over it. Then a second, and a third. We were stupefied. The canoe was full of water and moved in a different way! We were on a shingly beach. The storm had thrown us up on the shore of a little bay, a hundred and fifty yards across.

When we awoke the next day we saw that at each end of the bay were pointed rocks running out to sea.

Our clothes being already soaked, we tried to take advantage of the waves in dragging our canoe farther up the beach. It was hard work. We pulled and pulled; we were tormented by fatigue and the longing for sleep.

At last, when we had no fear that the rising tide would take away our boat, we lay down on the beach and slept.

Next morning when I awoke I saw that Petit Jean was not there. I woke up my other comrade, and we agreed that he must have gone to explore. It was so — and above the rocks he had found a little path and the tracks of a donkey's hoofs.

He came back joyful. The country was inhabited. We were free.

The first person we met was a Martinique Negro. He only spoke patois, but that was enough. We understood when he told us that we were in Venezuela.

Venezuela it was — our promised land.

Our escape took twenty-one days.

It seems best to let the convict's story end here. Actually, there are in my possession a further five or six hundred words or so of the narrative, dealing with the prisoners' reception by the Venezuelan authorities; their detention in an oddly casual sort of prison; their account of themselves as being fishermen shipwrecked in the great storm. But before any indication is given of the manner in which the writer eventually reached France again, the manuscript breaks off — it is a fragment, without beginning or end, and as such I have presented it to my readers, trusting that it will have held for them some of the interest which it aroused in me when first I read it.

THE INVADERS

by Robie Macauley

The young couple had been happy on the beach by themselves, until the boys came along. "Did you notice their clothes?" she asked. "They look as if they'd run away from a reformatory."

LIKE BRIGHT FIGURES on a poster they suddenly appeared at the top of the stairway, outlined against the sky. He was dark and she was blond as the summer morning around her, a tall, easy-standing girl, deerlike, trim, and nordic-faced as any printed model on a fashion page. She wore a fire-colored playsuit belted with white, blue sandals, and she carried a basket on her arm. She could not resist raising the other arm just as they reached the dune edge, as if she were demanding to be photographed by some ready camera, ever prepared for her newest step or gesture.

"Oh, how glorious!" she said.

He laid down the things he had been carrying and together they stood and looked.

That early June had been racked with storms and filled with an overplenty of rain. The doors and windows of the cottages to the right and left of them on the dune and farther back in the woods were still blind with nailed-up boards or shutters, and, driving along the road to the shore, they had met no one, because it was nearly the first day of real summer weather we had had that year.

The dune was tall, and it was as if they looked from a high theater balcony down onto a tremendous vacant stage. Over the slightly curved shoreline the very small waves folded themselves gently while the whole expanse of water out to the far horizon glistened like a sheet of stretched blue silk.

"We have it all to ourselves," he said. "That's fine."

She made a half-circle sweep with her arm. "Is that all it means to you? Look, Gib, doesn't it suggest something? I mean doesn't it suggest something more than just that to you?"

He had decided to pick up their things again and had managed to get most of them into his arms. "Yes, it's a nice view," he said, "but I've seen it lots of times before."

"Not *that*. Don't you see what I mean? I mean it's like our life together after we got married — no one has been there before; it's all ours to do with what we please."

"I suppose so," he said, starting down the stairs. "But I hope it won't be as empty as all that."

"Now you're being nasty, Gib."

"No, I wasn't. Now look out for these stairs. They're rotten and one good shake would knock them down."

"I wish you wouldn't snub me like that. Sometimes I think you don't appreciate things the way I do."

"I'm just busy with all this gear," he said.

She followed him down the steep stairs, and when they got to the level of the beach they went directly down to within five yards of the water. As he laid their blanket out on the sand and put their surfboard, picnic basket, and towels to one side, she stripped off the red garment; underneath it she had on a bathing suit that shone green like the water in a quiet shoal. They lay down flat in the sun for a while and watched two clouds that swam like lonely white fish in the sky.

He watched them for a long time as they glided through the airy blue pool and out of sight. He closed his eyes, but after a few minutes he awoke with the feeling of lying in a bath of warm honey. The sun had risen higher and it seemed to be nearly noon.

She lay on her back and he could see that she was now asleep. To his eyes she was like the elegant landscape of some familiar province as he lay there barely breathing. Sitting, he looked down on her as an aviator might look down on his own country and recognize the gentle heights, the rolling plains, and the symmetrically built town of her face. He closed his eyes and lay back again. A familiar country? Yes, something like that. When he had asked her to marry him he was not quite so aware of the borders and confines, he thought drowsily. Past the country club on one side, the suburban home on another, the good schools, the parties, the familiar names, was an unexplored wilderness, a wild Ireland beyond the pale. There was a certain dark frontier farther than which one could not go. As he fell asleep again he dreamed about riding a bicycle around an enclosed track with no exit.

In time she awoke, and she awakened him by tickling his ribs and kissing him on the forehead.

"Shall we go swimming now?"

While they were dozing a brisker wind had come up, stirring the surface of the water into rough little whitecaps that broke on the shallows about a hundred feet out. He picked up the surfboard, and she followed him to the edge of the beach. Janet was somewhat afraid of the water. She had explained it by saying that someone had pushed her into a deep place once when she was a child and she had nearly drowned. She always asked a hundred questions to reassure herself before she finally put her foot in. Is it cold? It looks terribly cold, doesn't it? Do you think there's any undertow today? Now let's not go too far out, shall we? It is freezing, isn't it?

She followed by inches; he was already pushing the white board through the waves toward the spot where the breakers curled over. If you took the right moment and jumped on the board just ahead of a breaking wave it would carry you on the crest nearly to shore. He showed her how.

A wave rolled toward them, bigger than any of the others. "Now!" he said, and boosted her onto the board. She slithered her body until she got firmly settled and grasped the handholds at the side. He swung the front end around a little so the wave would catch her evenly. It was almost on them. "Hold tight!" he yelled, and dived beneath the water.

As long as his breath held out he swam beneath the surface. The ridged sand of the bottom slid under his hands and a colder current knifed along his backbone. It was quiet here; the water scarcely seemed to move. He opened his eyes and thought that fish swimming in this green silence would never realize the dash and fury of the surface. But he preferred the waves. He put his hands flat on the sand and gave himself a push that plunged him up and into the air again. He looked for her.

But he had got turned around in swimming under water and he was facing down the beach. He was suddenly aware that the beach was no longer empty. He tossed his head to throw the water out of his eyes and began a slow sidestroke.

There were two figures on the beach, two men walking along the edge of the sand about a quarter of a mile away. They were not wearing swimming suits; they were fully dressed, and, though close to the shore line, they were not wading. They walked along slowly side by side as if going down a city street. He caught the glint of the sun on skin and then he realized that one was black.

He had only a minute to wonder about them because in the next he heard Janet calling to him, "Hi! It got away from me, Gib."

She was floundering in the shallows where the wave had carried her and trying to stand up in the riptide. She got up and waved to him. In the tossing water he could see the white back of the surfboard being carried down shore. It was about halfway between himself and the two men walking along the beach.

Then she saw them. She slowly lowered her arm and even at this distance he could feel her astonishment. Not that there was anything odd about other people on the beach — it was usually crowded this time of year — or that there was anything particularly strange about these two, but they had become so accustomed in the last few hours of thinking of themselves as the only two people in the world, had so accepted and enjoyed their isolation, that anybody's coming would be a shock. He planned to remark something about Crusoe and Friday when he came up with her. But now he had to swim for the board, and it was getting farther and farther away.

He went as fast as he could, but before he had gone very far he hoped that the two men had sighted it. He hadn't noticed before how strong the downshore current was. It seemed to push him along, but the board was traveling faster.

They stopped, and one of them stooped and rolled up his trousers legs. He was coming out into the water now and Gib could see him lifting the board up. Then they came on down the beach at the same pace toward the spot on shore where Janet was standing. Both of them had their arms hooked over the board.

He reached the shallow water and stood up; when he got to the shore they were just handing the surfboard to Janet. "Thanks," she said with a smile. "It knocked me over and ran away." They didn't smile in return. "O.K., lady," the white one said. "It's O.K."

They were not men, but boys. They both seemed to be about sixteen or seventeen, though they were short, shorter than Janet. He took Janet's arm and they went up and sat on the blanket and lighted cigarettes.

The boys stood and stared at the surfboard, which lay near the water where she had dropped it. They turned it over and looked at the other side. Evidently it was sandy because they scooped up water in their hands and tried to wash it off. "That's O.K.," Gib said. "It'll be all right." The boys came up and sat down carefully, about four yards away from them.

The white one had skin the color of skim milk. He was either completely and prematurely bald or else his head had been closely shaved recently. He had a small bunched face with sharp features that reminded Gib of some kind of tool, a monkey wrench, perhaps. The other one had close-cut hair, too, and a flat face like an imprint in some thick, warm tar. They sat close together, arms folded over their knees, and occasionally seemed to give each other a slight push or nudge, like a signal.

They were wearing high bootlike shoes, which they had put aside on the sand, but that was the only way they had prepared for the beach. Their shirts and trousers were made of similar gray stuff and the pants legs of the one who had gone after the surfboard were black from being wet. Except for the slight movements of shoulders or elbows, they sat very quietly, gazing at Janet and Gib.

Gib felt that he had to say something. "Where you fellows from?" he asked.

"Flint," said the colored boy.

The other one said something to Gib. It was a strange accent; Polish, he thought; and the words were run together. "We come up to the beach, we hitched up for the day," was what it sounded like. It might be a speech impediment; Gib wasn't sure.

"Aren't you going in swimming?"

"No, we ain't going in swimming." This was the colored boy, and though the words sounded unfriendly, the tone was soft and meaningless.

"We ain't got no suits," he finally said.

They asked about the surfboard. It was a neat board, they said. They had never heard of anything like that. Carried the lady right into shore.

After that no one said anything for a while. Janet had been rubbing suntan lotion on her shoulders, but when he started to light a cigarette, she took him quickly by the arm. "Let's go back in the water," she said, and ran into the waves, still pulling her rubber cap over her ears.

She was ahead of him all the way out to the sandbar where the waves broke. They dived through one together and when they came up she said, "Listen, I wanted to talk to you. What do those two want?"

In the trough of the wave before the next one came they stood and looked back to the shore. The two figures had moved; they were a few feet out in the water pushing the surfboard around between them. They were being careful not to let it get away.

The next wave slapped the swimmers before they knew it; it seemed to break just behind their ears, rush over them, and pull them violently toward shore. When they emerged, she took his arm with both hands.

"They're up to something, I know it. Did you notice their clothes? They look as if they'd run away from a reformatory." Her fingers gripped harder against his skin, and her voice was drawn and uneasy.

He was a little dismayed by her show of nerves. "Well," he said, "I think it's obvious that they think we're in *their* way. They came up here to go swimming. They haven't any suits and they can't swim naked until we go away."

"Maybe you're right," she said doubtfully, "but they give me the shivers anyway. They don't seem like *boys*, do they? There's something awfully grim about them."

"Forget it," he said, pretending to duck her. "We'll move our things up the beach and eat lunch. They probably won't stick around long if we ignore them." He dived over the next wave and they started for shore.

A little compunction, a little guilt, troubled him over his compromise with her fears. The boys had seemed only somewhat lost and lonely to him. If they lived in a crowded tenement, as he supposed, this stretch of empty sand and empty water must bewilder them more than he could understand. But he forgot about that as he raced her to the beach.

They did as he had said. The boys, now sitting close together in the same spot, watched their movements of gathering their things and going off without any question. They were still sitting there when Janet and Gib got out of sight around a place where the beach narrowed and the dune came close to the water.

"We might have offered them a sandwich," he said as they were eating. She shook her head.

"It was better not to. We'd have them around like flies all afternoon."

After they had finished eating they lay still on the blanket again, letting the sun cook them. He drifted again into the dozing state, dangling between real sleep and real wakefulness. Suddenly he was disturbed. It was nothing more than a momentary change in the light or the air, as if a shadow had passed across the sun. He felt that he must open his eyes, wake up. Slowly he did. They were sitting there, less than ten feet away, staring silently at his face.

"What do you want?" he asked, and sat up. They sat together just as before, one head dazzlingly black in the sun, close to the naked blue-white one. He felt that she was stirring on the blanket, and in a minute she would see them too. It seemed impossible to explain their strange insistence, this speechless patience, in his own terms. She would be frightened when she saw them here again, and a little of her panic would take hold of him, he knew — not entirely, but just a little more, and he was afraid of it.

He spoke slowly. "You fellows must be hungry?" He waited for an answer, but all he saw was a minute movement as if they had both at the same time shifted a little nearer the blanket. "Would you like a couple of sandwiches? We have some left over." They were silent.

He went to the picnic basket on hands and knees, taking care not to disturb her. He reached in and took out the leftover sandwiches, still wrapped in wax paper. The white boy extended his hand and took them. Gib was aware that she was awake now and listening.

"Why don't you go away somewhere and eat them?" For a minute he was not sure that they would pay any attention. Finally they rose slowly and went about twenty yards away; then they sat down again. They began to unwrap the sandwiches.

"*Get rid of them*," she whispered. "They're planning something, Gib; I know it. They're after us." Her whisper was hysterical; he could see a white bloodless band running across her cheeks beneath the tanned surface. "I can tell."

"Nonsense," he whispered back, but the very violence of her exaggeration shook him.

"They have criminal faces," she said.

"Now don't be silly, Janet. They haven't done a thing. They're pests, sure, but that doesn't mean they're up to anything." But the confidence had gone out of his words, and he was aware of an angry pulsing under his ribs. "By God, if I thought so . . ." he said.

"Look!" she whispered sharply.

They had stood up, dropping their sandwiches in the sand, and were looking at some spot down the beach, near the edge of the water. "What is it?" she asked. They could not tell. Gib got up on his knees to see. The two boys were going forward in an awkward stalk. They both stopped to gather something and then broke into a trot.

Gib saw what it was. There were five or six sandpipers hopping in their delicate, spinsterish fashion along the edge of the shore.

The boys were running at them now, and the birds took alarm. The boys stopped and began to throw the stones they had picked up as the frightened birds scattered on the beach or began to fly out over the water. One of the attackers gave a quick cut-off laugh, and then they were running down to the edge of the water.

"They're coming back!" she said.

They stood looking down at Gib and Janet. The colored one laid the sandpiper on the ground as if it were an offering or a prophecy. Neither of them said anything yet; the colored boy smoothed the dead feathers with his hand, and he smiled as he did so. When he smiled, Janet screamed.

"Get out of here!" The words shot out of her mouth. "Get out of here and leave us alone. You've bothered us enough today. We don't want you, understand? We don't want you; you can go wherever you're going and take your bird with you. *Go away*!" Gib realized that he had taken hold of her hand and that his other hand was clenched in a fist. His breath was pumping; he knew he was hers.

They were undecided, and they both kept glancing down at the bird as if they expected it to tell them something. The colored boy made some kind of gesture with his open hand in front of him, the palm showing pink in the center. At last he said, "We . . . I don't know. We ain't bothering you."

"Get out of here," Gib said. Now he was sure of himself. "We don't want you." The white boy sat down.

Janet's face was white now; it didn't seem pretty any longer. She was gathering up their things and with no more words Gib helped her. They put everything together and started down the beach, walking close to the water so that they could move faster on the hard sand.

"Are they?" she asked after a while. He had kept glancing back. "Yes," he said.

The stairway was nearer; they had only about fifty yards to go. He looked back again.

"They're about a hundred feet behind us," he said.

They got to the bottom of the stairs and she started to climb, panting from the exertion. He went a little more slowly, shifting the things in his arms so that he might drop them easily. He looked back and saw that the two were close behind them. They were standing at the foot of the stairs now. Their faces were raised toward him, and it seemed to him for a moment that they looked only puzzled and curious.

The colored boy stood a few paces in front of the other with his hands dropped by his sides. Suddenly he made that odd empty gesture with the palm of his hand, and Gib paused near the top of the stairway.

But it was the white boy who spoke, in his queer accent. His voice was windy and panting.

"Mister," he said, "give us a lift out to the highway?"

"No!" she said from behind him. "Hurry, Gib, hurry and for God's sake watch out." Her voice had risen to the pitch of a bird's shrill, dying scream. "Watch out!"

Gib ran up the last few steps. He could see the boys stand there for a moment and then they came forward and began to climb the stairs. He saw the black hand and the white hand clenched on the railing. "Gib!"

He threw the blanket and the surfboard on the ground and faced around. He watched them climb until they were less than ten feet below him. "Gib!" she whispered.

They were close. He knew what he had to do from the tone of her biting whisper. He wrenched at one of the two-by-four railings, and the rotted thing came away with the pull. He saw the two faces, one black, one white, tottering in front of him. He swung the club with all his force, and he saw the whole rickety structure give way. At the moment the blood splashed on his hand, the stairway fell. It seemed to burst into chunks and fragments of wood and avalanche down the steep dune. In the tangle of wood and sand and bodies he could see a raised black hand, open in the air with a pink spot showing in the center of the palm.

BIRD OF PREY

by John Collier

The chick had grown at alarming speed and was
not in the least like its mother.

THE HOUSE they called the Engineer's House is now deserted.
The new man from Baton Rouge gave it up after living less than a
month in it, and built himself a two-room shack with his own
money, on the very farthest corner of the company's land.

The roof has caved in, and most of the windows are smashed.
Oddly enough, no birds nest in the shelter of the eaves or take
advantage of the forsaken rooms. An empty house is normally
fine harborage for rats and mice and bats, but there is no squeak
or rustle or scamper to disturb the quiet of this one. Only creatures utterly foreign, utterly remote from the most distant
cousinhood to man, only the termite, the tarantula, and the
scorpion indifferently make it their home.

All in a few years Edna Spalding's garden has been wiped out
as if it had never existed. The porch where she and Jack sat so
happily in the evenings is rotten under its load of wind-blown
twigs and sand. A young tree has already burst up the boards
outside the living room window, so they fan out like the stiff
fingers of someone who is afraid. In this corner there still stands
a strongly made parrot's perch, the wood of which has been left
untouched even by the termite and the boring beetle.

The Spaldings brought a parrot with them when first they
came. It was a sort of extra wedding present, given them at the

last moment by Edna's mother. It was something from home for Edna to take into the wilds.

The parrot was already old, and he was called Tom, and, like other parrots, he sat on his perch and whistled and laughed and uttered his few remarks, which were often very appropriate. Edna and Jack were both very fond of him, and they were overwhelmingly fond of each other. They liked their house and the country and Jack's colleagues, and everything in life seemed to be delightful.

One night they had just fallen asleep when they were awakened by a tremendous squawking and fluttering outside on the porch. "Oh, Jack!" cried Edna. "Get up! Hurry! Run! It's one of those cats from the men's camp has got hold of poor Tom!"

Jack sprang out of bed, but caught his foot in the sheet and landed on his elbow on the floor. Between rubbing his elbow and disentangling his foot, he wasted a good many seconds before he was up again and had dashed through the living room and out upon the porch.

All this time, which seemed an age, the squawking and fluttering increased, but as he flung open the door it ceased as suddenly as it had begun. The whole porch was bathed in the brightest moonlight, and at the farther end the perch was clearly visible, and on the floor beneath it was poor old Tom parrot, gasping amid a litter of his own feathers, and crying, "Oh! Oh! Oh!"

At any rate he was alive. Jack looked right and left for traces of his assailant, and at once noticed the long, heavy trailers of the vine were swinging violently, although there was not a breath of wind. He went to the rail and looked out and around, but there was no sign of a cat. Of course, it was not likely there would be. Jack was more interested in the fact that the swaying vines were spread over a length of several feet, which seemed a very great deal of disturbance for a fleeing cat to make. Finally he looked up, and he thought he saw a bird — a big bird, an enormous bird — flying away; he just caught a glimpse of it as it crossed the brightness of the moon.

He turned back and picked up old Tom. The poor parrot's

chain was broken, and his heart was pounding away like mad, and still, like a creature hurt and shocked beyond all endurance, he cried, "Oh! Oh! Oh!"

This was all the more odd, for it was seldom the old fellow came out with a new phrase, and Jack would have laughed heartily, except it sounded too pathetic. So he carefully examined the poor bird, and, finding no injury beyond the loss of a handful of feathers from his neck, he replaced him on the perch and turned to reassure Edna, who now appeared in the doorway.

"Is he dead?" cried she.

"No," said Jack. "He's had a bit of shock, though. Something got hold of him."

"I'll bring him a piece of sugar," said Edna. "That's what he loves. That'll make him feel better."

She soon brought the sugar, which Tom took in his claw, but though usually he would nibble it up with the greatest avidity, this time he turned his lackluster eye only once upon it, and gave a short, bitter, despairing sort of laugh, and let it fall to the ground.

"Let him rest," said Jack. "He has had a bad tousling."

"It was a cat," said Edna. "It was one of those beastly blacks that the men have at the camp."

"Maybe," said Jack. "On the other hand — I don't know. I thought I saw an enormous bird flying away."

"It couldn't be an eagle," said Edna. "There are none ever seen here."

"I know," said Jack. "Besides, they don't fly at night. Nor do the buzzards. It might have been an owl, I suppose. But . . ."

"But what?" said Edna.

"But it looked very much larger than an owl," said Jack.

"It was your fancy," said Edna. "It was one of those beastly cats that did it."

This point was discussed very frequently during the next few days. Everybody was consulted, and everybody had an opinion. Jack might have been a little doubtful at first, for he had caught only the briefest glimpse as the creature crossed the the moon, but opposition made him more certain, and the discussions sometimes got rather heated.

"Charlie says it was all your imagination," said Edna. "He

says no owl would ever attack a parrot.''

"How the devil does *he* know?" said Jack. "Besides, I said it was bigger than an owl."

"He says that shows you imagine things," said Edna.

"Perhaps he would like me to think I do," said Jack. "Perhaps you both would."

"Oh, Jack!" cried Edna. She was deeply hurt, and not without reason, for it showed that Jack was still thinking of a ridiculous mistake he had made, a real mistake, of the sort that young husbands sometimes do make, when they come suddenly into a room and people are startled without any real reason for it. Charlie was young and free and easy and good-looking, and he would put his hand on your shoulder without even thinking about it, and nobody minded.

"I should not have said that," said Jack.

"No, indeed you shouldn't," said Edna, and she was right.

The parrot said nothing at all. All these days he had been moping and ailing, and seemed to have forgotten even how to ask for sugar. He only groaned and moaned to himself, ruffled up his feathers, and every now and then shook his head in the most rueful, miserable, despairing way you can possibly imagine.

One day, however, when Jack came home from work, Edna put her finger to her lips and beckoned him to the window. "Watch Tom," she whispered.

Jack peeped out. There was the old bird, lugubriously climbing down from his perch and picking some dead stalks from the vine, which he carried up till he gained a corner where the balustrade ran into the wall, and added his gatherings to others that were already there. He trod round and round, twisted his stalks in and out, and, always with the same doleful expression, paid great attention to the nice disposal of a feather or two, a piece of wool, a fragment of cellophane. There was no doubt about it.

"There's no doubt about it," said Jack.

"He's making a nest!" cried Edna.

"He!" cried Jack. "*He!* I like that. The old impostor! The old male impersonator! She's going to lay an egg. Thomasina — that's her name from now on."

Thomasina it was. Two or three days later the matter was settled beyond the shadow of a doubt. There, one morning, in the ramshackle nest was an egg.

"I thought she was sick because of that shaking she got," said Jack. "She was broody, that's all."

"It's a monstrous egg," said Edna. "Poor birdie!"

"What do you expect, after God knows how many years?" said Jack, laughing. "Some birds lay eggs nearly as big as themselves — the kiwi or something. Still, I must admit it's a whopper."

"She still doesn't look well," said Edna.

Indeed, the old parrot looked almost as sick as a parrot can be, which is several times sicker than any other living creature. Her eyes closed up, her head sank, and if a finger was put out to scratch her, she turned her beak miserably away. However, she sat conscientiously on the prodigious egg she had laid, though every day she seemed a little feebler than before.

"Perhaps we ought to take the egg away," said Jack. "We could get it blown and keep it as a memento."

"No," said Edna. "Let her have it. It's all she's had in all these years."

Here Edna made a mistake, and she realized it a few mornings later. "Jack," she called. "Do come. It's Tom — Thomasina, I mean. I'm afraid she's going to die."

"We ought to have taken the egg away," said Jack, coming out with his mouth full of breakfast food. "She's exhausted herself. It's no good, anyway. It's bound to be sterile."

"Look at her!" cried Edna.

"She's done for," said Jack, and at that moment the poor old bird keeled over and gasped her last.

"The egg killed her," said Jack, picking it up. "I said it would. Do you want to keep it? Oh, good Lord!" He put the egg down very quickly. "It's alive," he said.

"What?" said Edna. "What do you mean?"

"It gave me a turn," said Jack. "It's most extraordinary. It's against nature. There's a chick inside that egg, tapping."

"Let it out," said Edna. "Break the shell."

"I was right," said Jack. "It *was* a bird I saw. It must have been a stray parrot. Only it looked so big."

"I'm going to break the shell with a spoon," said Edna, running to fetch one.

"It'll be a lucky bird," said Jack when she returned. "Born with a silver spoon in its beak, so to speak. Be careful."

"I will," said Edna. "Oh, I do hope it lives."

With that she gingerly cracked the shell, the tapping increased, and soon they saw a well-developed beak tearing its way through. In another moment the chick was born.

"Golly!" cried Jack. "What a monster!"

"It's because it's young," said Edna. "It'll grow lovely. Like its mother."

"Maybe," said Jack. "I must be off. Put it in the nest. Feed it pap. Keep it warm. Don't monkey with it too much. Good-bye, my love."

That morning Jack telephoned home two or three times to find out how the chick was, and if it ate. He rushed home at lunchtime. In the evening everyone came round to peep at the nestling and offer advice.

Charlie was there. "It ought to be fed every hour at least," said he. "That's how it is in nature."

"He's right," said Jack. "For the first month at least, that's how it should be."

"It looks as if I'm going to be tied down a bit," said Edna ruefully.

"I'll look in when I pass and relieve your solitude," said Charlie.

"I'll manage to rush home now and then in the afternoons," said Jack, a little too thoughtfully.

Certainly the hourly feeding seemed to agree with the chick, which grew at an almost alarming speed. It became covered with down; feathers sprouted. In a few months it was fully grown, and not in the least like its mother. For one thing, it was coal black.

"It must be a hybrid," said Jack. "There *is* a black parrot; I've seen them in zoos. They didn't look much like this, though. I've half a mind to send a photograph of him somewhere."

"He looks so wicked," said Edna.

"He looks cunning," said Jack. "That bird knows everything, believe me. I bet he'll talk soon."

"It gave a sort of laugh," said Edna. "I forgot to tell you."

"When?" cried Jack. "A laugh?"

"Sort of," said Edna. "But it was horrible. It made Charlie nearly jump out of his skin."

"Charlie?" cried Jack. "You didn't say he'd been here."

"Well, you know how often he drops in," said Edna.

"Do I?" said Jack. "I hope I do. God! What was that?"

"That's what I meant," said Edna. "A sort of laugh."

"What a horrible sound!" said Jack.

"Listen, Jack," said Edna. "I wish you wouldn't be silly about Charlie. You are, you know."

Jack looked at her. "I know I am," said he. "I know it when I look at you. And then I think I never will be again. But somehow it's got stuck in my mind, and the least little thing brings it on. Maybe I'm just a bit crazy, on that one subject."

"Well, he'll be transferred soon," said Edna. "And that'll be the end of it."

"Where did you hear that?" said Jack.

"He told me this afternoon," said Edna. "He was on his way back from getting the mail when he dropped in. That's why he told me first. Otherwise he'd have told you first. Only he hasn't seen you yet. Do you see?"

"Yes, I see," said Jack. "I wish I could be psychoanalyzed or something."

Soon Charlie made his farewells and departed for his job on the company's other project. Edna was secretly glad to see him go; she wanted no problems, however groundless, to exist between herself and Jack. A few days later she felt sure that all the problems were solved forever.

"Jack," said she when he came home in the evening.

"Yes," said he.

"Something new," said she. "Don't play with that bird. Listen to me."

"Call him Polly," said Jack. They had named it Polly to be on the safe side. "You don't want to call him 'that bird.' The missus doesn't love you, Poll."

"Do you know, I don't!" said Edna, with quite startling vehemence. "I don't like him at all, Jack. Let's give him away."

"What? For heaven's sake!" cried Jack. "This rare, black, specially hatched Poll? This parrot of romantic origin? The cleverest Poll that ever . . ."

"That's it," said Edna. "He's too darned clever. Jack, I hate him. He's horrible."

"What? Has he said something you don't like?" said Jack, laughing. "I bet he will, when he talks. But what's the news, anyway?"

"Come inside," said Edna. "I'm not going to tell you with that creature listening." She led the way into the bedroom. "The news is," said she, "that I've got to be humored. And if I don't like anything, it's got to be given away. It's not going to be born with a beak because its mother was frightened by a hateful monstrosity of a parrot."

"What?" said Jack.

"That's what," said Edna, smiling and nodding.

"A brat?" cried Jack in delight. "A boy! Or a girl! It's bound to be one or the other. Listen: I was afraid to tell you how much I wanted one, Edna. Oh boy! This is going to make everything very, very fine. Lie down. You're delicate. Put your feet up. I'm going to fix dinner. This is practice. Stay still. Oh boy! Oh boy! Oh boy!"

He went out through the living room on his way to the kitchen. As he passed the window he caught sight of the parrot on the dark porch outside, and he put his head through to speak to it.

"Have you heard the news?" said he. "Behold a father! You're going to be cut right out, my bird. You're going to be given away. Yes, sir, it's a baby."

The parrot gave a long low whistle. "You don't say so?" said he in a husky voice, a voice of apprehension, a quite astonishing imitation of Charlie's voice. "What about Jack?"

"What's that?" said Jack, startled.

"He'll think it's his," whispered the parrot in Edna's voice. "He's fool enough for anything. Kiss me, darling. Phew-w-w! You don't say so? What about Jack. He'll think it's his, he's fool enough for anything. Kiss me, darling. Phew-w-w!"

Jack went out into the kitchen and sat down with his head in his hands for several minutes.

"Hurry up!" cried Edna from the bedroom. "Hurry up —
Father!"

"I'm coming," said Jack.

He went to his desk and took out the revolver. Then he went
into the bedroom.

The parrot laughed. Then, lifting its claw, it took the chain in
its beak and bit through it as if it were paper.

Jack came out, holding the gun, his hand over his eyes. "Fool
enough for anything!" said the parrot, and laughed.

Jack turned the gun on himself. As he did so, in the infinitesi-
mal interval between the beginning and the end of the movement
of his finger on the trigger, he saw the bird grow, spread its dark
wings; and its eyes flamed, and it changed, and it launched itself
toward him.

The gun went off. Jack dropped to the floor. The parrot, or
whatever it was, sailing down, seized what came out of his
ruined mouth, wheeled back through the window, and was soon
far away, visible for a moment only as it swept on broader wings
past the new-risen moon.

THE CONFESSION OF
CHARLES LINKWORTH

by E. F. Benson

Did the phone ring because the murder had been of peculiar
horror, and there was nothing of sympathy in the mind of
the public toward the perpetrator?

DR. TEESDALE had occasion to attend the condemned man once
or twice during the week before his execution, and found him, as
is often the case when the last hope of life has vanished, quiet
and perfectly resigned to his fate, and not seeming to look forward with any dread to the morning that each hour that passed
brought nearer and nearer. The bitterness of death appeared to
be over for him; it was done with when he was told that his appeal was refused. But for those days while hope was not yet
quite abandoned, the wretched man had drunk of death daily. In
all his experience the doctor had never seen a man so wildly and
passionately tenacious of life, nor one so strongly knit to this material world by the sheer animal lust of living. Then the news that
hope could no longer be entertained was told him, and his spirit
passed out of the grip of that agony of torture and suspense, and
accepted the inevitable with indifference. Yet the change was so
extraordinary that it seemed to the doctor rather that the news
had completely stunned his powers of feeling, and he was below
the numbed surface, still knit into material things as strongly as
ever. He had fainted when the result was told him, and Dr.

Teesdale had been called in to attend him. But the fit was but transient, and he came out of it into full consciousness of what had happened.

The murder had been a deed of peculiar horror, and there was nothing of sympathy in the mind of the public toward the perpetrator. Charles Linkworth, who now lay under capital sentence, was the keeper of a small stationery store in Sheffield, and there lived with him his wife and mother. The latter was the victim of his atrocious crime; the motive of it being to get possession of the sum of five hundred pounds, which was this woman's property. Linkworth, as came out at the trial, was in debt to the extent of a hundred pounds at the time, and during his wife's absence from home, on a visit to relations, he strangled his mother and during the night buried the body in the small back garden of his house. On his wife's return, he had a sufficiently plausible tale to account for the elder Mrs. Linkworth's disappearance, for there had been constant jarrings and bickerings between him and his mother for the last year or two, and she had more than once threatened to withdraw herself and the eight shillings a week which she contributed to household expenses, and purchase an annuity with her money. It was true, also, that during the younger Mrs. Linkworth's absence from home, mother and son had had a violent quarrel arising originally from some trivial point in household management, and that in consequence of this, she had actually drawn her money out of the bank, intending to leave Sheffield next day and settle in London, where she had friends. That evening she had told him this, and during the night he killed her.

His next step, before his wife's return, was logical and sound. He packed up all his mother's possessions and took them to the station, from which he saw them dispatched to town by passenger train, and in the evening he asked several friends in to supper and told them of his mother's departure. He did not (logically also, and in accordance with what they probably already knew) feign regret, but said that he and she had never got on well together, and that the cause of peace and quietness was furthered by her going. He told the same story to his wife on her return, identical in every detail, adding, however, that the quarrel had been a violent one and that his mother had not even left him her address. This again was wisely thought of; it would prevent his wife from writing to her. She appeared to accept his story completely; indeed there was nothing strange or suspicious about it.

For a while he behaved with the composure and astuteness which most criminals possess up to a certain point, the lack of which, after that, is generally the cause of their detection. He did not, for instance, immediately pay off his debts, but took into his house a young man as lodger, who occupied his mother's room, and he dismissed the assistant in his shop and did the entire serving himself. This gave the impression of economy, and at the same time he openly spoke of the great improvement in his trade, and not till a month had passed did he cash any of the bank notes which he had found in a locked drawer in his mother's room. Then he changed two notes of fifty pounds and paid off his creditors.

At that point his astuteness and composure failed him. He opened a deposit account at a local bank with four more fifty-pound notes, instead of being patient and increasing his balance at the savings bank pound by pound, and he got uneasy about that which he had buried deep enough for security in the back garden. Thinking to render himself safer in this regard, he ordered a cartload of slag and stone fragments, and with the help of his lodger employed the summer evenings, when work was over, in building a sort of rockery over the spot. Then came the chance circumstance which really set match to this dangerous train. There was a fire in the lost luggage office at King's Cross Station (from which he ought to have claimed his mother's property), and one of the two boxes was partially burned. The company was liable for compensation, and his mother's name on her linen, and a letter with the Sheffield address on it, led to the arrival of a purely official and formal notice, stating that the company was prepared to consider claims. It was directed to Mrs. Linkworth, and Charles Linkworth's wife received and read it.

It seemed a sufficiently harmless document, but it was endorsed with his death warrant. For he could give no explanation at all of the fact of the boxes' still lying at King's Cross Station, beyond suggesting that some accident had happened to his mother. Clearly he had to put the matter in the hands of the police, with a view to tracing her movements, and if it proved that she was dead, claiming her property, which she had already drawn out of the bank. Such at least was the course urged on him by his wife and lodger, in whose presence the communication from the railway officials was read out, and it was impossible to refuse to take it. Then the silent, uncreaking machinery of justice, characteristic of England, began to move forward. Quiet men lounged about Smith Street, visited banks, observed the supposed increase in trade, and from a house near by looked into the garden where ferns were already flourishing on the rockery. Then came the arrest and the trial, which did not last very long, and on a certain Saturday night the verdict. Smart women in large hats had made the court bright with color, and in all the crowd there was not one who felt any sympathy with the young athletic-looking man who was condemned. Many of the audience were elderly and respectable mothers, and the crime had been an outrage on motherhood, and they listened to the unfolding of the flawless evidence with strong approval. They thrilled a little when the judge put on the awful and ludicrous little black cap and spoke the sentence appointed by God.

Linkworth went to pay the penalty for the atrocious deed, which no one who had heard the evidence could possibly doubt that he had done, with the same indifference as had marked his entire demeanor since he knew his appeal had failed. The prison chaplain who had attended him had done his utmost to get him to confess, but his efforts had been quite ineffectual, and to the last he asserted, though without protestation, his innocence. On a bright September morning, when the sun shone warm on the terrible little procession that crossed the prison yard to the shed where was erected the apparatus of death, justice was done, and Dr. Teesdale was satisfied that life was immediately extinct. He had been present on the scaffold, had watched the bolt drawn and the hooded and pinioned figure drop into the pit. He had heard the chunk and creak of the rope as the sudden weight came on to it, and looking down he had seen the queer twitchings of the hanged body. They had lasted but a second or two; the execution had been perfectly satisfactory.

An hour later he made the post-mortem examination and found that his view had been correct: the vertebrae of the spine had been broken at the neck, and death must have been absolutely instantaneous. It was hardly necessary even to make that little piece of dissection that proved this, but for the sake of form he did so. And at that moment he had a very curious and vivid mental impression that the spirit of the dead man was close beside him, as if it still dwelled in the broken habitation of its body. But there was no question at all that the body was dead: it had been dead an hour. Then followed another little circumstance that at the first seemed insignificant though curious also. One of the warders entered and asked if the rope, which had been used an hour ago and was the hangman's perquisite, had by mistake been brought into the mortuary with the body. But there was no trace of it, and it seemed to have vanished altogether, though it was a singular thing to be lost. It was not here; it was not on the scaffold. And though the disappearance was of no particular moment, it was quite inexplicable.

Dr. Teesdale was a bachelor and a man of independent means, and lived in a tall-windowed and commodious house in Bedford Square, where a plain cook of surpassing excellence looked after his food, and her husband his person. There was no need for him to practice a profession at all, and he performed his work at the prison for the sake of the study of the minds of criminals. Most crime — the transgression, that is, of the rules of conduct which the human race has framed for the sake of its own preservation — he held to be either the result of some abnormality of the brain or of starvation. Crimes of theft, for instance, he would by no means refer to one head; often, it is true, they were the result of actual want, but more often dictated by some obscure disease of the brain. In marked cases it was labeled as kleptomania, but he was convinced there were many others which did not fall directly under the dictation of physical need. More especially was this the case where the crime in question involved also some deed of violence, and he mentally placed underneath this head-

ing, as he went home that evening, the criminal at whose last
moments he had been present that morning. The crime had been
abominable, the need of money not so very pressing, and the
very abomination and unnaturalness of the murder inclined him
to consider the murderer as lunatic rather than criminal. He had
been, as far as was known, a man of quiet and kindly disposition,
a good husband, a sociable neighbor. And then he had committed a crime, just one, which put him outside all pales. So
monstrous a deed, whether perpetrated by a sane man or a mad
one, was intolerable; there was no use for the doer of it on this
planet at all. But somehow the doctor felt that he would have
been more at one with the execution of justice if the dead man
had confessed. It was morally certain that he was guilty, but he
wished that when there was no longer any hope for him, he had
endorsed the verdict himself.

He dined alone that evening and after dinner sat in his study,
which adjoined the dining room, and, feeling disinclined to read,
sat in his great red chair opposite the fireplace and let his mind
graze where it would. At once, almost, it went back to the curious sensation he had experienced that morning, of feeling that
the spirit of Linkworth was present in the mortuary, though life
had been extinct for an hour. It was not the first time, especially
in cases of sudden death, that he had felt a similar conviction,
though perhaps it had never been quite so unmistakable as it had
been today. Yet the feeling, to his mind, was quite probably
formed on a natural and psychical truth. The spirit — it may be
remarked that he was a believer in the doctrine of future life and
the nonextinction of the soul with the death of the body — was
very likely unable or unwilling to quit at once and altogether the
earthly habitation; very likely it lingered there, earth-bound, for
a while. In his leisure hours Dr. Teesdale was a considerable
student of the occult, for like most advanced and proficient
physicians, he clearly recognized how narrow was the boundary
of separation between soul and body, how tremendous the influence of the intangible was over material things; and it presented
no difficulty to his mind that a disembodied spirit should be able
to communicate directly with those who still were bounded by
the finite and material.

His meditations, which were beginning to group themselves into definite sequence, were interrupted at this moment. On his desk near at hand stood his telephone, and the bell rang, not with its usual metallic insistence, but very faintly, as if the current were weak or the mechanism impaired. However, it certainly was ringing, and he got up and took the combined ear and mouthpiece off its hook.

"Yes, yes," he said, "who is it?"

There was a whisper, in reply, almost inaudible and quite unintelligible.

"I can't hear you," he said.

Again the whisper sounded, but with no greater distinctness. Then it ceased altogether.

He stood there, for some half minute or so, waiting for it to be renewed, but beyond the usual chuckling and croaking, which showed, however, that he was in communication with some other instrument, there was silence. Then he replaced the receiver, rang up the exchange, and gave his number.

"Can you tell me what number rang me up just now?" he asked.

There was a short pause; then it was given him. It was the number of the prison, where he was doctor.

"Put me on to it, please," he said.

This was done.

"You rang me up just now," he said down the tube. "Yes, I am Dr. Teesdale. What is it? I could not hear what you said."

The voice came back quite clear and intelligible.

"Some mistake, sir," it said. "We haven't rang you up."

"But the exchange tells me you did, three minutes ago."

"Mistake at the exchange, sir," said the voice.

"Very odd. Well, good night. Warder Draycott, isn't it?"

"Yes, sir; good night, sir."

Dr. Teesdale went back to his big armchair, still less inclined to read. He let his thoughts wander on for a while, without giving them definite direction, but ever and again his mind kept coming back to that strange little incident of the telephone. Often and often he had been rung up by some mistake, often and often he had been put on to the wrong number by the exchange, but there was something in this very subdued ringing of the telephone bell and the unintelligible whisperings at the other end that suggested a very curious train of reflection to his mind, and soon he found himself pacing up and down his room, with his thoughts eagerly feeding on a most unusual pasture.

"But it's impossible," he said aloud.

He went down as usual to the prison next morning and once again he was strangely beset with the feeling that there was some unseen presence there. He had before now had some odd psychical experiences and knew that he was a "sensitive" — one, that is, who is capable, under certain circumstances, of receiving supernormal impressions and of having glimpses of the unseen world that lies about us. And this morning the presence of which he was conscious was that of the man who had been executed yesterday morning. It was local, and he felt it most strongly in the little prison yard and as he passed the door of the condemned cell. So strong was it there that he would not have been surprised if the figure of the man had been visible to him, and as he passed through the door at the end of the passage, he turned round, actually expecting to see it. All the time, too, he was aware of a profound horror at his heart; this unseen presence strangely disturbed him. And the poor soul, he felt, wanted something done for it. Not for a moment did he doubt that this impression of his was objective; it was no imaginative phantom of his own invention that made itself so real. The spirit of Linkworth was there.

He passed into the infirmary, and for a couple of hours busied himself with his work. But all the time he was aware that the same invisible presence was near him, though its force was manifestly less here than in those places which had been more intimately associated with the man. Finally, before he left, in order to test his theory he looked into the execution shed. But next moment, with a face suddenly stricken pale, he came out again, closing the door hastily. At the top of the steps stood a figure hooded and pinioned, but hazy of outline and only faintly visible. But it was visible; there was no mistake about it.

Dr. Teesdale was a man of good nerve, and he recovered himself almost immediately, ashamed of his temporary panic. The terror that had blanched his face was chiefly the effect of startled nerves, not of terrified heart; and yet deeply interested as he was in psychical phenomena, he could not command himself sufficiently to go back there. Or rather he commanded himself, but his muscles refused to act on the message. If this poor earth-bound spirit had any communication to make to him, he certainly much preferred that it should be made at a distance. As far as he could understand, its range was circumscribed. It haunted the prison yard, the condemned cell, the execution shed; it was more faintly felt in the infirmary. Then a further point suggested itself to his mind, and he went back to his room and sent for Warder Draycott, who had answered him on the telephone last night.

"You are quite sure," he asked, "that nobody rang me up last night, just before I rang you up?"

There was a certain hesitation in the man's manner which the doctor noticed.

"I don't see how it could be possible, sir," he said. "I had been sitting close by the telephone for half an hour before, and again before that. I must have seen him, if anyone had been to the instrument."

"And you *saw* no one?" said the doctor with a slight emphasis.

The man became more markedly ill at ease.

"No, sir, I *saw* no one," he said, with the same emphasis.

Dr. Teesdale looked away from him.

"But you had perhaps the impression that there was someone there?" he asked carelessly, as if it was a point of no interest.

· Clearly Warder Draycott had something on his mind, which he found it hard to speak of.

"Well, sir, if you put it like that," he began. "But you would tell me I was half asleep, or had eaten something that disagreed with me at my supper."

The doctor dropped his careless manner.

"I should do nothing of the kind," he said, "any more than you would tell me that I had dropped asleep last night, when I heard my telephone bell ring. Mind you, Draycott, it did not ring as usual. I could only just hear it ringing, though it was close to me. And I could only hear a whisper when I put my ear to it. But when you spoke I heard you quite distinctly. Now I believe there was something — somebody — at this end of the telephone. You were here, and though you saw no one, you, too, felt there was someone there."

The man nodded.

"I'm not a nervous man, sir," he said, "and I don't deal in fancies. But there was something there. It was hovering about the instrument, and it wasn't the wind, because there wasn't a breath of wind stirring and the night was warm. And I shut the window to make certain. But it went about the room, sir, for an hour or more. It rustled the leaves of the telephone book, and it ruffled my hair when it came close to me. And it was bitter cold, sir."

The doctor looked him straight in the face.

"Did it remind you of what had been done yesterday morning?" he asked suddenly.

Again the man hesitated.

"Yes, sir," he said at length. "Convict Charles Linkworth."

Dr. Teesdale nodded reassuringly.

"That's it," he said. "Now, are you on duty tonight?"

"Yes, sir; I wish I wasn't."

"I know how you feel; I have felt exactly the same myself. Now whatever this is, it seems to want to communicate with me. By the way, did you have any disturbance in the prison last night?"

"Yes, sir, there was half a dozen men who had the nightmare. Yelling and screaming they were, and quiet men too, usually. It happens sometimes the night after an execution. I've known it before, though nothing like what it was last night."

"I see. Now, if this — this thing you can't see wants to get at the telephone again tonight, give it every chance. It will probably come about the same time. I can't tell you why, but that usually happens. So unless you must, don't be in this room where the telephone is, just for an hour to give it plenty of time between half-past nine and half-past ten. I will be ready for it at the other end. Supposing I am rung up, I will, when it has finished, ring you up to make sure that I was not being called in — in the usual way."

"And there is nothing to be afraid of, sir?" asked the man.

Dr. Teesdale remembered his own moment of terror this morning, but he spoke quite sincerely.

"I am sure there is nothing to be afraid of," he said reassuringly.

Dr. Teesdale had a dinner engagement that night, which he broke, and was sitting alone in his study by half-past nine. In the present state of human ignorance as to the law which governs the movements of spirits severed from the body, he could not tell the warder why it was that their visits are so often periodic, timed to punctuality according to our scheme of hours; but in scores of tabulated instances of the appearance of revenants, especially if the soul was in sore need of help, as might be the case here, he found that they came at the same hour of day or night. As a rule, too, their power of making themselves seen or heard or felt grew greater for some little while after death, subsequently growing weaker as they became less earth-bound, or often after that ceasing altogether, and he was prepared tonight for a less indistinct impression. The spirit apparently for the early hours of its disembodiment is weak, like a moth newly broken out from its chrysalis — and then suddenly the telephone bell rang, not so faintly as the night before, but still not with its ordinary imperative tone.

Dr. Teesdale instantly got up; put the receiver to his ear. And what he heard was heartbroken sobbing, strong spasms that seemed to tear the weeper.

He waited for a little before speaking, himself cold with some nameless fear, and yet profoundly moved to help, if he was able.

"Yes, yes," he said at length, hearing his own voice tremble. "I am Dr. Teesdale. What can I do for you? And who are you?" he added, though he felt that it was a needless question.

Slowly the sobbing died down; the whispers took its place, still broken by crying.

"I want to tell, sir — I want to tell — I must tell."

"Yes, tell me, what is it?" said the doctor.

"No, not you — another gentleman, who used to come to see me. Will you speak to him what I say to you? — I can't make him hear me or see me."

"Who are you?" asked Dr. Teesdale suddenly.

"Charles Linkworth. I thought you knew. I am very miserable. I can't leave the prison — and it is cold. Will you send for the other gentleman?"

"Do you mean the chaplain?" asked Dr. Teesdale.

"Yes, the chaplain. He read the service when I went across the yard yesterday. I shan't be so miserable when I have told."

The doctor hesitated a moment. This was a strange story that he would have to tell Mr. Dawkins, the prison chaplain, that at the other end of the telephone was the spirit of the man executed yesterday. And yet he soberly believed that it was so; that this unhappy spirit was in misery and wanted to "tell." There was no need to ask what he wanted to tell.

"Yes, I will ask him to come here," he said at length.

"Thank you, sir, a thousand times. You will make him come, won't you?"

The voice was growing fainter.

"It must be tomorrow night," it said. "I can't speak longer now. I have to go to see — oh, my God, my God."

The sobs broke out afresh, sounding fainter and fainter. But it was in a frenzy of terrified interest that Dr. Teesdale spoke.

"To see what?" he cried. "Tell me what you are doing, what is happening to you?"

"I can't tell you; I mayn't tell you," said the voice, very faint. "That is part . . ." and it died away altogether.

Dr. Teesdale waited a little, but there was no further sound of any kind, except the chuckling and croaking of the instrument. He put the receiver onto its hook again, and then became aware for the first time that his forehead was streaming with some cold dew of horror. His ears sang; his heart beat very quick and faint; and he sat down to recover himself. Once or twice he asked himself if it was possible that some terrible joke was being played on him, but he knew that could not be so; he felt perfectly sure that he had been speaking with a soul in torment of contrition for the terrible and irremediable act it had committed. It was no delusion of his senses, either; here in this comfortable room of his in Bedford Square, with London cheerfully roaring round him, he had spoken with the spirit of Charles Linkworth.

But he had no time (nor indeed inclination, for somehow his soul sat shuddering within him) to indulge in meditation. First of all he rang up the prison.

"Warder Draycott?" he asked.

There was a perceptible tremor in the man's voice as he answered.

"Yes, sir. Is it Dr. Teesdale?"

"Yes. Has anything happened here with you?"

Twice it seemed that the man tried to speak and could not. At the third attempt the words came.

"Yes, sir. He has been here. I saw him go into the room where the telephone is."

"Ah! Did you speak to him?"

"No, sir. I sweated and prayed. And there's half a dozen men as have been screaming in their sleep tonight. But it's quiet again now. I think he has gone into the execution shed."

"Yes. Well, I think there will be no more disturbance now. By the way, please give me Mr. Dawkins's home address."

This was given him, and Dr. Teesdale proceeded to write to the chaplain, asking him to dine with him on the following night. But suddenly he found that he could not write at his accustomed desk, with the telephone standing close to him, and he went upstairs to the drawing room, which he seldom used except when he entertained his friends. There he recaptured the serenity of his nerves and could control his hand. The note simply asked Mr. Dawkins to dine with him next night, when he wished to tell him a very strange history and ask his help. "Even if you have any other engagement," he concluded, "I seriously request you to give it up. Tonight, I did the same. I should bitterly have regretted it if I had not."

Next night, accordingly, the two sat at their dinner in the doctor's dining room, and when they were left to their cigarettes and coffee the doctor spoke.

"You must not think me mad, my dear Dawkins," he said, "when you hear what I have got to tell you."

Mr. Dawkins laughed.

"I will certainly promise not to do that," he said.

"Good. Last night and the night before, a little later in the evening than this, I spoke through the telephone with the spirit of the man we saw executed two days ago — Charles Linkworth.''

The chaplain did not laugh. He pushed back his chair, looking annoyed.

"Teesdale," he said, "is it to tell me this — I don't want to be rude — but this bogy-tale that you have brought me here this evening?"

"Yes. You have not heard half of it. He asked me last night to get hold of you. He wants to tell you something. We can guess, I think, what it is.''

Dawkins got up.

"Please let me hear no more of it," he said. "The dead do not return. In what state or under what condition they exist has not been revealed to us. But they have done with all material things.''

"But I must tell you more," said the doctor. "Two nights ago I was rung up, but very faintly, and could hear only whispers. I instantly inquired where the call came from and was told it came from the prison. I rang up the prison, and Warder Draycott told me that nobody had rung me up. He, too, was conscious of a presence.''

"I think that man drinks," said Dawkins sharply.

The doctor paused a moment.

"My dear fellow, you should not say that sort of thing," he said. "He is one of the steadiest men we have got. And if he drinks, why not I also?''

The chaplain sat down again.

"You must forgive me," he said, "but I can't go into this. These are dangerous matters to meddle with. Besides, how do you know it is not a hoax?''

"Played by whom?" asked the doctor. "Hark!''

The telephone bell suddenly rang. It was clearly audible to the doctor.

"Don't you hear it?" he said.

"Hear what?''

"The telephone bell ringing.''

"I hear no bell," said the chaplain, rather angrily. "There is no bell ringing.''

The doctor did not answer, but went through into his study, and turned on the lights. Then he took the receiver and mouthpiece off its hook.

"Yes?" he said, in a voice that trembled. "Who is it? Yes, Mr. Dawkins is here. I will try to get him to speak to you."

He went back into the other room.

"Dawkins," he said, "there is a soul in agony. I pray you to listen. For God's sake come and listen."

The chaplain hesitated a moment.

"As you will," he said.

He took up the receiver and put it to his ear.

"I am Mr. Dawkins," he said.

He waited.

"I can hear nothing whatever," he said at length. "Ah, there was something there. The faintest whisper."

"Ah, try to hear, try to hear!" said the doctor.

Again the chaplain listened. Suddenly he laid the instrument down, frowning.

"Something — somebody said, 'I killed her, I confess it. I want to be forgiven.' It's a hoax, my dear Teesdale. Somebody knowing your spiritualistic leanings is playing a very grim joke on you. I *can't* believe it."

Dr. Teesdale took up the receiver.

"I am Dr. Teesdale," he said. "Can you give Mr. Dawkins some sign that it is you?"

Then he laid it down again.

"He says he thinks he can," he said. "We must wait."

The evening was again very warm, and the window into the paved yard at the back of the house was open. For five minutes or so the two men stood in silence, waiting, and nothing happened. Then the chaplain spoke.

"I think that is sufficiently conclusive," he said.

Even as he spoke a very cold draft of air suddenly blew into the room, making the papers on the desk rustle. Dr. Teesdale went to the window and closed it.

"Did you feel that?" he asked.

"Yes, a breath of air. Chilly."

Once again in the closed room it stirred again.

"And did you feel that?" asked the doctor.

The chaplain nodded. He felt his heart hammering in his throat suddenly.

"Defend us from all peril and danger of this coming night," he exclaimed.

"Something is coming!" said the doctor.

As he spoke it came. In the center of the room not three yards away from them stood the figure of a man with his head bent over onto his shoulder, so that the face was not visible. Then he took his head in both his hands and raised it like a weight, and looked them in the face. The eyes and tongue protruded; a livid mark was round the neck. Then there came a sharp rattle on the boards of the floor, and the figure was no longer there. But on the floor there lay a new rope.

For a long while neither spoke. The sweat poured off the doctor's face, and the chaplain's white lips whispered prayers. Then by a huge effort the doctor pulled himself together. He pointed at the rope.

"It has been missing since the execution," he said.

Then again the telephone bell rang. This time the chaplain needed no prompting. He went to it at once and the ringing ceased. For a while he listened in silence.

"Charles Linkworth," he said at length, "in the sight of God, in whose presence you stand, are you truly sorry for your sin?"

Some answer inaudible to the doctor came, and the chaplain closed his eyes. And Dr. Teesdale knelt as he heard the words of the Absolution.

At the close there was silence again.

"I can hear nothing more," said the chaplain, replacing the receiver.

Presently the doctor's manservant came in with the tray of spirits and siphon. Dr. Teesdale pointed without looking to where the apparition had been.

"Take the rope that is there and burn it, Parker," he said.

There was a moment's silence.

"There is no rope, sir," said Parker.

NONFICTION

THE BROADWAY CENTRAL TRAGEDY

by Alfred Henry Lewis

An 1872 murder on the Ladies' Staircase tangled the lives
of big money manipulators and such people as Jay Gould,
Boss Tweed, and August Belmont.

IN THAT DAY they called it the Grand Central Hotel, but, since
questions of grandeur are ever questions of comparison, when in
the flow of years other hostelries grew up to overwhelm it with
their arrogant splendors, the brush of description was shifted
and the name changed to Broadway Central. So it is known today. The bloody field of events was the Ladies' Staircase. Also,
as exhibiting upon what casual, not to say trivial, hinges our
doors to life or death swing inward, had it not been for a
chance-blown nod and smile, tossed to him across the street by
the woman — whom he didn't know and had never seen — in
Room 207, Stokes wouldn't have entered the place at all.

The killing occurred January 6, 1872, while Kelso was chief of
police. Fisk was thirty-seven years old when he died, and, had
Stokes missed him and he lived until now, in the matter of years
and probably of fortune, he would have belonged to that group of
eminent gold-heapers made up of Rockefeller, Morgan, Car-
negie, and Hetty Green.

You have heard of men whose end was logical if not legitimate, and who died as they had lived. Fisk — whose death was
mean enough — at least was buried as he had lived, and in the
crude glories of his funeral you might have read his story. The

Ninth Regiment had taken gloomy charge. Twenty-five — the fighting age — when Sumter was fired on, Fisk's military ardor during the Rebellion had aroused itself no further than was necessary to take, at a fat figure, a contract to furnish blankets for the Union troops. The war over, however, his tardy valor awoke, and he became colonel of the Ninth. Now that he was dead, his regiment came forward and, wrapping him in its shot-torn battle flag, bore him to his grave.

Some souls, given to cynicism, might have found in the business certain elements of irony. Not so the fighting Ninth; the men who had bled in forty battles shed tears of grief as, with bowed heads, they followed to his last resting place a leader who had gone no nearer actual strife than Washington and the safe corridors of Willard's.

While two hundred police held back the mob, the coffin — rosewood, satin, and gold — was borne from the Fisk home, 313 West Twenty-third Street, to the Grand Opera House, only two doors away. The Erie Railroad had its official habitat on the upper floors of the building, and the coffin, after journeying up the Grand Staircase, was set in pompous state upon a catafalque prepared for it in the Erie Company's vestibule.

The dead man was dressed in his colonel's uniform, a priceless sword — unstained of blood — by his side. Everywhere were wreaths and crosses and crowns and anchors of hope, done in camellias, tuberoses, pale lilies, and immortelles. For Jay Gould had decreed that the Erie pay all; and, thus encouraged, the florists' bills clambered and mounted until the overflowing total would have fed for a fortnight the poor of all New York.

Aside from the wilderness of flowers, fortunes had been spilled out in more somber decorations. There were princely black ostrich plumes, rich black velvet draperies, richer draperies of white and black tulle, while from the wall, banked in by cut velvet, the face of the dead man — done by a world's most famous artist — looked down in painted approval of what was being so magnificently done in his honor.

Twelve o'clock — what the society reporters writing of a wedding call, no one knows why, high noon! The Erie doors are thrown open, and the sympathetic rabble pour in. At the dead man's head stand Lieutenant Montgomery and Sergeant Aspenwall; at the feet is Captain Fuller. For two hours, in single file, the mob drifts by. And, because humanity in the herd is shallow and easily stirred, a cataract of tears is shed like a deluge; and all as though a hero lies dead, and the age has been dealt a blow. Captain Flagg reads the burial service, and reads it very well. Then the march to the station begins; for the dead man is going home to those peaceful Vermont valleys which sent him forth.

While these matters were pressing forward, a busy little personage in black went tiptoeing in and out, whispering here a word, rearranging there a fold of the velvet pall, and trying throughout to look modestly mournful, but failing in favor of a smug pride which puffed and distended his bosom. This proudly modest yet self-conscious one was Undertaker Merritt; and a happy man — though in all humility — did he show himself that day. For the Fisk funeral was a creation, his creation, and in the grief-dimmed glances of the mourners Undertaker Merritt read the admiration which endorsed his work.

The slow march to the railway station was a model of outdoor sorrow. There were dirge-breathing brass bands. There were platoons of police opening a path through the mob, while other police platoons closed up the rear and checked the on-following throng. There were military companies, German singing societies, Tammany clubs. Such known if not uniformly honored spirits as Jay Gould, Boss Tweed, District Attorney Fellows, August Belmont, Peter B. Sweeny, Judge Shearman, John Hilton, Slippery Dick Connolly, David Dudley Field, and Judge Fullerton rode in the carriages. There were the officers of the Narragansett Steamship Company in uniform, and a round ununiformed one thousand of the employees of the Erie Railroad, and Fisk's horse — boots reversed and a wreath of woe-stricken tuberoses about its restless neck. There were twelve platoons of noncommissioned officers, and General Varien and staff — all of the National Guard; while by the coffin's side, with bared heads, walked as pallbearers General Funk, Colonel Sterry, Colonel Allen, Colonel Scott, Colonel Clark, and Lieutenant Colonel Webster. Good judges, learned in the art of street grief, declared the processional part of the mournful superior to anything of the drum-muffled sort ever witnessed in the avenues of New York.

The little hamlet of Pownal, greenly buried among the Vermont hills, claims the cradle honors of Fisk's birth. His father was a Yankee peddler. While still in his early teens, Fisk united himself with Van Amburg's circus and wild beast show, in the quality of a canvasman. He worked for the great lion-tamer seven years, and learned to drive tent pegs, pull guy ropes, sleep in straw, eat off tin dishes, and — as assistant ticket-seller — shortchange the crossroad rubes who came to see the show.

Ending with Van Amburg, Fisk became a peddler like his father before him. He made money as readily as some folk make trouble, and — a leftover impression of the circus — his prosperity instantly expressed itself in a dazzling peddler's wagon, drawn by four prancing horses wearing gold-mounted harnesses of stamped leather and frothily mouthing golden bits.

Fisk flashed through New England from Eastport in Maine to Stamford in Connecticut, a dry-goods–peddling comet, until he attracted the Boston attention of Jordan, Marsh & Co. The firm saw reasons for buying Fisk out; and so it took over his flashing wagon, his four frothing, bit-champing horses — with their gold-mounted harness — his trade, and his experience, paying therefor a full-stomached figure. Also it wrote him down on its books as chief salesman, at a salary which matched his meteoric merits. When, at the breaking out of civil war, he went to Washington and wined and dined Jordan, Marsh & Co. into divers rich blanket contracts, the firm, swept off its grateful feet by this display of genius, opened its arms to him as a partner.

As the junior member of Jordan, Marsh & Co., Fisk expanded and continued to expand until there dawned a day when the admiration of Jordan, Marsh & Co. gave place to fear. Thus, one prudent Saturday night his seniors invited Fisk into the back office and gave him $250,000 to quit and kiss the firm good-bye. Fisk was nothing loath. Those seven years with Van Amburg had marked him; the bandwagon had entered his soul. Dry goods too much confined him. The trade offered nothing in the way of tanbark, tights, and spangles. It was vacant of the snarl of the snare drum, void of the smell of the coal-oil lamp. For all of these, his circus-loving soul felt starved. Fisk in truth had grown to detest dry goods as much as ever dry goods had grown to fear him. Wherefore, when Jordan, Marsh & Co. — hands full of money, heart full of alarm — spoke of $250,000 for his "interest," he never waited for the second word. He took the money.

Fisk's few scant winters in the Vermont country schools had not stamped him overdeep with learning. He had read but few books, and the Bible was not among them. Therefore he had never heard of what woe attends upon those who call evil good and good evil, and his morals of commerce were as the morals of a gambler. With the $250,000 which Jordan, Marsh & Co. had paid to be rid of him, he burst upon Boston as a speculator; and all with a purpose of separating the puritans from their money by methods so coarsely callous as to be applauded only among professional cardsharps.

Fisk's Boston offices were at the corner of Summer and Chauncy streets. At once the staid puritans came seeking him; and such were their innocence and numbers that, within the first six months, they gambled him into bankruptcy and stripped him as bare as a coot. The puritans took Fisk's $250,000 off him so fast that — as he himself said later — he caught cold. For his share he gathered such a holy horror of them, and the almost religious fervor wherewith they skinned him, that he fled. Boston was no right field for him, he saw that himself; and thereupon — with his bankruptcy — he headed for New York.

Fisk found New York much easier than Boston. As a gambler, the New Yorker has ever been the soft and pulpy inferior of the Yankee. Fisk opened a brokerage game in Wall Street, upon a capital made up of his Boston experiences and an exhaustless mouthful of promises. When he talked of money, Fisk was not wanting in a kind of eloquence which sounded like the convincing clink of gold itself. In discussing any enterprise, he was as promissory as a rainbow, and the New Yorkers, then as now with a money appetite in advance of their money caution, were not backward in believing him.

The first big fish of gold to come Fisk's way was old Daniel Drew. Drew let Fisk sell his Bristol line of steamers; and Fisk, who knew how to lick his fingers as a good cook should, sold those vessels so wisely and so well that he established the firm of

Fisk, Belden & Co. on the strength of it, and wound up the year with $1 million in the bank.

Fisk, when he met Drew, was thirty-two years old — an age fortunate in that it has more hopes than memories — an age which, distinguished by energy and ambition, is prone to take opportunity by the beard and demand victory as a right. Drew was up to his financial ears in Erie. Having sold Drew's Bristol line of steamboats, Fisk, not waiting for any Drew invitation, decided to sell Drew himself out of Erie.

Fisk hooked up with Jay Gould, as young, as unscrupulous, as money-hungry as himself. Gould was already in Erie. Gould and Fisk pooled their hopes and their energies. When the two got through with Drew, they were in possession of Erie, and Drew was out. Cast thus into outer Erie darkness, Drew went about — like the wizards that peep and mutter — warning mankind against both Fisk and Gould, saying, "Beware of them two; their tech is death!"

Fisk and Gould, as the unchallenged masters of Erie, watered the stock from $19 million, to $34 million, and pocketed the water. They then rewatered it from $34 million to $57 million, and pocketed the water. Because a legislature must be bought, and inasmuch as buying a legislature includes the thought of district attorneys and juries and judges and jails, Fisk and Gould brought Tweed and Sweeny and Connolly and other high priests of politics into Erie. These latter Lords of Misrule owned the district attorneys and juries and judges and jails. They owned the New York City delegation in the Albany legislature. Fisk and Gould could attend to the stock-watering; Tweed and Sweeny and Connolly — dominant in New York politics — would hold the law at bay and keep Fisk and Gould from punitive bolts and bars.

By judiciously commingling politics with speculation, Fisk and Gould made one hand wash the other to such a jealous profit that each could write himself multimillionaire before another year was out. It took, to be sure, a deal of ruthless work. Some men they sent to Sing Sing; others they disgraced. Through their linking up with Tweed and his Tammany ring, Fisk and Gould not alone controlled for life or death the law and its machinery,

but greatly the public press. The last had become but the abject
dog of the Tweed Ring, to meanly fetch and carry.

As showing what he could do in the line of destroying character and sending guiltless men to prison, Fisk, as incident to his
Erie operations, caused the arrest of Eldridge, the Erie president, upon a charge of having embezzled $5 million of the Erie
Company's money, with which to bribe through the bill that authorized Fisk and Gould to water the Erie stock. It was Fisk, not
Eldridge, who had thus fraudulently employed that Erie $5 mil-
lion. But Eldridge, facing a felon's fate, knowing how powerless
was mere innocence in a Fisk-controlled day of Tweed, realized
his helplessness and bought his safety by resigning the Erie pres-
idency to Gould. This was what Fisk had been fighting for, and
Eldridge, having thus surrendered, was allowed to depart in
peace.

Dorman B. Eaton, more stubborn than Eldridge, was not so
fortunate. Eaton, representing a circle of shareholders, began a
prosecution of Fisk which threatened to expose his Erie operations. Fisk coaxed, flattered, threatened, offered a million of
money. All in vain; Eaton refused to be put aside. Perjurers as-
sailed the Eaton reputation; Eaton still stood firm. All else failing, Eaton was sandbagged on the midnight steps of his own
home; and, inasmuch as the result of such salutary sandbagging
was to render him helpless and half-unconscious for the space of
six months, he continued no longer a thorn in the Fisk-Gould-
Erie-Tweed-Sweeny-Connolly-Tammany flesh.

Men of today, who read of the raw work done in Erie those
forty-five years ago, wonder, in the phrase of Cherry Hill, how
Fisk "got away with it." For one matter, the country, rocking
and reeling on the groundswells of civil war, was greatly busy
with reconstruction and the task of saving itself. The popular
preoccupation worked vastly, and it might have been conclusively,
in black favor of Fisk. Had not the public's hands been quite so full
of its own affairs, our Prince of Erie might not have fared so well.
As things stood, however, he could laugh at walls of stone and iron
grates, and snap thumb and finger beneath the defeated nose of
justice. Fisk was no bad judge of chances, and he knew himself to
be much more safe than were much more honest men.

Fisk, with that show-ring hankering left over from the old Van Amburg days, coveted the Pike Opera House at the corner of Twenty-third Street and Eighth Avenue. He pressed the button of the Fisk-Gould dictatorship of Erie, and Erie bought the opera house with $820,000 in good gold coin of the realm. Then Fisk bought the opera house from Erie, paying with Erie's own watered stock. Later he rented as offices the upper floors of the opera house to Erie; and all at a figure which would have caused the modern New York landlord to bat his envious eyes.

Antony had his Cleopatra, and was our Antony of Erie to miss an equal fate? The Mansfield, a golden daughter of California, was tall, ripe, dark, graceful, with velvety eyes as soft and big and deep as the eyes of a stag. Molded like a goddess, her beauty was the beauty of a Venus. She had wit, sentiment, soul-quickness, and knew how to be feminine and daintily fine. She had a heart, too, and could have loved a man to the panting, bitter, blighting scaffold last of it, had she had but the luck to have met a man worth loving.

But she never did.

As a schoolgirl in California the Mansfield ran away with actor Lawler. She was careful to marry Lawler. Later she proved not quite so particular. Lawler was a poor actor, a worse husband, and the Mansfield fell upon bad days. She asked for a divorce and got it; and when Fisk first saw her — it was the day of the divorce — with beauty for her capital and but one dress to her lovely back, she was living on crusts and water in East Thirty-fourth Street at the rooms of an actress chum.

Fisk was of those whose god is their belly and whose glory is in their shame. In all things sensual, he was unmoral rather than immoral. He established the Mansfield at 359 West Twenty-third Street. The little house was mirrored and curtained and draped and rugged and frescoed and floored and furnished like unto a queen's palace; and, since his own home was but twenty doors away, and the Erie offices in the opera house a few doors farther on, he regarded existence as most comfortably arranged.

The Mansfield, cold and cool and wise and calculating, as a woman must be who has only her beauty to bank on, accepted Fisk for what he was and what he promised. She had ceased to be sensitive while yet Mrs. Lawler, and the rough touch of poverty had thickened her skin. She had become, too, a philosopher in petticoats; and, living in a day when Woodhull was preaching free love and the Reverend Beecher was trotting across the white-hot plowshares of the Tilton litigations, she saw much in the lives of others to keep her in decorous countenance. And so, with a dainty brazenness, which, while it confessed nothing, concealed nothing, she flung her little perfumed glove in the face of social order, and set up a circle of her own in West Twenty-third.

Fisk had nothing silken in his nature; his fiber was as coarse as horsehair. His great trait was vanity, and he would do anything, be anything, pay anything, for admiration. Of flattery, no matter how gross, he could not have too much. Whatsoever its source or its occasion, he gulped it down like wine. Much that Fisk did which was good — his liberalities, his so-called benevolences — had nothing better or nobler to support them than just his shoreless vanity.

It was vanity which prompted him to seek the colonelcy of the Ninth. Assuredly it was not his war spirit. When it came to actual carnage, he would — to steal from Falstaff — as soon have heard the devil as a drum. During the Orange riots — the only serious military service seen by Fisk — he was off his horse and lost to view at the crack of the first rifle. Two days later history laughingly laid hands on him somewhere in the wilds of New Jersey, being the first officially seen or heard of him since he went scrambling out of the saddle at Twenty-fifth Street and Eighth Avenue.

Once rid of his horse, upon that Battle of the Boyne occasion, Fisk fled through a ginmill, and — fat and girthy as he was, trussed up in his close-fitting uniform like any fowl for roasting — climbed a most difficult back fence. Over boxes and barrels, through friendly back doors, he made his breathless way to the Mansfield's little palace. There he shifted hastily from identifying epaulettes and gold braid into sober business clothes. Already he had sent word to the steamer *Long Branch* to meet him at the North River foot of Twenty-fourth Street. Thus, in the skulking language of the underworld, he made his getaway.

The Ninth, Sixth, and Eighty-fourth regiments had — men, women, and children — mowed down one hundred and twenty-eight people. The alarmed imagination of Fisk clapped a round one thousand to this, while his unflagging egotism taught him that the mob would think he himself had been guilty of it all. As he changed shiveringly from the blue-gold splendors of his uniform into the more quail-like colors of a gray-brown tweed, he was sure that an excited, not to say exasperated, public would not only sack his home at 313 West Twenty-third, but the Mansfield's house as well. He offered to take the Mansfield with him into New Jersey hiding; but her nerves were steadier than his, and she declined. She had a fortune in jewels and pictures and artistic whatnot to look after, and she decided to remain and look after it. So Fisk left her to take her chances. It was all, however, but an instance of vanity and exaggerated ego headed the wrong way. The mob never once thought of Fisk, never once of his family or the Mansfield.

Fisk's vanity, whether for good or ill, was always his North Star. It was his vanity which prompted him in his possession of the Mansfield. He never loved her. By the same hard, untender token, she never loved him. Why should she have so wasted herself? Those bleak, unfriendly years with actor Lawler had brought with them their lesson. They had taught her the barren futilities of sentiment without dollars. Wherefore, although finer, the Mansfield in a cut-glass way was quite as dour as Fisk, and while he pampered his vanity she kept her coldly observant eye on Number One.

Nothing if not a Lucullus, none knew better than Fisk how to dine. The Mansfield gave dinners at her little Twenty-third Street palace, and sat — the only woman — at the head of the table. To these Mansfield dinners came eminent ones in letters, finance, politics. And every man must mind his manners. For the Mansfield's position was peculiar, and in protecting it she narrowed conversation to the rigidly decorous. Many a jest, many a story, which would have passed at respectable tables, elected what careless humorist or raconteur had been guilty thereof to the Mansfield's blacklist. He had received his last invitation to dine in Twenty-third Street, Number 359; the Mansfield could not and would not abide the Elizabethan.

Fisk was always at the Mansfield dinners, which with a last word were Fisk dinners. There, too, came Gould and Tweed and what others were of the Erie-Tammany inner circle. It was over twelve-dollar wines and through the smoke of Emperor Napoleon cigars that these kings of politics and stock-jobbery laid out their campaigns. The bedplates of Black Friday and the Fisk-Gould gold corner — broken finally by President Grant — were laid at the Mansfield's in the midst of afterdinner laughter.

As wise as beautiful, the Mansfield garnered her golden harvests with the others. She, too, had brokers; she, too, sold on a down and bought on an up market, and became bear or bull with her powerful guests. For while it was her day of splendor, a day when her beauty bought a diamond necklace with a kiss, she had her side of independence, and liked best that gold which no man gave her. Thus she possessed final millions; and when Fisk was in the grave, and Stokes was in the Tombs and a subsequent Sing Sing, the Mansfield — lovely, languid, milk-fed — withdrew to Paris and to silken ease.

There was something to be admired about the Mansfield. She understood the game — hard, sordid, hopeless of aught that was sentimentally fine — into which her poverty and the accidents of life had thrust her. And she played the game to win. She had sold herself for money, and she made sure she got the money. If she felt regret, she never showed her feeling. If her soul hungered for aught better, no heart-sob made that hunger manifest. She neither demanded nor avoided attention. Whether she rode in the park or sat in her box at the opera, quiet, poised, beautiful after the manner of some self-centered rose, her expression carried nothing of defiance, nothing of apology. She invited no sympathy, proffered no scorn. She took the bitter with the sweet, making no wry faces; and if when she seized the flower she felt the thorn she did not cry out.

Fisk understood, while unable to appreciate, the Mansfield's superiority. While he didn't love her, he was proud of her — much as some toad might have been proud of the jewel in its head. It was Fisk's pride in the Mansfield which taught him to bring his friends about her. He liked to exhibit her; liked to show her off. More splendid in her loveliness than the golden glories wherein she sat framed, he regarded her as he might a monument which he had upreared to his own magnificence. Her owner, not her lover, it pleased his vanity more to be known as the proprietor of the Mansfield than as the Prince of Erie.

Fisk brought Stokes to the Mansfield's.

Stokes was the antithesis of Fisk. High, thoroughbred, Stokes was in every line of his nature the patrician. He knew all that schools and colleges could teach. Aside from books, he owned an outdoor side and boxed and fenced, and as much as any Comanche was at home in the saddle. Just as Fisk grew tubbily gross and girthy, so Stokes remained slim and clean and trained. Stokes's eyes were large and full of a brown fire. Alert, straightforward, the soul of courage, the feeling he furnished was a feeling of force. Commercially keen, he was what is called a good businessman. But he took his temper into his business. And, because his gun went with his temper, to rob or cheat him possessed a discouraging side.

Stokes's mother was a Pennsylvania Stiles — a fashion of Keystone Vere de Vere. His Grandfather Stokes, a man of position at home, came here from England in 1793, bringing Grandmother Stokes along. Grandfather Stokes possessed more aristocratical blood than money; for somehow he had stubbed his business toe in England, which was what sent him sailing to the West. He had some money, however, for he took his first step toward becoming an American by buying a farm overlooking the Hudson.

By the curious way, Sing Sing prison stands upon ground which was aforetime a meadow lot of Grandfather Stokes's farm. The stones, too, with which the prison walls were reared came from the old Stokes quarry; and Stokes — capable of the sardonic — must have been visited more than once during his Sing Sing years, by lip-curling reflections on how Grandfather Stokes had sold the state the very granite which held him captive, and, without foreseeing, reaped a blind profit on his own posterity.

Stokes was six years younger than Fisk. He came to New York from Philadelphia in 1860, and broke into business by way of the Produce Exchange. He wasn't long in making a record as a cavalryman of speculation, and, since he won all his battles, soon reared up a budding fortune.

Oil boiled to the western Pennsylvania surface, and Stokes was filled with petroleum dreams. He put up a $250,000 refinery at Hunter's Point, and all in a moment was briskly in the greasy swim. The panic of 1867 laid Stokes on his financial back. Also, before he again could scramble to his feet, his uninsured refinery burned to the ground. This left him as flat as a flounder.

Stokes had credit — that bower anchor of business. His trade genius was as high as his temper; his word as spotless as his courage. Scores of good men knew these things of Stokes, and now, in the hour of his adversity, those scores came forward and offered to set him on his legs again. He borrowed $250,000, rebuilt his burned refinery, and before the year ended he was again in possession of thousands and in close pursuit of more.

Rockefeller over at Oil City conceived the underhand idea of rebates. He made his rebate deals with four railroads, among them the Erie. Fisk, as sharp a huntsman as any Rockefeller of the wild beast called a dollar, beheld and knew at a hungry glance the pocket-bulging beauties of rebates. Through himself and Gould he was in control of the Erie. He, too, would go into oil; and thus — fixing what freight rate for himself he pleased — with oil and rebate working in conjunction, cord up a double profit.

Fisk had heard of both Stokes and his Hunter's Point refinery, but didn't know either. He wired Stokes, summering in Saratoga, to come and see him "on business." Stokes came, and Fisk, carrying him up into the high places of a probable profit, showed him the kingdoms of oil and the rebate glories thereof.

Fisk and Stokes constructed a new oil company. Stokes was given $6000 a year salary, $27,000 a year rent for his refinery, with 30 percent of what profits might be made. Thus, to the extent of oil and rebates, and through a rebate door, was Stokes brought into Erie.

Stokes had his honored place at those celebrated Mansfield dinners, where, with wine and laughter and blue cigar smoke over all, fresh schemes of piracy in stocks and politics were almost nightly shoved from shore.

When Fisk took possession of the Pike Opera House he re-baptized it the "Grand." Madam Monteland was brought over from Paris to sing in *Les Brigands*. Fisk gave her a dinner in the Erie rooms, and all the world was there — including the Mansfield.

Carried away on the tides of his own exuberance, Fisk proposed the health of la Monteland and, although no Cicero, made a speech. He informed la Monteland, among other matters of equal interest if not importance, that whereas in times past she had been wined and dined by Europe's counts of no account and dukes without a dollar, she was now being banqueted by one of the royal family of America — himself, indeed, the Prince of Erie — a prince so golden that he owned the opera house she was to sing in, a prince so powerful that he could change the name of New York to Fiskville whenever moved by the spirit of his own splendors so to do. This was all very impressive to la Monteland.

As for the Mansfield, she showed her appreciation of the prince's eloquence by frigidly leaving the table.

This cold conduct on the part of the Mansfield nearly sobered Fisk. When he called later at 359 Twenty-third Street to explain, she wouldn't let him in. The Mansfield didn't love Fisk; but one needn't be in love in order to be jealous. Fisk didn't love the Mansfield; but one needn't be in love in order to feel the cold scorn of two-edged beauty like any dagger of frost.

Fisk asked Stokes to prevail upon the icy Mansfield to thaw and see things in their proper light. The Stokes ambassadorship was successful; Fisk was restored to Mansfield favor. But he soon fell out again; and when for the second time Stokes sought to bring about a reconciliation, that mediator between hearts (?) didn't find his path so smooth. The Mansfield stood perched upon the high pedestal of her manifest wrongs and stonily refused to come down. After a soft and pleading siege of several days, however, Stokes was again victorious, and led the half-forgiven, wholly repentant Fisk into the Mansfield's presence.

Stokes, to the day of his death, protested that his own relations with the Mansfield were rippleless of romance and carried no warm colors of the heart. He declared and redeclared that nothing softer than dollars was ever talked of between them. The

Mansfield — not without a sneer at herself for being so pridelessly weak as to notice the subject — said the same.

Fisk, for his side, spoke often and fully to the blushing contrary. Since, however, it was only when the Mansfield refused him her smiles, even those who believed most in him felt that the charges were merely a Fisk first line of defense. With Fisk's own wife not twenty doors away, it was difficult even for the impassive Gould to keep his face straight when Fisk began telling how Stokes had deceived him. The most hardened realize the propriety of the chancery aphorism which insists that "he who comes into equity must come with clean hands." Wherefore, from Gould to the Erie office boy and back again, among those to whom he wailingly related how Stokes, pretending Damon to his Pythias, had traitorously stolen from him his Mansfield, Fisk met with no sympathy and but slender belief.

After the second reconciliation, Fisk, talking to Stokes, indulged in much pride-blown bombast. It might have been that then and there he signed his own death warrant. Stokes was as proud as any Lucifer at topmost notch of spirit. His courage, too, was as tall as his pride. Moreover, he carried within his heart that bitter drop which, given right — or wrong — occasion, incites to murder. Stokes, under his delicate manners of a gentleman, was a volcano of resentment. As Fisk sat with Stokes at 359 Twenty-third Street and drank and bragged, all that saved Fisk was Stokes's business entanglements with Erie. Stokes would have killed Fisk then and there had he not been held in check by that killing's dollar inconvenience. Stokes, through oil and rebates, was making $200,000 a year; and Fisk, by tearing up his Erie contracts and voting him out of his own refinery, could have stopped every dollar of the 200,000 on its way to Stokes's hand.

Save for the Mansfield — still a bit gloomy and storm-tossed, and only half-appeased — no one was at 359 Twenty-third Street that night save Stokes and Fisk.

"Ed, my boy," said Fisk, squinting to catch the color of the Burgundy, "it's lucky for you that Josie and I are friends again. Do you know anything of the little surprise party I'd arranged for you?"

"I don't understand."

"State's prison, my boy," purred Fisk, tasting his wine. "It was I who sent Morehead after you to insult you until you assaulted him; you fell nicely into the trap, my boy."

"Still I don't understand," persisted Stokes.

"You're dull, Ed; extremely dull" — here a sip of wine. "I suppose you know I rule here as much as any Robespierre ever ruled in Paris? I rule the courts; I rule the juries. There's an indictment right now against you in the office of the district attorney, which I'll have to send word to kill. The grand jury reported it a true bill two days ago, and you were to have been collared tomorrow. Josie's forgiveness is all that saves you, my boy — all that saves you."

Fisk complacently filled himself another glass, while the battle lanterns began to redly light themselves in Stokes's eyes. With an effort he held on to himself, thinking about bankruptcy. So far as dollars were concerned he was — and knew it — in the hollow of Fisk's hand.

"So you were behind that gutter-bred rogue, Morehead?" Stokes said after a pause. "Well, at least the work wasn't quite as coarse as when you had your Lynch gang blackjack Eaton. At the same time, Jim, make no mistake; for myself, I've no fear of you."

"Not fear me?" bellowed Fisk, as though an insult had been put upon him. "Not fear me? When I have power to drive companies worth millions in terror from the state, don't fancy I'm not powerful enough to put through a job which would land a fellow of your size in Sing Sing."

"I may yet go to Sing Sing because of you," Stokes retorted, his brown eyes glittering, "but it'll not be through you nor any job of yours."

The talk was growing too interesting, and the Mansfield interfered. Stokes walked home to the Worth House at Fifth Avenue and Twenty-fifth Street, while Fisk went soddenly to bed.

This was in brown October 1870.

When Fisk arose next morning he was sore in spirit. The allusion to the Eaton blackjacking had hurt him. The charge that he kept on his payroll a band of assassins in the Lynch gang had hurt him. The ready disbelief of Stokes in his, Fisk's, power to control district attorneys and grand juries and session judges had hurt him. The last, in truth, had fairly set his vanity to a troubled trot.

Most of all, although it dovetailed with his own claims of absolute power, Stokes had made a night-before reference to a $250,000 bribe, paid by Fisk to a United States judge in the Heath-Raphael litigation over certain blocks of Erie stock stolen from English interests, and that reference had peculiarly hurt him. For he had supposed that the bribery wasn't known.

Fisk spoke his mind bitterly to the Mansfield; Stokes should feel the weight of his thumb.

"My touch is cold and clammy to those who cross my path," said Fisk, who must have been reading Mr. Beadle's dime classics.

The Mansfield refused to sympathize. She sided with Stokes and made no secret of it. Also, she forced Fisk — for the Mansfield was not without gifts of analysis and eloquence — to a pointblank view of his own mean treasons.

Fisk liked this least of all, and retorted upon the Mansfield to such exasperating effect that she put him out of the house again. This time she instructed him that not all of the Stokeses to ever come out of Devon would prove persuasive enough to win his reinstatement. The Mansfield in every rose-hued sense was through with Fisk. And so she told him.

Fisk went to the Erie offices, breathing fire and jealous smoke. As comptroller of Erie he canceled the rebate contracts of the Hunter's Point refinery, and threw that oil industry — it was making $750,000 a year — on the rocks of a receivership.

Fisk went further, and charged Stokes with embezzling $50,000 of the company's money, and saw to it that he was arrested therefor late Saturday night, so as to insure his lying unbailed in the Tombs until Monday. Also, Monday's bail — Fisk pushing the lever — was fixed at $50,000.

Stokes gave it and went free.

Stokes was discharged in the matter of the alleged embezzlement, the judge rebelling against the too vulgarly visible hand of Fisk. Stokes began suit against Fisk for false imprisonment, fixing the damages at six figures.

The Mansfield came promptly to the field of battle. Fisk had "borrowed" $40,000 from the Mansfield to invest. Now that she had cast him out, he resolved to cling doughtily to the money. This being against the Mansfield's principles, which set her everywhere and always to claiming her own, she sued him.

Being a wise woman, the Mansfield had insisted, when Fisk got her money, upon getting his signature in return. The $40,000 was evidenced by three notes, one of which — it will do for all — read like this:

Treasurer's Office,
ERIE RAILROAD COMPANY.
Borrowed and received from Miss Josie Mansfield fifteen thousand seven hundred and fifty dollars.

$15,750.   JAMES FISK, JR.

The papers — Fisk was all-powerful with the press, having the Tweed Ring behind him — began to fill up with villain tales concerning Stokes. Stokes, falling back upon the libel laws, began to sue the papers.

The Mansfield received a printed slap.

Fish had been weak-minded enough to write boastful letters to the Mansfield, detailing his footpad exploits in Erie. She brought these vainglorious epistles, full of recorded crime, to Stokes. Stokes embodied them in an affidavit and made ready to publish them.

The letters referred disastrously to Gould, Boss Tweed, and a long black roll call in stocks and politics. There was much hurrying to and fro. Those letters, once out, would start stones to rolling which, in the downhill finale, might batter out the brains of all concerned.

Gould, Tweed, and those others in danger, souls atwitter, fell protestingly upon Fisk in flank. He must placate the Mansfield; settle with Stokes! Those fool letters must never get into print! Fisk, much cowed, paid the Mansfield her $40,000. Also he agreed — $50,000 each year for four years — to give Stokes

$200,000. But he didn't do the latter, being restrained not by his avarice, but his vanity. Stokes, he said, would overcrow him, and to be overcrowed was a thing he couldn't stand. With that there broke forth a fresh crossfire in the papers.

The Tweed interests, still worried over those fool Fisk letters to the Mansfield, again took hold. Stokes was bamboozled into an arbitration, in the course of which the Fisk letters to Mansfield — Stokes's one weapon — got into the hands of Sweeny. Gould and his Tweed clique breathed more freely after that. Those fool Fisk-Mansfield letters were the one written record of Erie iniquities.

The arbitration wagged to a close. The arbitrator — a Tweed individual — waited thirty days, sixty days, and then embarked for Europe. As the ship threw off her ropes he sent his finding ashore. It allowed Stokes $10,000 — which he refused to take. Fullerton and Beach were Stokes's counsel. On the back of that remarkable arbitration, Stokes sued Fisk all over again.

But Sweeny kept the fool Fisk-Mansfield letters.

Stokes, born in 1841, was but twenty-nine years old when his troubles with Fisk began. His own sense of honor was high; his word a bond. Quick in business, socially of the world, he was no less singularly innocent and credulous. The soul of truth himself, he believed every man his friend who shook his hand. Thus he was deceived again and again, and those who should have been most his friends betrayed him most.

If ever money and politics worked in black conjunction to send a man to the gallows, it was in the victim instance of Stokes. That they didn't succeed was among the nine days' wonders of New York. Erie ruled Wall Street, Tweed ruled the town, and, remembering the combination against him, it is difficult to see how a third of a century later Stokes came to die peacefully in his bed at last.

Stokes was tried three times upon that charge of murdering Fisk. From the first, after their wolfish manner to this day, the papers went clamoring for his blood — the papers, which have sent more men to chair and gibbet than has any other New York influence!

In the face of Erie, Tammany, and a hostile press, the first trial resulted in a "hung jury." Whereat Erie, Tammany, and the papers gnashed their disappointed teeth.

The second jury — Judge Boardman presiding — found Stokes guilty of murder in the first degree. He was eagerly sentenced to be hanged.

Stokes's courage never wavered. Pointing an accusatory finger at the corrupt twelve, he said:

"This verdict is not in accordance with the facts; it is in accordance with the money of Jay Gould!"

Even his foes were compelled to confess Stokes's unshaken courage. From the moment of Fisk's death he was torn at by treasons. Judge Fullerton and Judge Beach, up to that moment his own attorneys, announced themselves retained to assist the public prosecutor in putting the rope about his neck. This abandonment by "eminent" counsel struck no color from Stokes's face. He simply called to the elbow of his defense John Graham, Elbridge T. Gerry, William O. Bartlett, and John McKeon, and said no more about it.

To the atrocious tales flying on the front page of every paper, Stokes was eager to reply. He wanted to tell his story. His counsel said "No!" — all save McKeon. One day, spurred to resentment by a story more than commonly vile, he gave out an interview. With that Graham, Gerry, and Bartlett withdrew, and washed their hands of his affairs; only McKeon remained. Stokes refused to be cast down, and retained in their stead John D. Townsend, Henry Day, Lyman Tremain, and John R. Dos Passos.

Fisk dead, Stokes locked up, the Mansfield had crossed over to Paris. Stokes might have secured her testimony by deposition, but shook his head.

His counsel insisted.

"She could come if she cared to," said Stokes. "For myself, I'll hang before I'll accept safety at the price of any woman's tears and blushes."

The Mansfield never testified.

Stokes, capable of imagination, strung like a bow, feeling himself guiltless, must have suffered much. Little marvel that those

Tombs' months turned white his hair! Stokes being sentenced to hang, Boardman, judge, refused a new trial. Davis, judge, overruled Boardman, to be himself overruled in what is now the Appellate Division by his colleagues, Brady and Fancher. It was the final court which accepted the Judge Davis view, and set aside Stokes's arranged-for execution.

The Tweed Ring fell, and with it went crashing many a sinister figure. Tweed's overthrow meant everything to Stokes. The shallow tides of New York opinion, after the Tweed downfall, began setting in Stokes's favor. Also, when that third jury was sworn, no more were seen across the trial table the inimical figures of Beach and Fullerton — once Stokes's counsel but committed throughout those earlier trials, by Tammany influence and Erie power, to his destruction.

Another ray of sunshine: Davis, judge, would be this time on the bench — Davis, who had granted the stay when Stokes, hope all but gone, was within less than a week of black cap, rope, and drop. Altogether, when that third trial was called the skies had vastly cleared for Stokes.

The only evidence upon which to convict came from two hall boys, Hart and Redmond. These creatures, confined beyond the reach of Stokes and his friends in the House of Detention, boasted to Pat Logan, one of their keepers, that they would receive $1000 for their testimony. This came out at the third trial, Logan not daring to tell it while Tweed ruled New York. These hall boy witnesses complained, too, of the mental strain they experienced in learning by rote the yarn prepared for them, and which they felt was too foolishly long.

The third trial had a milder ending than had the one which preceded it, and the former hanging verdict was softened to manslaughter. Everyone was relieved, save the Erie ring — which had stuck for hangman's noose — and Stokes, who believed he should have gone free.

Incident to the trials, and a most venomously persistent witness against Stokes, was one Comer. Comer had been private secretary to Fisk, and was attached to both his employer and his employment. When, after he was sentenced to be hanged,

Stokes had been returned to his cell, 73 Murderer's Row, the
Tombs, a "congratulatory note" was thrust into his hands. It
read:

> Ed: Forgive me. I only did my duty. Remember me to Fisk when
> you see him, and tell him that the Gould affair is coming out all right.
>
> Comer

The day that Fisk was shot, Stokes had been all morning before Magistrate Bixby in the Yorkville Court. Fisk published that
the Mansfield and Stokes had conspired to blackmail him, and
put forward a Negro of the royal name of King to perjure the
charge through. Stokes caused the arrest of Fisk for criminal
libel, and the hearing was in progress in the Yorkville Court.

Fisk himself had not appeared. He had been ill — so ran the
reason of his absence — for two weeks. His counsel appeared
for him, and the hearing proceeded. It was still in the unfinished
air when Magistrate Bixby adjourned for the day.

Stokes was living at the Hoffman. Upon leaving the Yorkville
Court he, with his lawyers, went to Delmonico's, at Broadway
and Chambers Street. Lunch over, he drove to the Mansfield's in
quest of certain papers. He changed his mind, however, and
didn't see the Mansfield. If he had gone in, he might not have
visited the Grand Central, and Fisk in all chance would have escaped that day's bullets at least. But the shades were down at the
Mansfield's, Stokes hesitated to disturb her, and so Fisk was
duly shot on the Grand Central stairs.

Turning from the Mansfield's without ringing the bell, Stokes
drove down Seventh Avenue, through Fourth Street, to Broadway. He visited Niblo's and bought tickets for the evening.
Bailey, a merchant friend, lounged by, and, Stokes joining him,
the pair walked south.

As the two were opposite the Grand Central, the fatal lady in
207 bowed and beamed across the way. The lady in 207 didn't
know it, but that nod and smile meant death for Fisk.

Stokes, at the nod and smile, came to a full stop — like a setter
pointing a partridge. In the warm breath of his young nature,

every day was lady's day with him. He bade adieu to Bailey, and crossed to the Grand Central. He had never set foot in the hotel before.

Climbing the private stairway, Stokes glanced in at the open door of Parlor 207. The lady was there; but her instant expression showed that she didn't know him and didn't want to know him. There had been a mistake.

Stokes never went farther than the door. He didn't address the lady of the smile and nod. Understanding that he had erred, he started on his return to the street.

Fisk had friends — Mrs. Morse and her daughter — stopping at the Grand Central. Before he died he provided for them in his will. While too ill to attend the Yorkville Court, Fisk still felt himself well enough to call on the Morses. As Stokes began descending the Grand Central stairs, there was Fisk coming up.

Fisk had on a velvet coat, over which was swung a jaunty military cloak. Stokes was wearing a light topcoat. Both reached for their pistols. But since Fisk was bothered by the military cloak and velvet coat, while Stokes carried his pistol in the outside pocket of his driving coat, the latter got the drop. As Fisk raised his gun — which he did clumsily with both hands — Stokes jumped to the left and fired.

"Oh, Ed!" cried Fisk.

The Stokes pistol roared again.

"Don't, Ed; you've shot me!" exclaimed Fisk.

There was a bullet in Fisk's stomach; the other had pierced his arm.

Stokes tossed his pistol, hot and smoking, on the floor and walked slowly down the hall. He met his friend, De Corley.

"There's a man shot," said Stokes; "get a doctor."

Stokes found Proprietor Powers and told him to send for the police.

Fisk was carried into fatal 207. Lawyers and doctors came flocking. The latter could do nothing; the former drew Fisk's will. Fisk gave his millions to his wife, and died the morning after.

The Ninth Regiment held a meeting in its armory. There were deep lamentations, diversified by talk of lynching Stokes. The latter enterprise included the idea of taking the Tombs by storm. But, since Chief Kelso responded by throwing five hundred policemen into the prison, cooler counsel took the lead, and Stokes was left to the law.

Judge Davis sentenced Stokes to four years in Sing Sing. It was a cold November day when Deputies Shields and Cahill snapped the steel ruffles on Stokes's wrists and took him to the up-the-river train.

By way of showing how the wheel goes round, as Stokes started for prison that November morning, Boss Tweed was being put on trial before Davis, judge, for looting the city. Also, Judge Fullerton and John Graham, who aforetime had abandoned Stokes, were present for Tweed's defense, while as principal counsel for the prosecution came Lyman Tremain, who had saved the neck of Stokes.

November 1873:

The snow is early and deep this year. It lies thick in the Green Mountains, thick on the hills about Sing Sing, thick even along the Boulevard des Italiens before the Mansfield's modest door. And so they leave the story — these three: Fisk lies asleep in his Vermont grave; the Mansfield, furs framing her oval face, a retinue of new fools, French fools, sighing in her lovely wake, is taking her afternoon drive in the Bois, to return presently and piously by the church of the Madeleine to say a little prayer — that combination of humility and beauty is so fetching! — while Stokes, gray and grim for one so young, stands staring out through grates and bars across the wind-whipped drifts.

THE WOMAN AT THE STORE

by Katherine Mansfield

It was the little girl's drawing that settled matters.

ALL THAT DAY the heat was terrible. The wind blew close to the ground; it rooted among the tussock grass, slithered along the road, so that the white pumice dust swirled in our faces, settled and sifted over us and was like a dry skin, itching for growth on our bodies. The horses stumbled along, coughing and chuffing. The pack horse was sick — with a big, open sore rubbed under the belly. Now and again she stopped short, threw back her head, looked at us as though she were going to cry, and whinnied. Hundreds of larks shrilled; the sky was slate color, and the sound of the larks reminded me of slate pencils scraping over its surface. There was nothing to be seen but wave after wave of tussock grass, patched with purple orchids and manuka bushes covered with thick spider webs.

Jo rode ahead. He wore a blue galatea shirt, corduroy trousers, and riding boots. A white handkerchief, spotted with red — it looked as though his nose had been bleeding on it — was knotted round his throat. Wisps of white hair straggled from under his wideawake — his mustache and eyebrows were called white — he slouched in the saddle, grunting. Not once that day had he sung:

> I don't care, for don't you see,
> My wife's mother was in front of me!

It was the first day we had been without it for a month, and now there seemed something uncanny in his silence. Jim rode beside me, white as a clown; his black eyes glittered, and he kept shooting out his tongue and moistening his lips. He was dressed in a Jaeger vest, and a pair of blue duck trousers, fastened round the waist with a plaited leather belt. We had hardly spoken since dawn. At noon we had lunched off fly biscuits and apricots by the side of a swampy creek.

"My stomach feels like the crop of a hen," said Jo. "Now then, Jim, you're the bright boy of the party — where's this 'ere store you kep' on talking about? 'Oh, yes,' you says, 'I know a fine store, with a paddock for the horses and a creek runnin' through, owned by a friend of mine who'll give yer a bottle of whiskey before 'e shakes hands with yer.' I'd like ter see that place — merely as a matter of curiosity — not that I'd ever doubt yer word — as yer know very well — but . . ."

Jim laughed. "Don't forget there's a woman too, Jo, with blue eyes and yellow hair, who'll promise you something else before she shakes hands with you. Put that in your pipe and smoke it."

"The heat's making you balmy," said Jo. But he dug his knees into the horse. We shambled on. I half fell asleep, and had a sort of uneasy dream that the horses were not moving forward at all — then that I was on a rocking horse, and my old mother was scolding me for raising such a fearful dust from the drawing room carpet. "You've entirely worn off the pattern of the carpet," I heard her saying, and she gave the reins a tug. I sniveled and woke to find Jim leaning over me, maliciously smiling.

"That was a case of all but," said he. "I just caught you. What's up? Been bye-bye?"

"No!" I raised my head. "Thank the Lord we're arriving somewhere."

We were on the brow of the hill, and below us there was a whare roofed with corrugated iron. It stood in a garden, rather far back from the road — a big paddock opposite, and a creek and a clump of young willow trees. A thin line of blue smoke stood up straight from the chimney of the whare; and as I looked a woman came out, followed by a child and a sheep dog — the woman carrying what appeared to me a black stick. She made gestures at us. The horses put on a final spurt, Jo took off his wideawake, shouted, threw out his chest, and began singing, "I don't care, for don't you see . . ." The sun pushed through the pale clouds and shed a vivid light over the scene. It gleamed on the woman's yellow hair, over her flapping pinafore and the rifle she was carrying. The child hid behind her, and the yellow dog, a mangy beast, scuttled back into the whare, his tail between his legs. We drew rein and dismounted.

"Hallo," screamed the woman. "I thought you was three 'awks. My kid comes runnin' in ter me. 'Mumma,' says she, 'there's three brown things comin' over the 'ill,' says she. An' I comes out smart, I can tell yer. 'They'll be 'awks,' I says to her. Oh, the 'awks about 'ere yer wouldn't believe."

The "kid" gave us the benefit of one eye from behind the woman's pinafore — then retired again.

"Where's your old man?" asked Jim.

The woman blinked rapidly, screwing up her face.

"Away shearin'. Bin away a month. I suppose yer not goin' to stop, are yer? There's a storm comin' up."

"You bet we are," said Jo. "So you're on your lonely, missus?"

She stood, pleating the frills of her pinafore and glancing from one to the other of us, like a hungry bird. I smiled at the thought of how Jim had pulled Jo's leg about her. Certainly her eyes were blue, and what hair she had was yellow, but ugly. She was a figure of fun. Looking at her, you felt there was nothing but sticks and wires under that pinafore — her front teeth were knocked out, she had red pulpy hands, and she wore on her feet a pair of dirty bluchers.

"I'll go and turn out the horses," said Jim. "Got any embrocation? Poi's rubbed herself to hell!"

" 'Arf a mo!" The woman stood silent a moment, her nostrils expanding as she breathed. Then she shouted violently, "I'd rather you didn't stop . . . You *can't*, and there's the end of it. I don't let out that paddock anymore. You'll have to go on; I ain't got nothing!"

"Well, I'm blessed!" said Jo, heavily. He pulled me aside. "Gone a bit off 'er dot," he whispered. "Too much alone, *you know*," very significantly. "Turn the sympathetic tap on 'er; she'll come round all right."

But there was no need — she had come round by herself.

"Stop if yer like!" she muttered, shrugging her shoulders. To me — "I'll give yer the embrocation if yer come along."

"Right-o, I'll take it down to them." We walked together up the garden path. It was planted on both sides with cabbages. They smelled like stale dishwater. Of flowers there were double poppies and sweet Williams. One little patch was divided off by pawa shells — presumably it belonged to the child — for she ran from her mother and began to grub in it with a broken clothespeg. The yellow dog lay across the doorstep, biting fleas; the woman kicked him away.

"Gar-r, get away, you beast . . . The place ain't tidy. I 'aven't 'ad time ter fix things today — been ironing. Come right in."

It was a large room, the walls plastered with old pages of English periodicals. Queen Victoria's Jubilee appeared to be the most recent number. A table with an ironing board and washtub on it, some wooden forms, a black horsehair sofa, and some broken cane chairs pushed against the walls. The mantelpiece above the stove was draped in pink paper, further ornamented with dried grasses and ferns and a colored print of Richard Seddon. There were four doors — one, judging from the smell, let into the "store," one onto the "backyard," through a third I saw the bedroom. Flies buzzed in circles round the ceiling, and treacle papers and bundles of dried clover were pinned to the window curtains.

I was alone in the room; she had gone into the store for the embrocation. I heard her stamping about and muttering to herself: "I got some, now where did I put that bottle? . . . It's behind the pickles . . . No, it ain't." I cleared a place on the table and sat there, swinging my legs. Down in the paddock I could hear Jo singing and the sound of hammer strokes as Jim drove in the tent pegs. It was sunset. There is no twilight in our New Zealand days, but a curious half hour when everything appears grotesque; it frightens, as though the savage spirit of the country walked abroad and sneered at what it saw. Sitting alone in the hideous room I grew afraid. The woman next door was a long time finding that stuff. What was she doing in there? Once I thought I heard her bang her hands on the counter, and once she half-moaned, turning it into a cough and clearing her throat. I wanted to shout "Buck up!" but I kept silent.

"Good Lord, what a life!" I thought. "Imagine being here day in, day out, with that rat of a child and a mangy dog. Imagine bothering about ironing. *Mad*, of course she's mad! Wonder how long she's been here — wonder if I could get her to talk."

At that moment she poked her head round the door.

"Wot was it yer wanted?" she asked.

"Embrocation."

"Oh, I forgot. I got it; it was in front of the pickle jars."

She handed me the bottle.

"My, you do look tired, you do! Shall I knock yer up a few scones for supper? There's some tongue in the store, too, and I'll cook yer a cabbage if you fancy it."

"Right-o." I smiled at her. "Come down to the paddock and bring the kid for tea."

She shook her head, pursing up her mouth.

"Oh, no. I don't fancy it. I'll send the kid down with the things and a billy of milk. Shall I knock up a few extry scones to take with yer termorrow?"

"Thanks."

She came and stood by the door.

"How old is the kid?"

"Six — come next Christmas. I 'ad a bit of trouble with 'er one way an' another. I 'adn't any milk till a month after she was born and she sickened like a cow."

"She's not like you. Takes after her father?" Just as the woman had shouted her refusal at us before, she shouted at me then.

"No, she don't! She's the dead spit of me. Any fool could see that. Come on in now, Else; you stop messing in the dirt."

I met Jo climbing over the paddock fence.

"What's the old bitch got in the store?" he asked.

"Don't know — didn't look."

"Well, of all the fools. Jim's slanging you. What have you been doing all the time?"

"She couldn't find this stuff. Oh, my shakes, you are smart!"

Jo had washed, combed his wet hair in a line across his forehead, and buttoned a coat over his shirt. He grinned.

Jim snatched the embrocation from me. I went to the end of the paddock where the willows grew and bathed in the creek. The water was clear and soft as oil. Along the edges, held by the grass and rushes, white foam tumbled and bubbled. I lay in the water and looked up at the trees that were still a moment, then quivered lightly, and again were still. The air smelled of rain. I forgot about the woman and the kid until I came back to the tent. Jim lay by the fire, watching the billy boil.

I asked where Jo was, and if the kid had brought our supper.

"Pooh," said Jim, rolling over and looking up at the sky. "Didn't you see how Jo had been titivating? He said to me before he went up to the whare, 'Dang it! She'll look better by night light. At any rate, my buck, she's female flesh!' "

"You had Jo about her looks — you had me, too."

"No — look here. I can't make it out. It's four years since I came past this way, and I stopped here two days. The husband was a pal of mine once, down the West Coast — a fine, big chap, with a voice on him like a trombone. She'd been barmaid down the coast — as pretty as a wax doll. The coach used to come this way then once a fortnight — that was before they opened the railway up Napier way — and she had no end of a time! Told me once in a confidential moment that she knew one hundred and twenty-five different ways of kissing!"

"Oh, go on, Jim! She isn't the same woman!"

"Course she is . . . I can't make it out. What I think is, the old man's cleared out and left her; that's all my eye about shearing. Sweet life! The only people who come through now are Maoris and sundowners!"

Through the dark we saw the gleam of the kid's pinafore. She trailed over to us with a basket in her hand, the milk billy in the other. I unpacked the basket, the child standing by.

"Come over here," said Jim, snapping his fingers at her.

She went; the lamp from inside of the tent cast a bright light over her. A mean, undersized brat, with whitish hair and weak eyes. She stood, legs wide apart and her stomach protruding.

"What do you do all day?" asked Jim.

She scraped out one ear with her little finger, looked at the result, and said, "Draw."

"Huh! What do you draw? Leave your ears alone!"

"Pictures."

"What on?"

"Bits of butter paper an' a pencil of my Mumma's."

"Boh! What a lot of words at one time!" Jim rolled his eyes at her. "Baa-lambs and moo-cows?"

"No, everything. I'll draw all of you when you're gone, and your horses and the tent and that one" — she pointed to me — "with no clothes on in the creek. I looked at her where she couldn't see me from."

"Thanks very much. How ripping of you," said Jim. "Where's Dad?"

The kid pouted. "I won't tell you because I don't like yer face!" She started operations on the other ear.

"Here," I said. "Take the basket, get along home, and tell the other man supper's ready."

"I don't want to."

"I'll give you a box on the ear if you don't," said Jim, savagely.

"Hie! I'll tell Mumma. I'll tell Mumma." The kid fled.

We ate until we were full, and had arrived at the smoke stage before Jo came back, very flushed and jaunty, a whiskey bottle in his hand.

" 'Ave a drink, you two!" he shouted, carrying off matters with a high hand. " 'Ere, shove along the cups."

"One hundred and twenty-five different ways," I murmured to Jim.

"What's that? Oh! Stow it!" said Jo. "Why 'ave you always got your knife into me? You gas like a kid at a Sunday school beano. She wants us to go up there tonight and have a comfortable chat. I" — he waved his hand airily — "I got 'er round."

"Trust you for that," laughed Jim. "But did she tell you where the old man's got to?"

Jo looked up. "Shearing! You 'eard 'er, you fool!"

*

The woman had fixed up the room, even to a light bouquet of sweet Williams on the table. She and I sat one side of the table, Jo and Jim the other. An oil lamp was set between us, the whiskey bottle and glasses and a jug of water. The kid knelt against one of the forms, drawing on butter paper. I wondered, grimly, if she was attempting the creek episode. But Jo had been right about nighttime. The woman's hair was tumbled — two red spots burned in her cheeks — her eyes shone — and we knew that they were kissing feet under the table. She had changed the blue pinafore for a white calico dressing jacket and a black skirt — the kid was decorated to the extent of a blue sateen hair ribbon. In the stifling room, with the flies buzzing against the ceiling and dropping onto the table, we got slowly drunk.

"Now listen to me," shouted the woman, banging her fist on the table. "It's six years since I was married, and four miscarriages. I says to 'im, I says, what do you think I'm doin' up 'ere? If you was back at the coast, I'd 'ave you lynched for child murder. Over and over I tells 'im — you've broken my spirit and spoiled my looks, and wot for — that's wot I'm driving at." She clutched her head with her hands and stared round at us. Speaking rapidly, "Oh, some days — an' months of them — I 'ear them two words knockin' inside me all the time — 'Wot for!' but sometimes I'll be cooking the spuds an' I lifts the lid off to give 'em a prong and I 'ears, quite sudden again, 'Wot for!' Oh! I don't mean only the spuds and the kid — I mean — I mean," she hiccoughed — "you know what I mean, Mr. Jo."

"I know," said Jo, scratching his head.

"Trouble with me is," she leaned across the table, "he left me too much alone. When the coach stopped coming, sometimes he'd go away days, sometimes he'd go away weeks, and leave me ter look after the store. Back 'e'd come — pleased as Punch. 'Oh, 'allo,' 'e'd say. ' 'Ow are you gettin' on? Come and give us a kiss.' Sometimes I'd turn a bit nasty, and then 'e'd go off again, and if I took it all right, 'e'd wait till 'e could twist me round 'is finger, then 'e'd say, 'Well, so long, I'm off,' and do you think I could keep 'im? — not me!"

"Mumma," bleated the kid, "I made a picture of them on the 'ill, an' you an' me, an' the dog down below."

"Shut your mouth!" said the woman.

A vivid flash of lightning played over the room — we heard the mutter of thunder.

"Good thing that's broke loose," said Jo. "I've 'ad it in me 'ead for three days."

"Where's your old man now?" asked Jim, slowly.

The woman blubbered and dropped her head on to the table. "Jim, 'e's gone shearin' and left me alone again," she wailed.

" 'Ere, look out for the glasses," said Jo. "Cheer-o, 'ave another drop. No good cryin' over spilled 'usbands! You Jim, you blasted cuckoo!"

"Mr. Jo," said the woman, drying her eyes on her jacket frill, "you're a gent, an' if I was a secret woman, I'd place any confidence in your 'ands. I don't mind if I do 'ave a glass on that."

Every moment the lightning grew more vivid and the thunder sounded nearer. Jim and I were silent — the kid never moved from her bench. She poked her tongue out and blew on her paper as she drew.

"It's the loneliness," said the woman, addressing Jo — he made sheep's eyes at her — "and bein' shut up 'ere like a broody 'en." He reached his hand across the table and held hers, and though the position looked most uncomfortable when they wanted to pass the water and whiskey, their hands stuck together as though glued. I pushed back my chair and went over to the kid, who immediately sat flat down on her artistic achievements and made a face at me.

"You're not to look," said she.

"Oh, come on, don't be nasty!" Jim came over to us, and we were just drunk enough to wheedle the kid into showing us. And those drawings of hers were extraordinary and repulsively vulgar. The creations of a lunatic with a lunatic's cleverness. There was no doubt about it; the kid's mind was diseased. While she showed them to us, she worked herself up into a mad excitement, laughing and trembling, and shooting out her arms.

"Mumma," she yelled. "Now I'm going to draw them what you told me I never was to — now I am."

The woman rushed from the table and beat the child's head

with the flat of her hand.

"I'll smack you with yer clothes turned up if yer dare say that again," she bawled.

Jo was too drunk to notice, but Jim caught her by the arm. The kid did not utter a cry. She drifted over to the window and began picking flies from the treacle paper.

We returned to the table — Jim and I sitting one side, the woman and Jo, touching shoulders, the other. We listened to the thunder, saying stupidly, "That was a near one," "There it goes again," and Jo, at a heavy hit, "Now we're off," "Steady on the brake," until rain began to fall, sharp as cannon shot on the iron roof.

"You'd better doss here for the night," said the woman.

"That's right," assented Jo, evidently in the know about this move.

"Bring up yer things from the tent. You two can doss in the store along with the kid — she's used to sleep in there and won't mind you."

"Oh Mumma, I never did," interrupted the kid.

"Shut yer lies! An' Mr. Jo can 'ave this room."

It sounded a ridiculous arrangement, but it was useless to attempt to cross them; they were too far gone. While the woman sketched the plan of action, Jo sat, abnormally solemn and red, his eyes bulging, and pulling at his moustache.

"Give us a lantern," said Jim. "I'll go down to the paddock." We two went together. Rain whipped in our faces; the land was light as though a bush fire were raging. We behaved like two children let loose in the thick of an adventure, laughed and shouted to each other, and came back to the whare to find the kid already bedded on the counter of the store. The woman brought us a lamp. Jo took his bundle from Jim; the door was shut.

"Good night all," shouted Jo.

Jim and I sat on two sacks of potatoes. For the life of us we could not stop laughing. Strings of onions and half hams dangled from the ceiling — wherever we looked there were advertisements for "Camp Coffee" and tinned meats. We pointed at them; tried to read them aloud — overcome with laughter and hiccoughs. The kid on the counter stared at us. She threw off her blanket and scrambled to the floor, where she stood in her gray flannel nightgown, rubbing one leg against the other. We paid no attention to her.

"Wot are you laughing at?" she said, uneasily.

"You!" shouted Jim. "The red tribe of you, my child."

She flew into a rage and beat herself with her hands. "I won't be laughed at, you curs — you." He swooped down upon the child and swung her onto the counter.

"Go to sleep, Miss Smarty — or make a drawing — here's a pencil — you can use Mumma's account book."

Through the rain we heard Jo creak over the boarding of the next room — the sound of a door being opened — then shut to.

"It's the loneliness," whispered Jim.

"One hundred and twenty-five different ways — alas! my poor brother! "

The kid tore out a page and flung it at me.

"There you are," she said. "Now I done it ter spite Mumma for shutting me up 'ere with you two. I done the one she told me I never ought to. I done the one she told me she'd shoot me if I did. Don't care! Don't care!"

The kid had drawn the picture of the woman shooting at a man with a rook rifle and then digging a hole to bury him in.

She jumped off the counter and squirmed about on the floor biting her nails.

Jim and I sat till dawn with the drawing beside us. The rain ceased; the little kid fell asleep, breathing loudly. We got up; stole out of the whare, down into the paddock. White clouds floated over a pink sky — a chill wind blew; the air smelled of wet grass. Just as we swung into the saddle Jo came out of the whare — he motioned to us to ride on.

"I'll pick you up later," he shouted.

A bend in the road, and the whole place disappeared.

THE ESCAPE

by E. H. Lacon Watson

"Murderous-looking things, those Swedish knives! You
could stab a man with a thing like that."

HE WAS CONSCIOUS of making no very grand appearance as he
left the fine old Georgian house and heard the front door close
behind him with a well-oiled click. Quite smooth — like everything else in that infernal street — that street of lies and fair
words. Nothing could have been blander than the tones of the
eminent physician who had just pronounced his doom. At least,
it had sounded to him like that, though clearly Sir James was
minimizing it as much as he could. "A simple operation," he had
called it, lightly. But he knew well enough that men often died of
it. There was Jerningham, one of his fellow members at the club,
who had died in a nursing home the other day. The same thing,
precisely. And Jerningham was a lot healthier than he had been,
lately. Though he never said much about it, his heart used to
palpitate cruelly sometimes, at night.

He knew, as he left the house, that he had not taken it well.
The deferential butler, even, had noticed something, and seemed
really concerned. Would he care to have a small whiskey? He
looked rather white. And in fact he had been glad to hold for a
moment to the balusters as he came down the broad staircase. A
sort of giddiness came over him. But he refused a drink.

He ought to have been able to take it better than that. But he
had always been — rather that way — ever since he could re-

member. One of those nervous, highly-strung fellows whose lives have been a burden to them from the start. He remembered perfectly well going to school for the first time: the desolate sensation of utter loneliness when he was left in the old college buildings, and his father had gone off to catch the train home. He felt exactly like a small fish dropped into a pool where there were a lot of hungry pike. It seemed to him that all his life had been spent scurrying into corners and trying to hide himself. All through his life he had been struggling to escape notice, unsuccessfully. Always he was being dragged out, held up, and exposed. He had never enjoyed his schooldays. And even at the university it was not much better. He had been shy and nervous; he did not know how to deal with that loud-voiced, free-and-easy gang who used to swarm up into his rooms sometimes and "rag." Not the smallest use trying to adopt the same manner himself. He was detected at once as an impostor.

What a poor life he had passed! Probably his own fault, very largely. It did not pay to adopt that attitude toward the world that had always been his — the attitude of the shrinker. If he had to go through it again now he would go on the other tack — if he could. He would be one of the bullies; he would impose his own will on the others. Easy enough, if you started right; the difficulty lay in just those first few steps. Or did it lie deeper down than that? Perhaps it did. He was just a funk, by nature and habit. Never could he shake off that fatal disability now. It was too late.

True, he had been exceptionally unfortunate. Everywhere he went there was always one man who — well! who got on his nerves so that he hardly knew what to do with himself in his presence. Why were there such beasts in the world? That had been the root of his trouble, really — the remarkable prevalence of beasts. There had always been one, if not more, in his immediate neighborhood at school, and again at college, and again when he was in business, and now at his club. Always some one man whose business it seemed to be to annoy and afflict him. And just now, too, when he had come into his little bit of money, and been able to retire, and fancied that, at last, he might be going to get some enjoyment out of life.

Marrable was the man's name. (Even about the name there was something revolting: it sounded fat and luscious and over-ripe.) Pure imagination, no doubt, but from the first moment he had seen the man he had felt sure . . . No! He must manage somehow to get out of this habit of overemphatic statement. Keep calm, judicial, under any provocation. In fact, he had not disliked the man so much just at first; he could vaguely recollect having thought him amusing. Amusing! Good God! Marrable used to sit there, in the card room, just behind one of the players, and make comments. Of course no man ought to be allowed to do things of that sort; no man would in any really respectable club. That was the worst of the Camisis; it had fallen from its old position. Time was when it counted for something to be a member of the Camisis; now it seemed that anyone might join and — what was worse — behave much as he chose when he got there.

Of course, in a way, it was largely his own fault. He ought to have spoken to the other men — even complained to the committee if necessary. If he had acted firmly Marrable might have been abolished by now — perhaps.

But he was so infernally popular. (Why on earth a man like Marrable should be tolerated, let alone popular, entirely beat him, as it must beat everyone who considered for a moment.) He was big and fat and easygoing, and had one of those rather comic high-pitched voices that you occasionally find with fat men. Somehow, when he said things in that squeaky voice, it was difficult not to laugh — at first. He had laughed himself, heaven help him, before Marrable had begun to turn his attention to his own weaknesses. That was where the fellow was so infernally deceitful. He began by being as polite as could be to a stranger; but in a day or two little familiarities would begin to creep in. At the end of a week he was probably calling you by some absurd nickname and making all the others laugh at the way you did certain things.

It was too much! At the mere thought of it Pontifex flushed all over; he could feel himself getting hot right down the back. Did I tell you his name was Pontifex? That was yet another of the many troubles that had oppressed him all his life, since he was a schoolboy. He had begun to hope that this trouble, at any rate. would have passed when he attained to middle age. But that man Marrable had seized hold of it at once. He called him "Ponty" or sometimes "Pontifex Maximus." and pretended to receive anything he said on the subject of bridge with exaggerated respect. A man's name ought to be sacred from that sort of silly jesting, in any respectable club. He had spoken about it to more than one of the members. But they had only just laughed and turned it off with some careless remark.

"Marrable? Oh, nobody minds what old Marrable says. He is a licensed jester. Why, only the other day . . ."

And they would go off into some story of what he had said or done to someone else. All very fine, but it did not really help Pontifex in his own trouble.

It had been getting to such a pitch lately that Pontifex wondered if he would not have to resign. But he knew in his heart that he would never have the courage to resign from the Camisis now. He had belonged to it ever since he first came to London, more than thirty years ago. He was a creature of habit. He knew that he could not manage to exist now without dropping in there at teatime and having a rubber or two afterward, with a night out on Thursdays, when he stayed to dine and played on till about eleven. Fortunately Marrable never dined there, so that one night in the week at any rate was tolerably free from insult.

It was Thursday afternoon. The last Thursday before his operation — perhaps the last Thursday he would ever spend there. The next day he had to go to the nursing home, and it must be confessed he did not like the thought of going there in the least. He tried not to think of it more than he could help, but it kept recurring. They would keep him there a day or two "getting him ready" for the knife, as though he were some sort of sacrifice; and then one morning they would wheel him into the operating room and stick stupefying things into his mouth or over his nose, and do what they liked with him when he was all unconscious. And then — he might wake up again or he might not. And if he did, there was always the terrifying thought that he might awake to horrible agony — and death. If he was going to die he would rather die without coming round at all. But he did not want to die. He had always hated death.

Still, it was Thursday, and by the luck of things he had got just the sort of rubber he liked. A pleasant four, if they could keep it from being broken up by intruders. Perhaps the last evening's bridge he would have for a long while; possibly the last he would ever have. It sent a cold shiver through him when he thought of that.

He could not help saying something, after winning the first rubber, about that being his last night for some little time. They were all most sympathetic, and he was tempted to go into details a little (minimizing it all, of course, in a half-humorous way) when he was aware suddenly of that hated voice just behind him. It gave him quite a start, for he had never heard Marrable come in.

"What! Old Ponty going to have an operation? Hope it'll improve his bridge, eh? Say, that's not a bad idea. Never heard of a man having an operation to improve his bridge before, did you?"

And he cackled in his silly, high-pitched voice, while the others laughed. That was one of the things that irritated Pontifex so much — the immunity of the beast from the common laws of civilized life. The other men never seemed to think he was saying anything ungentlemanly or likely to be resented. Even Sellar, who was his partner, gave a sort of chuckle, and said something about the only operation that was likely to improve some players he knew. These fellows did not seem to realize that bridge was a game demanding intense concentration of all the faculties — if you pretended to play at all. But how the devil could a man play with that fat fellow blowing down the back of his neck, and the sound of his voice still filling the whole room?

"Sorry, partner," he said. "Of course I had it sitting. Such a row going on I simply couldn't think."

"Ponty, old man, that's a rotten excuse, and you know it." Marrable spoke in a sort of high-pitched chuckle, as though he were immensely amused. For one moment Pontifex was aware of a sudden blurring of the sight, as though a film had come over his eyes. He saw the room through a russet cloud. His fingers twitched. Suppose now — just suppose he sprang at the man suddenly, from behind, when no one was there, and got his hands once firmly on that bulging neck and held on! It seemed to him he could feel the vast bulk of the man struggling underneath him — at first — and then gradually growing still. Oh yes! He could be trusted to hold on if he once got him.

The cloud before his eyes faded slowly. He came to himself. That must be what they meant when they spoke of "seeing red," he thought. Well, there was a reddish tinge about that mist — a real sensation of color. And it was exactly as though something had gone in his head. He could almost hear the snap. With it vanished, in a moment, all the old inhibitions, the defensive walls of civilization that had been growing up round him since the days of his childhood. He seemed to see right down into his real self — an entirely different self from any he had known before.

With a tremendous effort he pulled himself back to the pretense of ordinary social life. That voice was still cackling about something. Drinks! Would he have a drink? No, certainly not; Marrable knew well enough that he never took anything. He was aware, in the inner recesses of his brain, of a curious glowing heat. He could see it with his mind's eye — a tiny red spark, deep down. Perhaps it was as well that he had settled to go into the nursing home the next day. Otherwise — probably this was just how those things happened. After all, a murderer was not a different being from the ordinary man. He was often merely one of ourselves who had been pestered and bothered until he simply could not stand it any longer — until something went cr-rrack in his head, as his own had gone. He had never realized he could feel like that himself. He would not have believed it a few hours ago. He would have put himself down as the one man in the world who was thoroughly free from primitive feelings like that. Sedulously, all his life, he had avoided anything like fighting, any suspicion of a row. Fortunately, during the Great War he had managed to get a safe job in a government office. He had not even undertaken a special constable's job; he disliked extremely having to patrol at nights. And those air raids, of course, had been terrible.

Well, if Marrable meant to stay he would have to go home;

that was all. In his present state, he said to himself, he simply could not stand it. Of course his last evening had been wrecked, but that was only what he might have expected. Marrable was absolutely certain to come in just that very night of all others; he might have known it. The sound of his voice behind him was almost more than he could bear. He was conscious that he could not keep the muscles of his face completely under control. Sellar, his partner, he thought was looking at him rather narrowly. And as he dealt the cards he could see his hand shaking. A curious sensation came over him — exactly as though someone had sliced away the back of his head and all the brains were running out.

"I'm on the verge," Pontifex said to himself, "absolutely on the edge of a breakdown. I wonder what I ought to do."

A good thing, after all, that he had to go to that nursing home the next morning. That was the one bright spot about the whole thing: the coming operation did not loom so terribly before him as it had. Perhaps it might almost turn out to be a blessing in disguise.

He started to walk back from the club along the Embankment, slipping away quietly at the end of a rubber, with Marrable still sitting there and making a nuisance of himself all round. How blessed it was to get out into the open air, all by himself! And how quiet it was there! Cleopatra's Needle, and the Belgian memorial opposite. (Surely that woman's neck was ridiculously long!) How well he remembered the Zeppelins coming over! He had watched one of them from his window up in the Temple there, with all the shells bursting round her — a silvery, cigar-shaped thing caught in the beam of a dozen searchlights. Just such another night as that. He leaned against the parapet and looked down on the smoothly flowing river. Something pressed against his chest, and he felt in his pocket for the cause. Of course! He had quite forgotten it — the Swedish knife that his nephew had wanted for a birthday present. He had looked in at Thompson's and bought it only a few minutes before going to the club, meaning to send it on from there. Well, it would have to be sent from his rooms now — or the nursing home. Murderous-looking things, those Swedish knives! You opened them out and

stuck them in that solid wooden handle and they were firm as a
rock. You could stab a man with a thing like that. Just as well,
perhaps, that he had not remembered it a few minutes ago at the
club. If it had been ready in his hand — like that . . .

A hand clapped him roughly on the shoulder, giving him such
a start that for a minute he went quite dizzy. Then came Marrable's voice.

"Now then, none o' that. Will you come along quiet, or shall I
'ave to tyke yer?" And then that high, cackling laugh.

It was the laugh that finished him. He could not stand that
noise. It oppressed him as though an actual physical pain had
shot through him, spurring him to sudden action. He turned and
leaped at the man like some wild animal. As he leaped he fancied
he could hear a sort of snarling cry of rage. It sounded quite outside himself, and yet he felt, somehow, it proceeded from his
own mouth. Marrable, compared with himself, was a big, powerful man; but the attack took him so much by surprise that he
went over with hardly a struggle or a sound. His arms went up
and waved in the air as he tried frantically to maintain his balance; then his foot seemed to catch in something, and he went
over backward, Pontifex on the top of him. He had got a firm
grip of his collar with his left hand at that first leap, and with his
right, holding the Swedish knife, he stabbed twice, fiercely, as
they lay on the pavement. He could feel the point sink in —
deep; his whole soul reveled in the feeling. That would do for
Marrable; that would stop him talking in the club for a bit — at
any rate in that silly, high-pitched voice. Damn it! Something
had snapped in his head again, and there was a red mist in front
of everything. The body beneath him had gone quite limp.

Pontifex let go and scrambled up unsteadily. He could not see
very well, but there was the body lying huddled on the pavement. The hat had flown off and was lying in the gutter. Marrable
was quiet enough now. Not a sound had he uttered since that
silly pretense of being a policeman. Damn him! He had brought it
on himself, clapping him on the shoulder suddenly like that, and
laughing just in the way he hated most. Any man would have
gone for him, playing a silly trick like that. All the same . . .

He became suddenly conscious of the knife still grasped in his hand. It was as though it stung him, like a snake, and he hurled it out over the parapet into the river with a gesture of repulsion. That was the luck of the thing, too — just the sort of thing that would happen to him of all people — that he should have been holding that knife, ready in its shaft, at the precise moment when Marrable came along. He just *had* to strike out at him. The purest nervous reflex action. But — they would hardly be likely to accept that if they got him in the dock, with some parchment-faced old judge sitting to try him. Murder — they would call it. Murder!

Pontifex felt he could not stay there another moment, on any consideration. He was seized with a panic. Fortunately, there was not a soul in sight — unless that was a figure of a man in the distance slinking along by the other side of the road, toward Charing Cross. The lamps along the Embankment threw dark shadows here and there, but none of them moved. So far as he could see, he was absolutely alone.

His instinct was to run — run away as swiftly as he could — before anyone appeared. He took two or three steps, but no, it would never do to be seen running, especially at that hour. The first policeman who saw him would obviously wonder what was up, and stop him, and begin to ask questions. What he had to do was to get back to his rooms in the Temple as soon as possible without attracting attention. He would turn up the next dark street and get into the Strand, where there was always traffic enough to make a man inconspicuous. And by the grace of God he reached the Strand, up the next street, without meeting anyone at all.

He was in the Strand, turning toward the Temple. But even as he turned the thought came to him that he did not want to go up those wooden stairs, to that lonely room of his, letting himself into a dark passage with his key and fumbling for the switch of the electric light. He would never have the courage to go to bed. Marrable would haunt him — or he would be fancying every moment that he heard the footsteps of avenging Law slowly coming up, the steps creaking, the halt outside, and then the thundering crash of the knocker on the door. How could he possibly stand that — all through the night? No, he certainly could not go to bed that night. Why should he go to bed at all? The next morning he was due at the nursing home. They could not very well trace him there, arrest him under the very surgeon's knife, and carry him off to trial. Only a few hours ago he had been dreading that operation; now he welcomed it.

There was Big Ben striking. It was only ten o'clock yet. A few minutes before he had been sitting at the bridge table playing a rubber, with Marrable close behind him. Why should he not go back there? He wanted company. Besides, it might possibly be useful if he got back in time to cut in again for the next rubber. No one had seen him go out, so far as he knew. At the Camisis the hall porter was often away from his post at that hour of the night; he might easily be able to slink in again and hang up his hat and pretend he had only gone into the other room when they had cut him out. At any rate he would be in the light and the company of his fellows. He turned around.

Of course, at the worst, it was all an accident. He had never meant to kill him. The merest outbreak of nervous irritation — and no wonder — with a man coming up behind like that playing the goat. And no one had seen him — he was certain of that — nor was it in the least likely that anyone would suspect him of a crime of violence. His reputation at the club would be in his favor. Never had he been anything but the most peaceable of men — too peaceable. He had stood things without a murmur that anyone else would have resented; he had almost become a byword — the sort of man who could be insulted with absolute impunity.

Well, Marrable would not insult him anymore now, at any rate.

Pontifex began to wonder what the police were doing. Had they found the body? Surely someone must have stumbled across it by now. What happened when one found a dead body? His mind, it seemed to him, was working with preternatural speed, rather as though a series of pictures was being projected on a screen in front of him. He saw a constable, slowly striding along the Embankment, suddenly confronted by Marrable's huddled form; then kneeling down, making a hasty examination, rising suddenly, and putting the whistle to his mouth to summon assistance. In a minute the deserted Embankment is alive with hurrying figures. Scotland Yard, the C.I.D., the Big Five — or whatever the papers called them. Cold-eyed, scientific men; trained observers. Sleuths, examining everything they saw with pocket lenses, in the manner of Sherlock Holmes. Heavens! They might even be able to follow his footsteps. Hastily he glanced round, half-convinced that he must be leaving a visible track behind. His senses seemed so acute now that he almost persuaded himself that he could see marks on the gray pavement. And that noise — surely that was the note of a policeman's whistle?

A hunted man! That was what he had become now. They were after him; the whole force of society was marshaled against him. Could he escape? Did they ever get away? Why, of course they did — in real life. It was only in fiction that the detective always triumphed. Think of the number of cases that happened years ago, in which the murderers had never been found out to this day. It only needed common sense and the avoidance of obvious mistakes. That was where criminals always slipped up; they made some silly blunder in the heat of the moment that gave the whole show away.

If he could only stop thinking a little! It seemed to him that his mind was racing, like the propeller of a steamer jerked clear of the water. That knife of his, now. Ought he to have thrown it away like that, into the river? They might find it. Oh yes, it sounded absurd, but that was just the sort of thing that always happened; they might sweep it up in a net or something and trace it to him. They could not help tracing it, once found. Of course he ought never to have thrown it away — only he felt that he simply could not keep it any longer. It burned his hand; it might have been made of red-hot iron. Why, the shop where he had bought it was only a few yards off. To be sure, he had not been there before, so far as he recollected — but that was nothing. They would parade him for inspection and he would be recognized. He saw the picture as clearly as anything: there he stood in a row of figures, inwardly shivering, trying to look composed; and there was Thompson's assistant, the man who had sold him the knife, walking down the line slowly, scrutinizing them one by one. Oh, it was hopeless. The man would recognize him at once, of course.

He had only walked a few yards while all this passed through his mind. And then he caught sight of himself reflected in a shop window, and the sight gave him such a shock that he all but fell down. In fact he did stagger, and had to catch hold of a lamppost to steady himself. He was without a hat.

Well, that did it for him, of course. His hat must have fallen off when he and Marrable were having that struggle, and in the excitement of the moment he had never noticed it. It must be lying there still, a damning piece of evidence — unless by some chance it had fallen into the river, or been blown away into the Embankment Gardens, or somehow managed to dispose of itself. But to think of him coming all that way without discovering that he had left it behind! He had put it on at the club before leaving. Yes, of course he had — a man did not go out into the streets from his club and leave his hat on the peg. He must have been dazed by the fall when they had gone down together. It had been a bit of a crash, and it was some time before he recovered himself. He remembered seeing a hat lying there, in the gutter, too. He shivered.

Perhaps there was just a chance still — if he went straight back — down the next turning. It was the only chance. There were not many people about that night, and it was only a minute or two since it had happened. If he could only get there before the police! They would never suspect him if he was the first to discover the body and give the alarm. His hat had blown off and he was following it up when he ran into this — terrible thing. That would be his story.

He turned immediately down the next street, almost brushing against a man at the corner. Fortunate that the fellow never seemed to look at him. No one had noticed him, apparently, walking along hatless on an autumn night. That was what he had always maintained: Londoners were extraordinarily unobservant. Unless you were dressed in regular fancy costume they would never stop to look at you — and not always then. After all, too, a number of young men had taken to going about the streets hatless.

He was on the Embankment again — and once more there did not seem to be a soul in sight. What extraordinary luck! His heart gave a bound, and he hurried on toward the spot. Ah! He was barely in time; there were two or three men approaching from the opposite direction. Well, he would get there first and give the alarm. There was his hat, just in front of him, and there was the huddled mass of clothes, still lying on the pavement. He waved his hands and shouted to the little party who were advancing. They took no notice.

"Silly fools!" he thought angrily. They must have seen him.

And then, suddenly, he heard a voice — the well-known squeaky, high-pitched voice of Marrable. There he was, in the center of the approaching group, explaining what had happened.

"I give you my word," he was saying, "I only just touched the poor chap on the back. Must have been nervous, for he gave no end of a jump and his arms went up, just like that. Thought he was going to hit me. Didn't like the look of him at all. And then the poor old chap collapsed suddenly, before you could say "knife," and fell on his face. I thought I'd better come and let you know."

A man in constable's uniform bent down and turned the huddled figure over gently.

" 'Art, it looks like," he said. And Pontifex found himself looking down at his own face.

THE DOLL

by Francis King

"No need for alarm. It was about this — er — this
squalid case of the vanishing girl."

IN THREE separate shop windows he had seen that photograph —
with above it the question HAVE YOU EVER SEEN THIS GIRL? and
below it the admonition IF YOU HAVE SPEAK NOW! But one did
not want to be observed studying a notice like that, did one?
People might suspect one of being in some way involved oneself.
So each time he gave no more than a shying glance, to be followed by that curious gesture of first lowering his pointed chin
down onto his collar and then pushing it outward, which indicated to those who knew him that he was feeling self-conscious
or embarrassed.

"Morning, Mr. Reynolds!"

"Morning, Eunice."

"*Good* morning, Mr. Reynolds. Quite a nip in the air, isn't
there?"

"Yes, quite a nip."

"Now what else for you, Mr. Reynolds? We have some nice
chicory in."

"My gentleman's off chicory."

But the chatty exchanges which he usually enjoyed so much
now were a burden to him. He wanted to gaze at that photograph
somewhere where no one could watch him doing so.

"Oh, Mr. Reynolds!"

That woman who had been recommended for the loosecovers and who had made them so badly was barring his path.

"Good morning." He nodded and tried to hurry round her.

"I wanted to explain. About those loosecovers. It was a question of cutting the cloth on the bias. Sir Malcolm just didn't seem to understand. You should have heard him on the phone! It was the bias. And then that finicky floral pattern he chose . . ."

Reynolds, a shopping bag in either hand, shifted from one foot to another, his eyes not on the moist, pale blue eyes in the quivering face opposite to him but darting among the passersby in an agony of restlessness.

"Is it his custom to talk in that kind of tone to a lady? I must say he gave me quite a shock. One doesn't look for a man of his refinement . . ."

Silly bitch!

At last he got away from her; and there, as he entered St. Ann's Well Gardens, loomed up another of the mammoth photographs. Hurriedly he glanced in all directions; then he gave himself up, with an almost voluptuous sigh, to a long contemplation.

Oh, it was a shame, a terrible shame, to think of a poor little thing like that lying out somewhere dead. If she *was* dead. They were not sure of that, of course; there was only the evidence of what they had called "a bloodstained article of clothing." What could that have been? Knickers, most like. Her mother had recognized them as hers together with that comic she had been carrying the day she had disappeared. On the beach that elderly woman with the dog had found them — they said the woman kept that shop called Dog's Den.

It was a shame, a real shame, to think of anything happening to such a pretty little thing, with that lovely long hair like silk and that little turned-up nose and that gay little smile. Well, if she hadn't been such a dainty little darling no one would have been interested in her. They said in the paper that, though she was twelve, her mental age had been that of a girl of five, but to look at the photograph you'd never think she wasn't just as bright as a new pin. Oh, that face looked just brimful of intelligence.

She was a doll, a real little doll. But dolls were dead things, whereas the one thing the photograph told one was that here was

a kiddy who was really *alive*, full of joie de vivre, with that lovely
smile of hers, and those laughing eyes of hers, and that, oh, so
fun-loving expression of hers, as though she were telling one that
the world was a marvelous place. Poor kid, poor little kiddy! Because of course it wasn't a marvelous place, not for her any more
than for anyone else, with that awful bloodstained "article of
clothing" and who knows what ghastly tortures she must have
suffered before it was over.

He put his head on one side, musingly oblivious of the weight
of the two shopping bags full of the groceries for which Mrs.
Evans was waiting. He couldn't rightly remember ever having
seen her with the other children from that special school, and
that was odd, because it was the kind of face, so gentle and trusting and well, yes, beautiful, that would stick in the memory. He
had talked to some of the children on his way back through the
gardens after shopping in the mornings, but he had never seen
anyone like her, of that he was sure. With most of them you
could tell that something was wrong as soon as you clapped eyes
on them; there was this curious way in which all their features
seemed to have been drawn together to the front of their faces,
and the features themselves were tiny. But everything about that
poor little mite's features was perfect. Oh yes, he would certainly have noticed her if she had been playing on the swings
with the others. Unless, of course, he hadn't realized that she
was one of them and had imagined that she was one of the normal children who also played there. But the normal children
were usually much younger — one didn't play on swings when
one was twelve; and in any case when the children from that
special school arrived the other children would usually drift off.
He thought it cruel the way that mothers of the normal children
would begin to wheel away their prams, shouting over their
shoulders "Come along, Fiona — time we moved on!" or "Rex!
Rex! Come *on!*" Often he himself brought some sweets with
him, and the children would remember this — oh, they could be
bright enough if they wanted to be — and then two or three
would spot him on the bench on which he always sat and they
would at once run over, to be followed by a whole jostling,
gabbling pack of them. The two women in charge would go on

knitting and chatting. Once he had tried to engage them in conversation, but he understood at once, from the way in which neither looked up as the larger of them answered, that they didn't want any company except each other's.

"What a pretty little thing!"

Reynolds started at the sound of the croaking voice behind him.

It was the old man with the tottering, gray-muzzled Labrador bitch on the end of a piece of string. Reynolds always tried to avoid him.

"Shocking," he said, swallowing on the word.

"And yet they do away with capital punishment. The world's going stark, staring bonkers."

The Labrador bitch was now straddling, back legs wide apart and an expression of patient suffering on her face as her whole body strained and strained again.

"I gave her some paraffin last night." the old man said. "I thought it might ease her, like."

But Reynolds was hurrying off.

"Well, you certainly took your time," Mrs. Evans said. She banged the fish down on the table as though she wished to hurt it. "It's me that gets the blame if his lordship's lunch is late. 'I think that a little Sole Véronique might perhaps tempt my invalid's appetite.' " The far from exact imitation of Sir Malcolm's "posh" voice voided, on this occasion as on many others, the accumulated venom which her small, neat person could no longer contain. " 'And don't forget the mousseline potatoes, now will you, Mrs. Evans?' How does he imagine that I'm to cook that kind of meal for him if you don't bring me the fish until nearly twelve o'clock?" As she spoke these last words, she picked up the sole and began to sniff at it.

"It's quite fresh," Reynolds said.

She sniffed at it again, a look of skepticism on her yellow face.

"He's in a fine old mood," she said. "One of his best."

"Why? What's the matter?"

"If he tells anyone it will be you, now won't it?" she said. "I'm not the one who gets his little confidences." She began to move him away from the refrigerator, the flat of one hand patting at his ribs. "Two men called to see him," she said.

"Two men? What men?"

"Police. They *said*. Didn't look like it to me."

"Police!"

"Scruffy like, one of them was. Just a boy really. They were with him quite a time. Oh, I knew he was upset from the way he started up again about that noise of the next-door radio. As soon as they had left him. It's not as though the radio's on at night-time. Not late, that is."

"What would the police want here?"

"Your guess is as good as mine."

At once, Reynolds did not know why, there had come into his mind that photograph of that poor little thing with her pretty doll-like face and blue, blue eyes and long hair like silk. Perhaps they were making a house-to-house check like the one they made when that woman had been murdered in the off-license in the Lanes. Two such polite men they had been — "just a routine check" they had called it. It had been the night when he had been attending the Whist Drive at St. Barnabas's, so he had had no difficulty in giving them an alibi. But in an odd way, for all their courtesy and for all the certainty of that alibi, they had made him feel somehow furtive and guilty, so that even as he talked to them he was conscious of his face beginning to redden, of his hands beginning to tremble, and of the words emerging from between his lips with the parched, laborious preciseness of someone nervously repeating a lesson learned by rote.

"It might be something to do with the car."

Mrs. Evans shrugged.

"Or perhaps he complained to the police about that radio."

This time Mrs. Evans made no response at all, as she continued to busy herself with removing the skins and pips from some grapes.

"What a footling job!" she muttered to herself at last.

Sir Malcolm did not mention the visit of the police all that day, and Reynolds knew better than to ask him.

"Oh, dear, oh dear, oh dear!" he exclaimed as Reynolds carefully eased the luncheon tray across his knees. "I see that our good Mrs. E. has again been digging into that confounded deep-freeze."

"Sir?"

"These beans look more than a little jaded."

"There were no fresh beans in the shops this morning, sir."

"Well, there must have been *something* fresh. What about chicory?"

"But I thought that you said that you didn't like . . ."

"I've nothing against chicory. Nothing at all. In moderation, that is." Sir Malcolm suddenly gave Reynolds one of his piercing glances from under the loosely wrinkled, pale gray skin of his eyelids. "Are you all right, Reynolds?"

"Perfectly, sir."

"Your hands are shaking."

Reynolds had just drawn Sir Malcolm's napkin out of its ring and had unfurled it with a single downward flick.

"My hands, sir?"

"You look as if something had upset you."

"Oh, no, sir. Not at all."

Sir Malcolm picked up a single grape on the end of his fork and peered at it from every angle. Then he popped it into his mouth and, sucking on it, said, "All right, Reynolds."

It was only when Reynolds was preparing Sir Malcolm for bed, holding out the tray with a tumbler of water and the two sleeping pills on it, that the old man at last mentioned the visit.

Having gulped first one pill and then the other, he went through his habitual gesture of stroking the wattles of his throat with a palsied right hand, presumably to coax the pills on their downward passage, before he said, "Oh, I had an inquiry about you today, Reynolds."

"An inquiry, sir?"

"Yes, an inquiry." The old man paused as though maliciously eager to prolong the other's anxiety. "A police inquiry."

"A police inquiry, sir?" Reynolds was conscious that his hands holding the tray had again begun to tremble and knew that it would be only a matter of time before Sir Malcolm again commented on the fact.

"No need for alarm. It was about this — er — this squalid case of the vanishing girl. How her parents allowed her to consort with a total stranger — or strangers — is quite beyond my understanding. It would be odd enough if she had been in full possession of her faculties, but in the case of a child who was actually simple — 'subnormal,' I think was the word used by our two friends — well, such irresponsibility is little short of criminal. Wouldn't you agree?"

"Yes, indeed, sir."

"Now don't look so worried! I — er — got you off the hook. I can promise you that. Fortunately I had only to look at my diary in order to satisfy them that on the two — or was it three? — days at issue, you were with me in London. It was when I was having those confounded tests at the London Clinic. Remember? Oh, you have nothing to fear, my dear Reynolds! I'd have lied for you, if need be; that goes without saying. After all, it's no easy matter to find a good servant in times like these. But in fact no lie was necessary."

"But why — why did they pick on me?"

"You may well ask. It was because — as they put it — they could not leave a single avenue unexplored. Or was it that they could not leave a single stone unturned? I forget. Anyway — it seems that some busybody had telephoned them to suggest that they might — er — investigate you."

Reynolds was appalled. "But who would want to do such a thing?"

"Oh, someone who wished to be *public-spirited*, I expect. I do hate public spirit, don't you?" Sir Malcolm turned to slap at the pillows against which he was propped. "It seems, you see, that this little girl — this Veronica or Valerie or Vivienne or whatever it was — numbered among her friends a middle-aged gentleman who was known to her parents merely as Ray."

"Ray!"

"Yes, Ray. Not a name for which I care. I could never call *you*

Ray, for example. But the anonymous caller suggested that Ray
might have been a — um — diminutive for Reynolds.''

''But that's slander; that's nothing but slander!''

''Now don't get so agitated. As I told you, I at once got you —
er — off the hook. The police informed me — something of
which I am bound to say I had always been ignorant — that it is
often your way to sit in St. Ann's Well Gardens and talk to the
children from the same school to which this unfortunate little
Vera or Violet or whatever it was used to go. No, no'' — Sir
Malcolm raised a purple-veined hand as Reynolds's mouth was
about to open in expostulation — ''I think such an interest in
the afflicted to be entirely to your credit. Entirely. And I told our
two gentlemen that.''

''Thank you, sir.''

''No, obviously you could not have been this Ray. And so'' —
Sir Malcolm leaned far back on the pillows, smiling — ''it seems
most unlikely that you will be summoned for an identification
parade!'' He drew the sheet up to his pointed chin. ''Do you
know,'' he asked, ''how this Ray first met the child Victoria?''

''I've no idea, sir.''

''No, of course you wouldn't. Well, believe it or not, he just
walked up to her parents on the front, said, 'What a pretty little
girl you have there!' and offered to take her to the Aquarium.
Now just think of that!''

''It's incredible, sir.''

''As you say — incredible.'' The creased eyelids fluttered and
descended. ''Well, now I must turn in. Now don't worry,
Reynolds. I've no intention of losing you. You're far too valuable to me.''

''Thank you, sir.''

Mrs. Evans was still in the kitchen, though it was long after
the hour when she usually left for home. When Reynolds came in
with the tray, she reached for her crocheted brindle beret and
began to tug it over her close-cropped gray curls. ''Has our lord
and master turned in?''

Reynolds nodded.

''Did he say anything about those visitors?''

"What visitors?"

"Those visitors this morning. Those so-called detectives."

It suddenly came to Reynolds that perhaps it had been Mrs. Evans who had telephoned to the police. He knew that she disliked him.

"Oh, those."

"Yes. Did he say anything about them?"

Reynolds shook his head.

"Perhaps he'll tell you tomorrow."

"Maybe."

"He tells you everything. In the end. Doesn't he?"

Sir Malcolm told Mrs. Evans nothing, and this infuriated her.

When Reynolds did not answer, she went on, "Yes, you'll know about it soon enough."

There was something in her tone which was not merely vindictive, as so often in the past, but even grimly menacing. Or had he imagined that? He stared after her, eyes wide and hands trembling as he clutched them together over his stomach as though in some sudden attack of abdominal cramp. Meanwhile she gave a last tug to the beret, and called out, "Bye for now!" and strode out into the darkness.

Reynolds lay in bed, trying to think of the date when he and Sir Malcolm had gone up to London. He had no memory for that kind of thing. No, his memory had never been good; it had always been a worry to him. He could memorize a long shopping list or all the items sent in a week to the laundry, but whole blocks of events had a way of slipping imperceptibly into oblivion. Once when he had complained of the vagaries of his memory to Mrs. Evans, she had fixed him with that sardonically appraising gaze of hers and had commented, "Oh, you can always remember what it suits you to remember."

"What do you mean by that, Mrs. E?" he had demanded, nettled.

"Oh, I don't mean you in particular. I mean you in the general sense. People. Everyone."

If Sir Malcolm said that they had been in London at the time, then they must have been there. Sir Malcolm never failed to fill in his diary every evening after dinner, however bad his health. But there had been something *queer* — almost as though he were making game of him — in the way he had said that about getting him off the hook and being prepared to lie for him. In fact, Sir Malcolm never told lies; in all his twenty-two years with him Reynolds had never known him to tell a lie — not a lie that mattered. But in this case had there not been some vague hint of conspiracy between them?

Reynolds turned over on to his back and stared up at the shadowy ceiling, his head cradled on his skinny arms. He hoped he wasn't going to have another of his spells of sleeplessness, like the one he had when Mrs. Evans had first come to work for them and Sir Malcolm had seemed to take a malicious pleasure in favoring her, although she was the newcomer. He had those pills from the doctor but after the first, which had made him feel giddy and light-headed all the next day, he had never taken another.

He would *know* if he had ever had anything to do with her. Wouldn't he? Surely? That was not the kind of thing one could forget. It was true that he could not remember — well, not properly — the death of his mother or of Iris in the air raid. But his mother had died when he was only six; and in the case of Iris he himself had been half-buried under all that masonry beside her, so that was not really so surprising. Shock could do things like that to your memory; that was well known.

Such a pretty little thing, like a doll, with those blue eyes of hers (yes, he was sure they must have been blue) and that long, silklike hair and that sweet, upturned nose. Who would want to hurt her? He certainly wouldn't. She was the kind of little girl he would like to have had for his own — the sort of girl Iris might have been when she was small, the sort of girl she might have had — and if he had met her all he would have wanted to do would have been to stroke her hair and talk to her and sit her on his knee and buy her some sweeties. It was terrible to think of those blue eyes shut forever and those chubby arms and legs sprawled out on that lonely stretch of beach and sand in the hair and sand on that lovely little mouth of hers . . .

All at once he remembered the doll and his whole body went rigid as though in a sudden spasm. He had forgotten the doll; he hadn't thought about it once for, well, going on forty years. Mimsie — that was the name he gave her because he couldn't bring himself to call her Mummy whatever his father said — had often scolded him about it — "A big boy like you, going round with a doll! You should be ashamed of yourself." He was seven at the time. Mummy, his real mummy, had given him the doll for Christmas and it had this lovely flaxen hair and these blue eyes that opened and shut and this peaches-and-cream complexion. He would carry it around with him and even trail it by one arm through the dank weeds that overgrew the bottom of the garden, so the dainty, frilly little skirt would get all soggy and the legs would be scratched by the brambles and stung by the nettles, just like his own. "I'll give it to the dustman the next time they call," Mimsie threatened. "You'll see if I don't." It was then that he buried the doll, before tea on a cold winter's evening, his whole body trembling and the gulping sobs rising in his throat as he first scrabbled away at the moldering leaves from under the beech tree and then began to dig, dig, dig ferociously with a trowel while the breath wreathed out from between his clenched teeth. "Dust to dust, ashes to ashes," he muttered, because he remembered those words from Mummy's burial; and then he scattered the first earth over that dainty little frilly pale blue skirt and on to the shut eyes and over the rose-bud mouth.

Once it was over he felt an extraordinary exhilaration, so that, having raced back to the house, he burst into the cramped sitting room with so much violence that everything in it shook and Mimsie looked up from painting her fingernails to tell him to quiet down.

He forgot about the doll; yes, that was odd — he completely forgot about her; she might never have existed. Until one day, when Daddy and Mimsie had gone into Colchester for the day, leaving him behind all alone, he had wandered, disconsolate and bored, down into the undergrowth at the bottom of the narrow strip of garden. Suddenly, with a curious mingling of terror and excitement, he had remembered that she lay somewhere here near his feet and, stooping, he had begun to burrow away with his bare hands, breaking some of his fingernails and clogging others with dirt and mold. There at last she was, her dainty dress all rotted and in tatters and her eyelashes and her mouth and her delicate nostrils filled with mud. He ran with her up into the house and placed her in the kitchen sink with some soapflakes in warm water. Gently he began to wash her, running his hands over the smoothness of her arms and legs and body, until bit by bit she came back to life for him.

The dress, of course, could never be the same; so he wrapped her up in an old vest of his that Mimsie had put in the shoebox to use on the shoes.

After that she often died for him, was buried, and was brought back to life. Daddy and Mimsie never knew anything about it; it was a secret not to be told them. Slowly, however, from the long stays in the earth and the scrubbings at the sink, the hair began to fall out, the silken eyelashes and then even the eyes themselves to disappear and the fingers and toes to crumble. Each such change he would watch with a fatalistic curiosity, pierced at times with a sudden brief pang of grief; until the time came when he knew that the burial would be the last, and he would never again disturb the grave of leafmold.

Yet how odd, he thought now, that between each death and resurrection he should completely have forgotten her! Involuntarily the memory of her would erase itself from his mind until, no less involuntarily, it would flash back with stabbing vividness, making him long for the first moment when he would be alone for long enough to dig her up again.

Reynolds sat up in the bed, clutching at his bony knees with hands equally bony. If he could so easily forget about *her*, might he not have forgotten about the other one, too? Perhaps in the case of that poor little kiddy no less than in the case of the doll the sleeping memory would one day — perhaps soon — rouse itself to glide back, snakelike, into his conscious mind. *Could* he have known her? *Could* he have done such a thing?

He jumped out of bed and scrabbled in a drawer for the bottle of sleeping pills. He put one on his tongue, and then, while beginning to savor its bitterness, put another and another. He had to obliterate that fear as soon as possible.

*

"You're half-asleep, man! What's the matter with you?"

"Sorry, sir." Reynolds fumbled to insert in the razor the blade he had forgotten.

"Aren't you feeling well?"

"Perfectly well, thank you, sir."

"You look pale. And I shouldn't be surprised if you weren't about to get a sty in that right eye of yours. Well, I hope you're not sickening for anything. That would be a fine kettle of fish."

A middle-aged woman sat on a swing and screamed each time that it rose higher and higher. She had on a shapeless, belted raincoat and a plastic sou'wester. Reynolds watched, his body hunched forward on the bench, with the two laden shopping bags resting against his shins.

Perhaps the woman was not really middle-aged. Many of them had a prematurely grown-up look; some who were only sixteen or seventeen one could mistake for thirty or forty . . .

On that afternoon he might have been sitting here like this and she might have slowly, dreamily, detached herself from that group of them playing some prolonged, meaningless game in the bushes, and wandered over in his direction. He might have smiled at her and felt in his pocket for a sweet and then held it out. That was what he usually did with them — it was like coaxing a nervous dog to come nearer and nearer to one. She might have sidled up and put out her hand and then he might have smiled at her, reassuringly, and she might have smiled back. "What's your name, dear?" "Vivienne." "That's a pretty name." Then one of the two women in charge might have called to her, looking up over her clicking needles, and Vivienne would have wandered off, with a whispered thank you.

But he would see her again. He was strolling along the pier (*was* now, not *might be*) and there she was, walking between two grownups, each of whom held one of her hands. It was a Saturday (Sunday?) and that was when those children were allowed out with their parents. The two grownups and the doll-like child paused to look down at the fishermen below, and he paused behind them. They turned, and, courage coming to him in some miraculous fashion, he found himself saying, "What a pretty little girl you have there!" Of course she did not recognize him, and he was not going to let on that he had met her before.

"Yes," said the mother, running a plump hand through that silk-soft hair. "But we mustn't tell her that or we'll make her vain, won't we?" The mother wore glasses so thick that her eyes bulged like hardboiled eggs behind them. Her voice was cooing and falsely genteel.

It was all so easy; they seemed to *want* him to take Vivienne off their hands.

"Wouldn't you like to see the Aquarium with your Uncle Ray?" he asked after some minutes of desultory conversation.

"Yes, you'd love that, wouldn't you, pet?"

"That's right," chimed in the father, sucking on his pipe. "You run along with your Uncle Ray."

Reynolds retched for a long time uselessly in the ammonia-smelling lavatory in one corner of the gardens. Then he pressed his ice-cold forehead against the ice-cold tiles. Yes, that was how it had been! That was it! He remembered how he had taken the car from the garage, slipping the key off Sir Malcolm's ring when he had shuffled from the bedroom to the lavatory, and how he had driven the poor, dear little thing out to that lonely stretch of beach, with the plastic sheet and the thermos and the beach ball in the back. He had not meant to do anything; of course he hadn't. But the screams, a magnified echo of the gulls circling above their sprawling bodies, and the sight of the blood and the scratch she had given him on the inside of his thigh — well, how could anyone be expected to keep his head with all that going on?

Poor dolly, poor broken little dolly! He had bundled her into the car — oh, gently, gently, of course — and had thrown the plastic sheet over her and had driven back through a narrow cleft in the Downs with the sky a blue as pale and serene as the blue of those darling eyes. He would have to bury her somewhere secret under a tree; and then later, when no one knew that he had gone up there again, he would go back and find her once more. Yes, that was what he would do. That was it.

The leaves had a curious sweetish smell on them, like the

moldering leaves at the bottom of the narrow garden. The eyes were shut in the same way and the long, silk-soft hair lay in the same way on its bed of earth. The frilly skirt stuck out stiffly; there was a patch of blood on it, like a scab. "I'll come back for you," he whispered. "I'll come back." He put his lips to the porcelain forehead, his hands in the hair. "I'll come back, my darling."

"Well, surely *I* should know!" he cried out in exasperation at them. But they shook their heads and yet again exchanged those glances, at once amused, annoyed, and pitying, with which they had greeted each fresh protestation of his guilt.

"Where does he live?" one of them asked.

"We ought to telephone to someone to fetch him."

"Maybe an ambulance would be the best plan."

"Look, old chap, we know that it just *can't* be you. For all kinds of reasons. So stop pulling our legs, eh?"

"Where does he live?"

"Who *is* the old boy?"

"Look, old chap, you'd better cut along and forget all about it."

"Where does he *live*? Just get him off my hands."

So it took a long time of patient and persistent arguing to persuade them that he could show them the place on the Downs where he had buried her. He could see it so well, out there before him, even while he was gazing into their red, stupid faces and shouting at them "Let me show you! Just let me show you!" He could see the stile, over which he had had such difficulty in carrying her in the dark, and the moonlit path, a vast silvery-skinned snake slithering away from him, and then the three trees, with the interlaced branches that made a curious pattering noise against each other as the wind blew through them. The plastic sheet felt oddly warm, as though it were no more than a living skin to what lay beneath it. But of course that must have been his imagination, because when he unwrapped her she was as cold as the doll.

Unerringly he found the way for them through the bright Feb-

ruary sunshine, a scurrying figure with bowed shoulders and
curiously tripping gait among the burly men with shovels and
spades and the cameraman and the other man with the tripod and
the lamps.

They still didn't believe him; he could see that. This was just
part of leaving no avenue unexplored, of leaving no stone unturned.

"There!" he pointed.

Again they exchanged those glances, at once amused, annoyed, and pitying.

"All right, boys. Get to work!"

They dug, not knowing what they would find. But he knew;
oh, he knew all right. There she would be, with her dainty little
frock all damp and rotted about her, and the mud in her beautiful
silk-soft blond hair and in her nostrils and over her mouth. But
one only had to wash her a little, wash her gently, gently, and the
pink porcelain flesh would brighten again under the frilly skirt
and the eyes would click open and the pretty little, winsome little
smile would appear.

How had he *known*? they asked him over and over again; and
when he screamed "Because I put her there, you fools!" they
shrugged their shoulders or looked angry or asked him if he was
right off his rocker. How had he *known*? they next asked that
middle-aged bus conductor with a limp, father of three children
and a member of the Baptist Church, when eventually they had
caught him. But the bus conductor could not give them the answer they sought. No, he had never seen Reynolds in his life;
Reynolds had never followed him, as far as he knew, on that
fateful winter evening; no, of course they were not accomplices
— he always had those turns of his alone.

"But how did you *know*?" Sir Malcolm would often ask
Reynolds in the months and years that followed.

But Reynolds could not tell him; he himself did not know how
he had known.

FICTION

UNDERTAKER SONG

by Damon Runyon

"Anyway, Mr. Phillips Randolph stands staring at Joey as
if he is greatly startled, and the chances are he is, at that,
for the chances are nobody here speaks to him in such a
manner in all his life."

NOW THIS STORY I am going to tell you is about the game of football, a very healthy pastime for the young, and a great
character-builder from all I hear, but to get around to this game
of football I am compelled to bring in some most obnoxious
characters, beginning with a guy by the name of Joey Perhaps,
and all I can conscientiously say about Joey is you can have him.

It is a matter of maybe four years since I see this Joey Perhaps
until I notice him on a train going to Boston, Mass., one Friday
afternoon. He is sitting across from me in the dining car, where I
am enjoying a small portion of baked beans and brown bread,
and he looks over to me once, but he does not rap to me.

There is no doubt but what Joey Perhaps is bad company, because the last I hear of him he is hollering copper on a guy by the
name of Jack Ortega, and as a consequence of Joey Perhaps hollering copper, this Jack Ortega is taken to the city of Ossining,
N.Y., and placed in an electric chair, and given a very, very,
very severe shock in the seat of his pants.

It is something about plugging a most legitimate business guy
in the city of Rochester, N.Y., when Joey Perhaps and Jack

Ortega are engaged together in a little enterprise to shake the guy down, but the details of this transaction are dull and sordid and quite uninteresting, except that Joey Perhaps turns state's evidence and announces that Jack Ortega fires the shot which cools the legitimate guy off, for which service he is rewarded with only a small stretch.

I must say for Joey Perhaps that he looks good, and he is very well dressed, but then Joey is always particular about clothes, and he is quite a handy guy with the dolls in his day, and, to tell the truth, many citizens along Broadway are by no means displeased when Joey is placed in the state institution, because they are generally pretty uneasy about their dolls when he is around.

Naturally, I am wondering why Joey Perhaps is on this train going to Boston, Mass., but for all I know maybe he is wondering the same thing about me, although I am making no secret about it. The idea is I am en route to Boston, Mass., to see a contest of skill and science that is to take place there this very Friday night between a party by the name of Lefty Ledoux and another party by the name of Mickey McCoy, who are very prominent middleweights.

Now ordinarily I will not go around the corner to see a contest of skill and science between Lefty Ledoux and Mickey McCoy, or anybody else, as far as that is concerned, unless they are using blackjacks and promise to hurt each other, but I am the guest on this trip of a party by the name of Meyer Marmalade, and will go anywhere to see anything if I am a guest.

This Meyer Marmalade is really a most superior character, who is called Meyer Marmalade because nobody can ever think of his last name, which is something like Marmaladowski, and he is known far and wide for the way he likes to make bets on any sporting proposition, such as baseball or horse races or ice hockey or contests of skill and science, and especially contests of skill and science.

So he wishes to be present at this contest in Boston, Mass., between Lefty Ledoux and Mickey McCoy to have a nice wager on McCoy, as he has reliable information that McCoy's manager, a party by the name of Koons, has both judges and the referee in the satchel.

If there is one thing Meyer Marmalade dearly loves, it is to have a bet on a contest of skill and science of this nature, and so he is going to Boston, Mass. But Meyer Marmalade is such a guy as loathes and despises traveling all alone, so when he offers to pay my expenses if I will go along to keep him company, naturally I am pleased to accept, as I have nothing on of importance at the moment, and, in fact, I do not have anything on of importance for the past ten years.

I warn Meyer Marmalade in advance that if he is looking to take anything off of anybody in Boston, Mass., he may as well remain at home, because everybody knows that statistics show that the percentage of anything being taken off of the citizens of Boston, Mass., is less per capita than anywhere else in the United States, especially when it comes to contests of skill and science, but Meyer Marmalade says this is the first time they ever had two judges and a referee running against the statistics, and he is very confident.

Well, by and by I go from the dining car back to my seat in another car, where Meyer Marmalade is sitting reading a detective magazine, and I speak of seeing Joey Perhaps to him. But Meyer Marmalade does not seem greatly interested, although he says to me like this:

"Joey Perhaps, eh?" he says. "A wrong gee. A dead wrong gee. He must just get out. I run into the late Jack Ortega's brother, young Ollie, in Mindy's restaurant last week," Meyer Marmalade says, "and when we happen to get to talking of wrong gees, naturally Joey Perhaps' name comes up, and Ollie remarks he understands Joey Perhaps is about due out, and that he will be pleased to see him some day. Personally," Meyer Marmalade says, "I do not care for any part of Joey Perhaps at any price."

Now our car is loaded with guys and dolls who are going to Boston, Mass., to witness a large football game between the Harvards and the Yales at Cambridge, Mass., the next day, and the reason I know this is because they are talking of nothing else.

So this is where the football starts getting into this story.

One old guy that I figure must be a Harvard from the way he talks seems to have a party all his own, and he is getting so much attention from one and all in the party that I figure he must be a guy of some importance, because they laugh heartily at his remarks, and although I listen very carefully to everything he says he does not sound so very humorous to me.

He is a heavy-set guy with a bald head and a deep voice, and anybody can see that he is such a guy as is accustomed to plenty of authority. I am wondering out loud to Meyer Marmalade who the guy can be, and Meyer Marmalade states as follows:

"Why," he says, "he is nobody but Mr. Phillips Randolph, who makes the automobiles. He is the sixth richest guy in this country," Meyer says, "or maybe it is the seventh. Anyway, he is pretty well up with the front runners. I spot his monicker on his suitcase, and then I ask the porter, to make sure. It is a great honor for us to be traveling with Mr. Phillips Randolph," Meyer says, "because of him being such a public benefactor and having so much dough, especially having so much dough."

Well, naturally everybody knows who Mr. Phillips Randolph is, and I am surprised that I do not recognize his face myself from seeing it so often in the newspapers alongside the latest model automobile his factory turns out, and I am as much pleasured up as Meyer Marmalade over being in the same car with Mr. Phillips Randolph.

He seems to be a good-natured old guy, at that, and he is having a grand time, what with talking and laughing and taking a dram now and then out of a bottle, and when old Crip McGonnigle comes gimping through the car selling his football souvenirs, such as red and blue feathers and little badges and pennants and one thing and another, as Crip is doing around the large football games since Hickory Slim is a two-year-old, Mr. Phillips Randolph stops him and buys all of Crip's red feathers, which have a little white H on them to show they are for the Harvards.

Then Mr. Phillips Randolph distributes the feathers around among his party, and the guys and dolls stick them in their hats or pin them on their coats, but he has quite a number of feathers left over, and about this time who comes through the car but Joey Perhaps, and Mr. Phillips Randolph steps out in the aisle and stops Joey and politely offers him a red feather, and speaks as follows:

"Will you honor us by wearing our colors?"

Well, of course Mr. Phillips Randolph is only full of good spirits, and means no harm whatever, and the guys and dolls in his party laugh heartily as if they consider his action very funny, but maybe because they laugh, and maybe because he is just naturally a hostile guy, Joey Perhaps knocks Mr. Phillips Randolph's hand down, and says like this:

"Get out of my way," Joey says. "Are you trying to make a sucker out of somebody?"

Personally, I always claim that Joey Perhaps has a right to reject the red feather, because for all I know he may prefer a blue feather, which means the Yales, but what I say is he does not need to be so impolite to an old guy such as Mr. Phillips Randolph, although of course Joey has no way of knowing at this time about Mr. Phillips Randolph having so much dough.

Anyway, Mr. Phillips Randolph stands staring at Joey as if he is greatly startled, and the chances are he is, at that, for the chances are nobody ever speaks to him in such a manner in all his life, and Joey Perhaps also stands there a minute, staring back at Mr. Phillips Randolph, and finally Joey speaks as follows:

"Take a good peek," Joey Perhaps says. "Maybe you will remember me if you ever see me again."

"Yes," Mr. Phillips Randolph says, very quiet. "Maybe I will. They say I have a good memory for faces. I beg your pardon for stopping you, sir. It is all in fun, but I am sorry," he says.

Then Joey Perhaps goes on, and he does not seem to notice Meyer Marmalade and me sitting there in the car, and Mr. Phillips Randolph sits down, and his face is redder than somewhat, and all the joy is gone out of him, and out of his party, too. Personally, I am very sorry Joey Perhaps comes along, because I figure Mr. Phillips Randolph will give me one of his spare feathers, and I will consider it a wonderful keepsake.

But now there is not much more talking, and no laughing whatever in Mr. Phillips Randolph's party, and he just sits there as if he is thinking, and for all I know he may be thinking that there ought to be a law against a guy speaking so disrespectfully to a guy with all his dough as Joey Perhaps speaks to him.

Well, the contest of skill and science between Lefty Ledoux and Mickey McCoy turns out to be something of a disappointment, and, in fact, it is a stinkeroo, because there is little skill and no science whatever in it, and by the fourth round the customers are scuffing their feet, and saying throw these bums out, and making other derogatory remarks, and furthermore it seems that this Koons does not have either one of the judges, or even as much as the referee, in the satchel, and Ledoux gets the duke by unanimous vote of the officials.

So Meyer Marmalade is out a couple of C's, which is all he can wager at the ringside, because it seems that nobody in Boston, Mass., cares a cuss about who wins the contest, and Meyer is much disgusted with life, and so am I, and we go back to the Copley Plaza Hotel, where we are stopping, and sit down in the lobby to meditate on the injustice of everything.

Well, the lobby is a scene of gaiety, as it seems there are a number of football dinners and dances going on in the hotel, and guys and dolls in evening clothes are all around and about, and the dolls are so young and beautiful that I get to thinking that this is not such a bad old world, after all, and even Meyer Marmalade begins taking notice.

All of a sudden, a very, very beautiful young doll who is about 40 percent in and 60 percent out of an evening gown walks right up to us sitting there, and holds out her hand to me, and speaks as follows:

"Do you remember me?"

Naturally, I do not remember her, but naturally I am not going to admit it, because it is never my policy to discourage any doll who wishes to strike up an acquaintance with me, which is what I figure this doll is trying to do; then I see that she is nobody but Doria Logan, one of the prettiest dolls that ever hits Broadway, and about the same time Meyer Marmalade also recognizes her.

Doria changes no little since last I see her, which is quite some time back, but there is no doubt the change is for the better, because she is once a very rattle-headed young doll, and now she seems older and quieter, and even prettier than ever. Naturally, Meyer Marmalade and I are glad to see her looking so well, and we ask her how are tricks, and what is the good word, and all this and that, and finally Doria Logan states to us as follows:

"I am in great trouble," Doria says. "I am in terrible trouble, and you are the first ones I see that I can talk to about it."

Well, at this, Meyer Marmalade begins to tuck in somewhat, because he figures it is the old lug coming up, and Meyer Marmalade is not such a guy as will go for the lug from a doll unless he gets something more than a story. But I can see Doria Logan is in great earnest.

"Do you remember Joey Perhaps?" she says.

"A wrong gee," Meyer Marmalade says. "A dead wrong gee."

"I not only remember Joey Perhaps," I say, "but I see him on the train today."

"Yes," Doria says, "he is here in town. He hunts me up only a few hours ago. He is here to do me great harm. He is here to finish ruining my life."

"A wrong gee," Meyer Marmalade puts in again. "Always a hundred percent wrong gee."

Then Doria Logan gets us to go with her to a quiet corner of the lobby, and she tells us a strange story, as follows, and also to wit:

It seems that she is once tangled up with Joey Perhaps, which is something I never know before, and neither does Meyer Marmalade, and, in fact, the news shocks us quite some. It is back in the days when she is just about sixteen and is in the chorus of Earl Carroll's Vanities, and I remember well what a standout she is for looks, to be sure.

Naturally, at sixteen, Doria is quite a chump doll, and does not know which way is south, or what time it is, which is the way all dolls at sixteen are bound to be, and she has no idea what a wrong gee Joey Perhaps is, as he is good-looking and young and seems very romantic and is always speaking of love and one thing and another.

Well, the upshot of it all is the upshot of thousands of other cases since chump dolls commence coming to Broadway, and the first thing she knows, Doria Logan finds herself mixed up with a very bad character, and does not know what to do about it.

By and by Joey Perhaps commences mistreating her no little, and finally he tries to use her in some nefarious schemes of his, and of course everybody along Broadway knows that most of Joey's schemes are especially nefarious, because Joey is on the shake almost since infancy.

Well, one day Doria says to herself that if this is love, she has all she can stand, and she hauls off and runs away from Joey Perhaps. She goes back to her people, who live in the city of Cambridge, Mass., which is the same place where the Harvards have their college, and she goes there because she does not know of any other place to go.

It seems that Doria's people are poor, and Doria goes to a business school and learns to be a stenographer, and she is working for a guy in the real estate dodge by the name of Poopnoodle and doing all right for herself, and in the meantime she hears that Joey Perhaps gets sent away, so she figures her troubles are all over as far as he is concerned.

Now Doria Logan goes along quietly through life, working for Mr. Poopnoodle and never thinking of love, or anything of a similar nature, when she meets up with a young guy who is one of the Harvards and who is maybe twenty-one years old and is quite a football player, and where Doria meets up with this guy is in a drugstore over a banana split.

Well, the young Harvard takes quite a fancy to Doria, and, in fact, he is practically on fire about her, but by this time Doria is going on twenty and is no longer a chump doll, and she has no wish to get tangled up in love again.

In fact, whenever she thinks of Joey Perhaps, Doria takes to hating guys in general, but somehow she cannot seem to get up a real good hate on the young Harvard, because, to hear her tell it, he is handsome and noble and has wonderful ideals.

Now as time goes on, Doria finds she is growing pale and is losing her appetite and cannot sleep, and this worries her no little, as she is always a first-class feeder, and finally she comes to the conclusion that what ails her is that she is in love with the young Harvard and can scarcely live without him, so she admits as much to him one night when the moon is shining on the Charles River, and everything is a dead-cold setup for love.

Well, naturally, after a little offhand guzzling, which is quite permissible under the circumstances, the young guy wishes her to name the happy day, and Doria has half a notion to make it the following Monday, this being a Sunday night, but then she gets to thinking about her past with Joey Perhaps and all, and she figures it will be bilking the young Harvard to marry him unless she has a small talk with him first about Joey, because she is well aware that many young guys may have some objection to wedding a doll with a skeleton in her closet, and especially a skeleton such as Joey Perhaps.

But she is so happy she does not wish to run the chance of spoiling everything by these narrations right away, so she keeps her trap closed about Joey, although she promises to marry the young Harvard when he gets out of college, which will be the following year, if he still insists, because Doria figures that by then she will be able to break the news to him about Joey very gradually and gently, and especially gently.

Anyway, Doria says she is bound and determined to tell him before the wedding, even if he takes the wind on her as a consequence, and personally I claim this is very considerate of Doria, because many dolls never tell before the wedding, or even after. So Doria and the young Harvard are engaged, and great happiness prevails, when, all of a sudden, in pops Joey Perhaps.

It seems that Joey learns of Doria's engagement as soon as he gets out of the state institution, and he hastens to Boston, Mass., with an inside coat pocket packed with letters that Doria writes him long ago, and also a lot of pictures they have taken together, as young guys and dolls are bound to do, and while there is nothing much out of line about these letters and pictures, put them all together they spell a terrible pain in the neck to Doria at this particular time.

"A wrong gee," Meyer Marmalade says. "But," he says, "he is only going back to his old shakedown dodge, so all you have to do is to buy him off."

Well, at this, Doria Logan laughs one of these little short dry laughs that go "hah," and says like this:

"Of course he is looking to get bought off, but," she says, "where will I get any money to buy him off? I do not have a dime of my own, and Joey is talking large figures, because he knows my fiancé's papa has plenty. He wishes me to go to my fiancé and make him get the money off his papa, or he threatens to personally deliver the letters and pictures to my fiancé's papa.

"You can see the predicament I am in," Doria says, "and you can see what my fiancé's papa will think of me if he learns I am once mixed up with a blackmailer such as Joey Perhaps.

"Besides," Doria says, "it is something besides money with Joey Perhaps, and I am not so sure he will not double-cross me even if I can pay him his price. Joey Perhaps is very angry at me. I think," she says, "if he can spoil my happiness, it will mean more to him than money."

Well, Doria states that all she can think of when she is talking to Joey Perhaps is to stall for time, and she tells Joey that, no matter what, she cannot see her fiancé until after the large football game between the Harvards and the Yales as he has to do a little football playing for the Harvards, and Joey asks her if she is going to see the game, and naturally she is.

And then Joey says he thinks he will look up a ticket-speculator and buy a ticket and attend the game himself, as he is very fond of football, and where will she be sitting, as he hopes and trusts he will be able to see something of her during the game, and this statement alarms Doria Logan no little, for who is she going with but her fiancé's papa and a party of his friends, and she feels that there is no telling what Joey Perhaps may be up to.

She explains to Joey that she does not know exactly where she will be sitting, except that it will be on the Harvards' side of the field, but Joey is anxious for more details than this.

"In fact," Doria says, "he is most insistent, and he stands at my elbow while I call up Mr. Randolph at this very hotel, and he tells me the exact locations of our seats. Then Joey says he will endeavor to get a seat as close to me as possible, and he goes away."

"What Mr. Randolph?" Meyer says. "Which Mr. Randolph?" he says. "You do not mean Mr. Phillips Randolph, by any chance, do you?"

"Why, to be sure," Doria says. "Do you know him?"

Naturally, from now on Meyer Marmalade gazes at Doria Logan with deep respect, and so do I, although by now she is crying a little, and I am by no means in favor of crying dolls. But while she is crying, Meyer Marmalade seems to be doing some more thinking, and finally he speaks as follows:

"Kindly see if you can recall these locations you speak of."

So here is where the football game comes in once more.

Only I regret to state that personally I do not witness this game, and the reason I do not witness it is because nobody wakes me up the next day in time for me to witness it, and the way I look at it, this is all for the best, as I am scarcely a football enthusiast.

So from now on the story belongs to Meyer Marmalade, and I will tell you as Meyer tells it to me.

It is a most exciting game (Meyer says). The place is full of people, and there are bands playing and much cheering and more lovely dolls than you can shake a stick at, although I do not believe there are any lovelier present than Doria Logan.

It is a good thing she remembers the seat locations, otherwise I will never find her, but there she is surrounded by some very nice-looking people, including Mr. Phillips Randolph, and there I am two rows back of Mr. Phillips Randolph, and the ticket-spec I get my seat off of says he cannot understand why everybody wishes to sit near Mr. Phillips Randolph today when there are other seats just as good, and maybe better, on the Harvards' side.

So I judge he has other calls similar to mine for this location, and a sweet price he gets for it, too, and I judge that maybe at least one call is from Joey Perhaps, as I see Joey a couple of rows on back up where I am sitting, but off to my left on an aisle, while I am almost in a direct line with Mr. Phillips Randolph.

To show you that Joey is such a guy as attracts attention, Mr. Phillips Randolph stands up a few minutes before the game starts, peering around and about to see who is present that he knows, and all of a sudden his eyes fall on Joey Perhaps, and then Mr. Phillips Randolph proves he has a good memory for faces, to be sure, for he states as follows:

"Why," he says, "there is the chap who rebuffs me so chur-

lishly on the train when I offer him our colors. Yes," he says, "I
am sure it is the same chap."

Well, what happens in the football game is much pulling and
hauling this way and that, and to and fro, between the Harvards
and the Yales without a tally right down to the last five minutes
of play, and then all of a sudden the Yales shove the football
down to within about three eighths of an inch of the Harvards'
goal line.

At this moment quite some excitement prevails. Then the next
thing anybody knows, the Yales outshove the Harvards, and
now the game is over, and Mr. Phillips Randolph gets up out of
his seat, and I hear Mr. Phillips Randolph say like this:

"Well," he says, "the score is not so bad as it might be, and it
is a wonderful game, and," he says, "we seem to make one con-
vert to our cause, anyway, for see who is wearing our colors."

And with this he points to Joey Perhaps, who is still sitting
down, with people stepping around him and over him, and he is
still smiling a little smile, and Mr. Phillips Randolph seems
greatly pleased to see that Joey Perhaps has a big, broad crimson
ribbon where he once wears his white silk muffler.

But the chances are Mr. Phillips Randolph will be greatly surprised if he knows that the crimson ribbon across Joey's bosom
comes of Ollie Ortega planting a short knife in Joey's throat, or
do I forget to mention before that Ollie Ortega is among those
present?

I send for Ollie after I leave you last night, figuring he may
love to see a nice football game. He arrives by plane this morning, and I am not wrong in my figuring. Ollie thinks the game is
swell.

Well, personally, I will never forget this game, it is so exciting.
Just after the tally comes off, all of a sudden, from the Yales in
the stand across the field from the Harvards, comes a long-
drawn-out wail that sounds so mournful it makes me feel very
sad, to be sure. It starts off something like Oh-oh-oh-oh-oh, with
all the Yales Oh-oh-oh-oh-oh-ing at once, and I ask a guy next to
me what it is all about.

"Why," the guy says, "it is the Yales' 'Undertaker Song.'
They always sing it when they have the other guy licked. I am an

old Yale myself, and I will now personally sing this song for you."

And with this the guy throws back his head, and opens his mouth wide and lets out a yowl like a wolf calling to its mate.

Well, I stop the guy, and tell him it is a very lovely song, to be sure, and quite appropriate all the way around, and then I hasten away from the football game without getting a chance to say good-bye to Doria, although afterward I mail her the package of letters and pictures that Ollie gets out of Joey Perhaps' inside coat pocket during the confusion that prevails when the Yales make their tally, and I hope and trust that she will think the crimson streaks across the package are just a little touch of color in honor of the Harvards.

But the greatest thing about the football game (Meyer Marmalade says) is I win two C's off of one of the Harvards sitting near me, so I am now practically even on my trip.

THE WOMAN'S GHOST STORY

by Algernon Blackwood

" 'How in the world did you get up here?' I stammered to
him across the empty room."

"Yes," she said, from her seat in the dark corner, "I'll tell you
an experience if you care to listen. And, what's more, I'll tell it
briefly, without trimmings — I mean without unessentials.
That's a thing storytellers never do, you know," she laughed.
"They drag in all the unessentials and leave their listeners to
disentangle; but I'll give you just the essentials, and you can
make of it what you please. But on one condition: that at the end
you ask no questions, because I can't explain it and have no wish
to."

We agreed. We were all serious. After listening to a dozen pro-
lix stories from people who merely wished to "talk" but had
nothing to tell, we wanted "essentials."

"In those days," she began, feeling from the quality of our silence that we were with her, "in those days I was interested in
psychic things, and had arranged to sit up alone in a haunted
house in the middle of London. It was a cheap and dingy lodging
house in a mean street, unfurnished. I had already made a pre-
liminary examination in daylight that afternoon, and the keys
from the caretaker, who lived next door, were in my pocket. The
story was a good one — satisfied me, at any rate, that it was
worth investigating; and I won't weary you with details as to the
woman's murder and all the tiresome elaboration as to *why* the
place was *alive*. Enough that it was.

"I was a good deal bored, therefore, to see a man, whom I

took to be the talkative old caretaker, waiting for me on the steps
when I went in at 11 P.M., for I had sufficiently explained that I
wished to be there alone for the night.

" 'I wished to show you *the* room,' he mumbled, and, of
course, I couldn't exactly refuse, having tipped him for the temporary loan of a chair and table.

" 'Come in, then, and let's be quick,' I said.

"We went in, he shuffling after me through the unlighted hall
up to the first floor where the murder had taken place, and I prepared myself to hear his inevitable account before turning him
out with the half-crown his persistence had earned. After lighting
the gas I sat down in the armchair he had provided — a faded,
brown-plush armchair — and turned for the first time to face him
and get through with the performance as quickly as possible.
And it was in that instant I got my first shock. The man was *not*
the caretaker. It was not the old fool, Carey, I had interviewed
earlier in the day and made my plans with. My heart gave a horrid jump.

" 'Now who are *you*, pray?' I said. 'You're not Carey, the
man I arranged with this afternoon. Who are you?'

"I felt very uncomfortable, as you may imagine. I was a 'psychical researcher' and a young woman of new tendencies and
proud of my liberty, but I did not care to find myself in an empty
house with a stranger. Something of my confidence left me.
Confidence with women, you know, is all humbug after a certain
point. Or perhaps you don't know, for most of you are men. But
anyhow, my pluck ebbed in a quick rush, and I felt afraid.

" 'Who are you?' I repeated quickly and nervously. The fellow was well dressed, youngish, and good-looking, but with a
face of great sadness. I myself was barely thirty. I am giving you
essentials, or I would not mention it. Out of quite ordinary things
comes this story. I think that's why it has value.

" 'No,' he said. 'I'm the man who was frightened to death.'

"His voice and his words ran through me like a knife, and I
felt ready to drop. In my pocket was the book I had bought to
make notes in. I felt the pencil sticking in the socket. I felt, too,
the extra warm things I had put on to sit up in, as no bed or sofa
was available — a hundred things dashed through my mind,

foolishly and without sequence or meaning, as the way is when one is really frightened. Unessentials leaped up and puzzled me, and I thought of what the papers might say if it came out, and what my 'smart' brother-in-law would think, and whether it would be told that I had cigarettes in my pocket, and was a free-thinker.

" 'The man who was frightened to death!' I repeated, aghast.

" 'That's me,' he said stupidly.

"I stared at him just as you would have done — any one of you men now listening to me — and felt my life ebbing and flowing like a sort of hot fluid. You needn't laugh! That's how I felt. Small things, you know, touch the mind with great earnestness when terror is there — *real terror*. But I might have been at a middle-class tea party, for all the ideas I had; they were so ordinary!

" 'But I thought you were the caretaker I tipped this afternoon to let me sleep here!' I gasped. 'Did — did Carey send you to meet me?'

" 'No,' he replied in a voice that touched my boots somehow. 'I am the man who was frightened to death. And what is more, I am frightened *now*!'

" 'So am I,' I managed to utter, speaking instinctively. 'I'm simply terrified.'

" 'Yes,' he replied in that same odd voice that seemed to sound within me. 'But you are still in the flesh, and I — *am not*!'

"I felt the need for vigorous self-assertion. I stood up in that empty, unfurnished room, digging the nails into my palms and clenching my teeth. I was determined to assert my individuality and my courage as a new woman and a free soul.

" 'You mean to say you are not in the flesh!' I gasped. 'What in the world are you talking about?'

"The silence of the night swallowed up my voice. For the first time I realized that darkness was over the city; that dust lay upon the stairs; that the floor above was untenanted and the floor below empty. I was alone in an unoccupied and haunted house, unprotected, and a woman. I chilled. I heard the wind round the house, and knew the stars were hidden. My thoughts rushed to policemen and omnibuses, and everything that was useful and comforting. I suddenly realized what a fool I was to come to such a house alone. I was icily afraid. I thought the end of my life had come. I was an utter fool to go in for psychical research when I had not the necessary nerve.

" 'Good God!' I gasped. 'If you're not Carey, the man I arranged with, who are you?'

"I was really stiff with terror. The man moved slowly toward me across the empty room. I held out my arm to stop him, getting up out of my chair at the same moment, and he came to a halt just opposite me, a smile on his worn, sad face.

" 'I told you who I am,' he repeated quietly with a sigh, looking at me with the saddest eyes I have ever seen, 'and I am frightened *still*.'

"By this time I was convinced that I was entertaining either a rogue or a madman, and I cursed my stupidity in bringing the man in without having seen his face. My mind was quickly made up, and I knew what to do. Ghosts and psychic phenomena flew to the winds. If I angered the creature my life might pay the price. I must humor him till I got to the door, and race for the street. I stood bolt upright and faced him. We were about of a height, and I was a strong, athletic woman who played hockey in winter and climbed Alps in summer. My hand itched for a stick, but I had none.

" 'Now, of course, I remember,' said I with a sort of stiff smile that was very hard to force. 'Now I remember your case and the wonderful way you behaved.'

"The man stared at me stupidly, turning his head to watch me as I backed more and more quickly to the door. But when his face broke into a smile I could control myself no longer. I reached the door in a run, and shot out on to the landing. Like a fool, I turned the wrong way and stumbled over the stairs leading to the next story. But it was too late to change. The man was after me, I was sure, though no sound of footsteps came; and I dashed up the next flight, tearing my skirt and banging my ribs in the darkness, and rushed headlong into the first room I came to. Luckily the door stood ajar, and, still more fortunate, there was a key in the lock. In a second I had slammed the door, flung my whole weight against it, and turned the key.

"I was safe, but my heart was beating like a drum. A second later it seemed to stop altogether, for I saw that there was someone else in the room besides myself. A man's figure stood between me and the windows, where the street lamps gave just enough light to outline his shape against the glass. I'm a plucky woman, you know, for even then I didn't give up hope, but I may tell you that I have never felt so vilely frightened in all my born days. I had locked myself in with him!

"The man leaned against the window, watching me where I lay in a collapsed heap upon the floor. So there were two men in the house with me, I reflected. Perhaps other rooms were occupied too! What could it all mean! But, as I stared, something changed in the room, or in me — hard to say which — and I realized my mistake, so that my fear, which had so far been physical, at once altered its character and became *psychical*. I became afraid in my soul instead of in my heart, and I knew immediately who this man was.

" 'How in the world did you get up here?' I stammered to him across the empty room, amazement momentarily stemming my fear.

" 'Now, let me tell you,' he began, in that odd, faraway voice of his that went down my spine like a knife. 'I'm in different space, for one thing, and you'd find me in any room you went into; for according to your way of measuring, I'm *all over the house*. Space is a bodily condition, but I am out of the body and am not affected by space. It's my condition that keeps me here. I want something to change my condition for me, for then I could get away. What I want is sympathy. Or, really, more than sympathy; I want affection — I want *love*!'

"While he was speaking I gathered myself slowly upon my feet. I wanted to scream and cry and laugh all at once, but I only succeeded in sighing, for my emotion was exhausted and a numbness was coming over me. I felt for the matches in my pocket and made a movement toward the gas jet.

" 'I should be much happier if you didn't light the gas,' he said at once, 'for the vibrations of your light hurt me a good deal. You need not be afraid that I shall injure you. I can't touch your body to begin with, for there's a great gulf fixed, you know; and really this half-light suits me best. Now, let me continue what I was trying to say before. You know, so many people have come to this house to see me, and most of them have seen me, and one and all have been terrified. If only, oh, if only someone would be *not* terrified, but kind and loving to me! Then, you see, I might be able to change my condition and get away.'

"His voice was so sad that I felt tears start somewhere at the back of my eyes; but fear kept all else in check, and I stood shaking and cold as I listened to him.

" 'Who are you, then? Of course Carey didn't send you, I know now,' I managed to utter. My thoughts scattered dreadfully and I could think of nothing to say. I was afraid of a stroke.

" 'I know nothing about Carey, or who he is,' continued the man quietly, 'and the name my body had I have forgotten, thank God; but I am the man who was frightened to death in this house ten years ago, and have been frightened ever since, and am frightened still; for the succession of cruel and curious people who come to this house to see the ghost, and thus keep alive its atmosphere of terror, only helps to render my condition worse. If only someone would be kind to me — *laugh*, speak gently and rationally with me, cry if they like, pity, comfort, soothe me — anything but come here in curiosity, and tremble as you are now doing in that corner. Now, madam, won't you take pity on me?' His voice rose to a dreadful cry. 'Won't you step out into the middle of the room and try to love me a little?'

"A horrible laughter came gurgling up in my throat as I heard him, but the sense of pity was stronger than the laughter, and I found myself actually leaving the support of the wall and approaching the center of the floor.

" 'By God!' he cried, at once straightening up against the window, 'you have done a kind act. That's the first attempt at sympathy that has been shown me since I died, and I feel better already. In life, you know, I was a misanthrope. Everything went wrong with me, and I came to hate my fellow men so much that I couldn't bear to see them even. Of course, like begets like, and this hate was returned. Finally I suffered from horrible delusions, and my room became haunted with demons that laughed and grimaced, and one night I ran into a whole cluster of them near the bed — and the fright stopped my heart and killed me. It's hate and remorse, as much as terror, that clogs me so thickly and keeps me here. If only someone could feel pity and sympathy and perhaps a little love for me, I could get away and be happy. When you came this afternoon to see over the house, I watched you, and a little hope came to me for the first time. I saw you had courage, originality, resource — *love*. If only I could perhaps tap that love you have stored up in your being there, and thus borrow the wings for my escape!'

"Now I must confess my heart began to ache a little, as fear left me and the man's words sank their sad meaning into me. Still, the whole affair was so incredible, and so touched with unholy quality, and the story of a woman's murder I had come to investigate had so obviously nothing to do with this thing, that I felt myself in a kind of wild dream that seemed likely to stop at any moment and leave me somewhere in bed after a nightmare.

"Moreover, his words possessed me to such an extent that I found it impossible to reflect upon anything else at all, or to consider adequately any ways and means of action or escape.

"I moved a little nearer to him in the gloom, horribly frightened, of course, but with the beginnings of a strange determination in my heart.

" 'You women,' he continued, his voice plainly thrilling at my approach, 'you wonderful women, to whom life often brings no opportunity of spending your great love, oh, if you only could know how many of *us* simply yearn for it! It would save our souls, if you but knew. Few might find the chance that you now have, but if you only spend your love freely, without definite object, just letting if flow openly for all who need, you would reach hundreds and thousands of souls like me, and *release us*! Oh, madam, I ask you again to feel with me, to be kind and gentle — and, if you can, to love me a little!'

"My heart did leap within me and this time the tears did come, for I could not restrain them. I laughed, too, for the way he called me 'madam' sounded so odd, here in this empty room at midnight in a London street, but my laughter stopped dead and merged in a flood of weeping when I saw how my change of feeling affected him. He had left his place by the window and was kneeling on the floor at my feet, his hands stretched out toward me, and the first signs of a kind of glory about his head.

" 'Put your arms round me and kiss me, for the love of God!' he cried. 'Kiss me, oh, kiss me, and I shall be freed! You have done so much already — now do this!'

"I stuck there, hesitating, shaking, my determination on the verge of action, yet not quite able to compass it. But the terror had almost gone.

" 'Forget that I'm a man and you're a woman,' he continued in the most beseeching voice I ever heard. 'Forget that I'm a ghost, and come out boldly and press me to you with a great kiss, and let your love flow into me. Forget yourself just for one minute and do a brave thing! Oh, love me, *love me*, LOVE ME! and I shall be free!'

"The words, or the deep force they somehow released in the center of my being, stirred me profoundly, and an emotion infinitely greater than fear surged up over me and carried me with it across the edge of action. Without hesitation, I took two steps forward toward him where he knelt, and held out my arms. Pity and love were in my heart at that moment; genuine pity, I swear, and genuine love. I forgot myself and my little tremblings in a great desire to help another soul.

" 'I love you, poor, aching, unhappy thing! I love you,' I cried through hot tears; 'and I am not the least bit afraid in the world.'

"The man uttered a curious sound, like laughter, yet not laughter, and turned his face up to me. The light from the street below fell on it, but there was another light, too, shining all round it that seemed to come from the eyes and skin. He rose to his feet and met me, and in that second I folded him to my breast and kissed him full on the lips again and again."

All our pipes had gone out, and not even a skirt rustled in that dark studio as the storyteller paused a moment to steady her voice, and put a hand softly up to her eyes before going on again.

"Now, what can I say, and how can I describe to you, all you skeptical men sitting there with pipes in your mouths, the amazing sensation I experienced of holding an intangible, impalpable thing so closely to my heart that it touched my body with equal pressure all the way down, and then melted away somewhere into my very being? For it was like seizing a rush of cool wind and feeling a touch of burning fire the moment it had struck its swift blow and passed on. A series of shocks ran all over and all through me; a momentary ecstasy of flaming sweetness and wonder thrilled down into me; my heart gave another great leap — and then I was alone.

"The room was empty. I turned on the gas and struck a match to prove it. All fear had left me, and something was singing round me in the air and in my heart like the joy of a spring morning in youth. Not all the devils or shadows or hauntings in the world could then have caused me a single tremor.

"I unlocked the door and went over all the dark house, even to kitchen and cellar and up among the ghostly attics. But the house was empty. Something had left it. I lingered a short hour, analyzing, thinking, wondering — you can guess what and how, perhaps, but I won't detail, for I promised only essentials, remember — and then went out to sleep the remainder of the night in my own flat, locking the door behind me upon a house no longer haunted.

"But my uncle, Sir Henry, the owner of the house, required an account of my adventure, and, of course, I was in duty bound to give him some kind of story. Before I could begin, however, he held up his hand to stop me.

" 'First,' he said, 'I wish to tell you a little deception I ventured to practice on you. So many people have been to that house and seen the ghost that I came to think the story acted on their imaginations, and I wished to make a better test. So I invented for their benefit another story, with the idea that if you did see anything I could be sure it was not due merely to an excited imagination.'

" 'Then what you told me about a woman having been murdered, and all that, was not the true story of the haunting?'

" 'It was not. The true story is that a cousin of mine went mad in the house, and killed himself in a fit of morbid terror following upon years of miserable hypochondriasis. It is his figure that investigators see.'

" 'That explains, then,' I gasped.

" 'Explains what?'

"I thought of that poor struggling soul, longing all these years for escape, and determined to keep my story for the present to myself.

" 'Explains, I mean, why I did not see the ghost of the murdered woman,' I concluded.

" 'Precisely,' said Sir Henry, 'and why, if you had seen anything, it would have had value, inasmuch as it could not have been caused by the imagination working upon a story you already knew.' "

THE TRIAL OF JANE'S AUNT

by Albert Borowitz

"Aunt Jane insisted that the clerk had given her the white lace by mistake, but Miss Gregory replied, ''Tis no such thing . . . You stole it, you are guilty.' "

JANE AUSTEN'S MATERNAL UNCLE, James Leigh Perrot, possessed two of the status symbols of the respectable Englishman, as listed by Jane in her last, unfinished novel *Sanditon*: "symptoms of gout and a winter at Bath." Uncle James had a touching (but unrewarded) faith in the therapeutic powers of the waters of Bath, and he and Aunt Jane Leigh Perrot spent almost as much time at that famous resort town and spa as at their home in Berkshire called Scarlets. In the winter of 1799–1800 Bath was particularly unkind to Uncle James's ailment, because, instead of conversing with his well-born friends at the Pump Room or the Assembly Rooms or promenading on the Royal Crescent, he spent the season with his wife at the rude home of the warden of Ilchester Gaol. For Aunt Jane had been arrested in August 1799 on the inelegant charge of filching a card of white lace from the William Smith millinery shop.

In May and June 1799, Jane Austen and her mother had also visited Bath in the company of Jane's brother Edward and his wife. It was feared that Edward was following in his uncle's painful footsteps and was teetering on the verge of gout. Jane's letters from Bath to her sister Cassandra report on Edward's condition (she had no cause for worry since he lived until eighty-two), but for the most part they are given over to shopping notes, which serve as an ironic prelude to Aunt Jane's impending troubles.

On June 2 Jane reported that she "saw some gauzes in a shop in Bath Street yesterday at only 4d. a yard, but they were not so good or so pretty as mine." She also compared the merits and prices of flowers and fruits as millinery ornaments and mentioned Aunt Jane's expert recommendation of a cheap shop:

> Flowers are very much worn, and fruit is still more the thing . . . A plum or greengage would cost three shillings; cherries and grapes about five, I believe, but this is at some of the dearest shops. My aunt has told me of a very cheap one, near Walcot Church, to which I shall go in quest of something for you.

Jane concludes with a sketch of the fiercely competitive social conditions which sent the young Bath tourists in desperate search of embellishments: "I have never seen an old woman at the pump-room."

In Bath Street, at the corner of Stall Street, was a "haberdasher and milliner's shop," which bore over its door the name WILLIAM SMITH but had been kept for two years by Miss Elizabeth Gregory. The shop had previously been owned by William Smith and his wife, Miss Gregory's sister. Mr. Smith had apparently fallen into financial difficulty and conveyed the shop to William Gye and Lacon Lamb, as trustees for his creditors. Gye and Lamb gave up the shop to Miss Gregory, who had already been a shop employee for three years. It is tempting to speculate as to whether William Smith's was the Bath Street shop to which Jane Austen referred in her letter of June 2, since it was at this shop that Aunt Jane stumbled into the clumsy arms of eighteenth-century shoplifting law.

On Thursday, August 8, after the departure of Jane Austen from Bath, Mrs. Leigh Perrot came to the Smith millinery shop between one and two o'clock in the afternoon. She asked Miss Gregory to let her look at some black lace that she had first seen the day before. She decided to buy the lace, which cost one pound, nineteen shillings, and Miss Gregory asked her clerk

Charles Filby to measure and wrap the lace. Aunt Jane paid for the purchase with a five-pound banknote and was given her package and change.

About a half hour later, the Leigh Perrots were passing the shop on the other side of the street when Miss Gregory crossed the street and addressed Mrs. Leigh Perrot: "Pray, ma'am, have not you a card of white lace as well as black?" Mrs. Leigh Perrot answered: "No, I have not a bit of white lace about me." Asked to "see" in her pocket, Aunt Jane gave a paper parcel to Miss Gregory, saying, "If I have, your young man must have put it up in mistake." Miss Gregory examined the parcel and found it contained not only the purchased black lace but also a card of white lace, bearing her shop's private inventory marking. Aunt Jane insisted that the clerk had given her the white lace by mistake, but Miss Gregory replied: "'Tis no such thing, 'tis no such thing, you stole it, you are guilty."

Miss Gregory took the white lace, leaving Aunt Jane with the black lace and the package. Within half an hour, she went with Mr. Filby to the Bath Town Hall to present a charge against Mrs. Leigh Perrot. The mayor was away, and they were told to come back the next day. Miss Gregory and Filby returned daily but were not successful in having their charge received until the following Wednesday, since the magistrates had their hands full making arrangements for the passage of a detachment of boisterous soldiers out of the town.

On Wednesday Miss Gregory and Filby finally obtained a hearing before the magistrates. A prima facie case of shoplifting was found to have been made out, and Aunt Jane was committed to Ilchester Gaol to await trial at the next county assizes, to be held in the spring at Taunton. The offense on which Aunt Jane was to be tried was far from trivial. Shoplifting of an item valued at five shillings or more was a capital crime, and the white lace was put down in the indictment at twenty shillings. For capital punishment the price was right. Although the penalty would likely have been commuted to transportation to Botany Bay in Australia, subjection to the rigors of the penal colony could be equivalent to a death sentence for convicts whose constitutions were not hardy.

Aunt Jane's social position had not exempted her from commitment pending trial, but it did win her the privilege of lodging in the house of the warden, Mr. Scadding, rather than in the prison itself. She was joined by Uncle James, who bore bravely a new onslaught of gout as well as a quality of accommodations far below the most modest Michelin rating. Aunt Jane wrote of the indignities suffered by her fastidious husband:

> Cleanliness has ever been his greatest delight, and yet he sees the greasy toast laid by the dirty children on his knees, and feels the small Beer trickle down his Sleeves on its way across the table unmoved . . .

Aunt Jane declined the kind offer of her sister Austen to send her daughters Jane and Cassandra to stay with them. Aunt Jane had stated that she could not procure the girls accommodations in the warden's house with her, and that she could not let those "Elegant young Women" be inmates in a prison or be subjected to the inconveniences she and her husband were obliged to put up with.

Indeed, the Leigh Perrots were themselves looking for a change of scene. In September, they went to London to seek an order from a judge of the King's Bench, releasing Aunt Jane on bail. However, the request was turned down, and Aunt Jane was remanded to prison. She wrote in disgust that "others must determine" whether the judge's refusal to grant bail was due to "inexperience or profound Wisdom."

The Leigh Perrots then had to accept the warden's hospitality until March, when the trial would begin. What did they make of the strange charge which Aunt Jane faced? Her family has officially declared it to be the crude product of a blackmail conspiracy. William and Richard Arthur Austen-Leigh wrote in *Jane Austen: Her Life and Letters* (1913):

> There were also strong reasons for thinking that the accusation was the result of a deep-laid plot. Gye, the printer, who lived in the market-place, was believed to be the chief instigator. His character was indifferent, and he had money invested in Gregory's shop; and the business was in so bad a way that there was a temptation to seek

for some large haul by way of blackmail. Mrs. Leigh Perrot was selected as the victim, people thought, because her husband was so extremely devoted to her that he would be sure to do anything to save her from the least vexation.

The trial took place on Saturday, March 29, at Taunton's Castle Hall, the scene of Judge Jeffreys's famous "Bloody Assize" in the seventeenth century. The hall, which seated 2000, was filled to capacity, but Jane and Cassandra Austen were not among the audience. Aunt Jane, persisting in her desire to protect them from sharing her ordeal, wrote that she could not accept the offer of her nieces to attend — "to have two Young Creatures gazed at in a public Court would cut me to the very heart." The cast of legal participants in the trial was impressive. The judge, Sir Soulden Lawrence, had sat on the King's Bench since 1794 and was a great friend of Samuel Johnson. The lead counsel for the prosecution was a future Attorney General, Vicary Gibbs, K C. Four able counsel acted for the defense, including a Member of Parliament, Joseph Jekyll.

In his opening to the jury, Mr. Gibbs stated his anticipation that the defense would in all probability be either that Filby had by mistake enclosed the white lace in Mrs. Leigh Perrot's parcel, or that the case "was a malicious prosecution, set on foot for the purpose of extorting money from the Prisoner's husband." With respect to the latter possibility, Mr. Gibbs avowed

> If that be proved, there could not be a more infamous or wicked attempt. All the witnesses must, in that case, be perjured, and the crime would if possible be greater even than that wherewith the prisoner was charged.

But Mr. Gibbs submitted that conspiracy could not be inferred from the conduct of the complainants

> who did not lie by to make the charge privately, but, on the contrary, immediately after the transaction, went to the Town-Hall, to lay information before the magistrates; and that, although many days elapsed . . . before the depositions could be taken . . . yet they related all the circumstances to the town-clerk and deputy town-clerk, and to every person they met. It was then impossible to recall the report.

Elizabeth Gregory was the first witness called by the prosecution. She testified as to the arrangement of the shop premises. The shop was in the shape of a triangle, with its right wall perpendicular to Bath Street. As one entered from Bath Street, one saw a counter along the right wall and a desk a little beyond it, at the truncated rear angle of the shop. On the left hand there was another counter (of crucial importance in the case), which ran diagonally in the direction of the desk and parallel to the shop's left wall. Over the greater part of the length of the left counter (the portion closer to the rear of the shop and the desk) ran a brass railing, on which veils and handkerchiefs were hung. The distance from the shop entrance to the beginning of the brass rail was about two-and-a-half yards, and the rail itself was about two-and-a-half yards long.

Miss Gregory recounted Mrs. Leigh Perrot's visit to the shop on August 8. When Mrs. Leigh Perrot asked to look again at the *black* lace she had examined the day before, Miss Gregory showed it to her. It was kept in a box on the left counter, in a space left clear by the rail at the end of the counter facing the bottom of the shop. Several veils and handkerchiefs hung down from the rail in such profusion as to obscure the view of any person behind them. Miss Gregory stood behind the counter with the left wall of the shop at her back, and Mrs. Leigh Perrot was in front of the counter. Mrs. Leigh Perrot decided on one of the several black laces that were in the box. While Miss Gregory was waiting on her customer, the clerk Filby was behind the counter, toward the end nearest the front of the shop, measuring *white* lace. According to Miss Gregory's testimony, she told Filby to measure the black lace she had just sold to Mrs. Leigh Perrot. Filby came down to the bottom of the counter to perform that task, and Miss Gregory then went to the desk and called to Miss Sarah Raines, her apprentice, to clear away the black lace box. Shortly, Filby came to the desk and asked Miss Gregory for change for Mrs. Leigh Perrot's note. She gave him the change and then went downstairs to dinner, leaving Miss Raines at the desk.

Miss Gregory was in the downstairs kitchen when Filby came in and told her that he had observed Mrs. Leigh Perrot leaving the shop with a card of white lace. She testified that about ten minutes had passed between her having gone downstairs and her return to the shop floor. About a quarter of an hour later she spotted the Leigh Perrots on the street and accosted her customer, with the results already related. Miss Gregory stated that the paper parcel which Mrs. Leigh Perrot gave her at her request was "rumpled" and that the ends were both opened and not folded. She said that Mrs. Leigh Perrot "trembled very much, was much frightened, and coloured as red as scarlet." When Miss Gregory turned out a corner of the paper (in a manner she demonstrated to the court) she saw a card of white lace, and the black lace over it. The black lace card was about an inch shorter than the white lace card beneath it. She saw her shop mark on the white lace card, and recognized that the mark was in Filby's handwriting.

On cross-examination, Miss Gregory testified that nobody had come into the shop during the entire time Mrs. Leigh Perrot was there. Filby, she stated, was about six or seven yards from Mrs. Leigh Perrot when he stood at the top of the counter, and was about four yards away from her when he measured and packed the lace at the bottom of the counter. The witness testified that her customer was wearing a "black cloak."

The cross-examiner, Mr. Dallas, tried to probe the witness's testimony as to the timing of events following the alleged theft. Miss Gregory stated that she was in the kitchen for about ten minutes when Filby came to her with his story, and that she then immediately went up to the shop. This response was consistent with her testimony on direct examination, but she seemed to waver a bit as to the amount of time that then elapsed before she saw the Leigh Perrots on the street. Perhaps it was five minutes, but she could not exactly say how long it was, and, she added defensively, she never had since, at any moment, been able to say exactly what time had elapsed.

On re-examination, Miss Gregory clarified her earlier testimony by stating that nobody had *entered* the shop while Mrs. Leigh Perrot was there, but that "an old lady" had been there when Mrs. Leigh Perrot came in, and stayed about three minutes.

On a second cross-examination, Miss Gregory was questioned about her business relation with Mr. Gye and Mr. Lamb, the trustees for the creditors of her predecessor, Mr. Smith, and she stated that she had purchased the shop from them on an installment basis and was carrying on business for her account. The cross-examiner was presumably hoping for testimony that Miss Gregory was, in effect, running the store for Smith or the trustees. However, it does not appear that she was asked a single question designed to elicit testimony in support of a claim that the trustee Mr. Gye was involved in a conspiracy against the Leigh Perrots.

Then the principal witness for the prosecution, Charles Filby, was called to the stand. He said that he had "lived with Miss Gregory as a shopman" for about six months prior to August 8. He had no prior experience in the millinery trade, and had twice been a bankrupt.

Filby remembered Mrs. Leigh Perrot's entering the shop. He could not recall that he had ever seen her before. When she came in, he was measuring white lace at the end of the left counter that was nearest the street. Standing behind the counter, he had the bottom part of the lace box on the right hand and the lid on his left. The lid contained the unmeasured lace folded on light blue cards. He took the lace from the cards, and, having measured it, put it on again, fixed a ticket to the lace noting the number of yards, and placed the measured lace in the bottom of the lace box on his right. Slightly contradicting Miss Gregory's testimony, he recalled that there was no other customer in the shop when Mrs. Leigh Perrot came in, but that a person came in afterward, stayed four or five minutes, was served and went away.

Filby confirmed that Mrs. Leigh Perrot asked to be shown the lace she had seen the day before, and that Miss Gregory took down the black lace box for her at the bottom of the counter. However, since he stood about four yards away, he had not heard the conclusion of the purchase when Miss Gregory called him over to measure the black lace her customer had selected. He had already put six measured cards of white lace in the bottom of the box. He particularly remembered the sixth card, because the original card had been worn so that he wrapped the lace round a new card. When Miss Gregory called him, he was working on the seventh card, which he placed on top of the unmeasured pieces in the lid. He moved the lid to the seat where he had been sitting, and the bottom of the box remained on the counter.

Filby then went over to measure Mrs. Leigh Perrot's purchase at the bottom of the counter, while Sarah Raines put away the rest of the black lace. He wrapped Mrs. Leigh Perrot's lace around a small card. The witness showed how he then packed the lace in a piece of whited brown paper by holding it in the paper lengthwise, then turning inward the two corners at each end to meet, and then doubling the ends down twice to make the parcel square. When he carried Mrs. Leigh Perrot's five-pound note to Miss Gregory at the desk, four yards away, Filby said, his back was to the customer. When he turned around from the desk, he observed that Mrs. Leigh Perrot had moved from the place where he had left her to the top end of the counter and was facing the desk with her left hand toward the fatal box of white lace. As he was passing along the inside edge of the counter to deliver the change to her, his sight was obscured by the cascade of shawls and handkerchiefs, but when he emerged beyond the beginning of the railing, he saw Mrs. Leigh Perrot's "left hand come out of the box with a card of the lace in her hand." She drew her left hand under her cloak but Filby saw a corner of the blue card, which the cloak did not conceal. Mrs. Leigh Perrot then took her departure as if she were one-armed. She held the purchased black lace in her right hand and then used the same hand to pick up the change that Filby had laid down on the counter.

Filby stated that he conversed with the two other shop assistants, Miss Raines and Miss Leeson, for about two or three minutes after Mrs. Leigh Perrot had left the shop, and then went downstairs to make his report to Miss Gregory. Although Filby said he did not examine the white lace box at this time, he swore positively that he had seen the customer remove the lace from the box.

After Miss Gregory recovered the lace, Filby went out to look for Mrs. Leigh Perrot and saw her and her husband turning the corner of the Abbey Churchyard. He asked Mr. Leigh Perrot's name, and was answered by that indignant husband "that he lived at No. 1, Paragon Buildings, and that his name was on the door." Filby went there directly and saw the name, and then went to Gye's, afterward proceeding with Miss Gregory to the Town Hall in their first effort to present their complaint.

At the beginning of the cross-examination of Filby, the examiner, Mr. Bond, attempted to attack the witness's credibility by questions about his past business dealings and failures. Filby denied having had any dealings with a pawnbroker picturesquely named Crouch, but admitted his partnership with another man named Crout. With such a name in the firm, we are not surprised to read that, like an earlier enterprise in which Filby had engaged, the business went sour. Mr. Bond then asked whether Filby knew of an incident after August 8 in which a customer of the shop, Miss Blagrave, on her arrival home, found two veils in her parcel instead of the one she purchased from Filby. Filby said he did not know whether Miss Blagrave in fact found two veils in her package but admitted that she returned a veil the next morning and told him that he "ought to be very careful, considering what had lately happened with Mrs. Leigh Perrot." Reminded of his testimony on direct examination that he never wrapped more things than were purchased, Filby began to equivocate about Miss Blagrave. He did not *know* she was right; he was not obliged to believe her; he did *not* believe that he wrapped her purchase. He also denied knowledge of a woman named Kent coming to the shop a few days before Mrs. Leigh Perrot to complain about having received more gloves than she bought.

Mr. Bond then turned to the witness's testimony with respect to the alleged theft. Filby stated that, upon coming back and looking in the box of white lace, he found a vacancy in the left corner of the box where he had put the last measured card of lace (the new card). When he saw the defendant's left hand in the box, only Miss Raines and Miss Leeson were in the shop, Miss Raines busy with needlework at the rear of the shop and Miss Leeson behind some muslin at the rear of the shop with her back to the defendant.

Counsel failed to shake Filby's testimony that he not only saw

Mrs. Leigh Perrot's hand in the box but also saw the card in her hand under her cloak. He was quite certain she was wearing a cloak: "Prisoner had on a black mode cloak . . . it was not a long cloak, but one that reached just below her elbows . . ."

Filby testified that the distance from Paragon Buildings (where the Leigh Perrots lived) to the shop on Bath Street was about a quarter of a mile, and conceded that he "[did not] know but that there was time to have gone home if she had chosen to do so." He stated that he stayed in the downstairs kitchen about four or five minutes after he reported the theft to Miss Gregory, and when he came back up into the shop he met Miss Gregory with the recovered card of lace in her hand.

On re-examination, Filby said that he was certain that from the time he went to serve Mrs. Leigh Perrot at the bottom of the counter he had never been nearer to the place where the white lace was left.

Sarah Raines was then called to testify. She confirmed the prior testimony as to the places where the defendant, Miss Gregory, and Filby were during the transaction. She saw Filby measure the purchased black lace and wrap it in paper and that there was nothing else in the paper. She added that Filby did not move from her side while she was putting away the rest of the black lace, that he was not half a yard away from her, and that before she left Filby, when he was about to deliver the parcel to the defendant, Filby and she were about four yards from the white lace box.

On cross-examination by Mr. Jekyll, she admitted that "there was nothing particular to draw her attention in the manner of Filby's putting up the black lace, and that she sees him every day putting up parcels — that she did not then pay any particular attention to him, nor did she observe particularly from whence he took the paper to wrap up the parcel in . . ."

Following these admissions, the judge asked the witness his own questions to test her evidence that there was no white lace in the package:

> *Q.* You say he did not put any white lace in the parcel with the black; how could you know that not being particularly observant?

A. I saw that he put in the black lace only.

Q. Are you certain of that?

A. Yes, my lord, I am.

The prosecution closed its case, and it was now the turn of the defense. The opportunities for the defense were severely limited under the criminal procedure of the time. The defendant could not testify in her own behalf nor could her husband testify in her defense. The defendant was permitted to make an unsworn statement. Mrs. Leigh Perrot attempted to address the court, but "after speaking a few sentences she became so much agitated that her voice failed her," and Mr. Jekyll was requested to repeat her address as dictated to him by his client. The address was brief and stressed Mrs. Leigh Perrot's lack of motive:

> Placed in a situation the most eligible that any woman could desire, with supplies so ample that I was left rich after every wish was gratified — blessed in the affections of the most generous man as a husband, what could induce me to commit such a crime? Depraved indeed must that mind be that under such circumstances could be so culpable.

Mrs. Leigh Perrot's statement also advertised the evidence as to her conduct and character that would be given by her "noble and truly respectable friends," but asserted that she would make no comment on the evidence against her. She did permit herself one remark on what she believed to be a weakness in the prosecution's case:

> I will only ask you whether to be found opposite to the Shop within the space of little more than half an hour, and with the Lace in my hand is like the conduct of a Guilty Person.

The defense then put on its case. The pawnbroker Mr. Crouch had been located in Cripplegate, London. He testified that Filby and his brother had done business in haberdashery goods at his house six or seven years before, but believed that the witness Charles Filby "might not have been with him on business more than once."

Miss Blagrave then gave her account of the superfluous veil as

to which Filby had been questioned. She said that she had purchased and paid for one veil at Smith's shop on September 19,
and received her package from a "tall shopman," whom she
identified as Filby. When she opened the parcel at home she
found a second veil, which she returned to Filby the next day.
He remembered waiting on her, took the veil, and thanked her,
saying that he had not missed it. On cross-examination, the witness said she did not know Mrs. Leigh Perrot and had never
been accused of stealing the veil.

Mrs. Mary Kent was put on the stand to testify as to another
case of alleged negligent wrapping at the Smith shop. She had
purchased four pairs of gloves at the shop in August and had
found five in her parcel. She was not sure who served her but
thought it was "Mrs. Smith's sister" (Miss Gregory).

The defense then led on a procession of distinguished wit-
nesses as to Mrs. Leigh Perrot's fine conduct, character, reputation, and religious principles, and — last but not least — Mr.
Leigh Perrot's reputation as a man of considerable property.
The fourteen witnesses included George Vansittart and Francis
Annesby, Members of Parliament for Berkshire and Reading;
Lord Braybroke; the Reverend Mr. Nind, vicar of Wargrave, in
Berkshire (the parish where the Leigh Perrots' house was
situated); and the Reverend Mr. Wake, curate of the Bath
parish. A linen draper, a mercer, and a jeweler, all from Bath,
testified unanimously as to Mrs. Leigh Perrot's honest dealings
in three separate lines of commerce.

The defense then rested, and the judge summed up the evidence for the jury. The jury then retired, and after fifteen minutes returned with a verdict of not guilty.

Despite the happy outcome, Mrs. Leigh Perrot was a severe
critic of the trial. In a letter to a cousin on April 1, 1800 , she gave
mixed ratings to the judge and her counsel. She praised Mr. Justice Lawrence's politeness but opined that:

> . . . he did not let enough be said of Filby's Villainy — he thought
> enough had been said to fully clear me, and was pretty sure that the
> winding up of his Charge to the Jury would put every doubt respect-
> ing my Innocence out of the Question; but I think it was a dangerous
> Experiment.

She was disappointed in the performance of two of her counsel, but thought one of them made up for forensic deficiencies by a real talent for sobbing. She regretted that neither her husband nor she was permitted to give evidence under oath: ". . . else I could have disproved my having on any Cloak, tho the Villain swore he saw the lace *under my black Cloak*." She did not, however, explain why she made no mention of her attire in her unsworn statement to the court.

What are we to make, with the hindsight of two centuries, of the merits of the case against Jane's aunt?

Sir Frank Douglas MacKinnon, in his book on the case, *Grand Larceny* (London, 1937), does not analyze the nature and quality of the evidence at the trial. He was content to reprint verbatim a contemporary account of the proceedings "taken in court" by John Pinchard, an attorney at Taunton, and to let that record speak for itself. MacKinnon's reticence is not surprising, since his book drew in large part on previously unpublished correspondence to which he was given access by the Austen-Leigh family. For him to have suggested, even by pausing to weigh evidence, that there would be any basis for doubting the tradition of conspiracy against Aunt Jane would not have been regarded by the family as an act of gratitude. Therefore, it may be worth an effort to take a closer look at the evidence on the principal issues of the case.

Was there a conspiracy to extort money from the Leigh Perrots?

It was the strong belief of the Leigh Perrots, which is accepted without question in Jane Austen biographies, that the case against Aunt Jane was trumped up in the belief that James Leigh Perrot could be induced to pay a large sum of money to spare his wife from imprisonment and trial. In fact, the tradition continues, the conspirators failed because the Leigh Perrots refused to yield to extortion and instead weathered the judicial ordeal together.

The prosecutor in the trial pointed out one of the difficulties with the conspiracy theory. The parties who initiated the prosecution did not make the charge privately to the Leigh Perrots but, immediately after the recovery of the white lace, went to the Town Hall to lay their charge before the magistrates. Even though many days elapsed before their depositions could be taken, Miss Gregory and Filby gave the matter as much publicity as they could in the meantime, relating the circumstances to the town clerk and his deputy and to every person in town who was willing to listen to them. They would have found it very difficult to retract the charge if they had been motivated by blackmail or indeed even if they had believed themselves in the right but wished to leave the door open to financial redress.

It is an assumption of the conspiracy theory that the ringleader, William Gye, had marked out the Leigh Perrots as victims in advance because Uncle James was known to be wealthy and deeply devoted to his wife. If this assumption is worthy of belief, then it is only reasonable to suppose that Mr. Gye and his confederates would have known the Leigh Perrots by sight and would also have known their home address. However, it was the testimony of Filby, unchallenged on cross-examination, that after the occurrence at the store he had gone looking for the Leigh Perrots and had asked them their names. When Mr. Leigh Perrot in annoyance gave him his address and told him to look for his name on the door, Filby lost no time in doing precisely as he was told. He noted the name, went to Gye's and afterward went with Miss Gregory to the Town Hall. Unless Filby was engaged in some rather pointless play-acting, it very much appears that he had made an effort to confirm the identity of the Leigh Perrots for the purpose of enabling Miss Gregory to provide proper information in laying her charge with the magistrates.

In support of the family tradition of a blackmail plot, the Austen-Leighs showed Sir Frank Douglas MacKinnon certain anonymous letters purportedly sent to the Leigh Perrots by two people claiming to have overheard Gye and his confederates plotting their villainy. Although the two letters are signed with different initials and apparently are written in different hands, they have such strong stylistic similarities as to suggest that they were dictated by a single source. Both writers claim to have been employees of Gye. The first, who wrote on February 12, 1800, to

Mr. Leigh Perrot, makes the self-serving statement that "had I the means of *gaining Bread for my Family* in any honest way I should gladly leave an employment under as malicious & vile a Man as ever existed." (Emphasis added.) The second writer, who sent his letter to Mr. Leigh Perrot on a date which looks like October 29, expressed similar discontent with the way he earned his "bread":

> . . . I am obliged to *earn Bread for a large Family* in any honest manner I can; and although it is my hard lot *to get that Bread* in the employment of one of the greatest Rascals that ever lived, I have the conscious pleasure of knowing that I have more than once been of service to those who might have suffered from his dishonesty."
>
> (Emphasis added.)

In addition to these anonymous letters, the Leigh Perrots received another letter from a friend in Bath, Daniel Lysons, which indicates that there was talk of the Gye conspiracy in the higher social circles of Bath as well. Presumably these letters were shown by the Leigh Perrots to their lawyers, who would have had an opportunity to investigate the rumors and to focus their inquiries on the employees of Gye. We do not know whether any such investigation was undertaken, but we are left with this curious result: *the only reference in the trial, as recounted by Mr. Pinchard, to the possibility of a blackmail plot was made by the prosecutor in his opening statement to the jury.* Of course, his effort was to induce the jury to discount that possibility, which might have been implanted in their minds by local gossip. However, absolutely no evidence was introduced by the defense to suggest the existence of a blackmail plot, and, instead, the defense was squarely based on the theory that the white lace was inadvertently enclosed in Mrs. Leigh Perrot's package through the negligence of the clerk Filby.

In fact, one of the circumstances of the case that was principally relied on by the defense to prove Aunt Jane's innocence proves still more definitively that there was no conspiracy against her. I refer to her being found on the street across from Smith's with the white lace in her possession about a half hour after she left the shop. Surely, if the object of the plot had been to find her with the incriminating lace on her person, Filby or Miss Gregory would have immediately pursued her as she left the premises and recovered the lace as soon as she moved far enough to accomplish what the common-law experts with their "little Latin" liked to call "asportation" (carrying away). Such apprehensions were not uncommon in the eighteenth century, as evidenced by the following account:

> We had not been long out of the shop but the mercer missed the piece of stuff, and sent his messengers, one one way, and one another, and they presently seized her that had the piece; as for me, I had very luckily stepped into a house . . . and had the satisfaction, or the terror, indeed, of looking out of the window, and seeing the poor creature dragged away to the justice, who immediately committed her to Newgate.

In these words, Daniel Defoe's famous shoplifter, Moll Flanders, describes the capture of her confederate.

But the supposed conspirators of the William Smith millinery shop did not set out in hot pursuit of Aunt Jane. How did they know, then, that she would conveniently return to the neighborhood a half hour later with the missing lace still in the original package, however "rumpled"? They could not have known. The recovery of the lace was fortuitous, and the conspiracy theory is apparently a fantasy.

Did Filby perjure himself in testifying that Mrs. Leigh Perrot hid the stolen lace under her black coat?

As noted, Mrs. Leigh Perrot complained bitterly that, due to her husband's legal incapacity to testify in her behalf, she had been unable to disprove the testimony of the clerk Filby that she had hidden the white lace under her "black cloak." She maintained that she was not wearing a cloak at all, and that Filby was lying. However, it would be hard to believe that the Leigh Perrots, promenading on one of the main streets of Bath, where they were well known, did not come across a single friend or acquaintance on the day in question who could have testified that Mrs. Leigh Perrot was not wearing a cloak. No such testimony was introduced. Filby would have been taking a great risk in lying about Mrs. Leigh Perrot's apparel, since the possibility of the defense's producing a contradictory witness should have struck him as very great indeed.

How persuasive was the evidence that Filby included the white lace in Mrs. Leigh Perrot's package through negligence?

In support of its theory that Filby inadvertently wrapped the white lace in Mrs. Leigh Perrot's package, the defense tried to establish that both the Smith millinery shop and Filby were negligent wrappers. Evidence of two other instances of similar "mistakes" was introduced, Miss Blagrave's testimony as to the veils and Mrs. Mary Kent's, as to the gloves. The judge, in his instructions to the jury, allowed the Blagrave evidence to stand, since she identified Filby as the wrapper, but he instructed the jury to disregard the Kent testimony, since it appeared that she had been served by some woman in the shop.

Although, under Anglo-American evidentiary rules, evidence of negligent "habits" can be introduced in support of an effort to show an act of negligence in a particular instance, one subsequent mistake in wrapping on Filby's part does not appear to go very far in dispelling the force of the prosecution's evidence against Mrs. Leigh Perrot. This appears with particular force when the physical circumstances of the Blagrave incident are contrasted with the uncontroverted testimony in the Leigh Perrot case. If Filby in fact packed two veils for Miss Blagrave instead of the one she bought, it is likely that he drew the second veil from the same box or counter area from which he took the veil she had selected. However, the white lace found in Mrs. Leigh Perrot's package had been carded in the shop at a location approximately *four yards* away from the area where Filby packed Mrs. Leigh Perrot's purchased black lace. If Filby made the error in packing that the defense attributed to him, he would have had to carry a card of white lace for the distance of four yards and to place it on the counter before him or hold it in his hand while he proceeded to card Mrs. Leigh Perrot's purchase and prepare her package. This "mistake" would have involved a degree of somnambulism (and possibly manual dexterity) on the part of Filby, which is hardly to be compared with the alleged miscounting of Miss Blagrave's veils.

Do the circumstances of the discovery of the white lace in the possession of Mrs. Leigh Perrot support the negligence theory by proving her lack of consciousness of guilt?

The judge seems to have been clearly correct in discounting the prosecution's evidence that Mrs. Leigh Perrot, when accosted in the street by Miss Gregory, was agitated and had "turned as red as scarlet," nor should we have been surprised had she turned white as lace. The court observed that the defendant's reaction should not

> be construed by them [*the jury*] into an indication of guilt for that, if any person were to be suddenly stopped in the public street, and taxed with the commission of so heinous a crime, such a charge, however conscious of innocence the party might be, would, in all probability, be productive of effects similar to those described by the witness.

I think, however, that some quarrel could be taken with his Lordship's accentuation of the defense argument that Mrs. Leigh Perrot's

> returning and passing by the shop, with the parcel containing the lace in her hand, so soon after she had left it, when it was proved by the witness Filby that sufficient time had elapsed for her to have gone home and concealed it, had she chosen so to do, certainly did not appear to be the conduct of a guilty person, for that thieves are wont to hide away and conceal the property they have stolen.

I have already argued that the fortuitous reappearance of Aunt Jane tends to undermine the notion that the recovery of the lace was the result of a "deep-laid" conspiracy. But could the circumstances of the recovery, by evidencing Aunt Jane's lack of guilty awareness, tend to support the alternative theory (on which the defense in court was based) that the white lace was included in Aunt Jane's parcel *by negligence*? It was common ground that Aunt Jane's residence at 1 Paragon Buildings was only a quarter of a mile away from the shop and that she would have had time to return home to hide the incriminating white lace. This, however, is at best a very ambiguous factor. There is no evidence as to what Mrs. Leigh Perrot's destination was after her famous visit to the millinery shop. It is possible that she did not enter the shop with any theft in mind and had already arranged to meet her husband in town at a fixed hour and place, which would not have permitted a prior return home. Why, then, could she not have said to the doting Uncle James when she met him that she desired to walk along home with him so that she could leave off a package? *Perhaps it was because the package was small, and James, afflicted with gout, was a painful walker.*

As to Uncle James's sorry condition only two months earlier, we can summon Jane Austen herself as witness. In her letter of June 2 she wrote to Cassandra: "My uncle overwalked himself at first, and can now only travel in a chair, but is otherwise very well."

What weight is to be given to Mrs. Leigh Perrot's social position and character evidence?

It appears quite likely that Mrs. Leigh Perrot's speedy acquittal was due less to defects in the prosecution's proof than to the great weight accorded by the court and the jury to Mrs. Leigh Perrot's social position and character evidence. The question ultimately came down to this: Is it believable that a woman of Mrs. Leigh Perrot's wealth and position, with a fine character testified to by neighbors and friends of high birth and standing, by clergymen from two parishes, and by three merchants from Bath, would have committed a disgraceful shoplifting? Mr. Justice Lawrence, in summing up the evidence to the jury, laid heavy stress on the testimony as to Mrs. Leigh Perrot's good character. Before turning to that evidence, he observed to the jury that "the case on the part of the prosecution was fully proved, if they believed the testimony of the witnesses called in support of it." He commented that as to the good character of Filby "there hung some doubt," but he concluded that "the evidence given by him stood uncontradicted except in one point of trivial consequence, namely, his having sworn that he never had any dealings with Crouch, the pawnbroker, whereas it afterwards appears form Crouch's evidence that Filby was once or perhaps twice at his house on business, which was eight or nine years ago." He particularly pointed out the corroboration of Filby's evidence by the testimony of Miss Gregory and her apprentice Sarah Raines and pointed out that Miss Raines had sworn positively that she took particular notice of Filby's putting up a parcel of black lace and that there was nothing but the black lace put into it by him.

The judge, however, thought it very persuasive that no person could have received a higher character from more distinguished witnesses than had Mrs. Leigh Perrot, and concluded:

> If upon taking all the circumstances of the case into consideration, the Jury should see any reason to disbelieve the witnesses for the prosecution, or which led them to doubt of the Prisoner's guilt, they should recollect the very excellent character which had been given her, and in that case it ought to have great weight with them towards an acquittal.

These were his Lordship's concluding words. The jury must have been impressed by this instruction, which reinforced the point made by the defendant's counsel in the address he had read to the court at her dictation. It seems obvious, then, that despite the long-lived tradition that Mrs. Leigh Perrot was freed because conspirators clumsily failed to impose perjured testimony on the court and jury, the outcome turned instead on the jury's disbelief that a rich and respectable woman would have committed a minor theft.

Unfortunately, lawyers who have had to struggle in modern days with the defense of retail establishments against shoplifting losses and false arrest charges know that rich and respectable women *do* commit thefts even of the most trivial kind, and that shoplifting is often an irrational crime. What the emotional roots of such crimes may be remains a puzzle.

It is possible that one source of middle-class shoplifting may be a warped sense of economy, a revolt, conscious or unconscious, against high prices. Could such feelings as this have impelled the affluent Mrs. Leigh Perrot to steal the white lace? Since the biographical data about her have been in the hands of the family, we have very little insight into her foibles. However, the family biographers, William and Richard Arthur Austen-Leigh, confide that "she was not exactly open-handed." An intriguing possibility may be built on this hint. We will recall from Jane Austen's letters that millinery prices in Bath were high. We also know that Mrs. Leigh Perrot, on the day before the incident, had been in the Smith shop, examining some black lace from London. Only on a second visit had she brought herself to conclude the purchase, and perhaps she regarded the price as extravagant. It is therefore possible that when she saw the opportunity of taking the white lace, she acted, like the stock investors of our time, to "average down" her purchase price.

Other affluent shoplifters appear to have been motivated by elements in their family relations that are not on public view. As an example I might cite the recent story, *A Case of Shoplifting*, by Michael Gilbert (1976). I suspect that Michael Gilbert, as a lawyer, has more than a little familiarity with apparently inexplicable shopliftings. In his story, Gilbert tells of Mrs. Kent-Smith, the wife of a busy self-made business tycoon, who simulates a shoplifting (and an intentionally unsuccessful one at that) for the purpose of attracting her husband's attention. We are told that the Leigh Perrots were a devoted couple, but a wife's notion of the degree of attention to which she is entitled does not necessarily coincide with the views of outside observers. Of course, since shoplifting was a capital offense, it would have been a dangerous form of attention-getting. Nevertheless, in light of the enormous volume of shoplifting in eighteenth-century England, there is little reason to believe that capital punishment acted as more of a deterrent to this offense than it did to more serious crimes.

It is risky to attempt to descend to lower levels of Mrs. Leigh Perrot's psyche since we know so little about her. Michael Gilbert, who could take greater liberties with his fictional Mrs. Kent-Smith, stressed her childlessness. Perhaps Mr. Gilbert was bowing in the direction of the theory espoused by Freudian psychiatrists that an adult female shoplifter who acts from no apparent economic motive is often a childless woman who compensates for her deprivation of children by taking things belonging to others. Whether the childless Mrs. Leigh Perrot might have fit this pattern we cannot know.

It is hard enough to convince a modern jury that shoplifting may have other than economic motives. It is possible that in Taunton in 1800 it would have been significantly harder to make the point that rich people not classically "mad" might be guilty of a petty theft. The principal contemporary authority on crime and its prevention, P. Colquhoun, in his *Treatise on the Police of the Metropolis*, which was published in London in 1800, the year of the trial, propounds a purely economic theory of the origin of petty theft. In Colquhoun's view, the chief explanation of theft was that the poor class was tempted to commit this crime because of the existence of specialized dealers in the various categories of stolen goods, ranging from metals to secondhand apparel. His proposed solution was the close supervision of these trading markets.

Ironically, however, the files of the Austen-Leigh family themselves contain some evidence of contemporary insight into the possibility of irrational shoplifting. The source once again is an anonymous letter-writer. In a letter to Mrs. Leigh Perrot of April 20, 1800, the female writer offered to act as an intermediary "to prevent the publishing of a scandalous print which discovered by accident is now in a forward state the subject of which is the crest of Mr. Leigh Perrot with a card of lace in the bill of the Parrot with other things and an inscription referring to the late accusation which was made against you." The writer claimed to have been authorized by the printmakers (who merited prosecution not only for extortion but for their execrable pun on the Perrot name) to offer the withdrawal of the print in exchange for a subscription of one hundred guineas to a city hospital that was in arrears. Professing a belief in Mrs. Leigh Perrot's innocence, the correspondent attributed to the publishers of the print a resolution "to lend their aid to punish you lest a sufficient impression should not yet be made on the mind of yourself & (as they were pleased to express themselves) other *genteel shoplifters.*" (Emphasis added.)

We do not have any direct record of Jane Austen's reactions to her aunt's trial. In her novels Jane Austen became the mistress of the art of piercing the veil of "first impressions," which enabled her, for example, to unmask the hidden immorality of two gentlemen, Mr. Wickham in *Pride and Prejudice* and Mr. Elliot in *Persuasion*. But Jane surely must have believed that her aunt was innocent. It is harder to have insight within the family.

There is no direct translation of Mrs. Leigh Perrot's ordeal in Jane Austen's fiction. It is in keeping with the character of a writer whose novels reflect only obliquely the wars and public events of her time that she should not have chosen to work the raw materials of a family criminal trial. However, a close look at the two Bath novels of Jane Austen, *Northanger Abbey* and *Persuasion*, may respectively give us glimpses of Aunt Jane and memories of her day in court.

In *Northanger Abbey* (which may have been written first in 1798 and revised about 1803) the heroine, seventeen-year-old Catherine Morland, is taken to Bath by Mr. and Mrs. Allen, a childless couple who are friends of her family. Although Jane Austen drew no characters wholly from life, there are a number of parallels between Jane and Catherine and between the Leigh Perrots and the Allens. By the time of the composition of *Northanger Abbey*, Jane, who, like Catherine Morland, was a minister's daughter, had visited the childless Leigh Perrots in Bath. Mr. Allen, like Mr. Leigh Perrot, took the waters of Bath as a cure for his gout. Although Mrs. Leigh Perrot appears to have been a more dour personality than Mrs. Allen, it is possible that the acute young Jane saw in her aunt aspects of Mrs. Allen's dominant trait, a passion for clothes and a compulsive need to surpass all her acquaintances in finery. Mrs. Allen's deepest emotion on crossing the crowded floor of the Upper Assembly Rooms is self-congratulation on having preserved her gown from injury:

> "It would have been very shocking to have it torn," said she, "would not it? It is such a delicate muslin. For my part, I have not seen anything I like so well in the whole room, I assure you."

And she interrupts her expression of concern about her failure to get Catherine a partner with a comment on a dress in the crowd:

> "There goes a strange-looking woman! What an odd gown she has got on! How old-fashioned it is! Look at the back."

When she meets her childhood friend Mrs. Thorpe, she is delighted to discover with her keen eyes that "the lace on Mrs. Thorpe's pelisse was not half so handsome as that on her own."

Perhaps a passion such as this drove Mrs. Leigh Perrot into the millinery shops of Bath. She may have agreed with Mrs. Allen's judgment of the attractions of the town for shoppers:

> "Bath is a charming place, sir; there are so many good shops here. We are sadly off in the country . . . Now, here one can step out of doors, and get a thing in five minutes."

The concluding portion of *Persuasion*, Jane Austen's last completed novel (published in 1818) is also set in Bath. Here very clear imprints of Jane's memories of her aunt's trial appear. It may be mere accident that in this novel there are more references to law and lawyers than are customary in the Austen novels. The early chapters introduce Mr. Shepherd, "a civil, cautious lawyer," one of the few portraits drawn by Jane Austen from his profession. Later in the book, when Mrs. Smith reveals to Anne Elliot the evidence she has preserved of treachery of Anne's unwanted suitor, the self-seeking Mr. Elliot, she speaks like a barrister addressing a jury:

> "I have shown you Mr. Elliot as he was a dozen years ago, and I will show him as he is now. I cannot produce written proof again, but I can give as authentic oral testimony as you can desire, of what he is now wanting, and what he is now doing."

Whether or not these associations of law with the town of Bath are related to recollection of Mrs. Leigh Perrot's case, other allusions in the book are unmistakably connected with the trial. Mr. Shepherd receives an application for tenancy of Kellynch Hall from Admiral Croft, "with whom he afterwards fell into company in attending the quarter sessions at Taunton," the town where Aunt Jane was tried. Later we learn that Mr. Musgrove "always attends the assizes, and I am so glad when they are over, and he is safe back again." Perhaps Anne Elliot's dislike of Bath mirrors Jane Austen's feelings toward a town that was associated with two family tragedies, the death of her father and the criminal charge against her aunt.

The conclusion of *Persuasion* presents final proof that the trial of Aunt Jane left a lasting impression on the mind of her famous niece. Dissatisfied with Chapter X of her original version of *Persuasion*, which reunited Anne Elliot and Captain Wentworth in a rather tepid drawing room scene, Jane Austen expanded and relocated the final episodes of their reconciliation. In a key scene of the revised version, Anne's sister, Mary, looking out a window of the White Hart in Stall Street, sees a woman standing under the colonnade with a gentleman she identifies as Mr. Elliot. She "saw them turn the corner from Bath Street just now."

On that very corner stood the shop where Aunt Jane had her unhappy encounter with a card of white lace.

Biographical Notes
Compiled by Laura Benford

STACY AUMONIER (1887–1928), British

Miss Bracegirdle Does Her Duty, page 153

The many-sided Stacy Aumonier was a landscape painter, an entertainer, and a journalist. He began his writing career in 1913 but did not attract public notice until publication of "The Friends" (1917), a short story, and *The Querrils* (1919), a novel, the chronicle of a wartime family. His warm and humorous style has a charm that reflects his diversified talents.

E. F. BENSON (1867–1940), British

The Confession of Charles Linkworth, page 203

Son of an Archbishop of Canterbury, and a prolific author of poems, biographies, and essays, E. F. Benson also pursued a career in archaeology and worked in Athens (1892–1895) and in Egypt (1895). He became famous in 1893 for his satirical novel, *Dodo*, to which he wrote several sequels. He also wrote novels of school life and tales of the supernatural including *The Luck of the Vails* (1901). Among his books combining personal reminiscence and social history are *As We Were* (1930), *As We Are* (1932), and *Final Edition* (1940). In his lifetime he published over eighty works.

ALGERNON BLACKWOOD (1869–1951), British

The Woman's Ghost Story, page 296

Until Algernon Blackwood began writing short stories at age thirty-six, he spent lean years at a variety of occupations including newspaper reporter in Toronto and New York, artist's model, actor, and soap-maker. His first of many short story collections, *The Empty House*, was published in 1906. Often called a mystic, he is best known for his novels and tales of the supernatural, and toward the end of his life he achieved a tremendous reputation in England for presenting ghost stories on television.

ALBERT BOROWITZ (1930–   ), American

The Trial of Jane's Aunt, page 306

Albert Borowitz was born in Chicago and earned three degrees from Harvard University. In 1954, M.I.T. published his monograph "Fiction in Communist China" as part of a research program under the leadership of Walt W. Rostow. Another monograph, "Chian Monlin: The Theory and Practice of Chinese Education" was published in the Harvard China Papers. Now a Cleveland lawyer with strong interests in the arts and crime detection, Mr. Borowitz has published a number of articles on criminal cases of literary and cultural significance in such journals as *The American Scholar*, *The American Bar Association Journal*, *The Musical Quarterly*, and *The Armchair Detective*. A collection of his articles appears in his recent book, *Innocence and Arsenic: Studies in Crime and Literature* (1977).

JOHN COLLIER (1901–   ), British

Bird of Prey, page 194

Mr. Collier is known in this country primarily for his two novels, *His Monkey Wife* and *Defy the Foul Friend*, and for his contributions to *The New Yorker*, *The Atlantic Monthly*, *Harper's Magazine*, and other periodicals. Poet and editor, he served for several years as literary critic for *The Telegraph* (London). In addition to novels, short stories, and poems, Collier published an informal history of Great Britain after World War I, written in collaboration with Ian Lang.

SUSAN GLASPELL (1882–1948), American

A Jury of Her Peers, page 130

Susan Glaspell began her literary career in college by writing stories for magazines. Later she was on the staff of a Des Moines, Iowa, newspaper. From short-story writing she turned to novels, publishing her first, *The Glory of the Conquered*, in 1909. In 1915 her husband, George Cram Cook, formed a theater group and her interest turned to writing plays. One of her first ventures was a one-act play, *Trifles* (1917), followed by *Suppressed Desires*, written in collaboration with her husband. Susan Glaspell turned away from plays after her Pulitzer Prize winner of 1931, *Alison's House*, but continued writing novels. Though she spent much time in England, France, and Greece, most of her novels and plays have their roots in her Mid-West background.

THOMAS HARDY (1840–1928), British

The Withered Arm, page 63

Architect for ten years and then writer, Thomas Hardy met with limited financial and literary success until publication in 1874 of *Far from the Madding*

Crowd. He became the center of a storm of controversy with the publication in 1891 of *Tess of the D'Urbervilles* and later in 1896 with *Jude the Obscure*, both labeled obscene. From his prolific pen came forth such novels as *The Return of the Native* (1878), *The Mayor of Casterbridge* (1886), and *The Woodlanders* (1887). In 1898 he turned his talents to poetry, a lifelong ambition, and issued *Wessex Poems*. A series of poetry volumes (including poems written many years before and his epic drama, *The Dynasts*) were subsequently published, all to public acclaim. In this he felt rewarded, for it was as a poet he wished to be remembered.

HENRY SYDNOR HARRISON (1880–1930), American

Miss Hinch, page 43

Harrison graduated from Columbia University in 1900 and started his career as a journalist. He left journalism after ten years to become a writer. In 1911 he published his first novel, *Queed* — about a young public-spirited newspaperman. *Queed* and its successor, *V.V.'s Eyes* (1913), which advocated factory reform, were very popular. His other principal novels include *Angela's Business* (1915), *When I Come Back* (1919) — which was a tribute to Harrison's brother who was killed during World War I — *Saint Teresa* (1922), and *Andrew Bride of Paris* (1925).

GILBERT HIGHET (1906–   ), American

Another Solution, page 38

Scholar and popular writer, Gilbert Highet was born in Glasgow, Scotland, and attended Oxford University. For many years he was professor of Greek and Latin at Columbia University and later chairman of the department. He is well known for successfully presenting informative and entertaining, rather than purely scholarly, treatments of poetry, satire, literary history, and criticism to the lay reader. His books include *People, Places, and Books* (1953), *The Powers of Poetry* (1960), *Anatomy of Satire* (1962), and *The Speeches in Vergil's Aeneid* (1972).

H. R. F. KEATING (1926–   ), British

The Old Shell Collector, page 93

Keating became a journalist after attending Trinity College in Dublin. He was an editor for three English newspapers, including *The Times* (London). His most famous crime novels are a series about India with their popular hero, Inspector Ghote of the Bombay CID. For *The Perfect Murder*, he won the Golden Dagger award of the Crime Writers Association in 1964 and the Edgar Allen Poe special award of the Mystery Writers of America in 1965. A contributor to *Ellery Queen's Mystery Magazine* and the crime book reviewer for *The Times*, Keating has written over twenty novels.

FRANCIS KING (1923–   ), British

The Doll, page 267

Born in Adelboden, Switzerland, Francis King spent his early childhood in that country and India. He attended school in England from age nine, eventually receiving his B.A. and M.A. from Balliol College, Oxford University. A conscientious objector during World War II, he joined the British Council in 1949, serving in Italy, Greece, Egypt, Finland, and Japan. He retired from the Council in 1964 to devote his time entirely to writing. He has published several novels and volumes of short stories as well as a collection of poetry.

ALFRED HENRY LEWIS (c.1858–1914), American

The Broadway Central Tragedy, page 219

Lawyer, journalist, and author, Alfred Henry Lewis spent part of his youth as a cowboy and sometime newspaperman in Kansas, Texas, Arizona, and New Mexico. Starting out on his legal career, his interest turned to politics and journalism. Published in the Kansas City *Times*, his "Old Cattleman" stories later led to the "Wolfville" stories of cowboy life. These tales belong to the best tradition of American humorous storytelling. Onetime Washington bureau chief for the Hearst syndicate, Lewis also wrote fictionalized biographies, novels of political life, and police procedurals.

ROBIE MACAULEY (1919–   ), American

The Invaders, page 184

Mr. Macauley was an assistant professor at the University of North Carolina, 1950–53, editor of *The Kenyon Review*, 1959–66, and is presently a senior editor at *Playboy Magazine*. He has been a lecturer for the U.S. State Department, a Guggenheim Fellow, and a Fulbright research fellow. An O. Henry Prize Stories winner in 1967, his works include *The Disguises of Love* (1952), *The End of Pity* (1957), and *Technique in Fiction* (1964). He is a contributor to numerous periodicals and newspapers including the *New York Times*, *Vogue*, *Esquire*, and *The New Republic*.

MILTON MACKAYE (1901–   ), American

The Man Hunt, page 22

Son of a Methodist minister, Iowa-born Milton MacKaye came east in 1922 to work on the staffs of various newspapers in Washington and New York, ending up finally with the New York *Evening Post*. MacKaye worked with the War Department and the Office of War Information during World War II. He began freelance writing in 1932 and over the years has contributed to many periodicals, including *The New Yorker*, *Redbook*, *Reader's Digest*, and *Saturday Evening Post*. His wife, Dorothy Cameron Disney, is also a noted writer.

KATHERINE MANSFIELD (1888–1923), British

The Woman at the Store, page 243

Abandoning a promising career as a cellist, New Zealand–born Katherine Mansfield turned her talents to writing. Ill health, limited success, and personal problems plagued her throughout her life. Her first collection of short stories, *In a German Pension*, published in 1911, was written during a rest-cure at a spa. She wrote literary reviews for a number of publications which attracted little attention until 1918. When *Prelude* (1918), *Bliss and Other Stories* (1920), and *The Garden Party* (1922) appeared, they brought long-awaited acknowledgment. Though much of her work was not published until after her death, these collections established her as a sensitive and highly gifted writer.

ALFRED MORAIN (1864–1938), French

A Record of Escape, page 169

This story was originally published in 1931 by E. P. Dutton as part of *The Underworld of Paris — Secrets of the Sûreté*. The stories were taken from dossiers preserved in the French Judicial Archives by Albert Morain, author and Préfet de Police of Paris from August 1924 to April 1927.

FITZ-JAMES O'BRIEN (c.1828–1862), Irish

What Was It?, page 1

Journalist and playwright, Fitz-James O'Brien was born in County Limerick, Ireland. His play *A Gentleman from Ireland* was first produced in 1858. "The Diamond Lens," his best-known story, was published in *The Atlantic Monthly* in 1857. He was drama editor of *The Saturday Review* in New York from 1858 until his death.

BERTON ROUECHÉ (1911–   ), American

The Raspberry Patch, page 15

Berton Roueché was born in Kansas City, Missouri, attended the University of Missouri, and after college worked as a reporter for various Missouri newspapers. Since 1944 he has been a staff writer for *The New Yorker*. He has written many books during his career, including his unique works on medical detection. Among them are *Curiosities of Medicine*, *Annals of Epidemiology*, and *Field Guide to Disease*. His mystery novels include *Feral* (1974), *The Last Enemy* (1975), and *Fago* (1977).

DAMON RUNYON (1884–1946), American

Undertaker Song, page 283

After serving in the Spanish-American War, Kansas-born Runyon worked as a sportswriter and reporter for a number of newspapers in New York, Denver, San Francisco, and other cities. He did not begin to write his famous stories of New York City "low-life" until about 1930. They are best known for their picturesque characters and their colorful slang — the famous "Runyonese." These stories were published in several magazines and later collected in a series of books: *Guys and Dolls* (1931), *Blue Plate Special* (1934), *Money from Home* (1935), and *The Best of Runyon* (1938). Runyon was also a Hollywood screenwriter; *Lady for a Day*, *Little Miss Marker*, *A Slight Case of Murder*, and *The Lemon Drop Kid* were his best-known screenplays. He died in New York City and seemed in danger of being forgotten until Frank Loesser's Broadway production of *Guys and Dolls* in 1950 re-established his prominence.

E. H. LACON WATSON (1865–1948), British

The Escape, page 254

After attending Caius College at Cambridge, E. H. Lacon Watson left his home in Leicestershire, England, in 1894 for London where he became a freelance journalist, essayist, and novelist. During World War I, he was a special correspondent for the Reuter Agency. He was the author of more than twenty-five novels and volumes of essays, which include *The Unconscious Humorist and Other Essays* (1896), *A Conversational Tour in America* (1914), *Cloudesley Tempest* (1914), *Notes and Memories of a Sports Reporter* (1931), *Contemporary Comments: Writers of the Early 19th Century as They Appeared to Each Other* (1931), *In the Days of His Youth* (1935), and *I Look Back Seventy Years* (1938).

LASSITER WREN (dates unknown), American

The Man Who Murdered Papa Désiré, page 116

This story was originally published in *Masterstrokes of Crime Detection* (1929). Lassiter Wren's other books include *Baffle Book* (1928), *Second Baffle Book* (published for the Crime Club in 1929), *Third Baffle Book* (1930), and *Mystery Puzzle Book* (1933) in which detective puzzles were given in the form of brief narratives that included diagrams, documents, and clues.